MAR 1 6

P9-DNB-694

No Shred of Evidence

Also by Charles Todd

The Ian Rutledge Mysteries

A Test of Wills

Wings of Fire

Search the Dark

Legacy of the Dead

Watchers of Time

A Fearsome Doubt

A Cold Treachery

A Long Shadow

A False Mirror

A Pale Horse

A Matter of Justice

The Red Door

A Lonely Death

The Confession

Proof of Guilt

Hunting Shadows

A Fine Summer's Day

The Bess Crawford Mysteries

A Duty to the Dead

An Impartial Witness

A Bitter Truth

An Unmarked Grave

A Question of Honor

An Unwilling Accomplice

A Pattern of Lies

Other Fiction

The Murder Stone

The Walnut Tree

No Shred of Evidence

An Inspector Ian Rutledge Mystery

Charles Todd

WILLIAM MORROW
An Imprint of HarperCollins*Publishers*

This book is a work of fiction. The characters, incidents, and dialogue are drawn from the author's imagination and are not to be construed as real. Any resemblance to actual events or persons, living or dead, is entirely coincidental.

NO SHRED OF EVIDENCE. Copyright © 2016 by Charles Todd. All rights reserved. Printed in the United States of America. No part of this book may be used or reproduced in any manner whatsoever without written permission except in the case of brief quotations embodied in critical articles and reviews. For information address HarperCollins Publishers, 195 Broadway, New York, NY 10007.

HarperCollins books may be purchased for educational, business, or sales promotional use. For information please e-mail the Special Markets Department at SPsales@harpercollins.com.

FIRST EDITION

Library of Congress Cataloging-in-Publication Data has been applied for.

ISBN 978-0-06-238618-2

16 17 18 19 20 OV/RRD 10 9 8 7 6 5 4 3 2 1

For Carolyn Marino . . .
for so many reasons, professional and personal, we've lost count,

and

For Danielle Bartlett . . .
who is absolutely awesome. There's no other word.

No Shred of Evidence

I

Near Padstow, Cornwall
Autumn 1920

It was a warm day for autumn, the sun shining from breakfast through the early afternoon, an unexpected break in the weather.

Afterward no one could be sure who had first suggested going out in the boat.

Very likely our last chance until the spring. What do you say? Don't you think it will be a lark?

And so the four young women staying the weekend at the Place mounted their bicycles shortly after luncheon had been cleared away and went down to the river landing that belonged to the Grenvilles. There they took out the rowboat.

They were proficient at it, having done it many times before.

Taking turns rowing, they went upstream some distance until they could look into the back garden of the house belonging to Elaine's family. Someone was on the terrace—her brother?—and they tried shouting to attract his attention, but he couldn't hear them. Or perhaps he didn't wish to. And then they turned downstream again.

They were only a matter of yards from the landing where they had taken out the boat when Sara said, "Look. That man. He's trying to get our attention." She pointed toward a small dinghy a hundred yards closer to the village. They could just see the man in it, standing up without regard to safety, waving frantically.

Kate said, frowning, "Is he in trouble, do you think?"

Elaine shielded her eyes. "Is that Harry? Surely not, he wouldn't be so foolish."

Victoria, at the oars now, said nothing, too busy trying to bring the boat in toward the landing to turn for a look. So she claimed afterward when it was over.

Reaching out for Sara's arm, Kate said, "Does the boat ride too low in the water to be quite—natural? I think we ought to have a look."

"Whoever it is, he's only trying to flirt," Victoria told them, bringing in one of the lines. "It's too far to go. Think about rowing all that way back."

"No, truly, we should have a look." Kate turned to Victoria. "I'll take the oars if you're tired."

"He's still waving," Sara reported, looking over her shoulder. "And the boat *is* lower. Victoria, I think he's foundering." There was alarm in her voice now.

Kate reached for the oars, but Victoria refused to give them up.

"Victoria?" Kate said. "Whoever it is out there, Harry or someone else, what if there *is* something wrong?"

"Oh, very well. A fool's errand if you ask me." She passed over the oars and sat back, her mouth turned down in what looked for all the world like a pout.

Kate wasted no time. Rowing swiftly, letting the current take her but not too fast, keeping control, she gained on the now visibly sinking craft. But it was going down more rapidly as it filled with water.

Elaine exclaimed, "Look, it *is* Harry, Victoria. That's the *Sea Lion*'s dinghy, I'm sure of it now. I don't understand—what's happened to it?"

"I hope Harry, whoever he is, can swim," Sara was saying anxiously. "I don't think we'll be in time."

Elaine's hands were clenched on the gunwale of the boat. "What will we do? If he's in the water?"

"If he goes under, Victoria is in the bow, she can watch that we don't overshoot him," Kate managed to say, intent on the effort she was making. "If we can take him aboard without swamping ourselves, the village will be closer than trying to reach the Grenville landing again. And we can find help for him there."

"Don't say *if*," Elaine begged. "I can't bear to watch him drown."

"Then keep your weight well balanced, Sara, Elaine, and let Victoria guide us in," Kate urged. "But help her. We don't want to lose him."

It appeared now that the man was standing in water—his boat had vanished under him. And then as the boat sank toward the bottom, he was sucked down with it. Too fearful to leap out of it, he simply stood there, stark terror on his face, letting it happen.

And then he was gone. Elaine cried out in alarm, and Kate put her back into the oars, trying to reach the man as soon as he came up.

"There he is," Sara called suddenly, pointing.

"Where?" Victoria cried. "I don't see him." And then they were upon him, on their left.

He was struggling in the water, mouth wide, arms flailing.

"Careful," Kate shouted, striving to steady the boat. "Victoria, grab his arm."

But the rowboat was going to overrun him.

Kate shipped the oars and reached out. A cold wet hand clasped hers in a death grip, nearly pulling her into the water. And then Sara had his other hand, and they were literally dragging him closer as the rowboat rocked dangerously.

"Stay where you are, Elaine, or you'll overturn us," Kate shouted as the third woman turned to help. "Victoria—*do something*."

Victoria sat there, staring at the drowning man, then fumbled in the bottom of the boat.

Kate thought she was reaching for a rope, but Victoria lifted one of the oars, raising it awkwardly, and lost control of it in midair. In a flash it fell, coming down with a wet sound, an audible slap as it struck the floundering man's head.

Kate and Sara cried out in the same moment, as the man visibly jerked in Kate's grip, and she almost lost his hand. "Pull," she shouted to Sara. "For God's sake, *pull*."

The oar was dragged clear, and Kate heard it clatter into the bottom of the boat as she and Sara got the man to the side and tried with all their strength to pull him in.

He was heavy with water, his head lolling, blood from a cut running down his pale face, and Kate knew at once that he was unconscious, unable to help them and at the same time almost impossible to hold.

From somewhere on the shore, they heard a shout, and Kate looked up to see a man dressed in the clothes of a farmer frantically shucking off his coat and boots, then diving into the cold waters of the River Camel.

He struck out with smooth, swift strokes, reached the boat after what felt to Kate like an eternity, and clambered aboard on the far side, rocking them perilously and dripping water all over their skirts. Then he was thrusting his way between Sara and Kate, reaching out to pull the man in by the collar of his coat, groaning with the dead weight, and then with a mighty effort that nearly swamped them all, he managed to heave the half-drowned man over the gunwale. Kate grabbed a leg and pulled, and then, without warning, the man came flying into the boat, landing hard, knocking Kate, Sara, and his rescuer after him into the well in a tangled heap of limbs.

Kate called frantically, "The oars—Elaine, the *oars*."

And with an effort that left her red in the face, Elaine found the one that Victoria had dropped and was trying to drag the other out from under the four bodies at her feet, just as Kate, Sara, and the farmer managed to sort themselves out. Water was sloshing about in the well of the rowboat, and they were all shivering now. Harry never moved, and Kate was trying to hold his face up, out of the water, just as Victoria got up and edged her way to Sara's place at one of the oars.

"I'll row. We've too much weight to make it back to our landing."

Elaine was busy trying to fit one of the oars into the rowlocks, and the farmer was kneeling over Harry now, pressing his hands on the man's back. He coughed up some water, but lay still.

"He's breathing," his rescuer reported, and helped Kate lift him to turn him on his back.

Sara made a sound, quickly choking it back, as she looked down on the man in the well. She was pale, wet to the skin from shoulders to knees, her hair coming down and straggling across her cheeks. "His face . . . Why is there so much blood? Did he strike one of the thwarts?"

There was a gash on his head, and it was bleeding profusely. Kate, ignoring the cold wind that seemed to have come up without her noticing it until now, bent down and tore lengths of linen from her petticoats and handed them to the farmer. Without a word he roughly bandaged the wound, and then finally, his chest still heaving for air even as he shivered violently, he sat up to face his companions.

They were only halfway to the village landing, but a crowd had collected there, staring out at the river and the boat making its erratic way toward them. Small at first, and growing larger by the minute as news spread.

Slowly looking at each of the four young women in the rowboat, the farmer demanded sternly, "Why the hell were you trying to kill that man?"

2

Rutledge had just returned from Derbyshire. Sitting at his desk, he wrote out his report, enclosed the statements taken by the local man, and was just dropping the file into his outgoing box when the door of his office opened and Sergeant Gibson stepped in.

"Chief Superintendent wishes to see you, sir. Is that your report? I'll just take that, then, shall I?"

"I was looking forward to going home for an hour. I haven't had time to change my clothes."

"I expect the Chief Super won't take long," Gibson said enigmatically.

Rutledge, glancing at him on his way out the door and down the passage, said, "What is it?"

"I don't know, sir. And that's the truth."

But Rutledge had a feeling he knew very well.

He knocked lightly at Chief Superintendent Markham's door, then opened it at the single word, "Come."

"Rutledge, sir. You wished to see me?"

"There's a tangle in Cornwall, complaints to the Home Office, requests for the Yard to send someone. I don't like it. Not our place to sort out every assault in the kingdom. Finished your report on Derby, have you?"

"Yes, Sergeant Gibson has it."

"Good. Then get yourself down to Cornwall and find out what this is all about. And be quick about it, I don't see a need to hold their hand any longer than necessary."

Rutledge didn't want to go back to Cornwall. His memories of his last inquiry there were still too strong, and he had hoped not to see the Duchy again.

"There are men here at the Yard who know the Duchy far better than I do. I should think they would be able to judge the situation more accurately."

"The Chief Constable specifically asked for an outsider."

Rutledge felt himself groan inwardly. This could only mean that a referee was needed, not a policeman.

"If that's your decision—" he began, but Markham cut him off.

"It is. Leave as soon as you can."

Which meant as soon as he was dismissed. Markham shoved a thin folder across the desk. "Four young women of good family accused of attempted murder. Victim was known to them. Witness saw what happened. The local man reported that the victim had been in the boat with the young women, and while they were out of sight on the river, they threw him overboard and tried to keep his head under. When that didn't work, they used an oar to try to kill him. That's what put him into the coma," he said. "What's more, he's still unconscious and unable to tell his side of the story. I must say that on the surface of it, it looks bad for the four women. Your task is to find out why they could have done such a thing, and if there's any evidence to the contrary. Problem is, in an inquiry like this, there's often a history that makes it the devil of a matter to sort out. Do the best you can to get to the bottom of it. I don't want to hear of more favors being called in by the likes of County families feuding with each other and the courts. You're not going to be very popular, whatever you do. But you have the weight of the Yard behind you, and I expect you to see it through, even if this was truly attempted murder."

Easier said than done, Rutledge thought as he picked up the folder. Markham nodded to him and he was dismissed.

Closing the door behind him, Rutledge went to his own office, tied up the loose ends awaiting his attention, and then rose to leave.

Sergeant Gibson was standing in the passage just outside his door, one hand lifted to knock.

"Gibson."

The sergeant said nothing, falling silently into step beside Rutledge until they were well out of earshot of the Chief Superintendent's office.

"You aren't the first to be sent to Cornwall," he commented with a sideways glance at Rutledge.

"Indeed?" Rutledge turned to stare at him. "Who went before me?"

"Inspector Barrington. He had a heart attack the day after he arrived. Dead."

Rutledge stopped short. "I hadn't heard." He'd known Barrington from before the war. Older, quiet, and lately often out of breath, as if he'd been running and hadn't quite caught it again.

"There's a wife," he said to Gibson. "And children, as I remember. Grown, I think."

"That's right. We've taken up a collection for them. Inspector Barrington was speaking only last month about retiring. He said it was time."

Rutledge reached into his pocket and handed Gibson some notes. "Add that for me. I'm sorry. He was a good man. Steady."

"He was that. Thank you, sir, I'll see the family gets this. Funeral is next week, I'm told. If you're back in time . . ."

"Yes. Leave the information on my desk. I'd like to be there."

They parted company at the head of the stairs, Gibson returning to his desk and Rutledge running lightly down the steps and out the door. His motorcar was not far away, and as he walked briskly toward it, he swore under his breath.

He'd returned to the Yard in June 1919, still shaken by the war, still finding his feet in this very different world of civilian life after four appalling years in the trenches. Only half healed physically and mentally. And Chief Superintendent Bowles, Markham's predecessor, had sent him first to Warwickshire and then to Cornwall, two very difficult inquiries that had drained him emotionally. He had had to deal with a drunken, shell-shocked ex-soldier in Warwickshire, the only witness to the murder of an officer on leave. And in Cornwall, he had come face-to-face with the secret life of Olivia Marlowe. He hadn't known then who she was, but her war poetry under the pseudonym of O. A. Manning was still so vivid in his memory that it had been something of a shock to realize she was dead. He had found it hard to put that case behind him too. Bowles, he was certain, had deliberately sent him to investigate both murders, knowing somehow that it would be a test of his ability to return to the Yard.

Less than two years ago that was. And yet it seemed like yesterday to him. He had promised himself he would never cross the Tamar into Cornwall again.

He tried to tell himself that Padstow was not particularly close to the Marlowe house. And besides, he'd heard that no one lived there now. It had been closed up.

It was cold comfort as he put his valise in the boot of his motorcar, shut the door to his flat, and set out for the West Country.

It was a long journey. He spent the night near Plymouth, tired still from his drive back from Derby. But that night, as he tried to sleep, Hamish kept him awake.

Hamish MacLeod, the young Scot he'd been forced to execute in the summer of 1916 for directly refusing an order. A God-bereft night, well into the battle on the Somme, the Germans bombarding the British lines, and then the British guns returning fire. In the end they'd caught their own lines in the barrage, killing what remained of Rutledge's company and nearly killing him as well. He'd been left with the shock of shooting one of his own men, left with the knowledge that the rest had died in a futile attempt to take out the machine gun nest before the order to attack at dawn—Hamish had told him over and over again how hopeless it was, but he couldn't listen, he couldn't disobey his orders. One company against the lives of hundreds of others? It was war, military necessity. And so he had persevered, aware of the cost, aware of the waste, aware of the insanity and only too aware that he was unable to do anything to stop any of it.

He hadn't dealt well with Corporal Hamish MacLeod's death. Shell-shocked and too long in the line himself, he'd barely kept his own head through that horrendous summer, and the voice of the young Scot had taken up residence in his mind, like a living man, dead though he was. Rutledge's punishment for leading so many over the top and watching them die. The merciless demands of rank and the pounding day and night of the guns had taken their toll. His measure of guilt for surviving when neither Hamish nor his men could.

He'd brought the voice home from France with him. Wishing he could have brought the living man and so be free. But there was no freedom after all, and in the end he'd been told by Dr. Fleming that he would have to learn to cope with that voice—or go mad.

He had thought, surely, that he was mad already. All the same, he knew that if he gave in to that madness, if he took out his service revolver from where he'd kept it safe in his trunk, killing himself would mean killing Hamish a second time, taking him with him into the dark. It was all that had kept him alive, that single fear.

This night, listening to the voice warning him not to cross the Tamar, to turn back to London before it was too late, he knew it was good advice. But he was an officer of the Yard now, and unable to refuse a direct order.

The alternative was to resign.

But the Yard, for all its shortcomings, had kept him alive too, forcing him to cope at any cost or face admitting to the world that he was a victim of shell shock. A man lacking moral fiber. A coward. No longer fit to be a policeman . . .

At dawn the next morning, he crossed the River Tamar, and a line of O. A. Manning poetry ran though his mind, welcoming him against his will.

This river
Does more
Than cut off the world.
It is a wall to shut it out.
For here I am at peace, I know this land,
And I am safe
In this, my house above the sea.

Only she hadn't been safe there. She had been driven to suicide, with her half brother Nicholas.

There was still the drive across Cornwall to Padstow on the north coast. The roads were not the best. Having eaten no breakfast, he had stopped in a village shop for a pasty hot from the oven, and in the pub bought a jar of Devon cider to drink with it.

The local people had watched him warily, this man from the

outside world. They questioned him as he made his purchases, and seemed glad to see the back of him when he pulled out of the village and found the next turning.

At the approach to the many-arched ancient stone bridge over the Camel in Wadebridge, he stretched his legs, then finished the last of the tea in the Thermos he'd refilled in a town he had passed through shortly before dusk. The shop had been about to close, but the owner had been willing to put the kettle on again. Standing there now, looking at the bridge, he thought about the man who had built it.

The ford over the Camel in the little town of Wade had claimed more than its share of lives. So dangerous was it that a chapel had been put up on each side of the crossing. People could pray for a safe journey over—and pray again in thankfulness for having survived. It was a clergyman who saw the need for a bridge instead of walking through the swift water, and in the 1400s, it had been built, a marvel in its day with all the arches stretching from one side to the other. And it was still a marvel when Oliver Cromwell took it during the Civil Wars, fully aware of its strategic importance.

Tonight it was quiet, and empty save for a cat trotting briskly across. She looked up as she passed his motorcar but otherwise paid no heed to him. Smiling, he got back behind the wheel for the last leg of his journey.

It was very late when he reached the village of Heyl, named for where the river broadened. According to the file Markham had given him, it was to the landing here that the four women had rowed after the near-drowning had occurred. The street was dark, no lamps to light it, as there were in London. Inspector Barrington had been staying at a small inn just before the village's center. Rutledge thought it must be used most often by travelers hiking the coast paths or following the Camel down to the sea. It was not particularly picturesque.

A fair man of forty-five or so answered Rutledge's knock and peered out at him as if seeing a ghost.

Rutledge smiled, though he didn't feel like it. "I'm down from London," he said pleasantly. "I'm told Inspector Barrington's room is still available."

"It's true. They sent for his things. I boxed them up myself. But there's no one to take them off my hands."

"I'll see to them. May I look at the room, please?"

Shielding his lamp with one hand, the man gestured toward the stairs. Carrying his valise, Rutledge mounted them. The inn, from what he could tell by lamplight, was probably a hundred years old, built of good Cornish granite, with paneled walls, a bar to one side of what must be the dining room, and a smell of damp about the lot.

The passage up the stairs was dark and silent except for their footsteps.

"Here," his guide told Rutledge, pointing to his right.

Rutledge pushed open the door nearest him and stepped inside.

To his relief, claustrophobic as he'd been since the war—he'd been buried alive when the shell had blown his sector into the night sky—he saw in the glow of the lamp that the room was quite large, with a pair of windows, an ornate wardrobe that could have been Jacobean, and a sturdy bed with a gay floral coverlet.

"This will do nicely," he said, and meant it. As the man lit the lamps, Rutledge asked for water and a basin to wash off the dust of travel, and then shut the door on the sleepy innkeeper when that was done. For a moment, he simply stood there in the middle of the room.

He'd been told that Barrington had died in the dining room below, gasping for air and then falling to the floor. But he'd been brought up here to his room while Dr. Carrick was sent for, and he was pronounced dead here.

Not one who believed in ghosts, Rutledge had seen men die, and dealt with the dead more times than he cared to remember. Still, he'd known Barrington fairly well, and met his wife on several occasions.

But the room was clean as a pin, the coverlet looked as if it had been freshly laundered, and Rutledge was tired. He undressed, opened the curtains to look out at the gleam of moonlight on the Camel, and went to bed.

If Barrington shared his dreams, he knew nothing about it.

The next morning it was clear that news of his arrival had spread quickly. His breakfast was accompanied by stares, as if everyone feared he too would fall facedown in his eggs.

When the meal was over, he asked the man who had shown him to his room the night before—who had brought his tea and introduced himself as Joseph Hays, the owner of the inn—if there had been any papers in Inspector Barrington's belongings.

Hays shook his head. "Scotland Yard asked that as well. But there was nothing. On the desk in his room or in the wardrobe."

Barrington had had a reputation for keeping his notes in his head until he could see the inquiry clearly enough to put them down on paper.

So. Rutledge was on his own with only the meager file that Chief Superintendent Markham had handed him.

He began by saying to Hays, "That's not a Cornish name, is it? Hays?"

"My mother's family was Cornish. My grandfather came down to Padstow on a matter of business to do with shipping, and never left."

"Well, then, perhaps you can give me a picture of what happened here last week?"

Hays shook his head. "I didn't know anything about it until the pub opened that evening, and everyone was talking about it. How Bradford Trevose had seen the four women struggling to drown Harry Saunders. Trevose was walking home from market and heard the commotion out on the river. It seemed to him they were trying to shove Harry's head beneath the water, but he was strong enough to withstand the worst and was on the point of climbing into the boat when one of the women struck him over the head with an oar."

"And Trevose accused them of attempting to murder Saunders."

"That's right. If he hadn't come along, they'd have succeeded, and it would have been a murder charge, right enough."

"But why should four young women from Padstow Place wish to kill a villager?"

Hays shrugged. "Who can say what was in their heads? Several people came forward later to say the women had rowed upriver looking for him, with no luck, then spotted him on their way back and took him aboard. I don't know the truth of that, but they did pass by the Place's landing."

When he had finished speaking to Hays, Rutledge asked to see Inspector Barrington's belongings, but the innkeeper was right, a cursory search showed there was nothing in them related to the case. They still smelled faintly of Barrington's favorite cigars.

Rutledge was shutting the valise again when Hays added, "The clothes he was wearing when he died went with the body to the undertaker's, thence to London. I put his shaving gear and the like into the valise."

Rutledge thanked him for his help, and went to look for the constable.

It was a typically Cornish village, scattered along the river and up the gently sloping land behind it. The church and churchyard were on higher ground, circled by a low wall of the same dark granite stone. Along the water were two pubs, The Cornishman and The Pilot, and behind them a row of shops. The police station was at the end of the row, perfectly situated between the water and the rest of the town to deal with whatever trouble might arise, from drunken Saturday nights to housebreaking.

Rutledge left his motorcar at the inn and set out on foot, walking along the water for some twenty yards before he came to the village landing. Boats bobbed in the tide as wind rippled the gray surface of the water. For a moment he studied the view, giving himself a sense of what lay upstream and down, then he turned toward the police station.

Pendennis was the name on the board outside. He was in, sitting at a table reading through several papers, a broad man with dark hair and sharp brown eyes. He looked up as Rutledge came through the station's door, and with a scowl said, "If you're representing one of the young ladies, I've nothing more to say to you. The matter is still under investigation."

"My name is Rutledge. From Scotland Yard. I take it you've had a lively time with the lawyers."

Constable Pendennis rose from behind his desk, and gave Rutledge a wry grin. "Beg pardon, sir. We've been beleaguered of late. The families of the young ladies are understandably upset. I expect I'd feel much the same in their shoes. Still, it's rained solicitors and barristers for days. I'm heartily sick of the sight of them. I tell them that I have nothing new to give them, that I was awaiting word from the Yard, but they don't listen. I'm very glad you're here to take charge."

Rutledge moved out the chair on the far side of the desk and said as he sat down, "Who are they? The accused?"

"Miss Grenville and Miss St. Ives, local families, and two visitors come for the weekend. So I'm told. A Miss Langley and a Miss Gordon."

He had known a Grenville at school. But from Devon, as he remembered, not Cornwall.

"Tell me, do *you* believe these women are guilty of attempted murder?"

Pendennis sighed. "I don't know what to say, sir, and that's the truth. Nor did Mr. Barrington, as far as that goes. Brad Trevose swears to what he saw. He tells me that if he hadn't leapt into the water, cold as it was, and swum to the rowboat, Harry Saunders would be a dead man. There were witnesses down by the village landing as well, drawn by the cries of the women, but they were too far away to see what Trevose saw. They could tell there was a man clinging to the side of the boat, they could see two of the women leaning over that side. But whether they were intent on saving the man or killing him, there was no way to know."

"And so the entire case rests on Trevose's statement."

"That's right, sir. But he's a man of good reputation, sound as they come. Why would he lie about what happened?"

"Good point. Where are the women now?"

"Not here in the station's only cell, sir," he exclaimed, as if Rutledge had suggested they might be in the castle dungeon, chained to the wall. "It's not for the likes of them. Mr. Grenville, Miss Victoria's father, has taken them into custody and kept them at the house. Padstow Place. He's the local magistrate, sir. I thought he could be depended upon to keep his word."

"And rightly so. Why was Scotland Yard called in?"

"The families of the young ladies felt that the Yard was necessary, to get at the truth. I don't know which of their fathers it was. Any one of them might have done it, for they are all wealthy enough and respected enough for the Chief Constable to give them his ear."

"Do you have the statements taken after the incident?"

"I gave them to Inspector Barrington, sir. He wanted to read them before each personal interview."

"I have found nothing in his belongings about this case, and London had very little information as well."

The constable's expression was bleak. "Then I don't know what to tell you, sir. Except that he didn't seem well when he arrived. The Inspector. He said it was only a spot of indigestion from an undercooked pasty he'd bought in St. Austell when the train stopped there."

Then where had Barrington put those statements—and any other information he might have come by, in his short tenure as the Yard's man on the scene?

"I'll start at the beginning, while a search is made for his papers. If need be, we can ask all the participants to give us a new statement."

Pendennis was skeptical. "It's not been done before. At least, not here. And they'll have had time to think. Not the same as taking it down while they're still uncertain."

"We might not have much choice in the matter. Very well, I'll start with the farmer. Trevose. Where can I find him?"

He was given directions and set out on foot.

The farm was tucked below the headland, the house upright and whitewashed, standing like a Neolithic stone on the landscape.

A line of washing hung to one side of the kitchen door, and Rutledge could just see the edge of a sheet flapping in the onshore wind. He had forgot how windy Cornwall could be, especially where the toe of Land's End jutted out into the Atlantic. Even this far north and this far inland, it shaped the trees and the people.

There was an ornate brass knocker on the black-painted door, and as he lifted it, Rutledge wondered who had chosen to put it there, Trevose or his wife.

An older woman came to the door, her white hair setting off a wind-browned face and startling blue eyes.

"Who is it?" she asked, looking up at Rutledge. She came barely to his chest, diminutive and yet oddly forceful, as if by right.

"Mr. Trevose, please. Inspector Rutledge, Scotland Yard."

She nodded. "They said someone was coming down from London. Step in, then." He followed her into the front room of the house, where the horsehair furniture covered in a dark green fabric boasted antimacassars crocheted in intricate floral designs, like arbors full of roses. The carpet on the floor was worn but of good quality, and a low fire burned on the hearth, making the room feel slightly stuffy.

The woman offered Rutledge a seat and disappeared into the back regions of the house.

A few minutes later, Trevose walked in. He was dressed in corduroys and a flannel shirt, a well-set-up man of medium height with dark hair just showing flecks of gray at the temples. Rutledge thought he might have been quite handsome in his youth. He was still a striking man in his late thirties.

"Inspector Rutledge, is it?" He didn't offer to shake hands, instead crossing the room to sit in the chair on the other side of the hearth. "They said someone would be coming down to replace Inspector Barrington."

"And as I am new to the inquiry, I felt it would be best to start from the beginning and form my own opinions," Rutledge answered pleasantly, neatly skirting the issue of the missing statements.

"Well, it's all in what I wrote down for Constable Pendennis. But I've no objection to going over it again."

He told his story briskly, and apparently objectively, withholding nothing.

"I was leaving the village on the river path when I saw the boat from Padstow Place. It was late in the year to be taking it out, and I saw there were four young women in it. That's when I realized that two were half out of the boat, and my first thought was they'd taken a little dog with them and it had gone into the water. I stopped, and that's when I saw that it was not a dog, it was a man's head. His arms came up, as if trying to reach for the side of the boat, and the women were trying to push him away, back down again. That's when the one in the bow dragged out an oar and hit the man over the head with it. I tore off my coat and kicked off my shoes, then jumped in. I'm a strong swimmer, even in cold water, and I reached the boat, swung myself into the well, and at that point, two of the women helped me pull the man into the bottom. I didn't recognize him at first, I was too busy trying to pump the water out of him. Then I turned him over to see what damage that oar had done, and I could see he was unconscious, a bloody great gash across the top of his head. If I hadn't been there, he'd have drowned. There's no doubt about it. He couldn't have fought to save himself, and they had only to hold his head under for a minute longer, and he'd have been a dead man."

"Was the boat lying within sight of the village?"

"It was, and there were people on the landing, drawn to all the shouting. But at that distance, I doubt they could tell what was happening. Although there was no doubt about that oar."

"What did the women say to you when the man, Harry Saunders, was breathing and you could pay attention to them?"

"One said, 'Thank God, you've come,' or words to that effect. But I made no bones about what I'd seen. I told them flat out that I knew they had tried to kill Saunders."

"What was their response?"

"They began to deny it, speaking all at once. But I know what I saw."

"What did you do then?"

"Both Saunders and I were wet to the skin, and two of the women were wet from the struggle by the side of the boat. I took the oars from them and pulled for the village landing. There were men waiting who took Saunders to the doctor, and I called for the constable. But he was already on his way, and I explained what I'd seen. He took the young women into custody and sent a boy to Padstow Place to let them know what had happened."

"Did you know these young women?"

For the first time Trevose hesitated. "One of them is the daughter of the house. Victoria Grenville. Two were visitors, or so I was told. The fourth is Miss St. Ives, who lives just up the way from the Place."

"The constable took them into custody. What did you do then?"

"I went to one of the pubs, where I stripped and dressed again in borrowed clothes while mine were drying in the kitchen. I walked down to the police station and Constable Pendennis took my statement. When that was done, I went home."

"Did you see the young women again?"

"I did not. I presumed they were in the cell in the back. Although Grenville himself came down while I was still there at the station and told me what he thought of me for accusing his daughter of attempted murder. It was either knock him down or go, and so I went out the door and didn't look back."

"Is he a man of temper? Grenville?"

"Not as a rule," Trevose said after a moment.

"And this is his only daughter?"

"That's right."

"Is there anything you'd like to add?" Rutledge asked.

"No. I did my duty as I saw it. There's an end to it."

"But why would Victoria Grenville, much less her three friends, want to kill this man Saunders?"

"I have no idea," Trevose answered with more force than he'd intended. Moderating his voice, he added, "You'll be asking them, I'm sure."

"In the course of my investigations, yes," Rutledge said. He rose. "Thank you, Mr. Trevose. I'll be back in touch, if I have any further questions."

"I'll be here," Trevose told him. "Or about the farm. Mrs. Penwith will tell you."

The woman kept house for him, then. Rutledge had thought she might be this man's mother or some other relation.

He left the farm, walking back to the village across the fields, his mind busy with what he'd learned from Trevose.

Had the man been overly quick to judge the situation? But if he hadn't feared the worst, he would never have swum out to the boat. And possibly, whether the women had tried to kill Saunders or not, he could well have drowned simply because they were not strong enough to lift a fully clothed, wet man into the boat.

But what was Harry Saunders doing out there in the first place? Had he been in the boat with the women?

When he reached the river, Rutledge stopped to consider it. Somewhere very close to this spot, Trevose must have witnessed the struggle with Harry Saunders. He could see the village some distance away, where Trevose had come from. And it was clear enough that the farmer had been the only person who could have seen the events and rescued Harry Saunders.

He retrieved his motorcar from the inn yard and with directions from Hays, he found his way to Padstow Place.

It was a lovely old stone manor house, set well above lawns that sloped toward the south, and the gardens in front rose layer by layer to where the drive looped up to the door. Ivy, red with the season, climbed the crenellated front.

When Rutledge reached out to lift the knocker, he saw that it was almost exactly the same design as the one at the Trevose farm, though larger. The shape was unusual, a riding boot and whip, with an initial, worn by time, on the handle of the whip.

The door swung open, and a maid in black with a white starched apron and cap asked his business.

"Inspector Rutledge, Scotland Yard, to see Mr. Grenville."

"He's in the library," she said. "If you'll come this way."

Rutledge had the impression that Grenville was expecting him. Had someone from the household been to the village and heard the gossip? Or had someone come posthaste to warn the house that he had arrived?

He was led down a passage to a very beautiful room, filled with sunlight from two arched windows, while on the walls on the other three sides, even by the door, shelves ran floor to ceiling, most of them filled with leather-bound volumes. On either side of the door the shelves were glass fronted, set in ornate gold-leaf framing. They contained an assortment of small treasures.

The man standing in the center of the room, by a table with six chairs, was nearly as tall as Rutledge, with an aristocratic face, the nose aquiline and the cheekbones high. He wore a mustache, and both it and his hair were a silver gray.

"Good morning, Inspector," he said, and gestured to the chairs around the table rather than to the leather chairs closer to the door.

"Good morning, sir. As you may know, I've been sent to replace Inspector Barrington. I'd like to interview your daughter and her three friends. I understand they are under house arrest here."

Grenville frowned at the words *house arrest* but said only, "They are upstairs. I'll send for them. But before I do, I should like to say that these are young women of impeccable backgrounds and reputation, and their families have been very upset by this matter, as have I. They have been here to visit their daughters, and I have persuaded them to leave me to deal with the local police and the Yard. I think you'd prefer that as well."

Rutledge, reserving judgment, said, "I'm sure this was appreciated." For Pendennis was, apparently, still being harried by their legal representatives.

"I will be honest with you. I'm afraid Inspector Barrington received the full force of their anger. I can only hope it did not contribute to his heart attack."

When Rutledge didn't answer, Grenville strode to the bell pull and summoned the maid.

"Would you prefer to see them one at a time or all together?"

"Have they been allowed to spend time together since they were taken into custody?"

"I am a father, Inspector, and not a gaoler. My daughter's friends have been treated as guests."

And had time to compare stories and settle on an acceptable one?

"Separately, if you please."

"Very well."

The maid came to the door, and Grenville said, "Would you ask one of the young ladies to come down to the library? You will not tell any of them why she is being summoned."

"Which one, sir?"

"Miss Gordon, I should think."

"Yes, sir."

When the door had closed behind her, Rutledge asked, "I gather these women were guests of your daughter's?"

"Yes, it was her birthday. She invited three friends down for the weekend. They arrived on Thursday evening, and the boating—accident—occurred on Saturday afternoon."

The door opened and a young woman stepped in.

"You asked to speak with me—" She broke off as she saw the man standing beside her host.

And at the same time, Rutledge felt the room shake around him, thrusting him into a past he had put behind him and did not want to revisit ever again.

3

Kate Gordon found her voice first, by an effort of will so great that she was suddenly pale.

"—sir?"

Grenville looked from one to the other.

"Do you know each other?" he asked, as if it were impossible for this woman to be acquainted with a policeman.

Rutledge answered for her. "I knew the Gordon family. Before the war."

He thought to himself that *knew* was hardly an adequate word to explain his connection to Kate Gordon. She was Jean Gordon's cousin, and he had been engaged to marry Jean in the summer of 1914. And in the spring of 1919, he had released her from that promise when he'd seen the shock and horror in her eyes as she looked at the shell of a man who had returned from France and been in hospital for months with some undisclosed affliction. The last time he had seen

Jean was quite by accident, after he'd returned to the Yard. She was coming out of the church where she was to be married to someone else the following week. Later, in Canada, where the war was a distant memory, she had died in childbirth.

The doctors had thought that seeing a familiar face would help him find his way back to the world he'd shut himself away from. Instead, it had sent him into a downward black spiral that had almost cost him his life. It had been his sister, Frances, not Jean, who had insisted that he be removed from the hospital and put in the care of Dr. Fleming, in a clinic that specialized in cases such as his.

He could hear Hamish thundering in the back of his mind, and he forced himself to shut out the voice.

"I should like to speak to her alone, if you please."

"I refuse—"

"You are not a relative, sir, and I believe she is of an age to speak for herself."

Grenville's mouth tightened into a thin line, and for a moment Rutledge thought he was about to argue. And then with a curt nod, he strode to the door.

They waited until they were certain he was out of earshot.

Kate lifted her hand, holding it out in a gesture of distress, then let it fall to her side.

"How are you, Ian?" she asked, her voice husky.

He was still battling the darkness but somehow he managed to say, "I'm well."

She didn't seem to believe him. But she said, "I wanted to come and see you, but Frances told me it wouldn't be advisable."

In a panic of uncertainty, he said, "*When?*" Surely not the hospital—please God, not the hospital!

"A week or so after you returned to the Yard. She said it was too soon after—after Jean had broken her engagement to you."

"I broke it," he said. "I set her free."

"Did you? It was very kind of you. She wanted to leave England, to go away and not think about the war any longer. I think it was best for her. She had taken the war very hard. But you know that. She wrote often, she said."

But in the last two years of the war her letters had been brief and infrequent, and often laced with her own fears and uncertainties. She hadn't been prepared for such a long war. For so many friends dead or wounded. It had taken a toll on her. And yet she had been laughing, happy, when he had seen her coming out of St. Margaret's with her friends.

He frowned, remembering. Kate had not been among them. He hadn't noticed at the time, had eyes only for the young woman he had hoped to marry and lost. It had taken all his courage to turn away before she could see him standing there. But she hadn't seen him . . .

"Yes," he answered. "And you, Kate, how have you been?"

"Like everyone else, I've coped," she said with an attempt at lightness. "There wasn't much choice in the matter, was there?"

"No."

She took a deep breath. "Are you here officially? How did you know I was in Padstow?"

"Officially. And I didn't know—I had only been given the surnames of the women involved. God knows, Gordon isn't an unusual name. It never occurred to me that you could be in Cornwall. Inspector Barrington died. I've been sent to take his place." It was disjointed, but the best he could do.

"I'd heard. I was so sorry, he seemed to be very considerate."

A silence fell. He thought he could hear the ticking of the clock, then realized it wasn't the clock, there wasn't one in the library. It was his own heart.

"Kate," he began, and cleared his throat. "We will have to talk about what happened."

"Yes."

"Why did you go out in the boat? At this time of year?"

She told him. "And so we rowed up the river, as far as Elaine's house, and it wasn't until we were coming back toward the landing that we saw the boat in trouble. And a man waving. I didn't know then who he was. But the boat sank around him, and I don't think he could swim well. We rowed down as quickly as we could, and when we spotted him in the water, we tried to bring him aboard. But he was too heavy for us, you see. His wet clothes combined with his weight. Sara and I tried to pull him up out of the water, but he was panicked, he was flailing and struggling, and it was impossible, really. I was about to tell Victoria that she had to row us in somewhere, beach us if necessary, as soon as she could, while we clung to him, and then this other man appeared—out of nowhere, it seemed. I didn't realize until later that he'd been on the riverbank and seen us. But as soon as Harry—that was the only name I knew him by just then—was breathing and safe, this man turned on us and accused us of trying to murder him. Ian, it was horrible, we were near to exhaustion ourselves, I was shivering with the cold, as was Sara, we were almost as wet as that man and Harry. And I didn't know what to say, I simply stared at him. That was when he took the oars and began to row us toward the village. Sara and I clung to each other for warmth, our teeth chattering. Elaine was crying, her face in her hands, and Victoria sat there in the bow like a woman turned to stone."

She broke off with a shudder at the memory. "It was awful, Ian. I can't tell you. And then we were at the village landing, being helped out of the boat. There must have been twenty or so people watching us. I couldn't remember afterward whether we'd tied up the boat properly or not. A silly worry, but I had no idea of what was to come. A constable appeared, Harry was taken first to a pub, and then to the doctor's surgery in Padstow. The farmer disappeared, and the four of us were hurried off to the police station. I thought they were going to take care of us until Victoria's father could come and fetch us. But

Sara and I were given these rather smelly blankets, and the four of us were ordered back to a cell. I was speechless with the shock, and then I asked the constable as he locked the door why he was doing this, but he wouldn't answer. In a while I heard the farmer's voice, or at least I supposed it was his, talking to the constable, and later other voices before Mr. Grenville arrived. It was then that I learned we were actually being accused of attempted murder. That the farmer had meant what he said."

She had been standing all this while, and now she sat down in one of the leather chairs as if her legs couldn't support her any longer.

It had been clear, concise, as objective as Kate could make it as she relived the events.

He looked at her. Really seeing her now. She had changed very little. And she had always been one of the most sensible women he'd ever met. Levelheaded, kind, trying to tell him how to manage Jean when she was in one of her moods. Almost six years older, now, in her twenties, and still very attractive.

He was a policeman, he had to keep his head and listen to her account with the objectivity of a stranger interviewing a witness. And yet he knew he believed her. That if Kate said it was not what it had appeared to be to Trevose, then it was true.

But she was only one of the four.

He said, "What about the oar?"

"The oar?"

"I was told that one of you struck the victim with the rowboat's oar?"

"I don't remember anything about an oar." And then, her eyes wide, she said, "But yes, I do. Victoria tried to put it out for him to cling to. She could see we were not going to be able to hold him much longer."

"It hit him in the head."

"Did it?" She stared at him. "Is that where the blood came from?

On his face? I thought it was where he'd been hauled inside. He landed with some force, on the thwarts. Well, we were heaving him in, trying to lift him above the side, and it had taken a great deal of effort. We hadn't intended to hurt him. But you're saying we didn't." She paused, looking back into her memory. After a moment she nodded. "You're right. Of course you are. There was blood on his face while he was still in the water."

She was quick, intelligent. "Is this why we're accused of attempted murder? Because of the oar? Inspector Barrington questioned us individually and asked us not to talk about what happened, not to anyone. And so I don't think any of us did. I didn't. He wouldn't tell us what he knew. Why the charges had been brought. He said in due course we would be told. But then he died, and we were rather in limbo. At least, Mr. Grenville had arranged for us to be taken out of that godforsaken cell, that smelled of drink and other things I didn't care to think about. Inspector Barrington let Mr. Grenville keep us here. And true to his word, Mr. Grenville asked us to remain in our rooms. We were allowed down for meals with the family, of course. But Mr. Grenville told us that there would be no discussion of events. That's how he put it."

"Do you think he's spoken privately to his daughter?"

"I don't know. He hasn't questioned me, that's all I can tell you. He thinks this is all Trevose's fault, I heard him tell his wife that, when he brought us here, but he's done his duty. My father came down, but I wasn't allowed to do more than greet him. Mr. Grenville asked us not to talk privately. He and my father had a very long conversation and then went to the village. I do know that. But I wasn't a party to it."

"Why should Grenville think Trevose was behind it?"

"On our way back to the Place, Mr. Grenville was quite angry. But not with us, nor even Constable Pendennis, who hadn't wanted to keep us in that cell any longer than necessary. It was the farmer who kept insisting he'd witnessed us trying to kill the poor man and that we ought to remain in gaol until it was sorted out. As if he were the magistrate, and not Mr. Grenville."

"And what has Harry Saunders had to say about the matter?" He said nothing about the coma.

"I don't know. No one has told us what he thinks."

"Indeed." He finally made himself sit down in the chair opposite her. "Kate, did you know Harry Saunders before you went down to the river that Saturday?"

"I hadn't met him, if that's what you mean. I did hear Victoria say to Sara that he was simply flirting with us. That was when he was waving, before we realized his boat was sinking. But I'm not sure she knew who the man was until Elaine recognized him. Her back was to the dinghy."

"Was there any reason to think that she did not like him?"

"I don't know. She didn't want to go down to rescue him—this was before the boat sank, you understand. She said we were very tired, and it would be too long a pull back upriver. Which was very true. I'd already thought about that but decided that with the current, we could at least make it to the village landing. Someone could bring the boat back to the Padstow Place landing later. I'd have been willing to pay them myself."

"Have you told anyone else about the fact that Victoria seemed to know the person in trouble and was reluctant to aid him?"

She frowned and shook her head. "Ian, I wouldn't have called it that, not at all. I don't think Victoria realized he was in dire straits, and besides, we'd bicycled down, and it was some distance back to the bicycles, much less the house. The back gardens face the river, of course, but the landing is down one of the estate lanes to the water."

He said nothing for a moment, and then stood up. "Thank you, Kate. Will you ask one of the others to come down?"

She rose and walked with him to the door. "Ian. Be kind to Elaine St. Ives, will you? We've all been quite distressed by what happened,

Elaine in particular. The only part she played in what happened was to sit across from Sara and me to balance the weight on the boat while we were trying to bring Harry in. And to try to find the oars, after he'd been saved. I don't know how she can be blamed for what happened—"

He cut her short. "No, don't tell me. I need to hear it from her."

She was about to answer him, but thought better of it. With a nod she left him standing by the door.

A few minutes later, Elaine St. Ives knocked timidly at the half-opened door, and then stepped into the room.

She was a trim young woman with fair hair, china-blue eyes, and a rosy complexion, the epitome of an Englishwoman, he thought, except that she had been crying and her eyes were red and swollen.

"My name is Rutledge," he told her gently. "I've been sent down from Scotland Yard to take Mr. Barrington's place."

"He's dead," she said in a voice husky with tears. "They told me his heart gave out."

"I'm afraid so. Come, sit down, and tell me if you will, what happened last Saturday, when you and your friends set out for the boat landing."

"We were on our bicycles—well, they belong to the Grenvilles, of course, but we'd used them that morning to go and see the deer, and while I'm not very good with a bicycle, Victoria told me the road down to the landing was even enough. And it was."

"So you had no trouble getting to the boat?"

"And Victoria knows it backward and forward, she said, so we all clambered in while she shoved us off and got in without wetting her boots. In a flurry of skirts, of course, but no one was watching."

"Where did you go?"

"Upstream at first. We could see someone on the terrace of my house, and we thought it must be my brother. But when we waved, whoever it was didn't notice us. Or didn't know it was us. It's quite a distance down to the water, you see."

"After that?"

"We turned around, and then headed downstream. We all took turns at the oars, but I'm not very good at it. My brother says it's all a matter of coordination, but I'm not very good at tennis either."

"When did you see the man?"

"We were almost opposite our landing, I think. At any rate, we were talking about going in. That's when Kate—or was it Sara?—saw someone waving." Her hands clenched in her lap. "Victoria said he was only flirting, and to ignore him. But Kate thought he was in trouble. And he was, because the boat he was in sank right under him."

"Go on."

"He tried to swim to us, and Kate maneuvered the boat close enough that she and Sara could pull him out of the water. But he was struggling, and I started to help, but Kate ordered me to stay where I was, so we wouldn't capsize. But I could feel the boat rocking hard from one side to the other, and then dip dangerously on their side, and I knew we were going to be swamped. It was horrible. The water is quite cold now, and I'm not a strong swimmer. And then this man suddenly appeared and helped us pull Harry in."

"How did you know that it was Harry?"

"I recognized his dinghy as we got closer, and of course I know who he is. His father owns the bank in the village. Well, it's a branch of the bank in Padstow. Victoria says he doesn't know his place. But I'm not sure about that. He'd never spoken to me in anything but the politest way."

She wrung her hands. "And then Mr. Trevose—I recognized him finally, even though his hair was wet and dripping into his eyes—accused us of trying to murder Harry. What's more, he told the constable, and we were taken into *custody*." She spoke the last word as if it were nothing short of a corner of hell. And Rutledge thought it must have seemed so to her.

"You've told me that Kate and Sara—Miss Gordon and Miss

Langley—had tried to help the man. Where was Victoria all this time?"

"She was in the bow. I don't think there was much she could do. Not without tipping the boat. If it hadn't been for Mr. Trevose, I expect we'd have all been in a great deal of trouble. But why he should think we were murdering Harry, I don't know. It was rather awful."

She began to cry, finding a handkerchief and burying her face in it. "I don't want to think about it any longer. Please?"

He could see she was genuinely upset, not trying to evade being interviewed. "One last question. Tell me about the oar."

"The oar?" She raised her head and blinked. "What oar? Oh. One was nearly half out of the boat. I was afraid it was going to fall out and be lost to us. I pulled it in, but I couldn't get the other one out from under Harry—he was in the bottom of the boat with Kate and Sara and Trevose on top of him. But Mr. Trevose decided to row after all, and I just sat there, feeling rather numb. I still couldn't believe what had happened. It had all been so sudden."

"Before that. When Miss Grenville took up one of the oars. What was she intending to do with it?"

"I expect she was trying to hold it out for Harry to grasp. He was clutching Sara's and Kate's hands, you see, and they couldn't let go to reach for his coat. He was about to pull them into the water with him. But the boat was rocking badly, and the oar's heavy, she couldn't quite manage it."

"Anything else you can think of that might help us see the situation more clearly?" he asked.

"That's everything, to the best of my recollection. Will we be put in gaol? Are they going to hang us?"

"You needn't fear hanging," he assured her.

She held his gaze with her own. "Are you telling me the truth?"

"Of course I am. Why should I not?"

"People do lie to me. They tell me it's to spare me, but it only makes matters worse when I find out the truth from someone else."

Rutledge said, "I don't lie in matters like this." Pausing, he added, "Has anyone asked you to lie to me? Or told you things you knew were lies? About what happened on the river?"

"Only Victoria. She told me she never touched that oar, and not to say that she had. And she pinched me. But when Constable Pendennis asked her particularly about that, she said that a shout from shore startled her."

"When was it that she asked you to lie?"

"As we were getting out of the boat. There was blood all over Harry's face, and they took him out first, and then pulled up Kate, followed by Sara. We were waiting our turns, and everyone on the landing was staring down at Harry. No one was looking at us. Not then, not until Mr. Trevose told them. And then they stared. I thought they were going to take us directly to Bodmin. My brother used to read me stories about murderers and highwaymen."

"Why should he do that?"

"To be mean, I think. He never did it when Nanny was in the room. It was always when we were alone. He kept the book in his pocket. I always knew it was there."

"How long have you been friends with Miss Grenville?"

"All my life. Victoria and Stephen and George and I were always in and out of each other's houses."

"George is your brother?"

"Yes. He was badly wounded in the war."

"And Stephen?"

Her eyes filled again. "Victoria's brother. He was killed at Mons. I was to marry him when the war was over."

He let her go then, and sent for Sara Langley.

4

Sara Langley was a tall strawberry blonde, with blue eyes and a smattering of freckles across her nose. They did nothing to diminish her attractiveness or her poise.

"Inspector Rutledge?" she asked, stopping in the doorway.

"Yes. Come in, Miss Langley." He explained as he had before that he had arrived to replace Inspector Barrington, and wished to conduct his own interviews.

"You have made Miss St. Ives cry," she said, coming into the room and taking the chair he offered. "That was unkind of you."

"I'm sorry," Rutledge said. "I'm afraid I asked who Stephen was."

"Ah. They were very much in love." She looked around her at the library, filled with books, her gaze sad. "She would have been mistress here one day."

"How did you come to know Miss Grenville?"

"We came out in the same year. It's exciting, of course, but a little daunting as well. I made several very good friends, and together we did what we could in the war to help. That brought us even closer. I got to know Kate then as well, and her cousin."

He could tell by the way she said the words that she had no idea that he was the man Jean would have married. He left it that way.

"Tell me about taking out the boat. Whose idea was it?"

"I don't remember. After lunch, it was such a fine day that we decided to ride our bicycles as far as the landing. Perhaps it was Victoria who suggested going out in the boat. I'm not the best of sailors, but I agreed when the others were willing. I didn't want to spoil their fun." She grimaced. "As it happened, I wish I had refused."

"And there was nothing unusual about the outing?"

"No. Elaine asked if we could go as far as the St. Ives gardens, to see if George was on the terrace. I expect he was—someone was. And then we turned back."

"Did you see the other boat, the one that was foundering?"

"Yes, I pointed it out to the others, in fact. There was someone standing in it, waving his arms over his head. Victoria told us to ignore him, that he was merely flirting. We were heading for the house landing, you see, and I thought he must want to join us or some such. I thought it rather foolish of him, and then as we watched, we could see the boat beginning to sink under him. After that everything happened at once. Kate took the oars, and we rowed down to him. But by that time, the boat had sunk, completely out of sight, and he was trying to swim toward us, and not making a very good job of it."

"Go on."

"Kate brought us alongside, and shipped the oars. She leaned over and caught one arm, while I was able to reach the other, just as he was about to go under again. He was flailing about, and we kept telling him to reach out and take hold of the side of the boat, that he was too heavy for us to lift out. But he didn't hear us, I don't think he heard much of anything; his strength was giving out, and he had panicked. It was rather awful, I thought we would either go in with him or have to watch him drown. Neither Kate nor I could manage to bring him in, and he wasn't able to help us." She shivered. "I'll never forget his eyes. He looked at me, pleading for his life, and I could do nothing but try to keep his head above water. As it was he was swallowing water at quite a serious rate."

"Where was Miss St. Ives?"

"She wanted to help, but she would have capsized the boat if she had come over to our side. And I don't think she could have made a difference anyway, there was so little room between Kate and me."

"And Miss Grenville?"

"In the bow. I didn't have time to look at her, I just knew she was there. And then the oar came down on my arms, and I cried out because I lost my grip on Harry."

"What was she doing with the oar?"

"I don't know—perhaps it was about to float away, but whether she was trying to bring it in, or shove it over where Harry could catch on to it, I don't know."

"Were you bruised? When the oar struck you?"

She hesitated, then pushed up the sleeves of her dress. There was heavy bruising on both forearms. It must have been very bad in the beginning, sore to the touch. It was still blue, fading into green and yellow on the right arm, and already green and yellow on the other. "Kate was bruised too. Perhaps it was wrong of us, but neither of us mentioned it."

Out of loyalty to Victoria Grenville?

Looking at her forearms, he wondered if she had inadvertently saved Saunders's life, as the oar struck her before coming down on the man's head.

"How badly was Saunders hurt by the blow?"

She shook her head. "I don't know. I was too busy trying to drag him into the rowboat. Later I saw that he was bleeding rather heavily. But wounds in that area do tend to bleed a lot, don't they?"

"Was he hurt when the dinghy went under?"

"I have no idea." Giving the question some thought, she finally said, "We couldn't see him once he went under. I can't give you an honest answer there."

"And then?"

"I managed to catch one arm again, but I knew we were all in desperate straits. And then someone was swinging himself into the boat, dripping cold water all over us, and I was pushed aside. He grasped Harry by the back of the collar and heaved. Kate and I caught the flailing arms, and then he was out of the water, falling headfirst into the bottom of the boat. I thought he was dying. He never moved. He was on his face, and Mr. Trevose was pushing down on his back, and he brought up water in several retches. When Mr. Trevose turned him over, I noticed the blood."

"What actually caused the blow on the head?"

Again she hesitated. "I never saw the oar strike him, my face was down only a foot or two above the river, and my arms were stretched as far as they could go as I pulled at the poor man."

"Yet it struck your arms."

"Yes, but there was no time to think about it. All that really mattered to me was catching his hand again." She bit her lip. "It was all rather horrible. I think Mr. Trevose saved his life. But pulling him into the boat could have hurt him too. You have no idea of the way he seemed to fly in. The wonder was we weren't all spilled into the river."

Was she lying? Or telling what she remembered of the truth?

"Had you ever met Harry Saunders before that Saturday afternoon?"

"I didn't even know his last name until the constable told us we were being taken into custody on suspicion of having tried to kill him. Elaine recognized him, of course, she called him Harry. She knew the dinghy as well."

"Why do you think Mr. Trevose accused you of trying to drown this man?"

"I truly don't know. He must not have seen the other boat sink. I wondered later if he thought Harry was in the boat with us, and we threw him overboard. But why would we do such a thing?"

"Was the other boat, the dinghy, ever brought up?"

"I have no idea. I expect I haven't even given it a thought." She held Rutledge's gaze. "If they haven't searched for it, why not?"

"Harry Saunders is still unconscious. Perhaps they're waiting for him to wake up and tell them what happened."

"Yes, well, someone should tell them about the boat."

Rutledge considered that a very good point, one he intended to pursue with the constable.

Victoria Grenville was the daughter of the house, and if the house was not entailed to the nearest male relative, she would inherit it.

Rutledge was interested to find that she was a slim young woman with dark hair and dark eyes, self-possessed and yet very alert.

All four of the women were attractive, and all were still unmarried at an age when most women were wed and had already had their first child. A measure of the war years, when men like Stephen Grenville were killed and others like George St. Ives were too gravely wounded to marry. He counted himself among the latter, knowing that whatever he came to feel for someone, there would be Hamish to deal with—and that was an unfair burden for any woman to take on. He had tried to tell Meredith Channing about Hamish, and had found it impossible.

Meredith, with that intriguing stillness that he had found so attractive. Meredith, who had seen the dark side of his life as a policeman and found it so disturbing. He was just learning to trust her, just finding that he could hope for a very different future, when her husband, missing in action, had been found alive and badly wounded in a hospital in Bruges. He had taken her there, and she had left him there. It had been the right thing to do, he had understood that much later. At the time it had seemed to be the ultimate betrayal, binding herself to a man she hardly recognized, whom she confessed she had never loved. He, Rutledge, might hold her heart, but not her loyalty.

He caught himself, and pushed back the shadows. He needed his wits about him now, unclouded by memory.

Victoria took her seat as if by right, and her dark eyes were impossible to read.

He said, smiling, "This has been a harrowing ordeal for the four of you."

"More so for Elaine and me, because we knew Harry. He wasn't simply a stranger we were trying to rescue."

"And yet you took no part in that effort."

He had caught her off guard.

"I was in the bow. Any attempt I made to rush to the aid of Kate and Sara, I could have put us all overboard."

"And yet they were half out of the boat, soaked almost to their knees as water spilled over the gunwale, and tiring quickly. The man was going to drown before your eyes."

"Sara—Miss Langley—is not a strong swimmer. How were we to save him, ourselves, and her, if we capsized? We were too far from the village landing for rescue. It was sheer luck, surely, that Mr. Trevose happened along."

"Have they raised the dinghy that Harry Saunders was in?"

She took a deep breath. "I asked my father that. He told me they hadn't."

"And so there's no proof that you hadn't taken Saunders aboard when first you went out, and then when he annoyed the four of you, you pitched him overboard?"

Her dark trim eyebrows rose high. "That's the most absurd thing I've ever heard. I won't even dignify the question with an answer."

"How well do you know the injured man?"

"We all know who he is. Well, Elaine and I. He's quite the flirt. Before the war he wouldn't have dared be so forward. His father is in banking."

As if that put him beyond the pale, socially.

"Where does he keep his boat?"

"I've no idea. Padstow, I should think? I've never actually seen it out of the water."

"Here was a man out in the river at the same time as you were coming back to the landing, and yet you felt no curiosity about him? Why in that case were you so certain he was simply flirting with a rowing boat carrying four young women?"

"I was told he was waving his arms about and shouting at us. I didn't look around. It would only have encouraged him."

"But he wasn't flirting. His dinghy was sinking under him. Too far from the village to hope from help there."

"We weren't to know that in the beginning, were we? And I had houseguests, Inspector. I wasn't interested in expanding the party to include someone else."

He ignored the question, countering with one of his own.

"Even when you were told that it was more than a flirtation, that he was in trouble, you left his rescue up to those same houseguests. Would you have preferred to let him drown?"

She snapped, "I had sense enough to stay where I was, rather than rush to help and endanger all of us."

"Tell me about Harry Saunders. What age is he? Was he in the war?"

"Thirty, perhaps? And yes, he was in the war. But not in the fighting, the way my brother was, or George St. Ives and so many of our friends. He spent his war in America, with a delegation trying to persuade the Americans to fight. His father saw to that, I'm sure. On the staff of the military attaché to the embassy in Washington."

"It was not a sinecure. They were tasked with finding weapons and powder, foodstuffs and ships, anything that would keep England afloat. Seeing to it that our desperate need remained paramount in the minds of newspapermen and the country's leaders."

"He was *safe,*" she said. "No one was trying to kill him."

"What about the oar that you struck him with?"

Surprised, she said, "The oar?"

"Trevose saw you lift it and drop it on the man in the water. Sara Langley has bruises on her forearms where it struck her as she tried to hold on to him. I expect Miss Gordon was struck at the same time."

"He couldn't reach the side of the boat. It was the only way I could think of to bring him closer, to where he could be dragged aboard. but he ignored the oar. Didn't anyone tell you? I had turned it around, handle first to make it easier for him. That only made it harder for me to control. We almost lost it altogether."

No one had mentioned that she had shifted the oar, handle first and not blade.

He talked to her for another ten minutes but she had nothing more to add. He wondered if perhaps her father had coached her. And if he had, was there anything she should have brought up—or might have left out—that the police ought to know?

When he had finished with Victoria Grenville, he went to find her father, who was just descending the elegant staircase that swept down from the first floor to a wide lobby.

"Can I help you, Inspector?"

"For the moment I've completed my interviews. Thank you for allowing me to speak to the women."

"Of course. Is there any progress that will clear them of this ridiculous charge?"

"In my view, Miss St. Ives may well be a witness and not a suspect. But it's too early to be sure. I need to continue my inquiry before that becomes official. Meanwhile I'd like her to remain in your charge." It was not what Grenville wanted to hear, but Rutledge had to assume that when it came to his daughter, this man was more father than magistrate.

Grenville suppressed a surge of anger. Rutledge saw it in the high color rising in his cheeks.

"Are you saying that my daughter, Miss Langley, and Miss Gordon are still being charged with attempted murder?"

"It's a beginning, Grenville. Be grateful for that," Rutledge retorted. "I understand your concern for your daughter, but it will take time to get to the bottom of what actually happened."

"This was a case where Good Samaritans are being punished for an act of courage. It's unconscionable."

"I'm sure it appears that way to you. But as a policeman, I'm expected to examine evidence and not my personal feelings to arrive at a conclusion."

"Inspector Barrington assured me—"

Rutledge cut through his words. "I'm not Inspector Barrington. I can't draw conclusions where I have not spoken to the witnesses and suspects. All of them. It will take time," he repeated. "And you would be wise to await the outcome with whatever patience you can muster."

With hundreds of years of aristocratic breeding behind him, Grenville swallowed his anger and said, "Of course. You must understand I am a father, and that I am responsible for the well-being of these friends of my daughter's. After all, the incident occurred in my boat. It's difficult to explain to the Gordons, the St. Iveses, and the Langleys that their daughters as well as mine are still being detained by the police."

"Was it you who requested that Scotland Yard be asked to take over this inquiry?"

He could see that it was, although pressure from the other families must have been brought to bear quickly enough. After a moment, Grenville answered him. "Are you a father?"

Rutledge said, "I am not."

"Then it will be impossible to explain to you what any of us felt when we learned of our daughters being put in that filthy gaol cell on a charge of attempted murder. Disbelief. Anger. A sense of helplessness." Grenville's voice was hard now, the courteous host vanished. "It was not something I will soon forget, the constable's lad knocking on my door with such news. But I can tell you this much. I will not let this charge affect my daughter's reputation or prospects in any way. Do you hear me?"

Without waiting for an answer, he walked past Rutledge and shut the library door behind him.

With Hamish loud in his mind, Rutledge drove back to the village and went directly to Constable Pendennis's office.

He was in, reading a newspaper, his feet on his desk. He swung them down smartly when he saw who had come in the door.

"Sir? Did you find the Trevose farm without any trouble?"

"Yes, thank you, and at Padstow Place I've spoken to the four young women who have been charged with attempted murder. A question came up in the course of those conversations. Have you brought up the Saunders boat?"

"Sir?" The constable stared at him blankly.

"The victim was in a dinghy that sank, throwing him into the water."

"I know there was some mention of a second boat, but Mr. Saunders hasn't regained consciousness."

"And Inspector Barrington didn't order that the boat be brought up to see why it sank?"

"Mr. Saunders's father would have to request it, sir. And the thing is, I don't know where to start looking."

"Why would his permission be required?"

"Since his son is not able to speak for himself—" the constable began, but Rutledge cut him short.

"I will need to have it salvaged," he said briskly. "Where can I find men to bring it up?"

"In Padstow, sir, I expect. Would you like me to see to it, sir?"

"Yes. At a guess, the dinghy should be somewhere between the village landing and the estate's landing. Possibly closer to the latter. And request a constable from Padstow to help you question everyone in the village who has a window on the water, asking if they saw the dinghy in question and the victim standing in it as it sank."

"That's a large order, sir. I should think someone would have come forward by now if he'd seen any such thing."

"Not if he—or she—felt such testimony to be unnecessary, that the case against the women was strong enough with the evidence given by Mr. Trevose. Which reminds me. There's a brass knocker on the door of the Trevose farmhouse, and it's a smaller version of the one on the door at Padstow Place. I'm curious about that."

"I never noticed, sir. You might ask the Grenvilles. Or Trevose himself."

"I'd rather not. Find someone who can tell us. Possibly the vicar. Does he live in the village, or is this one of several churches in his parish?"

Smaller parishes sometimes didn't run to a cleric of their own but shared one with another smaller church, providing the living between them. This had increased since the war, or so he'd been told, with fewer clergymen to go around.

"You'll be thinking of Mr. Toup. The vicar. The vicarage is at the bottom of the hill, this side of the church."

"Then he may know if there's any connection between the two families."

"I've not heard of any bad blood."

"Possibly not. But it could go back any number of generations."

The constable nodded. But Rutledge thought he saw no point in the Londoner's interest in family feuds.

He left the constable to his duties and walked out to the landing. The Camel here was called by a different name, although he'd never known why. The River Heyl, he thought. Widening as it ran toward Padstow and the estuary. It had many tributaries, rising on the shoulder of Bodmin Moor and heading south before making a sharp turn to the west. Padstow, for many centuries a port, lay on the far side of the Little Petherick. Across the river was another small town, Rock, but where he stood, he looked out at trees and the fields beyond.

The landing was not large—it accommodated local craft, and a few fishing boats. The water was shallow in places where the bright yellow sand had clogged the river's edges, but a channel ran through, enough for the boats to pass upstream some distance. The river itself was no more than thirty miles long.

He turned and looked up toward the church. The vicar, as visible as a crow in his black suit of clothes, was wandering through the dry grass, a sickle in one hand to cut through the taller clumps.

Rutledge started his way, but someone called to him, and he stopped.

"You're the man from London." It was a statement, not a query.

He turned. A man was just coming out of The Pilot. Over his head the sign, showing a figure holding his post at the ship's wheel in what appeared to be a gale, moved slightly in the breeze from the river, and it creaked on rusted hinges.

"I am." He waited for the other man to catch him up.

The landlord, or the barman, for he was wearing an apron. Of middle height, with glasses, and a bristling mustache, he looked more like a schoolmaster than a publican.

"Nasty business about young Saunders," he said. "He comes into The Pilot from time to time. Nice enough lad. Keeps himself to himself for the most part, but never unfriendly."

They stood in the middle of the street running down to the landing. It was a quiet time of afternoon, the shopping for dinner or tea done, men not yet home, children still in school. The bustle would start again in another hour.

"I understand his father owns the bank here and in Padstow."

"And in Rock," he said, gesturing toward the town on the far side of the river. Something in his manner indicated that he cared very little for his neighboring village, in spite of the broad sandy shoreline gleaming brightly in the late sun, that unusual—for Cornwall—yellow. "Came down from London a generation ago, and done very well for themselves."

Rutledge waited. The man had hailed him, there must be something more on his mind than the family history of the Saunderses.

When nothing more was forthcoming, Rutledge asked, "Liked in Padstow and in this village, are they?"

"Not much socializing between them and us, but respected people."

"Tell me about the son, Harry."

"Already have. Didn't see much of him, but he was never a troublemaker. Not one for airs and graces because he was at the bank."

"I've been told he was in America for most of the war."

"True enough."

"And there was hard feeling that he had an easy four years—thanks to his father's influence—compared to those who fought in the trenches or served at sea."

"Wasn't his choice to make, was it? Nor his father's, I expect. Still, if a family has lost a son, it's bitter to think that money made a difference."

"Did Harry Saunders own a boat?"

"He did. Many of the lads take out their father's, but he was given a trim little craft the summer before the war."

"And it has a dinghy?"

"Of course it does," the man replied, as if Rutledge had lost his wits.

"Had he taken it out on that Saturday?"

The man shook his head. "If he did, he didn't put in here."

Having exhausted all the questions he could think of, Rutledge said, "Was there something you wanted to tell me, Mr.—er—or ask me?"

"The name's Penhale. You might stop in at The Pilot one evening. It can give you as good a meal as the inn, and better company."

"Thank you, Mr. Penhale. I'll do just that."

He turned to walk on. He was almost out of hearing when Penhale called softly, "Bad blood between the Grenvilles and Trevose. But you didn't hear it from me."

Rutledge didn't pause or look around. With a barely perceptible nod, he continued on his way.

It had taken the publican time to work up his courage to pass on that bit of news. Rutledge wondered why. Whether there was a reason he wanted the police to know. If he himself was on one side or the other—or was afraid to take sides but wanted his own back in some way.

He considered speaking to the constable about what he'd learned but decided against it. Instead, he made his way toward the church.

A signboard by the gate in the wall informed him that this was the church of St. Marina, and the vicar's name was David Toup.

It was quiet in the churchyard. There were a number of recent graves, and some rather handsome Celtic crosses for such a small church. It was of the same Cornish granite as the village, with a sway-backed slate roof that appeared to be sinking into the nave. The tower looked to have been built in three stages, rising well above the church, and with slender pinnacles to give it even greater height at the battlemented top.

He could hear the vicar, still at work on the far side of the church.

Glancing at the stones, some of them sagging with age into the hummocky ground and one or two of Cornish slate, he made his way around the apse.

The vicar was in his shirtsleeves now, and a fair pile of grass in a barrow showed his progress. A tallish, thin man with graying streaks in his hair, he wore a pince-nez, and the golden chain was looped around a button of his vest, already tangled with the chain of his watch.

At his feet were six or eight hens, waiting expectantly for the seeds and insects falling to the wayside as he worked. They stretched their necks in alarm and turned to stare at Rutledge. The vicar straightened, sickle in hand, tossed a clump of dry grass into the barrow, and said, "If I don't keep at it, the seeds soon take over. Welcome to St. Marina. You must be the man they were expecting to come down from London."

"Inspector Rutledge," he responded and held out his hand. The vicar looked ruefully at his own, then dusted them on the seat of his trousers before taking it.

"So sad about your colleague. Inspector Barrington. I was called straightaway, but he was gone before I could reach him. I did what I could. I will say, and I think Dr. Carrick will bear me out, that he didn't suffer. Dead before he reached the floor, apparently. Did he have a history of trouble with his heart?"

"Not to my knowledge, no."

"Yes, well, sometimes the first attack is also the last." He took a deep breath. "And another tragedy, young Saunders. I'm told he's still unconscious. I can't judge whether that's a good sign or a bad one. How can I help you, Mr. Rutledge?"

"How well do you know the four young women who are accused of trying to kill Saunders?"

"I've known Miss Grenville and Miss St. Ives since they were christened. Miss Gordon and Miss Langley have been visitors from time to time. It's my understanding they met in London."

"Any problems with them? The visitors or the two local women?"

"Good heavens, no. Always well behaved, as they were brought up to be. During the influenza epidemic, Miss Grenville came down to nurse her father through his illness, and before it was over, nursed half the staff as well. Fearless, she was. I did what I could, but there was the village to see to. It was rather severe here, the Spanish flu."

"How long has she known Harry Saunders?"

Toup was surprised by the question. "Let's move out of this wind, shall we? There are benches in the church porch. As for Miss Grenville and Mr. Saunders, they were acquainted, of course. He grew up in Padstow and was often here with his father, learning his trade. He began as a clerk in the summer of 1914, sadly enough, then enlisted. It's possible they met in London a time or two before he went to Washington."

He led the way, and they could distinctly feel the wind drop as they stepped into the covered porch.

"And Miss St. Ives?"

"She was engaged to Stephen Grenville, of course, but I'm sure she and Saunders met, as young people do."

"She was young to be engaged before the war."

"Well, yes, but it had been understood since they were twelve that they would marry. Inseparable."

"And the other two?"

Toup shook his head. "I can't tell you if they'd ever met or not. I had heard rumors that Miss Langley and George St. Ives had met in London." He smiled. "Matchmaking women in the Temperance Society that meets at the vicarage on Thursdays. How they found out I don't know. Women seem to have a sixth sense about these things."

"And Miss Gordon?"

"I think perhaps she's the more levelheaded of the four. Charming girl, but she's also intelligent and capable."

"Then why should she conspire to help murder a man she barely knew?"

"Ah. I've heard the stories going round, you know. That Saunders had gone out with them, there was a quarrel, and he went overboard. Whether by accident or design I can't say."

"Why should he have gone out with the group?"

"He was in the water, fully clothed. An indication in most minds that he must have been in the boat at the start."

"The four women tell me that he was in his own boat, but it sank as he was heading toward them. They were trying to fish him out of the water. Apparently he wasn't a strong swimmer, or he'd have been able to pull himself into the rowing boat."

Toup stared at him. "I hadn't heard that account of events. Is this true?"

"Would it appear to make sense to you?"

"It makes more sense than murder. But where is the boat? The proof of what they are saying?"

"Out in the channel somewhere."

"Well, I must tell you that it makes very good sense to me. I was made very uncomfortable by these accusations. And yet—Trevose isn't the sort of man to lie."

Time to test Penhale's theory, Rutledge told himself.

"Is there bad blood between the two families?"

"Not to my knowledge. No, certainly not. Unless of course you count the deer."

"What deer?"

"There's a small herd at Padstow Place. Nearly tame, I'm told. Some years ago, well before the war it was, they were scattered during a winter storm, one of the worst in memory. A few of them found themselves on Trevose land and were helping themselves in his fields. He was all for shooting them, but Grenville came to collect them and threatened to fine Trevose if he so much as touched them. Regulars at The Pilot—that's a pub in the village, I daresay you've seen it down by the landing—will tell you that Trevose is still smarting from that encounter. Nonetheless, I'd hardly call it bad blood so much as a difference of opinion on the matter. Trevose claimed they would find their way back again, and if they did, magistrate or no magistrate, he'd stop the deer from destroying his livelihood. A way of saving face, I think, because they never came back."

"Then why is the knocker on the door of Padstow Place identical in all but size to the one on the door of the Trevose house?"

"Is it? Are you sure? I don't think I've ever noticed."

"I'm sure."

"How very extraordinary. But then, possibly not. There was a blacksmith in the village many years ago who made useful but very lovely things. By the vicarage door, I have a hook for my hat that is beautifully done, a scrolled *S*. It was there when I came. Someone told me it was made in the village. I daresay if there was a pattern for a door knocker, and someone else admired it, the old man would have copied it for him."

It was one explanation. Rutledge let it go.

The hens had followed them around to the porch, busily scratching in the path to the church, looking for seeds.

Toup said with apologies, "Their ancestors fed us during the war. Eggs and meat and feather pillows. I haven't had the heart to get rid of them. They live in a wooden hut outside my kitchen door, but when I come to the churchyard, they follow."

Rutledge smiled. They were beautiful birds, larger than most, and a dark blue-green with light brown patterning. Their combs were small and more orange than red.

Rising, he said, "Thank you, Vicar. I've enjoyed our talk."

"Any time, Inspector. I wish I could help you sort out this tangle, but unless you find that boat, we will be facing a rather unpleasant situation here."

The vicar was on his feet also, and the hens looked up, cocking their head expectantly. He strode back around the church, and the hens scuttled after him.

5

It was time to call on Harry Saunders, to hear from the doctor attending him exactly what had happened to him. And more urgently, to see the wound for himself.

Rutledge asked Constable Pendennis for directions to Carrick's surgery in Padstow, but when he rang the bell, the doctor's nurse informed him that Saunders had been taken to his father's house in the hope that familiar surroundings would bring him round sooner.

And so he found himself in an older part of town on a street with larger houses standing above the harbor.

Number 16 was two stories, painted white with dark gray facing stones used in a rather attractive pattern. There were bay windows on either side of the door. A handsome house. He knocked on the door, and it was opened by a middle-aged woman dressed in the uniform of a housekeeper.

"I'm afraid," she said, before he could speak, "that there is illness here, and the family are not receiving any visitors. If you will leave your card, I will see that they know you have called."

"I'm not a visitor. My name is Rutledge, Scotland Yard. I should like to speak to the elder Mr. Saunders, please."

She hesitated, uncertain whether to turn him away or seek advice about admitting him. "If you will step this way, sir, I'll see if Mr. Saunders will speak to you."

She led him to a room just off the entrance hall, and closed the door behind him.

It was a spacious room, tastefully decorated in pale green and cream, but the furnishings were Victorian and dark. He went to the window and looked down on the inner harbor, the stone arms of which gave safe anchorage in storms. Beyond lay the river, broadening as it swept out to the sea beyond. The low headland on the opposite shore was dull green at this time of year. A forest of masts picked out the fishing boats, but there were several pleasure craft as well, and a lifesaving station to one side.

Rutledge turned as the door opened. Mr. Saunders was of medium height, and appeared to have put on weight as he reached middle age. But his graying hair was well cut and his dark clothes indicated a good tailor, as one would expect of a banker.

On closer inspection as he went to meet his host, Rutledge could see the deep lines on either side of his mouth and the puffiness of sleepless nights and worry around his eyes.

"Mr. Rutledge," he said, coming forward but not offering his hand. "You've replaced Inspector Barrington, I believe."

"I've had to take up the inquiry without his guidance," he said, as Saunders indicated chairs by a marble-topped table. "And so I must ask questions that may repeat those he asked. How is your son?"

"Still unconscious. The doctor fears bleeding on the brain."

"May I see him?"

"He's not on display," Saunders retorted sharply, then shook his head. "I'm sorry. Of course you must. It's just that we've had any number of visitors moved more by curiosity than any interest in my son's condition, and it has been very trying for us, his mother in particular."

A gathering of crows, one Inspector had called it, come to find out whatever they could to add to the town gossip. Rutledge had seen it before.

Saunders led the way to the stairs, saying, "If you will hold your questions until we've returned to the parlor?"

"Yes, of course."

They mounted the steps, turned right, and entered a bright room where the curtains were opened wide to let in the sun. A fair-haired woman in a dark blue dress was sitting by a bedside, reading aloud from a book. She put it down and rose, looking at her husband.

"Inspector Rutledge, my wife."

He nodded to her across the still body of her son. She said, "Dr. Carrick has suggested reading to him. He tells us Harry may be able to hear our voices, if not the words."

Rutledge approached the bed. Under a pretty coverlet lay Harry Saunders. There was no longer a bandage on his head, but the cut where the oar had struck him was an angry raised line on his forehead within a quarter of an inch of his hairline. Rutledge judged it to be several inches long and quite deep. There was a raised lump as well.

Which meant that the oar had hit him before it had hit Sara Langley's forearms?

Or had this been the work of the thwarts? Rutledge was inclined to believe that it was the oar, considering the depth of the injury. It indicated too that he must have been struggling to keep his head out of the water. If the oar had come down only a matter of inches lower, it would have struck him across his nose and eyes. That at least had been a blessing.

He looked at the face of the unconscious man. Perhaps not handsome, but he had certainly inherited his mother's regular features, and his hair was the light brown that could well have been fair in his youth. He had a strong jawline and broad shoulders.

The sort of man that women would find attractive . . .

Apparently Victoria Grenville had not felt that way.

Mrs. Saunders put out her hand and smoothed back a strand of hair that had fallen across her son's forehead. "He's so *quiet,*" she said.

And he was. None of the twitching or involuntary movements of a sleeping man, untroubled and at rest.

Rutledge realized, glancing around the pleasant room, that it must be his mother's, feminine in detail, boxes of powder and jars of creams and crystal flasks of perfumes on the elegant dressing table, chintz covering on the chaise longue in a pattern of violets, wall papering with cream and pink and lavender cabbage roses. A summer garden, a familiar place, a comforting place.

Saunders would recognize it if and when he opened his eyes.

Rutledge had seen enough. He thanked Mrs. Saunders and followed her husband out of the room.

Out of earshot on the stairs, Rutledge said, "Does your son live with you?"

"He did before the war. And for some months after he came home. Now he has a cottage of his own just a few streets from here."

"And so you aren't aware of his comings or goings?"

Saunders stiffened.

Rutledge said, "For instance, if he takes his boat out or looks in on the bank in the village or in Rock, across the river. If he attends a party or has friends in to dine."

Innocuous pastimes, the sort of ways a young unmarried man might spend his time.

Saunders relaxed. "That's true. We didn't know he was in Heyl village. Not until word came."

"Does he take his boat out often?" They had reached the hall at the foot of the stairs. Rutledge noted that he was not invited to return to the parlor. But then Saunders appeared to be dead on his feet from worry and lack of sleep.

"Not the larger one, although in the summer he tries to make a few weekends for sailing down the coast."

"Did he take the smaller one to row up to Heyl village?"

"I can't imagine why he would do that, dressed to spend time at the bank. He has a horse, an Irish mare. Pretty little thing."

"Is the dinghy still tied up here in Padstow?"

"I've no idea, I have hardly left my son's side. Certainly I had no time to worry about boats."

"How well did your son swim? Do you know?"

Saunders looked away. "Not very well. He never took to the water as a child. Short distances. He preferred to be on the water, not in it."

Which confirmed Rutledge's earlier assumption.

"What was he wearing when he was brought to the doctor's surgery?"

"One of his dark suits, white shirt. Tie. What he'd expect to wear to do business."

"It was a Saturday. Is the bank open on a Saturday afternoon?"

"It is not. It closes at twelve. But there may have been a private meeting with someone thinking of buying a property. That sort of thing."

"Or perhaps to go calling on a friend?"

"Yes, that too. Although Harry doesn't have many friends in the village. It's not—comfortable—when your father owns the bank."

"I can understand that. How well does your son know Victoria Grenville? Or Elaine St. Ives?"

The man's mouth drew into a thin line. Then he replied, "I would have said, before last Saturday, that he and both young ladies were friends. Not close perhaps but most certainly on civil terms."

"Before last Saturday," Rutledge repeated in a thoughtful tone of voice, adding, "Miss Grenville is now an heiress. She would be considered quite a match for anyone in Cornwall. It wouldn't be unheard of for your son to wish to press his suit."

"Nonsense!" Saunders snapped. "He will most likely find a wife in London banking circles."

But not many fathers would be irritated by a liaison with a cadet branch of the Grenville family, one who owned an estate as fine as Padstow Place and had probably owned much of the town itself in the distant past.

Saunders opened the door. "Good day, Mr. Rutledge. I hope to hear from you very soon in regard to the attempted murder of my son."

"I'll keep you informed, of course," Rutledge answered pleasantly and went out the door, leaving Saunders himself to shut it behind him.

He wasn't certain whether Saunders actually believed that the four women accused of the attack on his son were guilty or whether in his fear and doubt he wanted someone to blame for that still form lying upstairs in his wife's room.

Rutledge drove on into the Old Town, left his motorcar in the yard of a pub, and walked down to the harbor. It was busy today, people coming and going, the shops doing a brisk trade, and a few women sitting or standing by the water, enjoying the view as they talked with acquaintances.

When he asked several of the men who were walking past if they could point out where Harry Saunders kept his smaller boat, they shook their heads.

"I expect it's too busy here in the harbor to tie it up," one man told him, anxious to be on his way.

"Didn't know there was one here," another told him.

And a third suggested that it might be tied up at a private dock instead.

He walked the length of the harbor but saw nothing that he could say with any certainty belonged to Saunders. And the first man had been right, the harbor *was* busy.

A fourth pointed out the larger Saunders boat, at anchor in the roads. A sailboat that Rutledge estimated could accommodate one or two people in its tiny cabin.

It was pleasant here in the sun, surprisingly warm now that the omnipresent wind had dropped, or because this was a sheltered place. Rutledge stood for a time with his back to the town, looking out to sea beyond the low headlands. One of his informants had told him there was a dangerous shoal out there, not a likely place for a small boat.

He had asked if it were possible to row upstream to Heyl, and he was told that it was a long pull if the tide was running out.

So where had Harry Saunders kept his boat, and why had he been rowing past the village that Saturday afternoon?

And then he turned and retraced his steps, looking for a salvage yard. Constable Pendennis had promised to see to it, but Rutledge wasn't convinced it would be a priority for the Heyl police.

He found what he was looking for and made arrangements for the yard to send someone upriver to find Harry Saunders's boat. The owner, a stocky man with a beard, brought out a map and asked Rutledge to pinpoint the area to be searched. He did that to the best of his ability, adding, "I was not there when the boat sank. It may have been left or right of the mark I've made. But I shouldn't think you will have too much difficulty locating it."

The man nodded. "We'll do our best. Why did it sink, do you know?"

"That's the point of retrieving it," he replied. "To find out."

Walking to where he'd left his motorcar, Rutledge took a detour to Church Street to see the church of St. Petroc.

It had been a great pilgrimage center, until the bones of St. Petroc had been taken away to Bodmin—and then stolen from there and carried off to Brittany. Henry II had restored them to Bodmin. And

Padstow became a backwater. The church was more a chapel, with gray stone, a square tower, and a churchyard full of tombstones tilting and leaning in the high grass. The mounded graves, the grass around them still thinner and shorter, marked where those who had died of their wounds in England lay buried alongside influenza victims.

He could feel Hamish stirring as he looked at them, and so he turned away, not lingering there.

It was on the way back to Heyl that Hamish finally spoke for the first time that day. A cloud had crossed over the sun, leaving a gray light behind that made the scenery more suitable to the time of year, a dreary dampness that promised rain.

"Yon man in the bed didna' look verra' good. It's a matter of attempted murder now. What if he dies? What then? His father will press for a trial. And it willna' go well for the lasses."

"It won't come to that." But he could see in his mind's eye a picture of Elaine St. Ives standing in the dock, in tears as she was being cross-questioned by the prosecutor. Any trial would be held in Padstow, where the Saunders name carried weight.

"You canna' be sure. And there's the Gordon lass."

He didn't want to think about Kate, charged with a murder. They would hold her and the others in gaol if Harry Saunders died. And he, Rutledge, would be responsible in a way, if he couldn't uncover a clearer answer to what had occurred there in the rowboat.

Kate didn't resemble Jean at all. They were very different in so many ways. Kate, if anything, was the plainer of the two, although very attractive. And added to that was her spirit, a natural openness and caring for others that was apparent after a few minutes in her company.

All of them would find prison life devastating. Even if their names were cleared, there would be a shadow over them for the rest of their lives.

But what he didn't know—couldn't know now, couldn't ask—was how Kate felt about him.

The last time he had seen her in that fall of 1914, when he was on his way to enlist in the Army, he had realized that this friendly, lively woman who had tried to help him understand Jean's mercurial temperament had been in love with him herself. And hidden it so well that he had had no idea how long or even how deeply she'd felt that way.

And he would not hurt her if he could help it.

He owed that much to Kate and to Jean.

By the time he reached the village, the cloud over the sun had become a dark bank, and the temperature had dropped to more seasonal levels as well.

He went to the inn and began a more thorough search of Inspector Barrington's belongings.

Barrington had not come for a very long stay. Two changes of clothing, nightclothes, extra pairs of shoes, an umbrella, shaving gear, a box of stationery that yielded a letter to his wife he'd begun but never finished, and his return ticket to London stuck inside a book he'd been reading on the journey down to Cornwall. Nothing in the shoes, nothing in pockets or between the folds of shirts. No loose sheets of paper, no small leather-bound notebook.

Rutledge took out the unfinished letter and read it. He hadn't wished to, but it represented the only contact with Barrington left to him.

My love,

I've arrived safely and set about the inquiry, but I fear Chief Superintendent Markham is wrong about dealing with this business quickly. I haven't visited the injured man yet—he hasn't regained his senses. But I've spoken to a number of the people involved. They don't seem to agree on many of the details. He may be better able to tell me with greater accuracy exactly what occurred.

It appears that I shall miss the Matthews' anniversary party, worst luck. You must go and wish them well for me. Twenty-five years of marriage. Wonderful indeed.

And it had stopped there, as if he had put it aside and expected to come back to it later.

His wife would be glad of it.

If the statements weren't in his valise, where were they? And why would anyone wish to take them? Everyone knew who the victim was, everyone knew by this time that Trevose had made the accusation against the four young women. There would be no surprises in the interviews as far as he, Rutledge, could judge.

But of course the room would have been cleaned daily. Perhaps Barrington had hidden the papers to keep prying eyes from reading them and gossiping about what he or she had seen.

He set about searching the wardrobe from top to bottom, and then the room, even lifting the mattress from the bed and searching in the hems of the floor-length curtains before pulling up each corner of the carpet.

Nothing. He looked behind the three pictures on the wall, went through the washstand.

Sitting down on the bed again, Rutledge admitted defeat.

If they were here, the statements and any notes that had been made about the interviews, if they were still in Inspector Barrington's possession at the time of his death, why would the constable lie about not finding them?

It didn't matter, he told himself. He had already talked to the principals, with the exception of Harry Saunders, and he probably knew as much now as Barrington had uncovered before his untimely death.

But it rankled. A policeman's notes were the Yard's business and no one else's, until he appeared in a courtroom.

What could Barrington have uncovered that might change the outcome of this case?

Or to put it another way, he thought, what had someone feared he'd uncovered?

Still, it was more likely that someone had been curious enough to take them, and didn't know just how to restore them to luggage now locked away for London to collect.

He spent half an hour interviewing the staff, but no one professed to knowing anything about Inspector Barrington's papers.

Hamish kept him awake until nearly four o'clock in the morning. And just before dawn the rain came down in a hard shower that turned into a steady downpour. When Rutledge looked out his window, the pavement was wet, water running in rivulets down the street in front of the inn, and those who were out this early hurried along with their heads bent and their umbrellas losing the battle with the elements.

The salvage people had promised to be there by eight o'clock, but they didn't come. He understood, it was not the best of weather to search for and raise a boat, even one as small as the dinghy the four women had described.

After breakfast he went out to the motorcar and set out to find the landing where Victoria Grenville and her friends had taken the rowboat onto the river.

Twice he drove down a rutted lane that led into a tenant's farmyard and had to search out a place where he could reverse. On the third try, he was luckier, and soon rounded a bend to see the small wooden jetty where a rowing boat was tied up.

He was surprised to see it there, swinging with the tide. He had thought it might be impounded as evidence. But very likely Grenville had prevailed and had it brought back. There was a canvas stretched over it to keep out the rain. He got out, pulled his umbrella from the boot, and walked onto the jetty. It was not quite twenty feet in length, a row of wooden pilings with planks nailed across to form a surface. From the look of it, he thought it had been there since well before the war. Some of the planks had been warped by weather and time, giving it an uneven appearance, although it was sturdy enough to take his weight without creaking.

He stood looking down at the boat, but it could tell him very little. It was large enough to accommodate the four women, and riverworthy if not seaworthy, with high sides and a blunt stern.

It would have been difficult to drag a grown man over the side and into the boat, most especially one whose clothing was already waterlogged.

But that was assuming the women were telling the truth.

Leaving the jetty, he looked for a place where the bicycles could have been left, but with the rain there was no way of being certain which stand of stunted scrub they had chosen.

He walked on along the shoreline for a time, damp sand clinging to his boots. In the distance, through another heavy shower, he could just make out the village landing and the pinnacles of the church tower. Beyond, the color of the water changed as the Little Petherick flowed into the Camel. Padstow was a blur downriver.

He soon picked up a rough track that followed the riverbank, and realized he must be off Grenville land. Several turnings that led inland must go to farms, he thought, a shortcut across the fields. The Trevose farm as well? Where exactly had Trevose been going that afternoon?

About here, then, was where Trevose had been walking.

He moved on, about halfway, he judged, between the Grenville landing and the village. The river was wide enough for the rowboat to be in the channel, and if the tide was full, a strong swimmer could make it to the boat in a matter of minutes.

If the women were intent on killing Saunders, they had only to let him go as soon as they heard Trevose shout. Saunders would have been pulled away from the boat by the current and drawn under. Trevose would have had to dive to find him, and even then it might have been too late, especially if the man had been stunned by the oar.

Why hadn't they?

Were they so intent on what they were doing that they wanted to finish it? Or were they holding on as best they could until help arrived?

Turning back the way he'd come, he found it hard to believe that Kate Gordon would be a party to murder.

Hamish, surprising him, taking advantage of Rutledge's change in mood, said in a voice loud enough to be heard over the rain beating down on the umbrella, "Ye canna' know she's the same person. It's been six years."

"People don't change that much. I can't believe Kate would." He broke off. There was a man standing by the jetty, watching him. He held a shotgun, broken, over his arm.

Had he answered Hamish aloud? Or had his words been caught by the wind or smothered by the rain?

He walked on, and when he was close enough, the man said, "This your motorcar?" His Cornish accent was so heavy Rutledge found it hard to translate what he was saying into plain English.

"Yes, mine," he replied.

The man waited until Rutledge was nearer, then added, "This is private land. You have no business driving in here."

"My name is Rutledge. Scotland Yard. I believe you'll find that Mr. Grenville will have no problem with my being on his land."

"That's as may be. I saw you down the home farm. Will he give permission to interfere there as well?"

"Hardly interfering," Rutledge said, stopping just out of range of the shotgun. "I'd like very much to know why you're armed."

"Trespassers. There were two men from newspapers at the door of the Place this morning. I was told to see they didn't disturb the family or wander about the property."

"I'm not a journalist."

"That's as may be," the man said again.

"Then we'll walk to the house, shall we, and ask Mr. Grenville's view of the matter."

After a moment the man said, "No need to disturb them again. If you're leaving."

Rutledge had seen all he'd come to see.

"As a matter of fact, I am."

The man stepped back, allowing Rutledge to pass. After turning the crank, he took his time closing his umbrella and stowing it once again in the boot. Then he walked to the driver's door and opened it.

Holding it open, he knocked the sole of first one and then the other of his boots against the frame, to shake off the thick coating of sand.

The man, waiting impatiently, said nothing. Rutledge got into the motorcar, reversed, his wheels spinning a little in the heavy wet sand, and then turned back toward the main road.

In his mirror he could just see the man standing there watching him before he was cut off by the bend in the road.

It was not very wise of Grenville to send one of his tenants out with a shotgun to keep interlopers off his property. On the other hand, he must feel beleaguered, and the estate was the only place he could protect his daughter. And her friends.

At least that was the way it appeared. But if the tenant took his work too seriously, there could be more charges than attempted murder.

When he reached the village again, he sat in the motorcar for ten minutes, telling himself that there must be other avenues to explore. People to talk to. Anything but going back to Padstow Place and speaking to Kate and the others. What more could they tell him?

Watching the raindrops racing down the windscreen, he put together all he'd learned thus far, and so far there was nothing to alter the initial charge against Victoria and her friends.

It still came down to their word against that of Bradford Trevose. In a courtroom in London, the four women might prevail. They were from good families, respected and respectable. A good barrister could claim that Trevose misunderstood what he was seeing and jumped to conclusions. That he had indeed helped the women save the drowning man. But there was the blow from the handle of the oar.

It was harder to explain away. It would depend on whether a jury believed that Victoria Grenville's intention was to help, to give Saunders something to hold on to if they weren't able to drag him in. A way to pull him to shore.

But it could also be viewed as fear that he might be saved.

By the same token, in a trial in Cornwall, would a man like Trevose be believed instead? He was known, one of their own, and a jury might well be persuaded that he would never have leaped into the cold waters of the Camel if there had not been a real threat to Saunders.

But where was the motive for murder?

Not even Saunders had suggested one.

Rutledge was about to step out of the motorcar when he spotted Constable Pendennis pedaling fast toward the inn. The constable saw him and veered into the yard.

"What is it?" Rutledge asked as the bicycle was braked to a skidding stop, a wave of muddy water splashing across the motorcar's radiator.

"I've just had word, sir. From Padstow. It appears that Harry Saunders has taken a turn for the worse. I thought you ought to know as soon as possible."

Rutledge stood there, grimly listening to the constable.

It behooved him to get to the bottom of what had happened on the river. Before the charges changed from attempted murder to murder.

6

Thanking the constable, Rutledge got back in the motorcar and pulled out of the inn yard, driving to Padstow Place.

The same maid admitted him and led him to the library. This time there was no delay before Mr. Grenville joined him.

"Are you here to question my daughter and her friends again? I don't know how much more they can tell you."

"That may be necessary. I've come because you should be aware that there has been a change in Harry Saunders's condition. It has worsened."

Grenville stood there, his face showing nothing. Then he asked, "Is this an attempt to frighten my daughter and my guests into confessing to something that would be a lie?"

"I'm quite serious, sir. I felt you should be told."

Grenville frowned, the fingers of one hand bracketing his mouth. "Will you give me your word that this is the truth?"

"I have no reason to lie."

Grenville turned away, walking toward the fire that burned on the hearth. His hands gripped the marble chimney piece, and Rutledge could see that his knuckles were nearly as white as the marble itself.

Then he straightened. "I shall have to send word to my solicitor. And to the other families involved. Will you arrest my daughter and her friends?"

"Not yet. I'll be forced to do that if the charge becomes murder."

"But Saunders can't die. He was hit on the head, half drowned. But he's healthy, young. He'll recover."

"I'm told there's bleeding on the brain."

"Dear God." He looked toward the tall windows where the rainwater was running in streams. "All right, what is it you need to ask? Who is it you will need to speak to?"

There was no choice in the matter.

"Miss Gordon."

"Wait here. But don't frighten her. I won't have that."

"You needn't worry. I'm sure she will understand the situation herself."

But he was speaking to Grenville's back.

In five minutes, Kate Gordon stepped through the doorway.

"Ian? Is there any news? Mr. Grenville was not himself when he came to my door. What is it? What's happened?"

He told her. There was no way to soften the blow.

She sat down abruptly. "Poor man," she said. "His parents must be frantic. But what can I do? What can we do?"

"I want you to think back to that Saturday afternoon. Is there any detail you might have forgot?"

She considered the question, her head to one side. "No, I think I've been as clear and honest as I can be."

"I shall need a written statement from each of you. It seems that your earlier ones have been mislaid. But let me warn you that they might well turn up, and if they do, and there are any inconsistencies between them, it will not go well for any of you."

Kate stared at him. "You're frightening me."

"No. I'm trying to warn you. That's all."

"I hardly remember the first statement. I was cold, my skirts hanging heavy around my ankles. And so very tired. I'd have given anything for it all to be over, a bad dream or a misunderstanding of some sort. But what's happened to the earlier ones?"

"Barrington had them, but they weren't in his belongings when Constable Pendennis looked for them. And I've searched as well. They've gone missing."

"That has an ominous ring to it."

"I don't know."

He went to the small escritoire standing in the middle of the room beside a small bookcase filled with what appeared to be older, more precious books. There was paper in the single drawer, and pens. He took out several sheets and handed them to Kate, along with one of the fountain pens. "Here. Take your time. If you think of something that might not be in the earlier version, tell me."

Kate took the pen and paper, walking to the little desk and sitting down in the matching chair. Its back was heavily carved, vines and faces peering out from behind them. She stared out the window at the rain, collecting her thoughts, and finally began to write. When she'd finished, she read it over, then looked up at Rutledge.

"Shall I sign it? I did the other one."

"Yes. Please."

She wrote her name with more confidence than he thought she felt, then rose from the chair.

"Will everything be all right, Ian? I must tell you, I'm worried. I sit there alone in my room, and I find myself reliving those ten—fifteen?—minutes. Knowing that in spite of all I can do, this man Harry is going to die. And then it felt like a miracle when Mr. Trevose pulled himself into the boat and lent his strength to ours. You can't imagine what it was like. Euphoria, which I think gave us what we needed to save him. I dream about it at night too."

He wished he could give her a comforting answer, but he refused to lie to her.

"I don't know, Kate. We'll have to wait and see. I'm doing all I can."

"I know you are, Ian. I don't doubt you for a moment." She managed a smile, and reached out to lay her fingers on his arm. "I'm glad you're here."

He put his hand over them for a moment, and then said, "Will you send Miss Langley to me next?"

"Yes, of course." She walked steadily to the door, but when she reached it, she turned to say, "It's the oar, isn't it? That's what is making us vulnerable. But I know Victoria, Ian, she's a little headstrong and spoiled, but I worked beside her during the war, carrying trays of tea to the trains full of recruits and of wounded, making sure each man got his hot drink and sometimes a bun. She was so cheerful, so quick to understand what this man or that one needed. The tea, a kind word, a smile. No matter how tired she was, or how awful the wounds. Even when we recognized someone we knew among the wounded. I can't picture her trying to hurt anyone."

The problem was, and he couldn't tell Kate, that if Victoria wasn't believed, if she couldn't convince everyone that she had meant to save rather than kill, she was very likely to condemn the others too.

The library door opened and Grenville stepped into the room, another man at his heels.

Rutledge rose from the table and waited.

The other man was Kate Gordon's father.

His expression was stern, controlled anger with not a little fear behind that.

"Rutledge," he said with a curt nod of acknowledgment, "Grenville told me you were here, and so I've traveled from London to speak to you. What's this nonsense about my daughter being accused of attempted murder? You know very well Katherine would not be a party to any such thing."

Rutledge hadn't seen Gordon in six years. Not since September 1914. The man's brown hair was grayer than it had been then, but he still had the carriage of a soldier despite the loss of his left arm. He had been part of the British Expeditionary Force sent to Mons, and he had fought straight through to the Second Battle of Ypres, where he'd been severely wounded.

"Hardly nonsense, Major Gordon. It's a very serious matter."

"It's incompetence, that's what it is. To have let it go this far."

"The police have not been able to interview Harry Saunders. Until they can, until he can tell them what happened, there are conflicting accounts of events on the water."

"You have four women telling you the truth, and one man, who was not on board that boat until the last few minutes, giving you a garbled version of it. I should think it would be straightforward enough to dismiss all charges, regardless of Saunders's condition."

"It doesn't quite work that way," Rutledge told him. "The women are being charged with attempted murder, and therefore their testimony is suspect. In the eyes of the law, Mr. Trevose is a witness with no known reason to lie. It will require Saunders's statement to break the impasse."

"I have never known my daughter to lie," Gordon said, his anger breaking through. "I'm sure Grenville here can tell you that as well, about Victoria. That must count for something."

"It will take a jury to determine who is telling the truth in this case, and I'm sure neither you nor Mr. Grenville wants to see the case go that far. I'm here to do my best to find not just the truth but proof of the truth. At this moment we're waiting for Saunders's boat to be brought up and examined. That may tell us something."

But Gordon wasn't to be persuaded that nothing could be done.

"I should think that you of all people should have no trouble coming to conclusions. You were engaged to Katherine's cousin. See that you remember that."

He turned on his heel and left the room in long, furious strides. Grenville followed him, shutting the door firmly behind them.

Rutledge took a deep breath and walked to the windows. Rain was still coming down in buckets, sweeping across the lawns in gray veils that obscured the light and the view across the gardens. Nearer to hand, taller plants in the border beneath the window were already bending under the weight of the water.

He could understand Gordon's distress. But this inquiry had nothing to do with Jean, his engagement to her, or any debt he owed the Gordon family for releasing her from her betrothal to him. Still, in those first weeks after news of her death had reached him, sometimes in the middle of a long sleepless night he had wondered if he'd done the right thing in telling her she was free. And yet what sort of life would she have had with *him*?

Rutledge could feel Hamish stirring in the back of his mind, and resolutely shut off the soft Scots voice as Victoria walked through the door.

"I know you were expecting Sara. I've come instead. I'm well aware that my actions have made this whole affair seem far more—sinister—than it is. I didn't try to kill Harry. I like him well enough, but lately there had been apparently accidental encounters with him. I could see where this might be leading, and I didn't want to embarrass either of us by having to tell him outright that I had no feelings for him. Not in that way. And so I'd tried to avoid him. When Sara and Kate saw him waving to us, I thought it was just one more of those chance meetings that generally ended with an invitation to lunch or tea or even a party his parents were giving. I never encouraged him, but it didn't seem to matter to him that I refused him time and again."

Rutledge, listening to her, couldn't decide whether she was telling him the truth or what she believed he wanted to hear, in order to clear her of any murderous intent.

When he didn't speak at once, she went on, her hands twisting together in some anxiety. "One doesn't go about killing unwanted suitors. It's ridiculous even to think so."

"Unless his attentions had become so persistent that you were exasperated enough to stop them for good."

"Don't be silly," she snapped. He might be Scotland Yard, but in her eyes he was only a few years older than she was, and she clearly expected him to understand.

"Did you put this information into your original statement, the one given at the police station before you were released to your father's care?"

"No," she admitted. "I thought it best not to. How would you like it if all the world were told you'd been flatly rejected? That's how Harry would feel."

He thanked her for giving him additional information, then asked her to write out her statement again.

She wasn't happy about that, but didn't refuse him.

Rutledge finished his collection of statements as quickly as he could. Major Gordon was still in the house, and he could feel the change in atmosphere. He rather thought even the four women, segregated as they were from the household at large, could sense the tension. He rang for the maid and told her that he was leaving. She stepped into the room and handed him a folded twist of paper.

"I was to give you this before you left, sir."

He opened it, holding it under the lamp to read the words scrawled on the small square of stationery.

I am in the morning room. Please ask Alice to show you the way.

It was unsigned, but the hand was feminine, he thought, and he looked up at Alice. "Before I go, could you show me to the morning room?"

"Yes, sir, this way, sir."

He shut the library door behind him and followed her down the passage to a small room done in a silk wallpaper in a shade of rose that showed off the swirled patterns in the fabric. Around the ceiling, in place of the usual molding was a band of darker rose that was picked up in the ribbons that displayed an assortment of paintings. A large mirror in an ornate gilded frame above the mantel reflected the comfortable but stylish furnishings and the woman waiting beside a Louis XV table desk.

She was as dark as her daughter, slim and very attractive still. The soft green dress she was wearing was London tailored, he thought. She waited until he had closed the door before speaking.

"Good morning, Mr. Rutledge. I'm Victoria's mother. Thank you for seeing me."

"What is it I can do for you, Mrs. Grenville?"

"I wish you could make all of this nightmare go away. But I'm afraid no one can. Please, will you sit down?" She pointed to two formal chairs on either side of the hearth, and joined him there. "I'm not sure how to begin. But I think it's important for you to hear what I have to say." She stared into the heart of the fire, and began to talk to it, rather than to him.

"Mr. Trevose has every reason to wish this family ill. And it's my fault. Some years ago, before I was married, I was invited to a house party at St. Michael's Mount. Do you know it? Have you ever been there?"

"I know where it is. On an island in Mount's Bay. I've seen it from a hotel in Penzance."

"Yes, well, it's an island as you say, and it was built up rather than out, rising well above the landing. The only access is by boat. We were all very young, and on a rainy Saturday evening, we were playing a game of hide-and-seek. It wasn't a wild game, just fun. There were so many good places for concealment. We hadn't heard the wind come up, but it had. I was looking for a place to hide and one of the footmen, hardly older than I was, showed me the door to one of the terraces, and I went outside. It was a warm summer rain, but it had made the flagstones slippery, and the wind caught at my gown. There was no railing at the edge of the terrace, and I thought I was going to be blown over into the sea. The footman snatched at my hand, and tried to pull me back. I found the handle of the door and clung to it for dear life. But he lost his footing and one moment he was there, the next he was gone. I was petrified. It took me what seemed to be an unconscionable amount of time to pull myself inside, and I ran screaming for help. The others thought it was part of the game, and ran after me, laughing and crying out that I was now it. I found someone finally, and I reported what had happened."

She moved her gaze from the hearth to Rutledge's face. "They discovered his body the next morning. On the rocky shore. Quite dead. I believed it to be my fault. Even now I do. But everyone said it was his for showing me such a dangerous place, and he must have had designs on my virtue, taking me out there in the dusk. But it was I who went out there, and he followed me only to keep me from falling. To protect my good name, it was called a tragic accident, and the footman's family was told of his death."

He wasn't sure where she was going with her story, but he could see that she was still haunted by it. And so he waited in silence.

"When I was married and came here to live at Padstow Place, I didn't know that the footman's family lived on a farm nearby. I was out riding one day and I encountered Mr. Trevose. He looked me up and down in a rude way and told me that he could now see why his brother felt I was worth dying for. It shook me, Mr. Rutledge, and I thought I was going to be ill. I was already pregnant with Stephen, and I said nothing to my husband or anyone else. When I came in from my ride, they saw how pale I was and they put me to bed and called a doctor. He ordered me to give up my rides. And of course I did, but not because I was pregnant. I have seen Mr. Trevose many times since that day—in church, of course, and around the village—but we have never spoken since. It was as if that day hadn't happened. But it had. And now I'm afraid he's found a way at last to pay me back for his brother's death."

"Who knows about this encounter?"

"No one. I told no one, not even my husband. I expect Mr. Trevose has said nothing about it either. There has been no gossip. If there had been, it would have come to my attention sooner or later."

He regarded her, wondering if she was telling the truth or was willing to sacrifice herself to save her daughter. After all, she'd lost her son. Victoria was the only child left to her.

"You realize that you have given me information that I shall have to investigate before I can discredit Mr. Trevose's statements. There will be no easy way to do this, and your name will eventually come out. I can't protect you and get at the truth at the same time."

"I wouldn't have told you any of this if I hadn't been prepared to accept the consequences."

"How, for instance, did Mr. Trevose learn your part in his brother's death? If it was treated as an accident?"

"I don't know," she told him frankly. "I've wondered. My best guess is that one of the staff wrote to him or his parents and told them what had occurred. At the time I hadn't met my husband; I had no connection to this part of Cornwall. I expect Mr. Trevose was as surprised to learn I was to be mistress here as I was to learn that his family's farm was nearby."

"Are you sure that there was nothing between you and this footman?"

"Paul. His name was Paul. I had seen him, of course I had, and he was simply one of the staff."

"What was he doing in that part of the house, when you were looking for a place to hide?"

"I don't know. He was carrying a tray with a glass on it. Someone had asked for something to drink. It was thought that he'd stepped outside on the terrace for some air. The house was stuffy, closed up on a stormy evening."

"You reported his death. How could you have known it had happened, if you hadn't been present?"

"It was said that I heard a cry, saw the door swinging open, and realized that someone had fallen. That I had initially thought it was one of the players. The doctor came and gave me a sedative. He asked me what had happened, and I was so frightened I also told him I believed it was one of my friends. He passed that on to the police."

"And did Paul try to force himself on you?"

"Good God, no, he was laughing and saying that no one would think to look for me on the terrace, and if I stood close to the doors, my gown wouldn't get wet. He was a footman, but he was a human being. He thought it great fun to help me." She covered her face with her hands for a moment, then dropped them to look at him. "We hadn't heard the wind, it had come up with the end of the storm. And out in the bay, cut off from land, the Mount got the brunt of it. Certainly the sea was very rough. They couldn't bring in the police or retrieve the body until later in the day. The fear was, it might wash away before anything could be done about it."

"And you believe this is why Mr. Trevose has accused your daughter and her friends of harming Harry Saunders?"

"Of course I do," she said impatiently. "What other reason could there be? Do you honestly think, for one moment, that those four young women are capable of trying to murder a perfectly respectable young man?"

"Your daughter tells me he has been running into her too often to be by chance. That he has feelings for her. Or at the very least, is infatuated."

Her eyebrows rose in surprise. "Harry Saunders? She hasn't—" She stopped herself in midsentence. "Would you find that so strange, Mr. Rutledge? She's a lovely girl. And he's unmarried."

"Would you or your husband be willing to entertain his suit, if he came to you to ask for your daughter's hand?"

Her eyes gave her away before she could answer him. There was no snobbery—she really believed that the heiress to Padstow Place could do much better than a banker's son. "We would treat his suit with every courtesy," she said.

"Victoria is no longer a young girl. I'm surprised she isn't married already."

Mrs. Grenville shook her head. "The war. Were you in it, Mr. Rutledge? Yes, of course you were. Most of her friends never came back. Or if they did, they're like George St. Ives, so badly wounded that they can't expect to enjoy a normal life. I don't think Victoria or Kate, Sara or Elaine, having seen their world change so drastically, are as eager to marry as they might have been in 1914 when all the world was a happy place."

Rising, she said, "I've kept you long enough. But I felt I had no right to say nothing when Mr. Trevose is apparently so willing to see my daughter and her guests charged with such a crime as attempted murder. Can you find your own way out? Or would you like for me to summon the maid?"

"I can find my own way, Mrs. Grenville." He started toward the door. "I am grateful for your confidence. But I will use it as I think best. I suggest you tell your husband what you've told me. Before it becomes public knowledge."

"I will choose my own time, Inspector."

He left her standing there in the middle of the room, just as he'd first seen her.

He wouldn't have been surprised to run into Grenville or Major Gordon as he found his way to the house door and made a dash through the rain for his motorcar.

Once clear of the house, he considered what he'd just been told.

Was it true? Or was there a great deal more that hadn't been said?

Either way, he came to the decision that he would say nothing until he was ready. If Trevose was out for revenge, then let him think he was successful for the time being. It would keep him out of further mischief.

And it wouldn't go amiss to ask Sergeant Gibson to look into the death of Paul Trevose at St. Michael's Mount. Meanwhile, he must find out more about the Trevose family.

And the best place for that might be the vicar, David Toup.

He drove through the village to the vicarage, where rivulets of water had turned the drive into a muddy glue. He could hear his rear tires spin as he made his way up the slight rise to the front of the house, and then picked his way through the puddles to the door. Someone had put a hemp mat there, and he wiped his feet as best he could before knocking.

Toup himself came to the door.

"Mr. Rutledge. Come in, man, and bring the ark with you."

Laughing, Rutledge stepped inside and Toup closed the door quickly.

"You'll be wanting to dry a bit by the looks of you. Come into the study and stand by the fire."

Rutledge followed him down the passage and into another dark Victorian room. The wallpaper was a medium blue with sailing ships plowing their way through the sea.

Toup saw him looking at it, and said ruefully, "The former vicar was from a seafaring family. I find myself seasick at the sight of them. I was about to eat my lunch. There's plenty, won't you join me?"

"Yes, thank you."

"Then we'll adjourn to the kitchen if you please, unless it's a matter of my services that brings you here."

"Just your memory," Rutledge answered, and followed him to the rear of the house to the large kitchen. Here the walls were painted a soft green, with a plain deal table and chairs set under the windows.

"I often take my meals here. There's fresh bread and eggs and cheese and so on. I can make a dish I learned to cook in France."

"By all means."

Toup busied himself at the counter, then checked the ancient cookstove before putting the kettle on for tea. "My housekeeper's day off, and I'm sure she's elated to be warm at home instead of trudging back down the lane to her house. Talk to me if you will, I can do two things at once."

Rutledge had considered his approach. "I've learned quite a bit about the Grenvilles and the St. Iveses. Even the Gordons and the Langleys. I know next to nothing about Trevose. Is his an old family?"

"Yes, they've been here for centuries. On the same land. They've produced some fine soldiers over the years. And even finer farmers."

"There's an older woman who came to the door."

"That's Bronwyn, the housekeeper. She was Trevose's mother's housekeeper as well. I have no idea how old she is, but my guess would be seventy. I may be wrong."

He was busy chopping onions, their sharp tang filling the room.

"Did Trevose have any brothers or sisters?"

Finishing the onions, Toup cracked a brown egg into a bowl. The yolk was a rich yellow. "There were three children, I believe. A sister who died of some childhood ailment, and a brother who was killed in an accident when he was sixteen, seventeen."

"What sort of accident?"

"It was before my time. And I've never asked. You don't, sometimes. In my first church I asked a woman about her dead son, only to learn he'd been hanged for murder. What I've told you I've discovered in the course of many conversations. Or seeing a name on a tombstone or in the church records."

"Then Trevose is not married?"

"No. I can't say 'never' because I don't know. But he's been alone save for the housekeeper ever since I took over the church."

He had finished beating the eggs, added bits of cheese and onion and a handful of breakfast bacon he took from the pantry. The teakettle boiled, and he set it to one side and put a large iron skillet in its place.

"And when did you come here?"

"Twenty-seven years ago. Straight out of seminary."

"And the Saunders family. Any children other than Harry?" He knew the answer but was interested in how the vicar would reply.

"The apple of their eyes, Harry. Someone told me that Mrs. Saunders had suffered several miscarriages before he was born."

"You told me that his family had come down from London in the past. Where is she from?"

"London. While the elder Saunders was there in training, he met her and brought her home with him."

"Love at first sight."

"Or so many people claim."

"And the Grenvilles?"

"I would say it was a love match. They are certainly well suited and seem to go on well together. And if you're about to ask where she's from, it's Plymouth. She's a distant cousin or something."

He remembered that Mrs. Grenville had told him the events in St. Michael's Mount had occurred before she met her husband.

"So they've known each other most of their lives."

Toup had scrambled the eggs and bacon and onion together, then turned them out on thick slices of a light brown bread. "I should think they must have done. But you never know."

Setting that on the table, he made the tea, brought out plates and utensils, cups and saucers, then began to cut the eggs in half, offering one half to Rutledge.

It was very good.

They were silent for a time, enjoying the meal, and then Rutledge asked, "Tell me, do you believe the young women were attempting to save Saunders? Or Trevose, that they were intending to kill him?"

Toup stirred uneasily. "I'm not a policeman, and it's not for me to judge."

Rutledge said, "I can appreciate your feelings. But you know all the participants in this tragedy. You must lean one way or the other."

Toup got to his feet and began to look in one of the cupboards. He brought out a small poppy seed cake and set it on a plate.

"I would be happier if Trevose is wrong. Victoria Grenville and her friends are young, with a life ahead of them. They did wonders in the war, the four of them, although they seldom speak of it. In addition to their duties offering tea to troops leaving for the Front and the wounded coming home, they gave their time generously. Raising money for widows and orphans, organizing families to knit and put together packets of things like paper and pencils, needles and cotton thread, shaving soap and razors to send to the troops, rolling bandages for hospitals, collecting warm clothes for fatherless children, encouraging people to write to soldiers and seamen . . . The list is amazing, when you think about it."

"The war has been over for two years. How do they occupy themselves now?"

"Ah." He picked up the plates and carried them to the sink as they finished their meal. "It was Miss Langley who said something about that to me after a visit that included attending a church service here. 'I've lost too many people I love,' she told me. 'I won't be hurt ever again by loving someone.' I found it very sad." Looking out the window he added, "I do believe the rain is letting up. My root crops will rot before they can be dug if it doesn't stop soon. Carrots and beets and parsnips and the like."

He was adroitly changing the subject. Rutledge let it go.

Ten minutes later, he thanked the vicar for his lunch and said goodbye, stepping out into a lighter rain. The wind had dropped as well.

Driving back into the village, he found himself wondering if Kate felt the same way about her future. He rather hoped, for her sake, that she didn't.

7

Harry Saunders died without regaining consciousness at a little after seven that evening.

Word was brought to Constable Pendennis, who in his turn came at once to the inn to pass the news on to Rutledge.

"Are you certain of your news, Constable? It was from a trustworthy source?"

"Yes, sir, it was one of the doctor's nurses. It's murder, now," he said. "I shall have to ask Mr. Grenville if he will bring Miss Grenville and her friends in to be charged. There's no room in the police station here for them. Only one cell, and no matron. I shall have to send them to Padstow or Wadebridge."

"I'd rather have them remain where they are," Rutledge told him. They were in the parlor of the inn, speaking quietly so that no one in the bar in the next room could hear them. "I will need to speak to them, and there's evidence still to be examined."

"Begging your pardon, sir, but now that young Saunders is dead, people will expect it. Murder changes the complexion of the inquiry."

"It does. And I will take them into custody myself when the time comes."

"I can't spare anyone to stand guard at the house."

"I think Mr. Grenville's word will be sufficient. What did you learn from the house-to-house canvass? Did anyone see Saunders out in his boat that same afternoon? Or have a better view of the river and what was going on?"

"The constables from Padstow couldn't find anyone who had seen anything. I find that very queer. All those windows overlooking the mole and the river? But no one has come forward."

How many people's livelihoods, he wondered, depended in some way on the Grenville estate or family? Or was it a simple matter of not wanting to be brought in to testify? The bank was important in the life of the village now, and people might not wish to stand up in court and give evidence at all.

"I'll drive to the Place and tell them the news. And make certain that Grenville understands his responsibilities."

"They have the money to spirit their daughters away to the south of France or even America. The Grenvilles and the St. Iveses. The others as well, to be sure."

"You're chasing shadows, Constable. And if these were your daughters, would you wish them in a cell anywhere?"

He had the grace to look away, reconciling his need to see things properly done and the fact that if the evidence was wrong, he would make the Grenvilles and the St. Iveses very angry with him.

"Very well, sir. If you insist."

"I'll take full blame, Constable."

He set out five minutes later to Padstow Place.

The family had just sat down to dinner.

Grenville came out to speak to him, saying, "Can't it wait until we've finished our meal?"

"I'm afraid not, sir. I've just received word from Padstow. Harry Saunders has died of his head injury. This means that the charge of attempted murder has now been changed to one of murder."

Grenville stared at him. "Are you sure, man?"

"Word was brought by one of Dr. Carrick's nurses."

Grenville turned to look toward the dining room, then swung back to face Rutledge.

"If you are here to take my daughter and my guests in to a cell, I will tell you as Chief Magistrate that I will not allow it."

"For the time being, I've persuaded the constable to leave them where they are. The weather is clearing; tomorrow I should be able to find Saunders's boat. Until I have that, I can postpone any official action. If it's not there, then we're back to the question of whether or not Saunders was in your rowboat, what he was doing there, and how he came to be in the water."

"Good God," Grenville said again, absently rubbing his chin with one finger as he tried to think. "Thank you. And I believe it would be best to say nothing to my wife or the young ladies. Not tonight. The news will keep until tomorrow. Let them rest." He looked up at the lamp that lit the entry and the stairs, an ornate but small chandelier. "I've lost my only son. I am sorry for Saunders and his wife. I know what that grief is like."

"Is Major Gordon still here?"

"He's on his way to London. God, I shall have to send a telegram to him, and to Langley. Have you told St. Ives?"

"That's where I'm going when I leave here."

"He'll find it as difficult to accept as I do. There's George, you see. Well. I must return to the dining room and keep this to myself as best I can. Good evening."

Rutledge left and drove on until he found the gates to the St. Ives house. It was not the size of Padstow Place, but even in the cloudy darkness, Rutledge could see that it was nearly as old as the Grenvilles'.

On the ornate gates, standing wide, was the image of a Cornish chough, the large glossy black bird with the down-curving red beak and red legs. It was depicted in soaring flight, with its long wings and short tail caught beautifully, and red enamel had been applied to the black of the iron plate to show the legs and beak.

One legend had it that as King Arthur died, he was transformed into a Cornish chough, and his spirit still watched over England.

On the gateposts were brass placards, one to each side, giving the name Chough Hall in English to the right, and presumably in Cornish to the left.

The house rose three stories above the drive, crenellated at the roofline, and spread out into two smaller wings on either side. The drive stopped at a set of three steps that led up to a broad terrace lined with stone urns, and the iron-studded wooden door was set deep in arched stonework.

He lifted a brass knocker in the shape of the St. Ives coat of arms, and waited several minutes before someone answered the door.

It was a manservant, dressed in black. "The family is not receiving this evening," he said.

"I'm from Scotland Yard. Please tell Mr. St. Ives that I'm here."

The man went away, and soon afterward St. Ives himself came to the door.

"Rutledge? Grenville told me he'd spoken to you. I was coming myself to speak to you today, but the weather stopped me."

St. Ives was older than Grenville by some years. A heavyset man, a head shorter than Rutledge, and balding.

"Come in, then. I was in my study."

Rutledge followed him into the interior, lit by only one lamp and filled with shadows.

"We keep early hours without Elaine here," St. Ives was saying. "My son just went up."

There was a fire on the hearth of the comfortable room, bookshelves lining two walls, a desk to one side, and leather chairs ranged around the hearth. There was paneling where there were no shelves, and several paintings hung in those spaces. Rutledge could see the resemblance to what appeared to be ancestral portraits going back to the 1700s, judging from the style of clothes.

"Sit down. Whisky? It's a raw night."

"Thank you, sir, but no."

"Bad news? Well, spit it out, man. We've been no stranger to it of late."

"Harry Saunders died earlier this evening."

St. Ives sat down hastily, as if the air had been let out of him. "I have been prepared for that. At least I thought I was. But it's a shock to hear it, all the same. Have you told Grenville?"

"I've just come from there."

"How did my daughter take such news?"

"The family was at dinner. Grenville thought it best to wait until tomorrow."

"Yes, well, he's right there. Elaine wouldn't sleep a wink, worrying about what's to happen next." He sprang to his feet again as he realized what Rutledge's call must mean. "Here! You're not taking them back to that damned cell, are you?"

"Not yet. But you must realize that it will happen sooner rather than later. Unless someone else comes forward to give us a different account from the one Trevose has given. Constable Pendennis has had men canvassing the village houses with windows overlooking the river. No one has admitted to seeing anything."

"Fools," he said succinctly. "But then we're used to the river being there. We don't sit and stare at it by the hour. We have better things to do. I've seen visitors do that, and it's all very well if you're on holiday. But listen to me. Elaine is not fit to sit in a prison cell for months on end. She wasn't always of such a nervous disposition. When Stephen was killed, I thought we'd lose her as well. Then her mother died of that damned Spanish flu, and her brother came home an invalid. She's seen how fragile life can be, and it's changed her. She cries over a dead mouse, for God's sake. What will happen to her in a prison, where the roughest of inmates will prey on her?" He looked at Rutledge. "I won't allow it. You must understand me on this, Rutledge."

"I find it hard to believe that your daughter was a party to any attempt to kill Saunders—but she has been accused of the crime, and that will have to be dealt with."

"We'll see about that," St. Ives retorted grimly. "If I have to apply to the King himself, I'll protect her. He has a family, he will appreciate a father's fears."

Rutledge said nothing. The King would have no authority here. Still, he remembered when, as a newly minted constable, he'd heard the older men talk about the conditions under which the suffragettes had lived in prison, and their treatment. It had been punitive, designed to deter them from some of their more dramatic behavior. But prison was still harsh, and the other inmates would make life wretched for women like Miss St. Ives, gently reared and unprepared for what she would find there.

"I'll go to see her in the morning," St. Ives was saying. "She'll be sick with worry. It might even be possible to persuade the others to clear her name. *Damn the man*," he added vehemently, and Rutledge wasn't certain whether he was referring to Saunders or Trevose.

"They can't clear her name. To say that Miss St. Ives had taken no part in the drowning will condemn them. What we need is fresh evidence, a new witness to come forward."

"I'll offer a substantial reward. That ought to bring the most reluctant witness out of hiding."

"Along with every poor fisherman or farmer eager to claim it, even if it requires them to perjure themselves. What's more, you can't be sure you'll be given the information you're searching for. It could make matters worse."

St. Ives swore. "I don't like this feeling of helplessness, Rutledge. It doesn't suit me, damn it."

"Nor does it suit me. But I'm bound to follow the law." He rose to take his leave. "Grenville will send telegrams to Langley and Major Gordon with the news of Saunders's death. It would be advisable for all of you to keep your heads. Otherwise you will do more harm than good threatening to take matters into your own hands."

"Easy for you to say," St. Ives answered shortly. And then he took a deep breath. "Damn it, Rutledge, I know you are doing your best here, but surely there's a way around this?"

"Much will depend," he said, "on how Saunders's parents take the death of their only child."

"Well, putting my only daughter in prison won't bring their son back."

"Did you know Harry Saunders?"

"I've seen him in the bank—he's been learning the trade—and in the village. I doubt I've exchanged a dozen words with him. Nice enough lad, as far as I could tell. Polite and all that. What he was doing out on the river that day still bewilders me. Foolish enough of Victoria to go boating."

He walked with Rutledge as far as the outer door, and said in parting, "Look, give me a few days to sort this business out. There must be something my lawyers can do. God knows that barrister charges enough."

"I'll do what I can, but I must remind you that the best hope your daughter has is the truth."

"She is not a liar," St. Ives said angrily. "She has no reason to lie."

"I haven't suggested she is. But she may feel some loyalty to her friends."

"We'll see about that," St. Ives snapped. "Good night to you, sir."

And the door swung shut almost on Rutledge's heels.

He had done what he could, he told himself, cranking the motorcar and then turning down the dark, twisting drive.

It was not a good night. Rutledge awoke twice, to sit straight up in bed, staring out through the windows at a darkness that was so pervasive in the countryside. No streetlamps, very few evening parties or concerts, everyone in bed by nine, ten at the latest.

The first time he'd had a tangled dream involving Olivia Marlowe, Kate Gordon, and her cousin Jean. He had been in the water, knowing that he only had enough strength left to bring one in to shore. And they were pleading with him as he struggled to find a way to save them all. The burden of decision had had nothing to do with the fact that Olivia Marlowe and Jean had been dead for several months. There in the swift running channel of the Camel, they were very much alive, eyes large and pleading in pale faces, hands frantically reaching for him. And in desperation he'd forced himself to wake up, to end the nightmare before it became unbearable.

He thought afterward that the second dream had been brought on by the tension of the first. For this time Hamish was there, lying just above him as the earth inexorably pulled them down into the suffocating darkness. The shell had deafened him, he couldn't hear anything or see anything, but he could feel the fabric of a man's tunic pressed against his face, and the weight of the man's body pressing him even deeper into the earth. He had tried to push it away, to escape from the burden above him, even as he knew it was hopeless. A small pocket of air between him and the body was all that was keeping him alive, and when that was gone, he would be dead too. He couldn't resign himself to dying that way, using all his strength, realizing he was using all that remained of his air as well. In real life, he had lost consciousness just seconds before he'd been found, but in this particular dream, somehow he could see the face of the corpse, black as it was in that crater, and he nearly flung himself out of bed to escape it.

His chest heaving, he tried to steady his heartbeat, and then he put his head into his hands and stifled the screams that were still echoing in his ears.

It was some time before he realized that he hadn't screamed, for no one came pounding on the door, no one called out to him to ask what was wrong. And yet the cries were so vivid in his mind that his ears rang for several minutes.

He got up, walked across the chilly floor, and with the heavy tongs set more pieces of coal on a fire that had gone cold and gray in the grate. It took matches, some stirring with the poker, and determined patience before it caught enough to lick at the kindling. Then he sat there and watched it until the blaze was bright and warming. He held out his hands, then stood up and went to the window.

A pale light told him where the river was, and he realized that the sky was beginning to clear.

The salvage firm would be able to start searching for the Saunders boat.

Still looking out at the river, he heard Hamish's voice as clearly as if the Scot stood just behind his left shoulder.

"What if there isna' a boat out there?"

Rutledge answered him aloud, as he often did when he was under a strain: "That could send Kate and the others to the gallows."

Rutledge had just finished his breakfast when there was a stir outside. He had chosen to sit by the windows, and he rose to see what had attracted attention.

A boat was coming upstream, and he recognized it. The men from the salvage yard had arrived. It passed the landing and continued up the river.

He tossed his napkin on the table and went out to watch. He could feel the curiosity in the onlookers, some of them silent, others speaking in low voices. He thought they probably guessed what the crew was searching for. It was obvious that a number of the watchers believed this attempt had been initiated by the police to corroborate

Trevose's belief that Saunders had been in the Grenville boat from the start.

His own tension mounted as the crew finally dropped anchor and leaned over the railing on both sides, peering down into the water below. Then they moved several yards upstream before looking again. And there they prepared for their first dive. It was an agonizingly slow process. Unfolding the heavy suit, helping their man clamber inside as the hoses were checked and rechecked, and then finally screwing down the helmet.

Three more times they moved upstream, bringing in the diver each time and divesting him of the heavy helmet. Then the ritual of leaning over the rail began the process all over again before sending him back down. Rutledge, watching the sun glinting on the bulbous copper and brass helmet as the man descended once again, felt cold, his claustrophobia at the thought of being in the man's weighted shoes almost making him turn away.

But on this dive, he had been down only a matter of minutes before he signaled to be hauled on board again. As soon as his helmet had been removed, there was a conference on deck, as if determining what to do next.

Rutledge had the uneasy feeling that they were giving up, that there was nowhere else the dinghy could have sunk out of sight, except there in the main channel.

And then they were lifting the helmet over the man's head again, bolting it in place, and sending him below, now lowering chain and other gear after him. Twenty minutes later he broke through to the surface, this time towing a chain behind him.

By God, they've found something! Rutledge thought.

Constable Pendennis came to stand at Rutledge's elbow. "Who summoned the salvage firm?"

"I did, when I was in Padstow."

"I'd have seen to it, sir. Save for the storm yesterday."

Rutledge didn't answer him.

The chain was brought in along with the diver, and the crane on the back of the boat began to winch whatever the diver had found up out of the river.

There was something close to a sigh passing through the growing crowd of watchers as the winch groaned and clanked, the sounds carrying across the water.

Something barely broached the surface and sat there, still invisible, for a good ten minutes, and then it was lifted free of its grave with great care, streaming water and river mud before it was gently swung aboard the salvage craft.

The *Sea Lion*'s dinghy.

The watchers had fallen silent.

The crew bent over it, examining it. Impatient now, Rutledge stood there, counting the minutes. And then they divested the diver of his suit, stowed their tackle, and finally pulled up the anchor, heading back downstream.

Rutledge ran for his motorcar, ignoring Pendennis, who turned as if to follow him, and drove up to the High Street on his way to Padstow.

By the time he'd reached the town, after driving to the nearest crossing up Little Petherick creek, the salvage boat had returned to its moorings and the dinghy was being winched ashore.

Rutledge joined the owner of the firm.

Henry Kelsey turned to greet him. "There she is," he said. "You can see the lettering."

On the stern of the dinghy was the painted inscription *SEA LION, Padstow.*

"That's the Saunders lad's boat, the *Sea Lion.* Pretty little craft." He pointed out past the harbor where a number of boats swung at anchor. "That's her, the black bottom and white trim. A pity. Word came with the milk this morning that he died last night."

"Where did he keep the dinghy?"

"At a private landing just west of the town. Before you come to Prideaux Place."

"Is it there now?"

"'Course not, there she sits."

"In police matters, it pays to be sure."

"No, I'd recognize her anywhere. And you might wish to have a look."

Rutledge followed him to the dinghy. It smelled of silt and river water, some of the boards already beginning to swell.

"Look here."

Under the seats, almost impossible to see, were a series of small holes.

"They wouldn't have brought in enough water at the start for him to notice. But eventually he'd begin to sink."

"How far could he have gone with those holes?"

"It would depend. If someone had plugged them with twists of paper, let's say, these would have soaked through soon enough and begun to come out a bit at a time. The point being, it would seem to me that whoever did this wanted Saunders to find himself well out to sea or up the river before he reckoned he was in trouble. And then the more water he took on, the faster he'd sink. And look here," he said, pointing to a place in the stern. "He'd have coiled the rope after untying the boat, and dropped it here. And there's a larger hole. No idea what that was plugged with. But as the boat took on water, that would open up too, and he'd go down fairly quickly."

Rutledge looked at the signs that Kelsey was pointing out.

"If the boat was in water, these plugs could have come out long before Saunders next took his boat out."

"He pulled it up on a bit of sand. See the scratches on the bottom." Kelsey had several men turn the craft. "No, someone wanted him to sink in yon dinghy."

"Someone wanted to kill Harry Saunders," Rutledge said finally, straightening up.

"That's what it looks like to me. In all my years in this business, I've never seen anything quite like it." He bent down again and touched the largest hole. "I'd give much to know what it was that had been used as a plug."

"So would I. It might lead us to whoever did this."

But the boat's discovery halfway between Heyl and the Padstow Place landing confirmed the account that the four women had given of Saunders being in trouble, the boat sinking under him.

Rutledge thanked Kelsey and paid for his services, asking him to keep the boat in his yard for a day or so and say nothing about the damage. Then he got directions to the small landing where the dinghy had been tied up.

He found it without any trouble, just west of the town. There was a house above the landing, and Rutledge went up to the door. No one answered his knock, and he walked on down to the water's edge.

Over his head the gulls wheeled, shrieking in glee at the sight of a possible meal being tossed their way. He counted five varieties, from herring gull to the smallest, the common gull, warily skirting their larger brothers.

For centuries the fishing industry had fed the gulls of Cornwall, and when the ships came in, the heads and entrails of the catch drew cats, dogs, and gulls to partake of the feast. To many people, the gulls were the souls of fishermen lost at sea, coming in once more with the fishing boats.

Rutledge wondered if some summer visitor had fed these, and the birds had remembered.

The landing was no larger than the one at Padstow Place, and it had space to tie up two small craft, one on either side.

The other one lay on its side on the sand to the left of the landing. A length of canvas covered it from stem to stern, and it appeared not to have been taken out for some time.

Where the Saunders dinghy should have been was bare sand. He went over to it and squatted, looking at the spot and the surrounding area. He could see that the boat was often dragged up above the water-line. The sand was more compact, and a little lower than that around it. Getting to his feet, he walked out on the landing to where the water lapped at the end, again scanning the area.

Had someone intended to sabotage the other boat, and by mistake worked on Harry Saunders's instead?

He went back to where the dinghy should have been. Who would want to kill Saunders? This was hardly a place where Victoria would bring her friends. The house was only a little larger than a cottage, and so were its nearest neighbors some forty yards away. The sort of places someone might use in summer and shut up all winter. The roof was made of Delabole blue, a pleasing contrast with the cream whitewash on the walls.

While other parts of the Duchy boasted tin and copper mines or clay pits or granite quarries, the vast Delabole slate quarry was all that this part of northern Cornwall had in the way of industry.

Rutledge went back to scuff at the sand with his boot, on either side of where the boat might have been drawn up.

He found a large nail, the sort that might have been used to make the holes. If someone had been here at night, he could easily have lost track of it.

He moved closer to the landing, and as he did, he saw something just visible in the shadow cast by the pilings that held up the planking. He squatted, and dug at it with his fingers.

When it came up, caked with sand, he couldn't decide what it was. And then he recognized it. A corner torn from a woman's gown. No more than three inches in length, yet he could still see the delicate embroidery: sprigs of lily of the valley tied in a green ribbon.

Turning, he looked back toward the house. It appeared to be closed up for the winter, and when he went up to peer in the window by the door, he could see dust sheets over the furniture.

He walked on to the next house, and there too the furnishings were covered, not as tidily as in the first cottage. Here sheets had been thrown over chairs and tables to keep the worst of the dust and sand out, whereas the others had been heavier and fitted.

He went to the third of the houses that stood above the landing. There was sand on the steps, and an air of occupation. He knocked before looking in a window. A man in his seventies answered the door.

"I saw you walking about, studying the cottages. Thinking of renting that far one for the summer? The nearer one is taken."

"I was curious about the landing."

The man chuckled. "I provide one for those who let the two cottages, but the truth is, they're not likely to use it. Town people, come for the summer. And more likely to drown themselves than row across the bay. Still. They seem to like the boat being there. They take photographs of the family sitting on it."

"But there has been a second boat. Who does that belong to?"

"That's Harry Saunders's. He pays me a little extra to allow him to tie up here."

"Where is the boat now?"

The man shrugged. "No idea. He comes and goes as he pleases. Took it out last Saturday a week, but I didn't see the *Sea Lion* put out to sea. I should think it's in for an overhaul. Wouldn't be surprised. Good time of year for it."

"You're certain he took it out that Saturday."

The man grimaced. "I'm not senile. Of course I'm certain."

"I'm sorry, I needed to be sure of the date. Has anyone come here to look at his dinghy? Or the cottages?"

"Not of late. There's more interest in the early spring. Letting is more reasonable now, of course, if you're interested. It's a nice class of visitor who comes here, you know. Last summer we had two spinsters and a newlywed couple."

Rutledge thanked him and left, walking back to his motorcar, where he'd left it near the middle cottage.

He needed to speak to Harry Saunders's parents, but they would be in the deepest mourning now. There were other questions he could put to Kate Gordon. She might be able to find out what he wanted to know.

Before turning back toward Heyl, he took the length of fabric from his coat pocket and dusted as much of the encrusted sand off as he could. Then he put it away again.

He made one brief stop on his way, at Dr. Carrick's surgery.

The doctor shook his head when Rutledge asked if he knew the cause of death. "I have not conducted a postmortem, if that's what you're asking. Mrs. Saunders has refused to let us take her son's body from the house. She sits there by the bed, reading to him. I agreed with her husband that we will try again this morning. For the moment, I expect it's the kindest thing, to let her have these last hours."

"And your best guess, as a doctor?"

"The bleeding in the brain from the blow on the head. There was nothing I could do to stop it. In the end it killed him."

"Did he regain consciousness before he died?"

"Sadly, no. He simply slipped away. I was downstairs at the time, talking to Harry's father, preparing him for the worst. And I heard Mrs. Saunders scream. I rushed up the stairs, but he was gone. No heartbeat, no respiration, nothing. She said she heard the silence in the room. And I expect she did."

"Poor woman."

"Yes, a blow for both of them." He sighed. "But this shifts the inquiry, does it not? From attempted murder to murder. I know the Grenville family and the St. Iveses as well. They're also my patients. This will be a terrible state of affairs now."

"Tell me about Miss St. Ives. I understand she has a nervous disposition?"

His choice of words was deliberate.

"Hardly that. She was very much in love with Stephen Grenville, and his death was a great loss for her as well as his family. She was quite ill for weeks after the news came, and we feared for her. She had hardly recovered when her mother died in the influenza epidemic. That was just after George had been brought to England, terribly wounded. It was likely he would die, and I think his mother couldn't bear it. At any rate, in my view Mrs. St. Ives never fought to live. As it happened, George survived. But he's hardly the man he was. Elaine has seen death take two of the people she loved most, and she has seen what the war has done to her brother. To be accused of killing Harry Saunders, whether by accident or design, will be too much for her. Prison could well turn her mind."

8

The house at Padstow Place was in an uproar.

When the maid opened the door to him, he could hear St. Ives's voice raised in anger. And then a reply in only slightly more measured tones from Grenville.

The maid was saying, "A moment, please, sir, I'll inquire—"

He smiled, setting her gently aside. "I believe I'm expected."

Before she could prevent him, he was across the entrance hall and already moving briskly toward the library.

The door stood open. Grenville was beside the hearth, looking distinctly beleaguered. In front of him St. Ives was pacing the floor, his face red with fury.

Both men turned to stare at Rutledge as he stepped in and closed the door behind him.

"What's the matter?"

Both men began to speak at once, and then Grenville said, "He came here demanding to take his daughter home. As my own daughter and his, as well as our two guests, were given into my custody, I have refused. Such a decision could find all four young women back in gaol."

"He's right, you know," Rutledge told St. Ives before he could splutter his own response. "He's their gaoler, and if you interfere, I shall have to take steps."

"You wouldn't dare," St. Ives told him.

"You're wrong. I'll have no choice but to back up Constable Pendennis, who made this arrangement before I took over the case. Don't put me in that position."

His voice was cold, authority in every word, and St. Ives, glancing at Grenville to see if there was any support forthcoming, and not seeing any, said, "Oh very well. But I hold you responsible, Grenville, and you as well, Rutledge, if my daughter suffers any more stress at the hands of the police."

Rutledge turned to Grenville. "Have you told them about young Saunders?"

"Yes, as we were finishing breakfast. I was afraid that they would overhear the servants talking about his death."

"Quite right. How did they take it?"

"How else would you expect?" Grenville snapped. "They were very upset. They're intelligent young women, Rutledge, they could see at once how this changed their situation. Kate, Miss Gordon, asked me if you would come to take them away, and my daughter was in tears, along with Miss St. Ives. Miss Langley just sat there, staring at me. I don't believe any of them realized Saunders could die of his injury."

"There has been a new development." The men's gaze focused on him as if he'd offered them a lifeline. "I have found the boat that Saunders was in. It sank, just as we have been told. I was able to have it removed from the water and taken to a salvage yard in Padstow. It will be evidence."

"Thank God," St. Ives whispered. "It shows that Trevose is lying."

"Actually, it doesn't. It simply shows that your daughters and their guests were telling the truth when they claimed Saunders was in the water because his dinghy sank beneath him."

"You mean it doesn't change the oar," Grenville said, suddenly weary. "Yes, I understand that. But surely, if the dinghy has been found, it explains how he came to be in the water in the first place. And that in turn reaffirms the fact that the accused were trying to bring him into their boat. Regardless of what Trevose thought he saw from the shore."

"It helps their case," Rutledge agreed. "But there will still be a trial."

St. Ives sat down, his face gloomy. But Grenville had remained standing by the hearth, a frown on his face. "Why did the dinghy sink?"

Rutledge was not ready to tell them. "A very good question. Would you give me a few minutes alone with Miss Gordon?"

"Why her?" St. Ives asked suspiciously.

"Because he knows her," Grenville said, his gaze on Rutledge's face.

"On the contrary," Rutledge blandly answered him, "she may be able to clarify a point in her statement."

In the end he was allowed to interview Kate in the morning room.

As she came through the doorway, he could see at once the toll the news had taken on her. She was pale, her eyes overlarge, as if her face had grown thinner than it had been when last he saw her.

"It's the worst possible news, isn't it, Ian? That Harry Saunders is dead. I am so sorry. For his family, as well as for us. I understand that he's an only child?"

"That's true."

"How very sad." She took a deep breath. "Is there something you wanted to ask me about my statement? I thought I remembered everything."

He went past her and quietly closed the door, then led her to the windows, where he hoped they had less of a chance to be overheard.

"We've found Harry Saunders's boat. At least we can now prove you were not lying about watching it sink. You're not out of the woods yet, Kate, but that's an important bit of evidence."

He thought for a moment she was going to faint from sheer relief. But in typical Kate fashion, she gathered herself together and managed a smile, although it wavered as she said, "I could use a little good news."

"Will you help me with a small problem? I hesitate to ask, because it could prove rather damning for one of your friends."

"No, Ian, please don't put me in that position," she said at once, reaching out to touch his arm. "I don't think I could live with such a betrayal."

It was what he'd hoped she would say.

"All right, then, on another line of inquiry. In London, I'd ask my sister. But we aren't in London." He reached into his pocket and brought out the little square of cloth. "What is this?"

She smoothed it out in her palm, holding it to the light. "What a pretty pattern. I think it's muslin, the sort of thing I'd wear in the summer."

"A woman's dress, then?"

"Yes, I think so. Or a child's, even. Very feminine and sweet. I can see it worn with a green sash, the color of those leaves, and perhaps the same color ribbons on one's hat."

He could picture it too. "Yes, I agree."

"Where did you find it?" She felt it with her fingers. "That's sand. And the cloth is stiff, as if it's been in salt water." She looked up at him, hope in her eyes. "Are you saying you found this in Harry Saunders's boat? That there's someone he was fond of? Oh, but how sad—"

"I have no way of knowing whose gown this might have come from. Where I discovered it, there are often summer visitors. But it appears to be from a more expensive sort of gown than they might have worn."

"Well, from what I can see of it, you're right." She held it up to the light. "See? The way it's woven? It wouldn't have been cheap."

He could just make out the slight ridges that formed a pattern around the sprig of flowers. Now it was time to distract her.

"Thank you, Kate. It probably has no bearing on the inquiry, but I'm required to pursue every possibility."

"I can tell you that we weren't wearing anything like that last Saturday. It wasn't warm enough for one thing, and for another, this isn't the sort of clothing to go bicycling in. It could catch on something too easily."

Changing the subject, she said, "If you found the dinghy, Ian, you must know why it sank. It went down rather fast, I can tell you. When I first saw Harry Saunders waving at us, the boat was still afloat. And then even as I watched, it was as if the water came rushing in."

"It must be examined," he agreed.

"There aren't boulders or sandbars in that part of the river, are there? There's the Doom Bar, of course, at the mouth of the estuary. More than one ship has come to grief there, not knowing it was in their path. I've heard Mr. Grenville mention it. There are stories about it. I've even heard people singing about the Doom Bar and ships caught in a storm."

He was suddenly interested. "Would Saunders go out that far in a dinghy? Surely not."

"I wouldn't know. It seems rather dangerous to me."

"Keep this to yourself, Kate, if you please."

"Of course I will. Mr. Grenville has told me he's sent a telegram to my father, asking him to come down again. I know he must, but I hate it. I hate him seeing me like this. I've never been accused of any crime, and I think he's found it rather dreadful to have me in this predicament and be unable to do anything about it. I can't blame him, to tell you the truth. But our visits are—uncomfortable."

He wanted to assure her that she had done no wrong, but he couldn't, not until all the facts were in. That was his duty.

He couldn't even put a hand on her shoulder to comfort her. That too would be wrong.

Instead, he said, "I didn't know your father well before the war. He was still on active service. We met—what, three or four times at most?"

"Three, I think."

"You should go before Grenville becomes suspicious. I told him there were questions about your statement. If he asks, you must say I asked you not to discuss it."

He walked with her to the door.

After she had gone, he looked at the length of cloth again.

Who had been with Harry Saunders last summer, who had caught her skirt on a splinter of old wood from the landing? It might be important to know.

While he was about it, he asked to see Miss Grenville.

She was not the same woman he'd interviewed before. Some of her spirit had either disappeared or been overlaid with worry.

"Tell me about Harry Saunders," he said. "I can't interview his parents just now, but I'd like to know something about him."

"I told you. I hardly knew him."

"But you've lived here all your life. There must be things you've heard." When she looked mulish—if such a pretty woman could ever look mulish—he added, "If I knew more about him, it might explain why Trevose believed the four of you were intent on killing him. For instance, did he have a reputation as a flirt, as you've claimed?"

"He flirted with me. I expect he flirted with other women. Whether it was all in fun or he was serious, I didn't know. And I wasn't interested in knowing."

"Was he courting someone before the war?"

"I have no idea. He didn't come home from America with a wife."

"No." He changed directions. "Was he generally liked?"

"I expect he was. His father owned the banks, but I'd never heard that they were difficult to deal with. You must ask my father about that."

"He had a larger boat, I'm told. The *Sea Lion*. Did he often take her out beyond the Doom Bar?"

"I don't know. I've never been aboard her. He talked about her. I gathered he'd been as far as Fowey on her. His mother has cousins there."

"How long has he had her?"

"Since after the war, I think. There had been speculation that he'd join the Navy when war was declared, but instead he went into the Army."

"Were people resentful that he spent his war safely in America?"

"I've no idea. He had American cousins, I've heard that, and also that it was thought he might know something about coping with the American government. But that's the Army for you. I heard Mr. St. Ives comment that Harry had never met his cousins. The Saunders family is gossiped about, just as I'm sure we are."

"How well did Elaine St. Ives know him?"

"You must ask her. I would have thought very like the way I had known him, the occasional encounter in the village or in Padstow. 'Hello, Harry, how are you?' And then he'd make conversation, in an effort to keep you talking for a few minutes. He always asked after my mother or my father, or he'd say something like 'I ran into Stephen the other day,' and use that as a starting point for a chat."

"How well did Stephen know him?"

"Probably the way I did, casual encounters and Sundays at morning services, if his parents decided to come to St. Marina that week. They made an effort to appear friendly, a part of village life. But of course they never could be, could they? They were richer than the greengrocer or the owner of the pub, and they weren't received here. Neither fish nor fowl, you might say."

He was getting nowhere, and so he thanked her and let her go. But at the door he said, "Miss Grenville, do you know where Harry Saunders kept the dinghy?"

She turned, her dark brows drawn together. "In the harbor at Padstow, I expect. He pointed the *Sea Lion* out to me when I happened to meet him there. As I said before, we seemed to meet more often than could easily be explained by coincidence."

Rutledge left his motorcar at the inn and walked on to the police station.

Pendennis rose from the table when he came through the door.

"Sir?" A single word, but heavy with questions he didn't know how to begin. About the salvage operation, about the dinghy, about where Rutledge had been for the better part of the morning.

"Constable." He nodded a greeting, and then took the chair across the table that served as a desk. "As you could see, there was a dinghy in the river. And as you could probably tell, it didn't appear to have been there for many years. I went to the salvage yard to confirm that it was Saunders's boat, and it had the name of his larger craft across the stern. This in turn is reasonable evidence that the accused were telling the truth about his boat sinking under him."

"But with all respect, sir, why should a perfectly sound dinghy suddenly go down like that? He didn't keep his boat here in the village. He must have rowed some distance. Convenient, I'd say, that it sank just where the young ladies were pulling into the Grenville landing."

"A good point, Constable. The answer is that someone had tampered with the dinghy. Saunders was lucky to have got this far."

Pendennis's eyebrows rose in surprise. "Tampered with? By whom, sir?"

"We don't know. Yet. I would prefer that this be kept quiet for the time being. But everyone saw the dinghy being brought up. We can confirm, I think, that it belonged to Saunders."

"Yes, sir. I understand, sir."

"That brings us to Trevose's statement. That he believed Saunders had been in the Grenville rowboat, had been pushed into the water, and was being held down by two of the women, Miss Gordon and Miss Langley. I didn't see his original statement, of course. It hasn't been found yet. We will now consider those comments pure conjecture on his part. I now have to ask myself why he should have been so certain the four women in that rowboat were attempting to murder Harry Saunders rather than rescue him?"

"Because of the oar, sir. He saw the oar being lifted, and it struck Mr. Saunders on the head."

It was the sticking point, as Rutledge expected it would be.

"Still, I wonder how much of his account Trevose would like to reconsider, in light of new information about the dinghy."

"I don't know, sir. He appeared to be vehement at the time."

"Yes, I understand."

"And Mr. Saunders is still just as dead, sir. Do we know what killed him?"

"I stopped by Dr. Carrick's surgery whilst I was in Padstow. He hasn't done a postmortem. But he believes it was bleeding in the brain caused by a blow on the head."

"Then if Miss Grenville dropped the oar on his head, she's likely to be responsible for his death. And a good lawyer could claim the other two were holding him there in place."

"So they could claim. But who damaged the dinghy? And why?

If the four women were there when it sank, it could be said that he might have drowned, had they not been. According to his father, Harry Saunders was not a strong swimmer. And the river was cold. He would have been in some trouble, I think. Whether the Grenville rowboat was in hailing distance or if he were out in the river alone."

"As to that, I don't know, sir.

"Then we'll leave the four women where they are at present, while we explore other avenues. From what I've been told about Harry Saunders, he wasn't the sort of person who collected enemies. And yet here we have two possible examples of ill will. The tampering. And the matter of the oar."

"That's reasonable, I think, sir."

Concealing his relief, Rutledge nodded. "I think it's time we paid another visit to the Trevose farm."

Rutledge drove this time, and Constable Pendennis sat stiffly by his side.

At the farmhouse, Mrs. Penwith told them that Trevose was out looking to see how much rain damage there had been to parts of the farm nearest Little Petherick Creek.

They set out down a muddy lane, then crossed two fields. Where a third intersected with the first two, Rutledge saw Trevose in the distance, a shovel in one hand and a hoe in the other. He was walking their way, although he hadn't acknowledged seeing them.

"We'll wait," Rutledge said, looking down at his boots, already beyond hope of ever being clean again.

"Yes, sir." The constable seemed happy to agree.

When Trevose was near enough to speak, he said, "Praying by the well, are you, Inspector? Although I'm surprised at you, Pendennis, good Chapel man that you are."

Pendennis, flushing, was about to answer him, but at a glance from Rutledge shut his mouth again smartly.

Trevose didn't stop but continued toward the house, and the other two men fell in step beside him.

"I expect you've heard that the Saunders boat has been located and brought up," Rutledge began quietly. "I'm sure gossip reaches even this far."

"Mrs. Penwith's cousin brought it out with a sack of flour," he responded. "I don't see that it changes anything. But the lad's death does. That news also came with the sack of flour."

"There's a strong possibility now that the four accused were telling the truth that Saunders was in the dinghy, and it was sinking rapidly."

Trevose shrugged. "It could have been there for weeks, that boat, and he'd been out with the women to search for it."

"Why at this time of year would he ask four women to help him search, when there's a perfectly good salvage firm in Padstow that he could afford to hire? What's more, Harry's father never mentioned that the dinghy had been reported missing."

"Perhaps Harry didn't see fit to tell his father. I saw what I saw, and there's an end to it."

"I have a witness who saw Harry Saunders take the boat out that Saturday afternoon. That tells us the dinghy was in Saunders's possession shortly before the encounter with the Grenville rowing boat, and that he had no one in the dinghy with him."

"I saw what I saw, and there's an end to it."

"Do you have any personal connection with the families of any one of these young women?"

Trevose glanced at him, then gestured around him with his free hand. "Do you think it's likely?"

"Miss Gordon is from London. And Miss Langley. Have you ever traveled to London, Trevose?"

"I'm a farmer, Rutledge. Cows to milk, chickens to feed, pigs to keep out of the gardens. It's a long way to London."

"Is that a yes or a no?"

"No."

"Miss St. Ives, then. Any connection with her family? They're close by, you could be home in time to milk and all the rest."

"And what, pray, would I be doing there? I'm too old to ask for the hand of his daughter, and I never went to school with his son. We have nothing in common." It was said with disdain, as if the loss was St. Ives's.

"And the Grenvilles?" Rutledge had purposely left them to the last.

Trevose glanced in Pendennis's direction before answering, "You might say the same for the Grenvilles. Although we've had words over his precious deer getting out of the park and grazing on my crops."

"You had a younger brother, I believe."

Trevose stopped and stared straight at Rutledge. "He died young. Leave him out of this." And then he walked on, ignoring them.

Rutledge let him go. Whatever reason drove Trevose to stick to his story, it was beyond argument. But he had given the man some information to think about.

Turning to Pendennis, he said, "That will do for now."

He drove the silent constable back to the police station and then decided to take the owner of The Pilot up on his invitation to come in.

The pub was old and dark, paneling and beams blackened by years of smoking fires and men's pipes. The bar was bright with brass pulls and stacks of clean glasses, while the space around it was shaped like a U, with tables and chairs. They were heavy, at least thirty or forty years old, the tabletops well worn and uneven. But the smells wafting in from the kitchen were irresistible, and Rutledge nodded to the barkeep as he crossed the room to a table. It was late for lunch, still early for dinner. And the bar was empty. He had The Pilot to himself.

The day's special was a turnip-and-potato pasty, piping hot from the oven. To his surprise when he cut into it, Rutledge found it contained mince as well. With it came a side dish of stewed apples and another of green cabbage.

He was halfway through the meal when Penhale came in from the kitchen, saw him sitting alone, and came over to the table.

"Found the Saunders dinghy, did you?"

"We have."

"Pity he's dead. Nice enough young man."

"I need to find his friends and ask them a few questions about him."

Penhale scratched his chin. "Acquaintances here, of course, but no close friends that I know of. You'll have to ask in Padstow. Or Rock."

Rutledge had thus far avoided bringing in the Padstow police. Or crossing over to Rock. "The problem is, everyone tells me what a 'nice young man' Harry Saunders was. Surely if that's true, he had friends. There would be respectable young women who invited him to dinner or parties or walked out with him on Sunday afternoon."

"In Heyl he kept to himself. Before the war he sometimes went fishing with George St. Ives. Now, of course, St. Ives is a vegetable, or so I hear."

"Have you seen him since the war?"

"I have not. He stays close to home, and the staff don't gossip. He had a nurse for the first weeks. She came with him from the clinic."

"Anyone who might wish Saunders harm?"

Penhale chuckled. " 'A nice young man'?"

"All right then, his father."

The chuckle faded. "I've not heard any talk against him."

Someone walked in the door, calling to Penhale. He nodded to Rutledge and left to speak to the newcomer. Rutledge suspected the man, who looked like a fisherman, was asking news of Saunders, for both looked toward his table as Penhale answered.

Finishing his meal, Rutledge paid for it and left.

Until he could speak to Mr. and Mrs. Saunders, he was at a standstill. But there was Elaine St. Ives, whose brother had gone fishing with Harry.

He drove to Padstow Place, and asked to speak with her.

Grenville, intercepting him on his way to the library, asked if there was any news.

"I'm trying to look into Saunders's background," he said.

"I can't see what good that will do you. The question we're facing is what to do about the charges against my daughter and her friends."

"Trevose stands by his initial statement."

Grenville swore. "Bloody-minded fool. Surely you can put that nonsense to rest about throwing Saunders out of the rowboat. If his dinghy sank, he was never in ours until Trevose helped drag him there. A fact, Rutledge."

"Another fact, Grenville, is that he died from the blow to the head. If that injury is due to the oar hitting him, your daughter could still be charged. The seriousness of the charge will depend on just what she intended to do when she picked up that oar."

"My daughter has never hurt anyone."

"Then we must hope we can prove that."

He waited in the library for Elaine St. Ives, staring out the window that had been drenched in rain only the night before.

As she came in she said quietly, "I'm so sorry to hear that Harry is dead. It's quite terrible to think we had something to do with it. His parents must be unable to believe it. I wish I could write to them, but Mrs. Grenville tells me it wouldn't be wise."

He turned. She was thinner, he thought, than when he had first met her, the bones of her face tight against the skin, her eyes dark-circled. He remembered what St. Ives had said about the other tragedies she'd suffered.

"No, I'm afraid it's not a good idea," he said, paying her the courtesy of believing her and understanding her feelings. "I haven't spoken to Mr. or Mrs. Saunders since he died. I know they must be suffering. But if what you tell me about that Saturday is true, his death was not your fault."

"I don't think I've lied." She took a deep breath, walked toward the hearth, and held out her hands to the blaze. "I tried my best to balance the rowboat, to give Kate and Sara a chance to bring him in.

Death is so final. You can't go back and try again and hope it will all turn out well this time round. You can do that with art or music or poetry—start a fresh page. But not with a life." She turned to face him. "I'm told you wished to see me. I can't think of anything else, although I've tried. I was so frightened in the boat, it almost seems as if I wasn't really there, just watching someone who looked like me and who wasn't handling her fear very well. I see myself trembling when it should have been Harry I worried about, or Sara and Kate. You should have seen the bruises on their knees and arms, leaning out that way. I didn't even have a splinter to show how I'd tried."

"It's often that way with a very bad experience. Soldiers feel much the same after a battle. They see themselves running forward, firing their weapons, watching others fall around them. It's a way to cope with it. You will too, in time. But I came here to ask about Harry Saunders. Who should I speak to who could tell me more about him? Who his friends were, his enemies—if there was someone he particularly cared for. I need to know more than simply seeing him as the victim in this."

"I wish I knew how to answer you."

"I understand your brother sometimes went fishing with Harry Saunders."

"That's true. On summer holidays, of course. We didn't see much of him during the school year. My brother was at Winchester, and Harry was sent to a school in Yorkshire."

"Did they get along?"

"I think so. Fishing is not very divisive, is it?"

He smiled. "Not at all. What did they talk about?"

"I've no idea. School. Sports. Girls."

"Has Harry visited your brother since the war?"

Her face clouded. "No. George isn't up to seeing anyone. He spends most of his days in his room. Sometimes he joins us for dinner. But that's difficult for him."

"How badly was he wounded?"

"He was terribly burned. A German flamethrower. He and some of his men had taken refuge in a shell crater, where they were trying to cover men retreating after a botched assault. Their angle of fire was deadly. The Germans sent out a man with a flamethrower, and he came up behind them. There was chaos on the battlefield at the time, and no one saw what he was about to do. There was no warning. Four of my brother's men were already wounded. George turned and fired, but it was too late. No one quite knows how it was he survived. They got him to a field hospital and from there to the Base Hospital. It was awful, Mr. Rutledge. I'm ashamed to say I felt ill the day when I saw him carried through the door on a stretcher. Even his legs are twisted. He stays in his room or on the terrace in the shade, although he goes out into the gardens for a little air, but only at night when everyone is asleep. I'm told his skin—scars—are still quite sensitive to the sun."

Rutledge had seen such men. Sometimes they went out at night, faces hidden by a scarf and a hat pulled down low, gloves on their hands. It was said that children screamed and dogs barked when they saw burned men. Whether it was true or not, no one with severe scars wanted to find out. The pulled and puckered skin that twisted features and fingers was something out of nightmares. He himself had flinched once or twice when he'd seen a severe case.

Flamethrowers had been more useful against buildings or bunkers, places where men were pinned down by fire. It was also said that snipers targeted men with the equipment on their backs, and that few were ever taken alive, even if they were captured. It was not seen as an honorable weapon of war.

"I'm sorry," he said. "To return to Harry Saunders?"

With a visible effort, Elaine St. Ives brought her thoughts back to the library. "Victoria believed he was in love with her. I don't know if it's true or not. I have no idea who his friends are. I seldom attended parties here in Cornwall. Most of my friends are in London now."

"Where did Saunders keep his dinghy?"

"I have no idea. I don't believe anyone has ever mentioned it to me."

He found he believed her. She didn't have the kind of face that concealed what she was thinking. He had watched the play of emotions as she answered his questions. And having been engaged to Stephen Grenville, she had moved in very different circles than the banker's son. It was one thing for boys to go fishing together. Quite another for a daughter of the house.

Still, Padstow wasn't a large town, and Heyl was even smaller. Had she heard no gossip?

Apparently not. Gossip too moved in particular circles.

He thanked her, and she had already opened the door when she shut it again and turned.

"I just remembered . . . It was this past summer. A young woman came to Sunday services at St. Marina. I hadn't seen her before. And she didn't come every Sunday. Quite pretty, with brown hair and lovely taste in clothes. I never knew her name, she never offered to introduce herself. And then by September she was gone. Harry Saunders usually brought her to the vicarage, and then she came alone to the church. He came sometimes, but not always. If he didn't stay, the vicar would take her home. Wherever home was. When I asked him who she was, Mr. Toup told me she was his cousin and visiting with friends over in Rock. I thought no more about it. Whenever Harry did stay for services, Victoria was there, and I expect he'd come to see her." She smiled. "She would tell me not to leave her alone with him, but any woman is flattered by attention, and I thought she rather liked knowing she'd captivated him."

And then she was gone, leaving him to weigh what she'd just told him.

9

Rutledge was crossing the hall when Mrs. Grenville came down the stairs. She was wearing a dark red dress with a gold chain necklace, and the combination was very attractive with her dark hair.

"Good evening, Inspector."

"Good evening, Mrs. Grenville."

"We've been given the sad news. And I understand, too, that poor Harry Saunders's dinghy has been found."

"That's true," he answered her, and then he had the strongest feeling that she had been watching for him.

She crossed to where he was standing and said, "I'll see you out."

"Thank you."

They walked together as far as the house door, and with a quick glance over her shoulder to see if anyone was within earshot, she said quietly, "And has Mr. Trevose reconsidered his earlier statement, that my daughter and her friends were trying to drown Harry? I should think that finding the dinghy would change his mind, at least about the fact that Harry was in our boat. Instead he must have been trying to reach it after his own went down."

"Mr. Trevose remains adamant that what he reported was what he saw."

Her expression changed from polite interest to uncertainty. "But I should think he would find it hard to claim any such thing, now."

"He refuses to discuss the matter. But the inquiry is ongoing, and there is every possibility still that new information will come to light."

She closed her eyes for a moment, saying, "Dear God, I hope so," under her breath. And then she forced a smile and thanked him.

He walked out to his motorcar with the distinct impression that she was still watching him. He could only hope, for her sake, that the past could stay buried, but if that was what was driving Trevose, the man wouldn't give up his pound of flesh very easily.

It was well after six o'clock when Rutledge reached the vicarage. He expected to find Mr. Toup sitting down to his dinner, but the vicar was just hanging his coat on the rack by the door as he opened it to Rutledge's knock.

"You only just caught me," he said. "Or have you come looking before?"

"I've been out to Padstow Place and only just returned to the village."

"Well, then, come in. May I offer you a drink? Vicars are supposed to drink only sherry, but I much prefer a good whisky. I've been to one of the outer farms, sitting with a parishioner who is recovering from pneumonia. We had feared at her age that she might not live, but she's a sturdy soul. The cottage was so hot from the coal fire, I thought I'd perish from the heat. But she feels the cold in her bones, she says."

He led Rutledge into the study, where the fire was burning down. Toup looked at it, decided to leave it where it was, and went over to a cabinet where he kept his whisky.

"Some of my parishioners are strong temperance supporters, and so I try to make certain they aren't shocked by my habits."

Rutledge smiled, taking the whisky that Toup poured for him.

"Now, tell me. How are Miss Grenville and her friends bearing up? I've called several times, but Mr. Grenville has taken his duties to heart and refused to allow me to speak to them. I understand, of course, but I continue to call to assure them that I care about them."

"It's been difficult. They expected to be returned to gaol when Saunders died, but finding the dinghy has called into question some of Trevose's assumptions. Early days." It was the standard police response when certain information hadn't been made public.

"What brings you here this evening?"

"I was told that there was a young woman who visited St. Marina this summer, and Harry Saunders generally brought her to the vicarage to attend."

Alarm spread across the vicar's face, quickly suppressed.

"A summer visitor," he answered casually. "Sometimes Saunders would bring her over in his carriage. As a courtesy."

"Who is she?"

"A cousin of mine," Toup replied. "She's very young, and I thought it best for her not to stay here. My housekeeper doesn't live in." He smiled. "Even a man of my age is not immune from malicious gossip. Rock was more suitable."

"Who was she?" Rutledge persisted.

Toup finished his whisky and said, "She's not important to this inquiry, Inspector. She left here in September and hasn't returned."

"Anything to do with Harry Saunders is important to me."

"May I ask who mentioned her to you?"

"I'm not at liberty to say."

"If I asked you, as a favor to me, to this church, to say nothing more about her, would you agree? I can vouch for her, and I can tell you truthfully that Harry Saunders was being kind when he brought her here. She's a little reserved, and I think she felt more comfortable coming to services here rather than attending in Padstow. There's no mystery about that. She didn't wish to appear to be a friend of his—he has his own life, or had. He simply provided transportation because I asked him to."

Rutledge considered his request. "Are you being absolutely truthful, Vicar?"

"On my soul, I am. She has nothing to do with what happened here on that terrible Saturday afternoon. She wasn't even in Cornwall. I see no purpose in putting her through an inquisition by the police."

"Hardly an inquisition." Still, he recalled Elaine St. Ives's anxiety when he'd first questioned her. He finished his own whisky and considered the vicar.

"I will agree to this. If I discover that this woman was in any way involved with Harry Saunders, I will expect you to tell me whatever I need to know."

Rutledge could see that Toup was not happy about the bargain, but he had found himself in a corner and really had no choice.

Reluctantly the vicar agreed. And then he rose, set his glass and Rutledge's on the cabinet, and said, "I won't keep you, Inspector. But thank you."

Rutledge stood and said quietly, "I'll see myself out."

"No. I have not forgot my manners," he said, and walked with Rutledge to the door.

Dissatisfied, Rutledge went to his motorcar and found what he wanted in the boot. Then he set out on foot in the direction of the Trevose farm.

His eyes were soon accustomed to what light there was, allowing him to avoid the worst of the obstacles in his way as he cut across country. The cow pats and sheep droppings were invisible, but he persevered, hoping that in the rougher patches, the animals had found nothing worth the effort of grazing in that direction.

It was fully dark now, and he was still some distance from the house. Without warning he stumbled over an old, rotting stump where shoots had begun to grow up from the roots in a last desperate attempt to survive. He was just about to move around it when his boot struck stone, and not a stone in the earth but what remained of a low shelter of some sort. Unwilling to risk using his torch, he ran his gloved hands over it. Stone walls. Moss-covered stone roof. An opening on one side. A cold, wet spring running over his fingers. He realized that it was a small shrine, and the whispering sound he'd been hearing for the past two minutes was the soft bubbling of water out of a sacred well.

Such wells were common all over Cornwall, dedicated to obscure Cornish saints with often unpronounceable names. Was this St. Marina's well? From its condition, he thought it must be a more neglected saint whose fame had been lost to time. Or perhaps, Hamish was suggesting, it was Trevose who'd neglected it.

Then Rutledge remembered something Trevose had said when he and Constable Pendennis had walked out into the fields to find him. Something about praying, although the constable was a Chapel man. Assuming it was a personal taunt between the two men, Rutledge had said nothing at the time, but now he smiled to himself.

Glancing up to take his bearings, he could see that the well offered a direct line of sight to the front of the Trevose house. As good a spot as any, he thought, and downwind of any dogs on the property.

He settled himself there and opened the clasp on the case holding his field glasses. They were familiar in his hands, and he focused them on the door of the house, watching for some time before it opened in a flash of lamplight, then closed again. He could just pick out the shape of a man, Trevose he thought, and he followed the shape as it set off down the lane, then cut across the fields in the direction Rutledge had just come from.

To the pub?

He waited for nearly a quarter of an hour, in the event the man had gone to fetch some farm implement he'd left behind when he came in for his dinner.

When there was no sign of him, Rutledge rose to his feet and made his way to the door.

Mrs. Penwith, a tea towel in her hands, said crossly, "You can't lift the latch for your—?" Breaking off as she recognized Rutledge, she started to close the door, but he put his foot in the space before she could manage it.

"I'd like to speak to you," he said quietly. "It won't take long."

"I have nothing to say," she told him querulously. "I wasn't there."

"You weren't," he agreed. "What I'd like to know is why Trevose dislikes the Grenvilles."

"Does he?" she asked, surprise in her voice. Was it genuine, or ironic?

"He appears to hold some grudge. He seems determined to see Grenville's daughter and her friends held by the police for murder."

"He told me young Saunders was dead," she agreed. Her eyes were impossible to read, unlit by the lamplight in the room behind her. "It would appear to me that someone was at fault for that. Else, why are *you* here?"

He had no intention of telling her about the holes in the dinghy. Instead he countered, "How well has he got on with the Grenvilles in the past? Is there a land dispute?"

He watched her frown. "What sort of land dispute? He's told me nothing of that."

"Or is it more personal, do you think?" he suggested.

"There never was any trouble with the Grenvilles. Unless you want to count the deer. Ever seen what deer can do to a farmer's field? Trevose was within his rights to complain."

"One of the family, then. The daughter? Victoria Grenville?"

She stirred a little. "He's never mentioned the daughter."

"If not her father, her mother, perhaps?"

"He's never liked her. But I can't say why."

"Would his dislike of the mother turn him against her daughter? Or perhaps make him decide to use her daughter to reach her, punish her?"

"Punish her for what?" There was a sharpness in her voice now.

He changed direction. "You've worked for Trevose for some time. Does he have any family to speak of? Perhaps they're the ones with a grudge against the Grenvilles."

There was a silence. Then she said, "There was a brother. He died long ago. No one else."

"How did he die?"

"In service. He didn't want to farm, he wanted to leave Cornwall behind. Easier said than done. But he thought service would give him a better chance."

"Did they quarrel over his leaving, Trevose and his brother?"

"They fought over it one night. Came to blows. The next morning, the boy was gone. We never saw him again, until Trevose went to bring him home to bury him."

"Trevose must have felt bad about the manner of their parting."

"He was that upset he didn't sleep for a dozen nights. Just sat there staring into space, saying nothing. Hardly eating, drinking heavily. It was a bad time. A terrible time."

There was little more he could learn from Mrs. Penwith. After another question or two, Rutledge was about to withdraw his boot from the doorway when he remembered the door knocker.

"That's an unusual design," he said, pointing to it.

"I can't think what possessed Trevose to put it up there. We'd had an old horseshoe in its place for as long as I could remember, and it'ud served us well enough. But he said it was a reminder of a debt owed. That every time he looked at it, coming in his door or going out of it, he remembered."

"When was it put up?"

"As I remember, it was about the time Miss Victoria was born. There was a fine christening in the church, and afterward, Mr. Grenville paid for all of us to wet her head at the pub."

Trevose had been safe enough putting it up. Mrs. Penwith was unlikely to see the original on the door of Padstow Place, and if the Grenvilles came to his door, they could make of it what they liked.

He thanked her for her time and let her close the door. But she wanted the last word.

"*He* won't thank you. Not if he finds you here asking questions. And if he wants to know whether you came, I'll swear you never did, and I'll call you a liar to your face, if you say otherwise."

And she shut the door with force, leaving him there in the dark. Behind him he heard a dog growl low in its throat, as if at a signal. He realized it must have come stealthily up behind him, then sensed the tension in those last words with Mrs. Penwith.

"Like dog, like master," Hamish said quietly in the back of Rutledge's mind.

Rutledge was not eager for a confrontation with the animal, and he had a long walk back to the village. For that matter he couldn't be sure Mrs. Penwith would call it off if it attacked. She could swear the dog had heard him banging on the door after she'd refused to let him in.

Dropping to one knee, he said softly, "There's a good fellow. Good dog."

After a moment he could see the dog's tail drop from its ridged stance, and he kept speaking to it in the same tone of voice, not moving from where he knelt. He could sense Mrs. Penwith on the other side of the door, waiting. Finally the dog lowered its head. Rutledge held out a hand, palm up. "Good dog. Come here and let me scratch behind your ears."

He had always had a way with animals. The dog stretched forward and sniffed his fingers, then allowed Rutledge to stroke him. He reached behind the ears, then put both hands behind the dog's head, ruffling the fur as he talked. When he rose slowly to his feet, the dog's tail began to wag. And it followed him for some distance before breaking off and returning to the farm.

Relieved to see him go, Rutledge made his way through the darkness until he was far enough away from the Trevose property to use his torch.

Trevose had felt some guilt over his parting with his brother, and that might be strong enough to turn him against Mrs. Grenville, blaming her rather than accepting blame himself for what had happened. And it would be tempting, consciously or unconsciously, to take away someone she loved—her daughter?—for the brother she had accidentally taken from him. Grenville himself would have been a more formidable target. And to kill Mrs. Grenville would not assuage the suffering Trevose had endured.

If that were true, Rutledge thought as he reached the outskirts of the village, it would be difficult to convince Trevose to change his mind about his statement. The man had already found it easy to face the prospect of sending Victoria's friends to the gallows along with her, if that was the only way he could manage to achieve his revenge.

Perhaps in his eyes, it was another young woman very much like them who had killed his brother. They were all guilty, because they could all have been in that room when the terrace door shut.

"Or perhaps," Hamish put in, "the weight on yon mother's soul would be all the heavier, if all the lasses hanged."

Depend on a Scot, Rutledge thought wryly, with their long tradition of blood feuds, to see an advantage to showing no mercy to the other three women.

The question was, did Trevose love his brother that much? Or was he intent on assuaging his own guilt at whatever cost?

He was not ready to step into the brightly lit dining room for his dinner.

Instead, he walked down to the village landing. He had it to himself, and there was a quiet broken only by the whisper of the water running there beyond where he stood. The moon was just rising, turning the water to silver and pewter. Rock, across the river, was a scattering of lamplight marking the houses there.

Against his will he thought about Olivia Marlowe, who had died in the moonlight, preferring that to what lay ahead if she chose to live.

Lines of her poetry came unbidden into his head.

The night is quiet, the moon
A brightness on the horizon.
And I am here, waiting.
Love, come to me
In the moonlight,
And leave war behind.

Written for the man she loved above all others. He had envied that love. Envied the trust and joy and peace it brought her, even though it was beyond the pale in this life. He had been grieving for Jean, and Olivia Marlowe had touched him deeply, just as the O. A. Manning poems had touched him in France, long before he had known who O. A. Manning was.

The headland where she was buried wasn't visible from where he stood, but he knew it was there, he knew that he could get into his motorcar and drive there, and stand outside the house and as the moon rose, remember.

And Meredith Channing held him in thrall as well, though she had chosen her husband over him. As it should be, as he knew it must be. For both their sakes, he must learn to let her go.

He walked down to the landing's edge and watched the water below it, dark in the shadows, and still swift and swollen with the rain. One more step, two, and he would find his own peace and rest.

He had never felt quite so alone . . .

Over his dinner that night, Rutledge wondered if he'd made a devil's bargain with Toup over the name of the woman who had sometimes come to St. Marina's with Harry Saunders. He couldn't force the vicar to give him the information he'd asked for. Not until he could show that it was essential to closing the inquiry. But he was distinctly uneasy.

The vicar had said that she was staying in Rock. Then why attend services in Padstow at all? It would make sense for her to attend here in Heyl, if she crossed the Camel.

The other problem on his mind was the dinghy.

It wasn't Trevose who had put those holes in the bottom of the dinghy. Of that much he was fairly certain. What purpose would it have served? He couldn't have predicted where or when the dinghy would sink. It had been sheer luck that someone else had been out on the water that day. But someone had wanted Harry Saunders to die. And he, Rutledge, was going to have to find out who it was, before he could either clear the names of the four accused, or condemn them.

A niggling suspicion crept into his mind as he finished his tea.

Had Victoria, despite her protests about her relationship with Harry Saunders, been jealous enough of the other woman to tamper with his boat? On the theory that if she couldn't have him, no one else would? Was this the motive that had eluded him?

Did she know enough about boats to have done the work?

The one small piece of evidence in favor of that possibility was her reluctance to go to his aid when the dinghy was sinking. And dropping the oar on his head had been her reaction to the chance that he would be saved by her friends. After all, it would be difficult to find another opportunity to kill him.

Rutledge reached into his pocket and took out the small square of cloth he'd found in the sand.

Whom did it belong to? Victoria, as she was trying to put holes in the bottom of the dinghy? Or had it caught on a nail as a summer visitor strolled down to the water to watch a sunset or moonrise, a gust of wind whipping the delicate fabric against the rough planking of the landing? Too much could be read into bits of evidence. Wishful thinking on a detective's part, hoping to find truth in what was actually irrelevant.

Hamish, in the back of his mind, was telling him that he had not allowed the other four women to escape questioning. Why hadn't he insisted that the vicar tell him the name of the fifth?

"Yon lass," he said, referring to Kate. "You do na' believe she's guilty, but you were verra' cold wi' her. Was it because of the ither?"

He knew what Hamish was suggesting, that he had been giving Kate no quarter because she was Jean's cousin, and he must not be seen favoring her.

He didn't think he had been harsh with her. He had tried to walk the narrow line between friendship and duty, bearing in mind too how Kate had once felt about him.

"But does she feel the same way now?" Hamish asked.

He didn't know. It was not a subject he could broach.

He remembered her distress when he'd asked if she would help him find out the truth—she had seen it as a betrayal of her friendship with the others. He should not have put her in that position, even to conceal his real interest—asking her about the bit of cloth he'd found. And yet he was faced with the very real possibility that all four women would be taken to Bodmin and put in cells in the women's prison there. He had managed so far to keep them safe from that horror—but it had only been the holes in the dinghy that had saved them after Saunders died of his wound.

He was tired, he told himself, and Hamish always found him vulnerable then.

Kate Gordon's father arrived with the morning post. He had had to leave a meeting in Dartmouth, and he was in a foul temper.

His driver, a corporal, walked into the inn just as Rutledge was finishing his breakfast, seeking a room.

Passing through Reception, Rutledge stopped at the sight of the uniform, and said, "Good morning. Inspector Rutledge. I take it that Major Gordon has come down to Cornwall?"

"He has that," the corporal replied, his mouth twisting in a grimace. "Corporal Dixon, sir. I'm to collect him tomorrow morning at ten. Sharp. I can only hope he's in a better temper. I swear I could smell sulfur in the air, most of the way."

"I doubt he will be in a better mood."

He gave Gordon half an hour to greet his daughter before arriving himself at Padstow Place.

The maid who opened the door was visibly rattled, and even from where he stood, Rutledge could hear raised voices.

"I can find my way," he said to the maid, and walked purposefully toward the library.

He opened the door to find Gordon standing by the hearth, St. Ives by the window with his back turned, and Grenville at the table, leaning forward with his hands flat on the surface, his expression as hard as Gordon's was furious.

"And I say no jumped-up Inspector from Scotland Yard is going to dictate to me about my daughter's movements."

"If you take her away from here, all four of them will be put in—"

Absorbed in their confrontation, neither had looked toward the door. Grenville did now, breaking off and clearly intending to tell whoever had opened it to get out.

Instead, he straightened up and waited.

Gordon, looking in his turn at the interruption, frowned. "Inspector," he said after a moment, and then, "What's to prevent me from removing my daughter from Cornwall?"

"Good morning, sir. Mr. Grenville will tell you that we have gone to great lengths to see to it that the accused have remained here in this house. The few hours they spent in the small cell in the village were shocking. By all means, take Miss Gordon back to London with you. I can't stop you. But when she leaves this house, a warrant will be issued for her immediate arrest, and when she is taken into custody, she will be transferred to the nearest prison that can accommodate her. And her friends will be sent there as well, where they'll remain until this case comes to trial. Neither Mr. Grenville nor I will be able to do anything about that."

"This is ridiculous nonsense, and you know it. Kate is no more a felon than I am. It's time this farce is finished and she's allowed to return to her family."

"Hardly a farce, Major. Harry Saunders has died of his head wound. The charge is now murder. There will be an inquest shortly. I expect the accused will be remanded to prison to await trial. Trevose's testimony and the blow to Saunders's head will see to that. Men have been convicted on less. Your best hope was Harry Saunders living to give *his* evidence."

"I don't see why the statement of a farmer is more trustworthy than that of my daughter. Or Grenville's for that matter," Gordon fumed.

He was a soldier, accustomed to instant respect and men at the ready to carry out his orders.

"Because at the moment, he's an impartial witness. If there *was* an attempt to kill Saunders, there would be collusion among the women in that boat to deny it."

"Is this some sort of retribution for Jean's breaking off of your engagement?"

Stung, Rutledge could hear Hamish raging in the back of his mind, but he forced himself to say calmly, "You're understandably angry, sir, and I will overlook that remark. As I was not there in that rowing boat, I can't tell you what actually happened. And therefore I must depend on the evidence in the case, not any regard I may have for your daughter."

"What's more," Grenville interjected, "I will not allow you to jeopardize *my* daughter's well-being by countenancing your removal of Kate from this house. If Rutledge can't stop you, I can. As magistrate, I have some authority here."

St. Ives turned to face the room. "You're outnumbered in this, Gordon, and I expect Langley will side with us as well. Face it. This is one stronghold you can't charge and overthrow with cavalry and foot."

Gordon controlled his temper with an effort. "This Saunders. Why is that name familiar to me?"

"His father is connected with our local bank."

"I'm not acquainted with your local banker. During the war, was he an officer seconded to the military attaché at the embassy in Washington?"

"He was."

"I knew the attaché. He spoke highly of the lieutenant. I am sorry to hear he's dead. Nevertheless, I will have Kate out of here before London gets wind of this and the story is spread all over the newspapers that she's an accomplice to *murder*."

"I understand your feelings, sir," Rutledge said. "But the story will reach the newspapers sooner if Kate and the others are locked up in Bodmin. They are safer here, and a good deal more comfortable."

"Bodmin? While they await their trial? You can't be serious, man."

"Where else can they go? Four female prisoners? Neither Padstow nor Wadebridge is able to take them."

There was a knock at the door, and Grenville called, "What is it?" in a tone of voice that clearly indicated his displeasure at being disturbed a second time.

The maid stood on the threshold.

"Constable Pendennis is here, sir. For the Inspector."

"Show him in," Grenville ordered, and after a moment Pendennis walked into the room, his face as expressionless as he could contrive to make it.

He'd taken in the situation at a glance. The three men waiting for him to speak were glaring at him. Turning to Rutledge, he said, "Mr. Saunders's solicitor was just at the police station, sir. And he informed me that Mr. and Mrs. Saunders are pressing for the four young ladies to be bound over for trial. As Mr. Grenville is the magistrate, he will be required to hear the charges."

Gordon was the first to recover. "I am sorry for the loss of his son. I have already said so. But victimizing my daughter will not bring the lad back." He turned on Rutledge.

"And you, sir, will see to it that this matter is concluded before there is any further persecution of my daughter."

Still smarting from Gordon's dressing-down, Rutledge kept his temper and asked to speak to Elaine St. Ives.

Grenville took him to the drawing room, and he waited there for Elaine to come down.

When the door opened, he was surprised to see Mrs. Grenville stepping into the room and quietly closing the door behind her.

"I have heard the shouting from the library. I gather there is no good news."

"Pendennis has come to relate the Saunderses' insistence on having the accused returned to gaol. Your husband will have to deal with it. I left Pendennis in the library."

"Daniel in the lion's den," she said ruefully. "Will he succeed in taking them to Bodmin?"

"I doubt it."

"Would it do any good if I were to call on Mr. and Mrs. Saunders?"

"At the moment, they're blinded to everything but their own grief. I think it best to wait."

She said, with sadness in her voice, "We are all parents. And I know what it is to lose an only son. Do *you* think those four women are guilty of intentionally killing Harry Saunders?"

She had not invited him to sit down. He thought it was a measure of her distress that she had forgot her manners.

"As a policeman it's my duty to find out the truth. Not to judge."

"You've interviewed them, Mr. Rutledge. You must know that they aren't criminals."

He understood what she wanted from him: some relief from the worry that was tearing her apart. But there was no way he could offer her that.

He asked his own question instead of answering hers. "Do you think Trevose is concerned with whether they are guilty or not?"

If he had struck her, she couldn't have looked more shocked. After a moment she said in a husky voice, "Are you saying that my daughter and her friends are paying for his brother's life?"

"You may be better able to answer that than I am. I can't read Trevose's heart any more than I can read your daughter's."

"It's a long time to nurture a grudge." It was said almost in hope, as if she wanted very badly to believe it.

Rutledge disliked having to disabuse her of the hope, but she needed to hear the truth. "He and his brother quarreled before the boy left. It was never made up. It may be that for Trevose, his own guilt is driving him to find someone else to blame for his brother leaving."

"Ah. That explains so much." There was despair in her eyes as she turned away.

He gave her time to compose herself, and then brought out the small square of cloth. "Do you recognize this fabric?"

She examined it closely. He found himself wondering if she was trying to decide how to answer him.

"I don't," she said after a moment. Then she looked up and held his gaze. "Is it important, is that why you are asking me?"

"I doubt it," he said, deliberately making light of it. "But a policeman must consider even the smallest detail that comes his way. Otherwise, how is he to know what's important and what isn't?" He put the bit of cloth back in his pocket. Then he added, "I've known smaller things to clear a person."

She blinked, and he realized that she thought he'd been offering her a chance to clear her daughter's name, and somehow she had failed.

He said, "No, it wasn't a test. Only a query. It changes nothing."

The door opened and Elaine came in.

"Why are they shouting in the library?" she asked uneasily. "I could hear them as I came down the stairs." She glanced over her shoulder, her face suddenly pale. "We're being taken to gaol, aren't we? Harry's dead, and it's too late to ask *him* what happened. But why does that farmer want us to be hanged?"

Mrs. Grenville caught her breath, her eyes pleading with Rutledge.

He shook his head slightly, warning her to say nothing more.

For an instant he thought she was going to ignore it, her sense of responsibility getting the better of her good judgment.

IO

Recovering her self-possession with an effort, Mrs. Grenville managed a smile. "Kate's father has just arrived," she said. "I expect he's angry that more progress hasn't been made in clearing all of you. I shouldn't worry about it, if I were you."

Elaine returned the smile. "Then I won't." To Rutledge, she said, "You sent for me, Inspector?"

With a nod to Rutledge, Mrs. Grenville went out the door and closed it behind her.

"It's a tangle, isn't it?" he said pleasantly to Elaine. "We need facts—and sometimes there are no facts to be found. Or if there are, they point in different directions, until we're all in a muddle."

He was thinking that he wasn't more than five or six years older than Elaine St. Ives. And yet he felt old enough to be her father or an uncle. He could sympathize with her bewilderment. She had had only to sit still and balance the rowboat while the others fought to save—or kill—Saunders. Was she strong enough emotionally to lie for the others, if they had decided to drown Saunders? To keep their secret even in the face of trial and possible conviction? He couldn't be sure. Sometimes fragile people were made of steel, where their own interests were concerned.

"It's like a nightmare. I wish it would end," she said, with feeling.

He didn't want to begin with what had brought him here. And so he said, "I find it hard to believe that someone who could barely swim had a larger craft that he took as far as Fowey, or that he ran about in its dinghy. He wasn't dressed for swimming that Saturday, was he?"

"I expect he was meeting friends. He grew up on the Camel. As we all did. He and my brother were always out on the water in the summer." She smiled, remembering. "That was before the war. I don't think it worried Harry that he wasn't a strong swimmer. He was so used to boats, you see."

"That still doesn't explain why he never learned."

"He was quite strong, a good horseman, a very fine tennis player. That sort of thing. But he told George that in the water he always sank like a stone. He had no buoyancy. My brother claimed he had no faith in the water. That he didn't expect it to hold him up. He was a thrasher. Fighting the water instead of going with it."

Which he found intriguing. "Then he couldn't have made it ashore, if you and the others hadn't been there?"

"Possibly. Although I doubt it. He must already have been unsettled by the boat sinking as it did. That even shocked me. He wouldn't have been able to let the water take him, and use it to reach the shore or hang on to something until he reached the village landing. The water was cold, mind you. That wouldn't help."

"You know a good deal about it," he said.

"My brother taught me to swim when I was four. We live not far from the water, he was always around it, and I think he was afraid I'd try to follow him one day and drown. We never told our parents. My mother would have been horrified."

Rutledge smiled. "I expect she would have been." But that brother, he thought, had been wise beyond his years. As a rule, girls seldom learned to swim.

"Why did you go upstream, instead of down?"

"Mr. Grenville didn't want us to go farther than my parents' house or the village landing. These were places we knew well. The harbor at Padstow wasn't suitable, he said. And beyond there of course was the Doom Bar."

He said, "There's one other matter I need clarified before moving on. Tell me a little more about the young woman who came to services at St. Marina's last summer."

The question took her by surprise. "What young woman? The vicar's cousin?"

"Yes. You were never introduced, but could you describe her for me?"

"I'll try. She was quite pretty—lovely dark hair and a nice smile. Her clothes were rather conservative but beautifully made. You can always tell, can't you? A soft voice, cultured. Rather shy and uncomfortable in crowds of people. I thought perhaps she might be from London, that we might have acquaintances in common. But Mr. Toup told me her father was a vicar in Norfolk, near the North Sea coast, and she acts as his housekeeper most of the year."

"A suitable wife for Harry Saunders, do you think?"

She smiled wryly. "Harry might feel she was. But his father might feel quite differently. Even bankers are ambitious for their sons. Unless of course she was an heiress."

He returned the smile.

"Where does she stay in Rock when she comes to Cornwall?"

"I have no idea. You must ask Mr. Toup." She tilted her head, curious. "Why are you so interested in this young woman? It isn't just because of Victoria and Harry, is it?"

A very perceptive question.

"I don't know," he told her in all honesty. "Anything to do with Harry Saunders interests me until I have discovered how he died." Another thought occurred to him. "Who transported this young woman across the river? I haven't been told that the vicar has a boat. Was it Harry, do you think?"

"There's a ferry," she said doubtfully. "That's how most people go back and forth. Although Harry might well have offered his services. I did wonder why she chose to stay across the river."

He could feel Hamish stirring suddenly in the back of his mind. Hamish had worked it out already, and Rutledge needed time to think.

Thanking Miss St. Ives, he walked with her to the door. As he shut it behind her, he stood there with his hand on the knob, his mind racing.

What if Toup had lied to him? What if this mystery woman lived not in Rock but in those cottages for hire between Padstow and Prideaux Place? Was this how Harry had met her? He kept his boat there.

But that would mean that the man in the third cottage had lied as well. A young married couple and a pair of spinsters . . .

Saunders was a banker's son. He could afford to bribe the landlord.

It would be fairly unusual for a young single woman to live alone in an isolated cottage let for the summer. And Toup had said he couldn't allow her to live at the vicarage without a chaperone, indicating that she was indeed traveling alone.

But if she did live by herself in the cottage above where Saunders beached the dinghy, and she appeared on his arm at Sunday services, a stranger who kept to herself, speculation would be rampant, her connection with the vicar notwithstanding. Was Toup aware of where she was staying? Or had he been lied to as well?

Rutledge could see, all at once, why Victoria Grenville would have been angry with the banker's son for flirting with *her,* while he was involved with this stranger. Using his flirtation as a cover for an affair. A Grenville would not have found that either amusing or even endurable.

It didn't sound like the Harry Saunders everyone had described to him, but Rutledge could see how appearances might be one thing, reality another.

Even the saints sometimes had feet of clay . . .

But would Victoria Grenville be angry enough—would she feel she had been embarrassed enough by Saunders—that when the opportunity came her way, she might drop an oar on his head?

He found it hard to believe.

But had that been what she had been counting on, before Trevose appeared on the scene? That no one would think Victoria Grenville was capable of murder?

Her mother had been the cause, however inadvertently, in one man's death. Was *she* involved in another's?

Rutledge realized that he was still standing there, his hand on the doorknob.

He stepped out into the passage, just as Kate was walking toward the library door.

Moving swiftly, searching the passage to make sure they were alone, he caught her arm and laid his finger on his lips, to warn her not to speak.

"Have you been summoned to the library?" he asked softly.

She nodded.

"Whatever happens, don't let your father take you to London. It will mean an order for your immediate arrest and that of the others as well. You're safer by far here than in a prison cell."

"They won't let us go. Not now that Harry's dead," she answered him. "I knew that as soon as I heard the news. Poor man." She hesitated. "Ian. It will be all right, won't it? In the end?"

He released her arm, stepping back. He couldn't lie to her. "I'm doing my best. Let's pray it's enough."

He had only just reached the drawing room door when there was a general exodus from the library. He could hear Major Gordon greeting his daughter as St. Ives and Grenville left the room, with Pendennis in tow. He turned and waited, preparing himself for the verdict.

Grenville was grim. Pendennis looked defeated. St. Ives was still quite angry.

"Stubborn fool," he heard St. Ives say under his breath.

It had ended in a draw, Rutledge thought. But in favor of the accused.

Grenville stopped. "I've to inform you, Inspector, that I feel it is for the best for these young women to remain in my charge. I recognize that the circumstances now are different, that this is a murder investigation. But I do not feel that there is anything to be gained by incarcerating them. I can appreciate the despair the Saunderses are feeling, but I would be failing in my duty as magistrate if I agree to their imprisonment for the sake of appearances."

"You do realize," Rutledge said, "to be perfectly clear about it, the police have not been able to question the victim. We have never been able to ask him what he believed actually happened there in the boat. It would have been very useful, if we could have done so. It is now a matter of the word of the farmer, Trevose, and the word of your daughters."

Grenville's face darkened. "Are you telling me that you want to see the accused taken away to gaol?"

"No, I am not. I am telling you that as their gaoler, you must remember that you are just that, and not a father. Or in loco parentis for Gordon, Langley, and St. Ives. You must see that they are kept close. For their own safety as well as a matter of duty."

Grenville stared at Rutledge. He was not accustomed to being told where his duty lay. Certainly not by a policeman. And then he seemed to realize that Pendennis was still standing there with them, all ears.

That undoubtedly the constable would report this conversation to the grieving parents of the dead man.

He cleared his throat, as if that action also cleared his head, and then responded with dignity. "I do understand, Inspector. I will not show favoritism, I will not allow them privileges that are not permitted by their circumstances, and I will stand surety for their appearance if called upon to answer these charges in court."

"Then I rely on your good faith. Constable?"

Pendennis nodded. "I have no choice but to do the same."

Grenville glanced at St. Ives, then turned to walk Pendennis and Rutledge to the door, the good host. Or as near to that as he could muster. St. Ives remained where he was.

Grenville saw them out punctiliously.

Pendennis, turning toward his bicycle, glanced at the closed door. He said, for Rutledge's ears only, "I'm not happy about this. What am I to tell Mr. and Mrs. Saunders? Their son is *dead*."

"There's rope in the boot," Rutledge said. "We'll lash your bicycle to the motorcar and I'll drive you back to the village. We'll talk about it on the way."

"I'd prefer to ride on my own, sir. If you please."

"Then you'll stop at the gate. We can talk there."

He cranked the motorcar and followed Pendennis down the drive, wondering as he did if the constable would wait for him there.

He did. Rutledge left the motor running to signify that he had no intention of holding up the constable for very long. The time for argument had, in fact, long since past. He got down, walked to where the constable was standing, and said, "You disagree with Grenville's decision." It was a statement, not a question.

"I do, sir. Harry Saunders is dead. There must be an inquest, binding those four young women over for trial. It's not right that they aren't in Bodmin Gaol."

"I have not forgot. Grenville will see to scheduling the inquest. But

I also remember that these same four women, even in a state of distress, still claimed that what happened out there on the water was an accident. However it might have looked to Trevose on the riverbank. And Trevose has also claimed that Saunders was in the Grenville rowing boat at the start of this business, and had been shoved overboard and held under the water to drown. Since then we've discovered the dinghy at the bottom of the river. Just as the four accused told us. What else is incorrect in his statement? Until the inquest decides, we will treat the young women with respect."

"If they were anyone else, they would be in custody while you investigated the truth of the accusation. Sir," Pendennis said stubbornly.

"When was the last time you were in Bodmin Gaol? Would you care to see your own daughter sent there?"

"I have no daughter, sir!"

"Yes, Constable," Rutledge responded patiently. "I was speaking in general terms. Any young woman of your acquaintance, then. A sister. A friend."

Pendennis hesitated.

"Bodmin was considered a proper place to keep the Crown Jewels safe during the war. Surely that recommends it?" Rutledge asked.

"But Harry Saunders—do you seriously believe, sir, that they will be found not guilty? That they have spoken the truth, and Trevose is lying?"

Rutledge could almost hear his thoughts—that Inspector Barrington wouldn't have handled the situation in this manner. That Barrington wasn't acquainted with one of the accused. Or was that his own conscience speaking?

"I shall want to know more about who put those holes in the bottom of Harry Saunders's boat before I parcel out guilt or innocence. Did you mention that problem to Grenville?"

Constable Pendennis drew himself up stiffly. "I don't gossip. Sir. And you asked me not to say anything."

"Good man. Whoever interfered with the dinghy knew what he or she was doing. Holes placed carefully so that it would take on water slowly, well into midriver and far from help. Until I'm satisfied on that point, I can't in good conscience close this inquiry. If the four women are guilty of causing Saunders's death, then part of the responsibility surely belongs to whoever put him in peril in the first place." Rutledge looked up as a cart came rattling by, the man holding the reins staring with interest at two policemen standing at the gates of Padstow Place. He waited, watching it until it had gone around the next bend in the road. "Can you understand why I am reluctant to listen to Saunders calling for their blood, reluctant to hurry them off to Wadebridge or Bodmin, until I know who else wanted Harry Saunders to die in the river that day? You can see these holes for yourself, if you wish."

He half expected Pendennis to ask if he himself had done the damage to the boat, to protect the four women.

But the man said, "Will you take me there? It's too far to go on my bicycle."

"Yes, I will do that. Now, if you like."

"Now would be convenient, sir."

They lashed the bicycle to the motorcar after all, and the constable got in beside Rutledge. They traveled to the village in silence, and Rutledge wondered if the constable was mulling over what he'd been told.

Dropping the bicycle at the police station, they set out for Padstow and the salvage yard.

As they were nearing their destination, the constable spoke for the first time. "It was deliberate? You are sure of it? And it happened before the—incident—on the water?"

"See for yourself."

He left the motorcar where he had before, and they walked down to the salvage yard. It was busy, and one or two of the men at work there glanced up as they passed, their boots crunching in the wet sand where a boat had been pulled into drydock. On their way there, Rutledge had said, "You were aware where Saunders kept the dinghy?"

"I was, sir. I expect other people knew." And then he stopped, as if he wished he'd bitten his tongue.

They reached the dinghy where it had been stored in an out-of-the-way corner and together turned it over. Pendennis clambered aboard, and Rutledge stood back, letting him find the damage for himself. Watching as the constable thoroughly examined the bottom of the boat, Rutledge had a sense of being observed, and he turned his head to look. The owner of the yard was standing some thirty paces away, watching, along with one of his men. Rutledge nodded to him.

Pendennis hoisted himself out of the boat, then said, "Could we turn her over again, sir?"

Together they got it hull up, and Pendennis went to look for the narrow holes. "How come he didn't see this before he took her out? Harry Saunders was a careful sailor, from all reports."

"I don't know the answer to that. The yard owner suggested that some sort of filler was used, something that would disintegrate after being in the water. Clay, possibly, or bits of paper or wax stuffed back in. Or perhaps he was in a hurry, or had other things on his mind, and so he saw what he believed must be there—an intact hull. See for yourself. Did you spot them when you first walked up to the dinghy and we turned it over the first time?"

"No, sir. I was thinking, when first you told me, that something like an axe was taken to the planks. This work wasn't meant to be visible, was it? But it was enough to let the boat sink in due course."

"Precisely. Why put holes in the fabric of a boat? A warning, that someone had been here, and had damaged it, someone who had it in for you? But these were well hidden, so that in the course of your afternoon out, or halfway round to the Padstow docks, where your larger craft is anchored, you either swim for it or drown?"

"The young ladies took the boat out for pleasure, because it was a fair day. So they say. But maybe not so, maybe they wanted to watch Saunders drown."

"How could they possibly be sure when next he was to take the dinghy out? And how could they know, putting the holes where they did in the fabric, that he wouldn't go down sooner, on his way to Padstow? They aren't experts in this, Pendennis. Do you think they would know when to be lying in wait?"

He shook his head. "It would be hard to say, precisely, where he set out to go, and how long he would stay afloat."

"Then it's possible, isn't it, that the sinking of this dinghy was by design, and that the encounter was happenstance. No one was watching that day. The accused had only to let him drown. After all, there was no one else on the river, and these young women could claim that they hadn't been able to reach him before he went down. Why pull him over to their boat and then hit him with an oar?"

"It still doesn't clear them."

"No. I agree. But it puts enough doubt in the picture to make me reluctant to send them to Bodmin Gaol. They'd just come down from London. When would they have had time to do this much damage? Even if they knew where to find the boat."

"I dunno, sir. But I expect you're right." He looked down again at the dinghy. "But if it wasn't the accused, who had it in for Harry Saunders?"

"I'd like to know that myself, Constable. And with any luck, we will."

Pendennis turned to study the yard. "I wish I'd seen this straightaway, sir. Before I went to see Mr. Grenville this morning."

"At the moment, the fewer people who are aware of this dinghy, the better, until I can sort it out."

"I see, sir."

But Rutledge wasn't sure he did. Still, the constable appeared to be satisfied.

"I'll drive you back to Heyl."

The constable took one final look at the dinghy, as if still convincing himself of what he'd seen there, then followed Rutledge back to the motorcar.

"Know anything about the summer visitors who come here to let cottages?" Rutledge asked as he went to turn the crank.

"No, sir. They generally stay in the vicinity of Padstow. I know of them, and that's about it. Over the years I doubt I've seen four or five in the village."

"And the young woman who sometimes accompanied Saunders to St. Marina's for Sunday service?"

"Was she from one of them?" Pendennis had opened the motorcar's door and he stopped, staring at Rutledge. "I thought she was from Padstow. That he might have brought her down to the village to keep her out of his father's or mother's eye." He shrugged. "They strike me as rather—" He groped for the right word, and failed. "He's an only son. An only child. They would be particular about the company he kept."

"Did you ever meet her?"

"Lord, no, he wouldn't be likely to introduce us, would he?" Pendennis got in and shut the door. "Pretty little thing. Struck me as rather possessive, all the same. The way she'd hold his arm, as if afraid to let go." Then the thought occurred to him. "You're not saying that she had anything to do with the damage to the boat. Where was the cottage she was staying in?"

"Do you think she was strong enough to do that kind of work?" Rutledge countered.

"There's that. But a jealous woman?" He shook his head. "They're a force to be reckoned with, they are."

"Keep this to yourself," Rutledge warned again. "I haven't even spoken to Grenville about it."

That seemed to please the constable, and in a way appeared to assuage some of the sting of being told out of hand that there would be no formal arrest warrant.

They were nearly to the village. "Will you keep me informed of any progress?" Pendennis asked.

"I will. What will you tell Mr. and Mrs. Saunders?"

There was a deep sigh as the constable considered. "I dunno, sir. They won't be happy, whatever I tell them."

Rutledge waited until he had seen Constable Pendennis enter the police station and shut the door. Then he turned back the way they had just come.

It had been a risk, telling the constable so much about the boat. But one that it had been necessary to take.

Now that there was a murder charge, the families of the accused would send a phalanx of lawyers back to Heyl, intent on making certain the daughters they represented were protected. It would stir up animosity in some quarters, and if there was any inkling that there might be more to the case than they knew, the Londoners would muddy the waters for the police. He had seen it before.

But there was nothing he could do about it now. The one good thing, he told himself, was that the families would be as eager to keep the press out of Cornwall as he was. Unless or until it was in their best interests to look for public support.

He left the motorcar in what was fast becoming its accustomed place, and walked past the first two cottages, staring out at the river as it broadened toward the Doom Bar. And then, as casually as he could, he turned and walked back toward the only cottage that was still occupied.

Before he could knock, the white-haired man he'd spoken to before opened the door with a smile.

"I thought you might be back. Thinking of letting one of them, are you?" He gestured toward the vacant cottages, then invited Rutledge in, offering him a chair.

"It's possible," he agreed. "Tell me, what sort of neighbors would I have, if I chose to spend the summer here? It's rather isolated. I wouldn't want to find myself with people I wouldn't care for."

"Mostly families from London," the man said. "I think I told you. A young couple in that first cottage. Celebrating a second wedding anniversary, I was told. They spent most of their first summer here just walking, the two of them. I expect he'd been in the war, and they were getting to know each other again. I think they like being alone out here. Or perhaps he needs to get away from the city's bustle."

"What does he do there? If he can spend his summers here?"

"He's writing a book, his wife told me. I thought it might be a memoir of the war, but she said it was about Africa. He grew up there, it seems. Lots of famous people in the book, she said, and he knew them all."

"And in the second house?"

"A pair of spinster sisters."

"Then they'll be coming back?"

"No. They left a note saying that they wouldn't be returning."

"And the young woman? Where did she live?"

"A young woman?" He shook his head. "Do you mean the wife?"

"I understood there was a young woman who spent much of the past summer here. Alone or with her family."

"You must be thinking about another cottage for let." He rose. "Now I've a few repairs to make, if you'll pardon me for rushing you off."

"Do you own the cottages? Or do you act for the person who does?"

"That needn't concern you, sir, if you'll forgive me for saying so. If it's too soon to decide, as you say."

Rutledge stood and allowed himself to be ushered toward the door. "Tell me about the spinsters."

"Two women in their sixties, I believe. Two sisters. Former schoolmistresses, I should think."

Rutledge thanked him, and left.

It was odd, he thought, walking back to the motorcar, that the man knew so many details about the young couple, but almost nothing about the spinsters. They might have chosen to keep themselves to themselves. Or he could be lying, and they didn't exist.

But why lie?

He went into Padstow with an eye to finding an estate agent who could tell him more about the cottages and even provide the names of the people who had let the first two during the past summer.

An hour later, Rutledge found what he was after. The cheerful man behind the desk smiled and said, "'You must mean Frank Dunbar's cottages. I wouldn't mind taking him on as a client, but he manages quite well on his own. Puts advertisements in London newspapers in the early spring, and usually has someone in both houses by the start of May. He never lets the third. Prefers to live there himself despite the money he would make."

"Do you know anything about the people who let his cottages?"

"Nothing at all."

"What sort of advertisements does he run?"

"Very simple ones. *Out-of-the-way private cottages on the River Camel, looking for quiet people seeking a peaceful summer.* That sort of thing. The truth is, I think I could get far more money for them. Artists, writers. People like that are willing to pay well for privacy and inspiration."

"I thought artists preferred the light along the southern coast."

The man shrugged. "Those who want to be noticed, yes. It's the famous ones seeking privacy I'd like to attract."

Leaving the office and returning to his motorcar, Rutledge wondered who precisely this young woman was. The vicar's cousin? Someone who cared for Harry Saunders and had been disappointed in love? Or someone more sinister? She might well have been from Padstow or even Rock, not the cottages.

The vicar had protected her. She had clung to Saunders, but he had not always stayed for services. Hardly the behavior of a lover. Dunbar was adamant that she had not let one of his cottages.

Then what was her connection to the damaged dinghy? Had she been back since September, openly or secretly? Or was she across the river in Rock, and had never left Cornwall?

Rutledge would have given much to know the answer to that.

In his room Rutledge wrote a letter to Sergeant Gibson, querying what he might know about the death of a young footman on St. Michael's Mount, and what he might know about Trevose and the Saunders family. Then he went to find Corporal Dixon and asked him to post the letter for him in London.

"Dull reports," he said with a shrug, making light of their importance. This was Major Gordon's driver, after all. "But necessary, or I'll have someone from the Yard breathing down my back."

Dixon laughed. "Better you than me."

Passing Reception, Rutledge was given a note asking him to call on Constable Pendennis as soon as he returned to Heyl village. Rutledge walked on to the police station. Pendennis was just eating his lunch, a large meat pasty. Flakes of crust were caught on his chin as he looked up.

Swallowing with the help of a bottle of Cornish cider, he said, "A telegram for you. Came just after I'd walked in the door. Where have you been?"

"Wandering around Padstow," Rutledge answered. "I needed to think." He took the telegram the constable was holding out and quickly realized that it was from the Yard. Markham wanting to know what progress he was making. Sergeant Gibson had sent it, indicating that Markham had asked a rhetorical question and this was interpreted as a need for information soonest.

Rutledge folded the sheet, returned it to the envelope, and put them in his pocket. "The Yard," he said briefly as Pendennis stared up at him, waiting to hear the contents.

There was no telegraph office closer than Padstow.

"I'll respond tomorrow." With a nod, he left the station and walked back to the inn.

He was just stepping into Reception when a motorcar very like his own pulled up at the door, and someone called his name.

Rutledge turned to see Harry Saunders's father getting out.

"You are a hard man to find," the elder Saunders said, catching him up.

Letting the jibe go, he led the way to the tiny parlor, all the inn boasted in the way of privacy, and offered Saunders a seat.

"I'll stand. My mission is brief. Why have you not brought those young women in to gaol, where they belong?"

"Do they?" Rutledge asked. "I haven't completed my inquiry into the death of your son. The facts may alter before I'm finished."

"How can they? My son's death is directly connected to what happened to him at the hands of four women. Trevose has made it plain enough: attempted murder. And now that my son is dead, it's murder."

Rutledge asked with interest, "Do you know any of those who are accused of your son's death? Victoria Grenville, for one. Do you know her?"

"I know her father; I may have met her from time to time. I can't immediately recall when."

"Elaine St. Ives."

"The same, and to save you the trouble of asking, I have never to my knowledge met the other two."

"Your son knew two of them. Were there any other young women in his life?"

"None. His mother or I would have known. We had high hopes. And he was young, the war hardly over. Time enough to wed."

"Why did his boat sink, do you know?" The change of subject caught Saunders unaware.

"I have been sitting at his bedside for days. Hoping, praying for his safe return to us. There has been no time to think or do anything other than offer him what comfort we could. Do you have any idea what that's like, sir? An only child, one's son." There was anguish in his eyes, and bitterness. "He was to follow me in the bank. And his son after him. And now there's nothing. No future, nothing. A gravestone in the churchyard."

"I am so sorry for your loss, sir, but as I must find out who is responsible, I must ask these questions. Among the answers will be information that will help me satisfy you and your wife about how your son died." His voice was gentle. It was always difficult to interview the bereaved, but there was no one who knew the victim better.

"You know who is responsible. I don't understand why you are still *investigating*." His emphasis made it sound like an improper word.

"All the facts aren't in. I have not found Inspector Barrington's notes, and so I have had to begin at the beginning, as it were. Would you have me arrest the wrong person? Do you know, for instance, if all four of the women in that boat intended to see your son dead?"

"I can only surmise that they must have been in collusion. One wielded the oar. The others tried to hold his head under. It's what Trevose has told us in his statement."

"Elaine St. Ives was on the other side of the rowboat."

"Yes, balancing the craft so that it didn't overturn."

"But not trying to murder anyone."

"Come now, man, in a boat that small, she had to be aware of what was happening. And she did nothing to stop it."

"Did your son have enemies, sir? Is there anyone who might have wished him ill?"

"Good God, Inspector, you have four examples before you now. How many others must you find?"

"Why were they enemies? These four examples. What transpired between your son and the young women, to make them turn to murder?"

It was clear from his shock that Saunders hadn't thought about the four accused as anything other than his son's killers. Why they should have been enemies hadn't occurred to him.

"I must assume there was something between them. These four and my son."

"Did he mention them at home? To you or to his mother? Was he interested in courting one of them? Victoria Grenville for one would have been a satisfactory match, if not a very fine one."

"Harry had his own flat. He had his friends. He never spoke to me of women in his life. He had just come back from the war—he needed time to settle. To decide what to do with his future."

He had been in Washington, in America, far from the battlefields. But it was clear that having their only child back with them had meant much to Mr. and Mrs. Saunders. It was they who needed time to get to know him again, and to feel safe with him at home again.

"Who were his particular friends?"

"One of them, Walter Poltruan, was killed in France. Ypres. The St. Ives boy came home in sad shape. Although I wouldn't call him a particular friend. And there was Sandy Wade. His father's the doctor in Rock. He himself lives in Padstow."

"Can you tell me where?"

Saunders gave him the direction, then seemed to recollect what had brought him to the village. He turned and sat down very heavily in the nearest chair, uncomfortable by the looks of its straight back, as if he had outrun his strength. "I fail to understand why all this is necessary," he said querulously. "You ask questions as if my son is responsible for his own death. Do you doubt what you have been told,

Inspector? If you do, then explain to me, if you will, how my son has died."

Rutledge took the chair opposite him, one in dark green upholstery that matched the drapes at the single window.

"Your son died of a bleeding in the brain, according to Dr. Carrick. I am not questioning that. What I can't understand is why that dinghy sank under him. He was a good sailor, was he not?"

"Yes, from an early age. He would have gone into the Navy, if he'd had a choice, I think. He loved the water."

"Experienced, then. And he kept his crafts seaworthy?"

"Of course he did. He understood that it was necessary. For that matter, he took pride in them. Every weekend he would find a little time to work on the *Sea Lion*. His mother often teased him about caring more for that boat than he did for either of us. It was not true, of course, but he would laugh and reassure her that he loved her as well."

"And yet the dinghy foundered, throwing him into the water. Could he have swum ashore, if the four women hadn't come up at that moment?"

"I don't know. I—he was not a strong swimmer."

"He could have drowned, within sight of shore?"

"Yes, yes, I expect so. But he didn't. He was killed by that woman sitting in the bow, the one with the oar. She deliberately struck him in the head."

"If she had wanted to kill him—if any of those four women had wanted Harry Saunders to die—why not simply let him drown when his boat sank?"

Saunders stared at him.

"They were four women. They might have failed to reach him in time. People would have praised them for trying, but your son would have been just as dead. It would have taken some time to find his body."

The older man got to his feet as if he'd been stung.

"What sort of policeman are you, Inspector?" He seemed at a loss for words for a full three or four seconds, and then he said, "Have you been bribed, to find a way to prevent those four women from paying for what they have done? I will hear no more of this. I will not listen to you. I refuse to hear another word."

And with that he made for the door like a hunted man, flinging it open and leaving it standing wide as he rushed through Reception and out to his motorcar. In his distress he had trouble cranking it, and he leaned his head on the bonnet for a moment, his eyes shut, too distraught to start his vehicle.

Rutledge, who had followed him out, said quietly, "Let me take you home. You can send for the motorcar later."

Saunders raised his head. "I wouldn't allow you to drive me anywhere."

This time the motor caught, and he got behind the wheel, almost leaping forward as he mismanaged the clutch. And then he turned away and was gone, on his way to Padstow.

Rutledge watched him out of sight. There would be no help from that quarter, any more than there would be from Trevose. But Saunders, he thought, had better reasons for hating.

He turned and walked into the inn. The way the clerk behind the desk looked at him made him wonder if their voices had carried that far. But there was nothing he could do about it.

He had missed his lunch and would miss his dinner. He took the stairs two at a time, spent five minutes in his room trying to clear his mind. And then he turned and left the room, intending to drive to Padstow and interview Sandy Wade.

II

It was not difficult finding the house where Wade lived. It was on a street of small bungalows, many of them late Victorian.

No one answered his door, and so Rutledge waited for Wade to come home.

Two hours later, a young man with very fair hair and a slim build came down the street whistling to himself, and turned into the path to the door.

Rutledge got out, calling his name, and Wade turned, surprised.

"Do I know you?" he asked, frowning.

"Inspector Rutledge, Scotland Yard. I understand you were a close friend of Harry Saunders?"

"I was," he answered warily.

Rutledge said, "I'd like to speak to you about him. His parents, understandably, are not able to talk to me."

"I should think not," Wade said. "Hard enough for me, to realize he's dead. All right, come in."

Rutledge followed him inside. The front room was comfortable, a mixture of older pieces, possibly from his parents' attic, and newer pieces he must have purchased when he moved in.

He gestured to a chair, and sat down himself after a moment. "What is it you'd like to know?"

"About Harry. His war. His friends. His boats. What he was like as a person."

"Kind, thoughtful. A good friend. He loved those boats. As for his war, he was always uncomfortable talking about it. He'd been in the States, and except for a harrowing experience going over when his ship was torpedoed, he saw no real fighting. Several friends we had in common died in France. I was wounded three times. When we sat around of an evening telling stories, he had little to say. But that wasn't his fault—being sent to America. We were hoping the Yanks would come in sooner, but it took the sinking of a liner to bring that about. Harry was supposed to find ways to encourage them to think of England as an ally. Over a hundred years since Yorktown, barely that since the burning of Washington. But we had common interests, a common language, heritage. A good many American fliers came over to fight for the French. Well, you must know that. And more than a few Yanks went to Canada to join up. But a drop in the bucket to what we needed. He said once that he had had a letter from his mother describing the difficulty planning a decent meal, and he's been dining out on the best beef available. It worried him."

"Not enough to take his own life?"

"God, no, he did his duty. What was asked of him. He knew that. Hell, someone had to do it. It happened to be Saunders."

"His friends?"

"We lost a good few, Harry and I," Wade answered tersely.

"Was he thinking about marriage? Was there a particular young woman he fancied?"

"If there was, he didn't tell me. He flirted sometimes with Victoria Grenville. He liked her, come to that. But he knew a banker couldn't aspire that high."

"Elaine St. Ives?"

"He was fond of her. She's a very sweet girl. I've met her once or twice, when I was in the village. Harry liked her in a different way. Her brother had been badly wounded, her fiancé killed. Harry felt rather protective toward her."

"There was someone he was seeing over the summer."

Wade got up and walked to the window, standing with his back to the room. "I don't know where you heard that. There was no one that I know of."

"Are you lying to me?"

Wade turned. "Why should I lie?" He took a deep breath. "I don't think Harry was ready to marry. His father wanted him to follow him in the bank, but Harry wasn't sure about that. They nearly had words a time or two."

"What did he want to do?"

Wade shrugged eloquently. "I don't think he knew. A good many of us came home restless, uncertain about the future. My father wanted me to follow him into medicine. But I've seen enough torn bodies to last me a lifetime. A dozen lifetimes." He gestured to the room around them. "A bequest from my grandmother. It gives me breathing space until I know where I'd fit in."

"Why do you think his boat sank under him?"

"That's a mystery," Wade declared. "But I've also been told that he was already in the boat with the women. That he'd joined them in their outing on the Camel."

"Where was he going that Saturday afternoon? Do you know?"

"I don't, and that's the truth. He'd said something on Thursday about intending to call on a friend. He said it was past time."

"Who was this friend?"

"He didn't tell me. Afterward I wondered if he meant Miss Grenville. After I'd heard he was in their boat."

But Saunders hadn't been in the Grenville boat, according to the four women.

"Could it have been George St. Ives?" He'd been on the terrace that afternoon, but had not returned his sister's wave.

"St. Ives? I doubt it. He's made it fairly clear he doesn't want to see anyone from the past. But Harry knew him better than I did. He might not have taken no for an answer."

And it was a fine day. Saunders might have hoped to find St. Ives in the garden, or even on the terrace. A casual encounter. *Just passing, and I saw you there . . .* Easier than calling at the house and being turned away.

Speculation, but entirely possible.

"Where were you that afternoon?"

Wade grinned sheepishly. "Under the weather. I'd got drunk the night before at a bachelor's party."

"Was Harry at the party?"

Wade shook his head. "Across the river, in Rock. This was a man I'd gone to school with. I don't usually drink that much, but we got onto the war, and it was tempting to forget. Although it doesn't help, does it? Trying to forget. Were you in France? You must have been. You have the bearing of an officer."

Rutledge smiled grimly. "The Somme."

"Then I don't need to tell you why I drank more than I should."

But Rutledge had never turned to alcohol. He'd been afraid to, having seen too many drunken men still wearing parts of their uniforms mixed with civilian clothes, stumbling along the streets, mumbling to themselves, oblivious of any of the staring people trying to avoid them.

As if he'd heard the words, Wade said, "I was rather ashamed of myself in the morning, and the hangover didn't do much for my self-esteem either. I expect that was the third time I'd sought to forget in a bottle. In two years. I've been ashamed of that too."

"Why won't anyone tell me about the young woman Harry Saunders escorted to services at St. Marina's?"

Wade looked away. "Possibly," he said, "because she doesn't exist."

"But she does. Mr. Toup, the vicar, has already warned me off the subject."

Wade rose. "Then perhaps he knows best. Thank you for coming, Inspector. Now, if you'll forgive me, I have an engagement for the evening."

And he was politely ushered out of the house.

Who was this mystery woman? She existed, although no one would talk about her. And did she have anything to do with Saunders's death? She had only been in Cornwall for the summer. A few months at best.

He was back to his theory of jealousy. Although he still found it impossible to picture Victoria Grenville working so carefully to make the holes in Harry Saunders's boat. She would have been more likely to take an axe to it.

Hamish, who had been quiet for some time, said, "Aye. But she wielded yon oar with devastating results. And she hadna' wished to rescue the lad in the first place."

If it came down to the fact that Victoria had deliberately killed Saunders, and it could be proven beyond a doubt, where did that leave Kate and the other two women?

The question bedeviled him all the way back to the village.

Before going to bed, Rutledge made another search for Barrington's notes, but he was coming to the conclusion that the man hadn't been here long enough to put down on paper any of the observations and information he'd collected. But original interviews were missing as well, and that was far more troubling.

Come to that, he thought wryly, he himself had only jotted down whatever he thought pertinent, but it was a start, enough to write his report when the time came.

He lay in the comfortable bed, an arm beneath his head, staring at the ceiling and trying to shut out the voice of Hamish MacLeod.

How important was the damage to the dinghy to this particular case? Had any other boats in the vicinity suffered like damage? Was it a pattern of vandalism that pointed in an entirely different direction?

Or if it was specific to the dinghy, was it a first attempt to kill Harry Saunders? And because he had been too busy—or the weather had been too unpromising—to take out a boat, nothing had happened. But when the dinghy did go down, it wasn't out at sea, and there was rescue at hand. Had one of the occupants of the Grenville rowing boat realized that another, far more desperate attempt must be made? And that would point strongly to Victoria Grenville. She was rather headstrong, but would she be that concerned if Harry Saunders's attentions had turned in another direction? Or if she thought he had flirted with her to cover the true direction his affections had taken?

But the other young woman had left Cornwall, and apparently nothing had come of any relationship with Saunders over the summer.

Then why was everyone unwilling to talk about her?

He could think of several reasons—she was married, in which case he couldn't quite see Harry Saunders, with his upbringing, dallying with her. She was someone of importance, seeking a summer away from her usual life and duties. But he didn't know of any royal princesses, English or European, who might choose a desolate coast of Cornwall as a retreat from their routines. There was one other circumstance that might account for someone needing a few weeks of quiet and rest to regain her strength: a severe illness. That could explain the reluctance to talk about her.

Rutledge didn't know of any current cases of Spanish flu to account for that as a possibility. Tuberculosis? He remembered something he'd been told, that the young woman in question had clung to Harry

Saunders and seemed reluctant to meet or chat with other people. For fear, in her still delicate state, of picking up a chill or other infection?

"Ye havna' considered a young widow," Hamish suggested from a corner of the room.

"No one has mentioned that she wore black. But it would mean that the square of cloth I found wouldn't have belonged to her. That's worth looking into."

The next morning he went to speak to the vicar again.

Toup was just leaving the vicarage, and he said at once, as he opened the door to Rutledge, "Can it wait? I've promised a parishioner I'd call."

"I've come to ask a question. It won't take very long."

Wary, the vicar studied him. "What is it?" he asked after a moment.

"The young woman who came to services with Harry Saunders. Was she a widow?"

"Good God, what put that into your head? You're making much out of nothing. She was a summer visitor, no more than that, and Harry was kind enough to escort her to services a time or two. My own duties prevented me from fetching her myself."

But it had been more than a time or two.

"Had she been ill?"

Exasperated, the vicar said, "All right, if you must know, she had lost her mother in rather sad circumstances, and she thought a change of scene might help her in her bereavement. Is there anything criminal in that? I'd been asked to respect her privacy. She wasn't up to social calls, nor was she eager to entertain. She just wanted to escape from a houseful of memories for a little while. Now I must go."

"Then how did Harry meet her?"

"We can't discuss this matter on the doorstep. It's unseemly." He led Rutledge into the parlor, offered him a seat, but stood himself by the hearth, as if this would of necessity not take much longer. "The cottage she let for the summer is where he kept his boat. The small one, the dinghy."

If Harry had simply done her a kindness, it would explain why he had asked his friends not to talk about her or speculate on an attachment. Certainly he wouldn't have wished his parents to get wind of someone in particular. And it probably explained why they had come to services here, and not in Padstow, where she would have been an object of interest in the company of an eligible young bachelor. Or even encountered his parents.

"I am concerned because the dinghy that belonged to Saunders, the one kept just below that cottage, had been seriously tampered with, enough so that the next time he took it out, it sank under him. That was when Victoria Grenville and her friends claim to have tried to rescue him."

The vicar's exasperation disappeared in a look of sheer alarm. "But my cousin left just before the first of September. Thereabouts. Harry has been out in the dinghy since then. I've seen him myself. Who could have done such a thing? *Why?*"

"Would Victoria Grenville have done something like that out of sheer jealousy?"

"My God, I can't imagine that she would even have *thought* of such an act. She's always had her pick of beaux."

"Precisely my point. If Harry had been among them, and then a stranger had tried to take him away from her, she might have wanted to teach him a lesson. Not knowing how dangerous it could be." But he thought she would have known. From the start.

"No, no, this is ridiculous, Inspector. And it would do immeasurable harm even to speculate on such a suggestion." Toup was as agitated as Rutledge had ever seen him. "It was all a dreadful accident. It must have been, Trevose notwithstanding." He turned. "Really, I must attend to my parishioner. I refuse even to give these speculations my attention."

He was ushering Rutledge out the door, distracted and upset. "I must be on my way," he said again, closing the door behind them. And with a nod, he was gone.

Rutledge watched him walk away.

Something was unsettling the vicar. He didn't know what it was.

He wondered if the living at St. Marina was in the gift of the Grenville family. If that was the case, it was likely that Toup was torn between his duty to the law and his concern for the family that had brought him here.

Rutledge could see this inquiry ending with Victoria being tried as a murderess. A clever KC could connect her to the dinghy's holes, and when that attempt to kill Saunders had failed, when her friends had happened on the scene and wanted to rush to Saunders's aid, it could be claimed that she had resorted to the oar. Right or wrong, it could easily happen.

When it did, it was going to be difficult to disentangle the other three women from the repercussions of what she had done.

There was not much he could do to change that fact.

And then, out of nowhere, came a new direction.

12

From the vicarage Rutledge went into Padstow, intending to send his response to the Yard.

He worded it carefully, that response, for he didn't want to hear later that it had been twisted out of context.

Inquiry proceeding. Have not located original statements to compare with later ones. Families have arranged for counsel. They are not without influence. Meanwhile, there is one piece of evidence that so far can't be explained. Early resolution expected.

It also told the eager telegrapher nothing in the way of useful gossip. He had all but snatched the sheet from Rutledge's hand, once he discovered the message was addressed to Scotland Yard.

Rutledge walked on to the harbor, looking out at the larger craft that had belonged to Harry Saunders. After studying it for a time, he engaged a boatman to take him out to it.

The wind off the estuary was strong, and Rutledge had had to remove his hat or else watch it sail away onto the water.

When he reached the *Sea Lion,* it was swinging at anchor, sleek in the watery sunlight with sails furled and covered with canvas, the paint in good condition, and everything tidily in its place. He went up the rope ladder dangling over the side, and swung himself onto the deck.

It was as if the owner had just walked away. Rutledge went over it with care, from the small cabin to the wheelhouse, and then down to where there was a good-size engine. From there he found his way into the bilge, but if someone had tried to damage this boat, Rutledge was unable to find any signs of it.

But why risk interfering with this boat, where you might well be seen from the harbor, when damaging the dinghy had served just as well? The summer visitors were gone from where it was kept, and there was only one cottage still occupied. Easy enough to wait until one man had left for the day, and you could take your time with the task. And the waterman who had taken Rutledge out to the *Sea Lion* confirmed that the dinghy was the usual way Saunders reached the larger craft.

"Only once did he ever use one of us, and that was the first day, when he took ownership. He brought the dinghy back in three hours later, and soon after found a place to bring it ashore." The waterman grinned, scratching a grizzled chin. "The bank overlooks the water, you know. He wouldn't want to be seen playing truant, now would he?"

Rutledge agreed, and when he was taken back to the harbor, he paid the old man his fee, then crouched on the harbor wall just above him and asked a last question.

"Anyone else wanting to be taken out to her? Before Saunders had his accident, perhaps."

The man shook his head. "Nay. If he wanted friends to come aboard, he rowed them out himself. But it wasn't a boat for that sort of thing. There was never any gossip about that. A quiet sort, Saunders. Not one for carrying on. I'll say that for him."

"Did he ever bring a young woman here to see her?" He gestured to the boat.

"Nay. Not that I ever heard. And he'd be a fool to take her aboard, now wouldn't he? Wouldn't do much for *her* reputation, without a maid or a brother or the like to play chaperone."

"You liked Saunders, I take it?"

"I did. He didn't choose himself a fancy craft to lord it over the rest of us. He got one he could handle himself. And he never needed the lifeboat out to rescue him. As have some who shall not be named."

"Any trouble in Padstow with someone tampering with boats?"

"Tampering? Never heard of any such foolishness."

Rutledge thanked him again, rose, and with a last look out beyond the harbor at the mast of Saunders's boat, walked back to where he'd left his motorcar.

One more detail dealt with. He toyed with the idea of running out to the cottage again, but it could tell him nothing more. And the dinghy couldn't speak, confiding to him who had done such damage.

Pausing briefly at the salvage yard, he asked the owner to return the dinghy to its usual mooring. Constable Pendennis and the owner of the yard were now his witnesses to what had been done to it. Better to let the person who had made the holes wonder if they'd been discovered. Then he went to fetch his motorcar.

He needed to question Trevose again, but he knew that was not likely to give him a straightforward answer. The time would be better spent interviewing Sara Langley or Victoria herself. Preferably in that order.

Coming into the village, Rutledge noticed that people were collecting near the entrance to the police station, standing there staring, and there was a carriage pulled up just beyond, a small boy holding tightly to the reins and rubbing the nose of the horse.

His first thought was that in his absence Pendennis had managed to bring in the accused.

He threaded his way through the crowd and left the motorcar at the inn, then ran lightly back to the station. Heads turned again as he approached, eyes wide with curiosity and alarm.

Making his way to the door of the station, he stepped inside. "What's happened?" he called to the constable. "Why are there so many people outside there?"

From where he was standing in the passage, Pendennis pointed toward the single cell at the end of the corridor. "The doctor's with him now. One of the Terlew lads, taking the cow back to pasture, found him when one of the dogs began scratching at the underbrush around an old stone. He was lying there. It doesn't look good."

"He?" Rutledge asked, rapidly readjusting his first concern. "Who is it?"

"Vicar."

"But I saw him. Not an hour or more ago. He was on his way to call on a parishioner." The man had been upset. "What is it? His heart?"

Pendennis shook his head. "He was set upon. Savagely beaten."

"The *vicar*?" Rutledge asked. "By whom?"

"Nobody knows. Doctor says he won't be telling us anytime soon. He's unconscious still. And having trouble breathing. Broken ribs, Doctor says. It's a good thing the lad didn't try to move him. And his mother didn't know what to do. She sent the lad to me, and a half dozen of us went out and brought him back on a stretcher. He's lost a lot of blood, Doctor says. Some of it internally."

Rutledge thanked him, and walked on down to the cell. Dr. Carrick was working on the man lying still on the prisoner's cot. His shirt was off, and the doctor, with the help of another man, was wrapping his ribs with tape. Then the doctor moved to one side, to look at a leg, and Rutledge saw the vicar's face.

It was bloody, swollen, unrecognizable. Rutledge drew in a breath. He had seldom seen such a savage beating.

The leg was broken. They began to splint it while Toup was still unconscious, then moved on to an arm. But it wasn't broken, just badly bruised, a muscle torn.

Rutledge waited until Dr. Carrick straightened his back, looking down at his patient while taking a break.

"Who did this, do you know?" Rutledge asked quietly. "Has he spoken?"

Carrick shook his head. "Not even when the boy found him. He's not said a word that anyone knows of. He ought to be dead. He's a frail man to begin with."

"How many, do you think? How many did it take to do this?"

"No idea. But I'd start looking, if I were you. He wasn't robbed. And he was wearing his collar. Whoever it was knew he was a priest. Whoever it was is dangerous."

"Quite," Rutledge said grimly, and turned to leave.

Carrick stopped him. "He couldn't have crawled far. If he could crawl at all. You might find the weapon there. If you don't, then I'd put a curfew on this village."

With Pendennis at his side, Rutledge went out to speak to the growing crowd of onlookers gathered around the entrance to the station.

He was bombarded with questions about the vicar's condition.

"Dr. Carrick is still examining him. His injuries are quite severe. I want to see your hands. Hold them up, all of you."

After a moment's hesitation, the men in the crowd did just that, and people turned to look at the hands thrust forward.

Rutledge examined them one at a time, but he found no bruising, only the calloused palms of men who worked for a living.

"Very good. Now I want volunteers to fan out in groups of three or four, searching for whoever did this. He may be armed with something, we don't know yet. But he will have bloody hands, blood on his clothes. If he's already washed them, or changed his clothing, examine his knuckles for bruising, and his tools for blood. If he's suspicious at all, bring him to me and let me question him. You know the countryside; you're the ones who will find a hiding place I might overlook or speak to someone who has noticed a stranger. If it isn't a stranger, it's one of you. Knock on every door. Look at any male over the age of twelve. Be certain you've missed no one, the man in the byre, the lad bringing in the cows for milking, the farmer working in the field. Ask if anyone has been behaving strangely. But hear this, and I will brook no argument about it. If you find him—or them—you will bring whoever it is to me. Whole, and untouched. I want to see if the vicar fought back. I want to see the evidence for myself. And if you batter this suspect, I will have no proof of anything but your stupidity. I want this man, I want him badly. But Vicar would tell you that he must be taken into custody and tried. And I agree with that. Let a judge decide his fate, not set him free because of what one of us has done. Do I make myself clear?"

There was a growl of agreement. And then the men in the crowd began counting themselves off in groups of four or five, debating among themselves just where each would search. Rutledge watched them sort themselves out. Pendennis circulated among them, coordinating the search. Some of them might have been Chapel men, but they all knew Toup, and they were all for finding who had done this to him. Then with a nod toward Rutledge, they set off.

He had little hope of their finding the person or persons who had attacked the vicar, but these men could search a wider area faster than he could, and search it more thoroughly. It was the only chance he had.

One of the women still standing there in front of him said, "What can we do?"

"Sandwiches," another put in. "And tea. They'll be hungry and dry when they get back."

"The Pilot," another said. "They'll be coming in there first."

And a dozen of the women hurried away to see to it.

The rest began to move on, whispering among themselves as they went, dismay still there in their faces.

"Even the most desperate criminal wouldn't have attacked Vicar," the constable was saying. "He'd have given them whatever they wanted."

Then who had?

Rutledge turned to Pendennis. "Show me where he was found."

They set out on foot, and soon began to pick out across the scrubland and the fields small groups of men searching.

"They won't find anybody," Pendennis said, echoing his own thought.

"Probably not. But a search had to be made. Did Toup have any enemies?"

"'Course not. He was Vicar."

"Then who would attack him?"

"How do I know? A prisoner, escaped from Bodmin Moor?"

"It would only serve to give him away. No."

"If Vicar knew him, and could tell me where he was?"

It was possible. And just now, there was nothing else to go on.

The stone where the vicar had been found looked to be the stump of an ancient cross, or even part of an ancient circle. It was some twenty feet off the narrow path where cattle followed the same route day in and day out to their pasture. Out of the way, no house to overlook the spot.

There was blood at the base of the rough plinth. Toup had bled quite a bit before he was discovered. To one side lay his gold pince-nez, one of the lenses missing. Casting about, Rutledge found the lens some four or five feet away. Collecting both pieces, he put them into his pocket.

The constable swore under his breath. "Bastard," he said, more loudly.

Rutledge continued to search for anything that might have been used for a weapon, but in the high grass, already trampled nearer the stone where men had come to bring in the unconscious man, there was nothing large enough except for more stones. And such a beating would have required something more easily grasped than a stone.

He widened his circle, and about five yards away he found a ragged scrap of dusty cloth caught in a thornbush about shoulder high. It was black, and he thought at first it had been torn from the vicar's coat or trousers, but when he looked at it more closely, he saw that it was a thin, very cheap cotton. How long had it been there, hooked by the thorn? The black dye was slightly faded, beginning to brown. But that was not a good indication of anything but the age of the fabric.

He gently pulled it free and put it in his pocket. Another bit of cloth, he thought wryly, and just as useless.

He widened his search again. And at last, nearer the path some twenty feet farther on, he found what he was seeking.

It was a cudgel, about five feet long and nearly two inches thick, rough wood smoothed by time. The sort of thing a countryman or a walker might use to make the going easier. It had been broken, but not in two, some splinters still holding the halves together. And there was blood all over one end of it.

He hadn't used his hands. Whoever he was.

And he'd had no choice but to rid himself of this, flinging it as far away as he could in his haste to be gone.

Rutledge crouched beside it, studying it. He could see where it must have struck the stone where the vicar had been discovered. Toup must have stumbled toward it in the first seconds of the attack, desperate to escape the sudden, brutal blows. He couldn't have gone far with that broken leg, Rutledge thought. That must surely have been the last blow.

"Over here," he called to the constable.

Pendennis came at a trot, then looked down at the cudgel. "Almighty God," he said under his breath. "Who could do such a thing to an unarmed man? A man of the cloth?"

The questions weren't asked of Rutledge. Pendennis turned, made it as far as a small clump of grass five feet away, and bent over, vomiting.

Rutledge gave him time to recover, then picked up the cudgel.

There was absolutely no way to identify it.

"Where does this track lead? The one the boy was on?"

"To Half Acre Farm. There's no one there could do this. I've known the family all my life. They wouldn't have touched Mr. Toup."

"Why was he on the way there? Are they his parishioners?"

Pendennis said, "They are."

Rutledge set out for the farm, still holding the cudgel, keeping it free of the ground. After a moment the constable came after him, and they walked in single file to the house.

It was a typical Cornish farmhouse, tall, foursquare, two storeys, no adornment. A rough door set in the stone was the entrance. And it stood open.

Rutledge knocked at the frame and called out, "Is anyone at home?"

A middle-aged woman came from a back room, saw the stranger at her door, and paled. And then the constable stepped up behind Rutledge, and she smiled nervously.

"Constable? How is Vicar? And who is this?"

"Mrs. Terlew," he greeted her. "Vicar is with the doctor now. Dr. Carrick. And this is Inspector Rutledge, from London. He's been looking into the death of young Mr. Saunders. He'd like to ask you a few questions."

She didn't appear to be too pleased, but she nodded to Rutledge.

"Mr. Toup had told me earlier that he was on his way to call on someone. Was he coming here, do you think?"

"My mother-in-law," she said, gesturing to the room she'd just left.

"She's been poorly for several days and won't hear of having in the doctor. Mr. Toup promised he'd stop by when he could. But he never set a time. We hadn't seen him this week, until my lad found him on the road."

Had someone followed Toup from the vicarage to that lonely place in the road where an attack was possible? Where no one could hear the vicar's cries, and his attacker could disappear as easily as he'd come?

"Here, you aren't thinking my boy did this?" she asked sharply when he didn't immediately respond.

"I don't think he physically could." Rutledge held up the cudgel, and she stared at it.

"Was that what was used?" She shook her head in dismay. "I have never seen a man so badly beaten. I didn't know if he was alive, when I ran toward where he lay. I wasn't sure he would live to be taken back to the village. Who could have been so vicious, and toward a man of the cloth?" Another thought struck her. She said anxiously, "He couldn't have mistaken Mr. Toup for my husband? He wasn't waiting for *him*, was he?"

"Where is Mr. Terlew?"

"He's gone to a fair over to Camelford. They have a few ewes for sale. He left in the afternoon, yesterday, and I'm not expecting him back until tomorrow."

Near the hearth in this room was a small spinning wheel, and he could just see the edge of a loom in the room where her mother-in-law was coughing with the deep, chesty sound of old age. He wondered which of the women was a weaver. Certainly the shawl across Mrs. Terlew's shoulders was a fine piece of workmanship in shades of gray and green.

"Does your husband look anything like the vicar?"

"He's as broad as Vicar is thin," Pendennis answered for her. "I can't think he would be mistook for Vicar."

"And you've seen no strangers passing the house?"

"The only person to come by here was the St. Ives lad. That was early on. He walks at night and sometimes goes too far before dawn catches him out."

"I didn't know he could walk," Rutledge said, surprised.

"It's painful, must be, but he manages somehow. I never see him in the village, only out in the fields where no one can watch him. He doesn't care for pity. I turn my back when he's passing. He seems to prefer it that way."

"Does he carry a cane, when he walks? To help him?"

"He used two sticks in the beginning, but only one of late. But here, you can't think he could have done this?"

"He may have seen someone on the road," he replied, not wanting to feed the rumors that would be flying until whoever had done this was caught. But he found himself wondering if St. Ives had resorted to the cudgel to make it easier to bring the vicar down. If swinging it was easier than a cane . . .

There was nothing more to be gained by keeping her from her mother-in-law. She'd already cast a glance or two over her shoulder when the coughing was particularly thick. He thanked her and they left, but not before she made the constable promise to let her know how Vicar was faring.

When they were out of earshot, Rutledge said to Pendennis, "Could Toup's attacker have been St. Ives?"

"Why would he harm Vicar?"

"What precisely is the matter with St. Ives?" He had been told about the burns, but only in general terms.

"I'm not all that certain. As Mrs. Terlew says, he stays close to home. But sometimes he takes it in his head to wander farther afield late at night. Better him than me. We stay close at night; there are things in the dark you'd not want to encounter," Pendennis said darkly. "But then he'd been sent away to school as a boy. He might not remember what's out there."

But Trevose wasn't afraid to walk to the village after dark . . .

"Difficult terrain for a man with a walking stick." It was rough ground even here on the path they were following, let alone in the fields.

"Still. As Mrs. Terlew said. People do see him from time to time. He does no harm."

If it wasn't St. Ives, who else had traveled this path, so early this morning?

Meanwhile, the cudgel would go into the boot of his car for safekeeping.

13

The vicar was still in the cell, although his housekeeper or someone had brought down pillows and bedding, in an attempt to make him more comfortable. Dr. Carrick was worried about moving him again—being transported from Half Acre Farm had been difficult enough for someone in his condition. And that had not changed for the better.

The first of the searchers came in several hours later, reporting to Pendennis that they had found no one who was likely to have attacked the vicar. More to the point, they had seen no strangers, nor had those they'd questioned.

"But it's fairly open ground, where they were looking. A stranger would have stood out for some distance," Pendennis explained to Rutledge after he had thanked the men and sent them to the pub for something to eat.

Still, there was the occasional wind-twisted tree that broke the horizon in some places, and if a walker could gain that before he was spotted, he might not be seen.

He waited until three more search parties returned with no news before walking down to the inn and his motorcar.

Driving on to Chough Hall, he discovered that Mr. St. Ives himself was at home, and in a far from friendly mood.

"Rutledge," he said, when he strode into the sitting room where Rutledge had been taken by the maid who answered the door. "I hope you have better news than on your last visit to Grenville's house."

"I'm afraid not. I wonder if I might speak to your son."

"To George?" St. Ives repeated blankly. "What the devil for?"

"I understand from your daughter that the four women rowed as far as the back garden of this house, and called to your son, who happened to be on the terrace at that moment."

"And what if they did?"

"I'd like to verify that by speaking to him," Rutledge replied blandly.

"My daughter doesn't lie," he said harshly. "And George is resting just now. He had a bad night."

"I'm sorry to hear it. But I must speak with him. I will gladly go to his room, if that would be more comfortable for him."

"I tell you he's not receiving visitors today. Including the police."

"What precisely happened to your son in France, St. Ives?"

His face twisted in a grimace. "He was badly wounded," he said evasively after a moment. "And before he could be sent back to an aid station, he was taken prisoner by the Germans. He didn't receive the medical treatment he should have done. Not their fault, possibly. He tells me they did their best. Still, there you are."

"Can he walk?"

Affronted, St. Ives snapped, "Of course he can walk." But the bitterness in his eyes belied that.

"How far can he walk, if he leaves this house?"

"I thought you had come about the man on the terrace."

"And so I did. But you refused to allow me to speak to him. And I must know why."

"I have told you, he's resting."

"And I have a witness who saw him walking near Half Acre Farm quite early this morning."

St. Ives gawked at him. It was the only word to describe his expression. Recovering, he said, "You're a liar."

"I have no reason to lie. If you like, I'll take you to speak to the person who saw him."

"Wait here."

St. Ives left the room and shut the door behind him. Rutledge could almost follow him in his mind. Down the passage, up the stairs, down another passage to the room where George St. Ives was resting. To ask him if the man from London had lied.

He was gone for some time. Rutledge waited patiently. Whatever was going to happen in that room upstairs, he wanted to know the outcome.

The door opened unexpectedly. St. Ives walked in, his eyes on Rutledge.

"I owe you an apology, sir. You were telling the truth. George has been walking after dark, when he couldn't sleep. To strengthen his legs. He didn't want me to know because he wanted to surprise me." He looked away. "George is my heir. I had despaired of him taking over after I'm dead." There was a change in his voice. Rutledge recognized what it was he heard: hope.

"I'm sorry to have ruined his surprise. I still need to speak to him."

"That's quite impossible."

"Perhaps you haven't heard what happened today. Mr. Toup was savagely beaten this morning on his way to call on a parishioner. We've been searching for his attacker. As your son was in the vicinity of the attack, he may have seen someone. It could help us find out who did this."

"Toup?" St. Ives frowned. "I thought you had come to verify that my son was on the terrace when the Grenville girl rowed that boat upriver."

"That too." He walked to the window and then turned. "I may have two crimes on my hands, St. Ives. The Chief Constable hasn't requested the Yard's assistance in regard to Toup, but it's likely that he will as soon as a report reaches him. And then there's the matter of your daughter and the others. That, of course, is my priority. But as I was on the scene at the time of the attack, I must do what I can. Men are searching the fields and farms right now."

"Your task is to keep my daughter and the others safe," St. Ives told him bluntly. "I can't think who would want to harm Mr. Toup. And I'm sure it's of great concern to everyone—"

"You haven't seen the vicar, St. Ives. How he survived is a question that Dr. Carrick has been asking all morning. Anything your son can do to help us find this person would be appreciated."

But it was clear that St. Ives had no intention of allowing Rutledge to speak to his son.

As he left the house and turned the motorcar back toward the village, Rutledge wondered why.

And that led him to stop at Padstow Place and ask to speak to Grenville. He had gone out, Rutledge was told, to a tenant farm. Rutledge took a sheet from his notebook and left a message for him, informing him of the attack on the vicar. That done, he asked the maid to summon Elaine St. Ives.

When she came into the drawing room, he could see that she had been crying.

"Are you all right?" he asked, offering her his handkerchief.

She unfolded it with the intentness of someone opening a gift, but then her control broke, and she buried her face in it.

He let her cry. There wasn't much else he could do. When she was at the stage of hiccupping sobs, he turned from the window where he'd gone to stand, and asked gently, "What's upset you?"

"I miss my home—my father and my brother. My dog. I like it here well enough, but it isn't *home,* is it? And I must stay in my room now. I can't even walk out in the garden, and they're bringing our meals up to us. It makes me feel as if I've done something wrong, and I haven't! I didn't hurt Harry Saunders, I didn't want him to die, but he has, and now there's nothing to be done but wait."

"Tell me about your brother," he said, leading her to a chair with a hand at her elbow, and then taking the one opposite her.

"George has changed since the war. I expect it was what happened to many men. But he's my brother, and I've had to learn to look at him now without flinching."

"Because of his legs?"

"Yes, they're twisted somehow. I'm not supposed to tell anyone. And I can't explain it. He walks rather like a crab, and he was such a good horseman. And an excellent cricket player. But the worst of it is his face. It's terribly scarred. I hardly knew him when he finally came home from hospital. I hadn't seen him there, you see. He didn't want us to come. And the marks on his face were still raw-looking, red and puffy and still draining in some places. Victoria hasn't seen him. He won't talk about her or see her. It's rather dreadful. But the worst of it is his temper. He rails against his wounds sometimes, and throws things. Or uses his canes to thrash about his room. I hear him sometimes at night, and I want to cry. Papa tries to pretend everything is as it was, but it isn't. It won't ever be again."

He thought she was going to weep once more, but she pulled herself together with a sniff, and said, "I shouldn't be telling you this. I promised Papa that I would never speak of George's injuries to anyone. Most especially not to Victoria. If pressed, I was only to say he'd been burned."

They were back to Victoria Grenville. Everything seemed to come round to her. Even what had happened to the vicar? "Does she ask about him?"

"Sometimes, but only to be polite, I think. I have a feeling that he was in love with her. And he doesn't want her to think of him as he is now, but as he was before the war."

"How far can he walk?"

"He manages the stairs. And he goes out to the terrace sometimes. The staff finds it as hard as I do to see him now. I wouldn't be surprised to find out that they avoid him—they never seem to be around when he's downstairs."

"Does he go out at night? Walking to strengthen his legs?"

Astonished, she stared. "Whatever gave you such an idea?"

He said nothing to her about Mr. Toup. It would only have upset her. But he wondered as he drove back to the village if George St. Ives could have lashed out at the vicar in his anger, as a surrogate for God. He'd heard men curse God in the trenches. And the same men would pray just as fervently.

In Rutledge's absence there had been no change in the vicar's condition. The doctor had gone, and one of the village women with a gift for nursing now sat by his side. The vicar moved restlessly, clearly in pain, but he was not conscious.

"Has he been given a sedative?" he asked the woman. Mrs. Daniels, Pendennis had told him her name was.

She was lean as a post, with a calm face and hair as black as a crow's wing. But her hands were gentle as she reached out to smooth the covers over her patient. And he appeared to respond to her touch, his head lying still on the pillow for a moment afterward.

"Doctor said not, with the blows to the head. And there could be internal bleeding as well."

Rutledge remembered the X-ray machines in the Base Hospital at Rouen. The Americans had brought them over when they set up the hospital there, along with a contingent of nurses and doctors to run it. But there was no such thing here in this part of Cornwall, and Carrick could only guess at the extent of the vicar's injuries.

As he was leaving the cell the last of the search parties came straggling in, with nothing to report.

"If it's an outsider," Pendennis said with a sigh as he watched four of the searchers walk down to the pub, "then he's well away. I'd rather think about that than consider the possibility that one of our own did this."

"I can't think why someone local would hate the man enough to do this to him."

"No. Did you find George St. Ives? Could he tell you anything?"

"His father said that he was resting. I couldn't force him to let me speak to his son."

"That's not like St. Ives."

"I think he's protecting his son, and in his own way, he's denying that anything is wrong with George."

They had returned briefly to the cell where Toup lay, his face and hands swelling and already discoloring as his bruises appeared. Pendennis looked out the door of the police station, at the people passing on the street.

"We've been a quiet village," he said. "Nothing like what's happened here, with Saunders and now Vicar. I wouldn't have guessed that four young ladies could be held over for murder, or that Vicar would be set upon. It's as if something's happened to us. I don't like it. I'll be glad when we can settle this business and be done with it."

But the question was, Rutledge thought as he walked back to the inn for a late luncheon of sandwiches and tea, what had been set loose in this place? And more importantly, was there any connection between the attack on the vicar and the holes in the dinghy's bottom?

If there was, he couldn't find it. And until he did, he would have to treat them as two entirely separate inquiries.

The doctor had reported what had happened to Toup to the police in Padstow, and Inspector Carstairs came to the village police station in late afternoon to have a look for himself at the vicar's condition.

Rutledge was there when Carstairs strode in. He had a youthful look about him that made it hard to judge his age. Mid-thirties? Or even forty. There was some gray in his dark hair, but his face belied it.

He spoke to Pendennis, looked at Rutledge, and said, "Who are you?"

"Rutledge. Scotland Yard."

"Sorry." He considered Rutledge for a moment. "Carrick came to see me. I understand search parties have been sent out. Any word from them?"

"No luck, I'm afraid. Were any strangers in Padstow yesterday or today?"

Carstairs shook his head. "No one has been reported to me. Beyond the usual time for tourists, although we do get a few latecomers through early November." He smiled without friendliness. "You've been sighted a number of times, of course. Went out to Saunders's boat once."

"So I did."

"Is it possible to have a look at Toup for myself?"

"At the end of the passage, sir. We've dared not move him yet," Pendennis responded.

The constable companied Carstairs to the cell, and Rutledge could just hear their low voices as the two policemen discussed the situation.

When they came back down the passage, Rutledge was waiting.

"Lucky you. Not a single crime to speak of in two years, and two in a matter of days on your watch."

Rutledge decided to take it as lightness rather than a challenge. He'd dealt with enough local men to have a fair idea of what this one was feeling. While technically Carstairs oversaw the village in the shadow of Padstow, the Chief Constable had made the decision to ask for the Yard to take charge. And Rutledge was fairly sure this was because the families of the four suspects had reservations about Carstairs and his impartiality. He had seen that often in Yard cases.

"Any information or suggestions you may have are welcome," he answered in a neutral tone of voice. "You know the people and the geography."

Carstairs sighed. "I don't envy you dealing with the parents of those four women. I expect you'll be the one held to blame if they must stand trial. I've had an occasional chat with Grenville and St. Ives. Two more like them would be tiresome. Closer to any solutions in that direction?"

"I've looked into Saunders's background. Do you know anything about those cottages where he left his boat? There's a small landing there."

"They're to let, every summer, and they're generally occupied. There has been no trouble with the people who do come to stay. As a rule, they're older, settled, looking for a quiet few weeks by the sea. The younger ones prefer to stay in town, closer to the restaurants and the shops and so on. Any particular reason for inquiring about them?"

"The boat that sank came from there."

"Yes, of course. And in regard to Toup. Any theories?"

"Pendennis doesn't know of any problems the vicar has had with his parishioners. He was wearing his clerical collar, there was no mistaking him for anyone else. George St. Ives was out that way this morning. I called on the family to see if he'd spotted anyone coming through. A walker. A vagabond. For that matter, anyone who shouldn't have been on the farm's land. But he was resting. His father preferred not to disturb him."

"Oddly enough, I've seen young George myself. On the outskirts of Padstow. And yet I wasn't aware he was walking."

That was news indeed. "Apparently he's been strengthening his legs of late. A surprise for his father."

"Face that would frighten children. I don't blame him for walking at night, poor bastard. No stares or glances of pity. Wasn't he to marry the Grenville lass?"

"His sister was engaged to Grenville's son."

"Yes, that's right. I remember now. Pretty girl, young Elaine. My wife was in school with her. A year or so ahead, but she knew Elaine. A sad business, all around. Well, I'll leave you to it. My wife is about to present me with our second child, and I want to be there for this one's birth. I was outside Ypres when my son was born. Didn't see him until he was three years old. He wouldn't even come to me when I walked through the door." He shrugged, as if to show that it hadn't hurt. "Cost of war," he went on. "Let me know if you need anything." And he was gone.

Pendennis blew out a breath. "He's a good man," he said to Rutledge. "But I'd not like to cross him."

Rutledge rather thought he himself had, and it was as much a need to see the man from London that had brought Carstairs to Heyl as the need to find out what had happened to the vicar.

It was just after the dinner hour when a message came from the Chief Constable.

Rutledge was summoned to the police station by Pendennis and found the messenger, an older man, waiting for him there.

There were only two lines on the sheet of paper.

If you believe the two inquiries are in any way connected, I will clear the attack on the vicar with London.

Rutledge stared at the lines, ignoring Pendennis hovering behind him, waiting to find out what the Chief Constable had written.

Was there a connection? It was still too soon to be certain. But there was the question of George St. Ives, whose sister was one of the four women in the rowing boat. The last thing Rutledge wanted just now was to find Carstairs using the opportunity offered by the Toup inquiry to meddle in his own case.

He asked Pendennis for pen and paper, bent over the constable's desk, and wrote a short reply.

Thank you, sir. I am not in a position at this stage to tell you whether there is a connection between the attack on Mr. Toup and the death of Harry Saunders. However, anyone looking into what happened to the vicar will be interviewing many of the same people involved in my present inquiry. It would be better if I dealt with both until such time as I can see that these are separate issues. I will then call on you and ask to turn whatever evidence I may have discovered over to someone else.

Hamish, apparently looking over his shoulder, startled him by commenting, "The Yard willna' like it."

Rutledge, striving to ignore the voice, signed his name to the note and handed it to the messenger.

"Thank you."

The man nodded and walked out to the carriage waiting to carry him back to the Chief Constable.

"Is it wise? To take on a second inquiry?" Pendennis asked when Rutledge told him what the Chief Constable had decided. "Not that I'm eager to see Inspector Carstairs darken my threshold again. But I could help with the vicar's case."

"So you could. And you can begin by finding out if anyone brought a message to the vicarage, asking Mr. Toup to call on the elder Mrs. Terlew. She wasn't expecting him that morning. We need to know if the vicar was lured to the farm where he could be attacked in a quiet corner."

"I'll be on it first thing tomorrow," Pendennis said.

"No. Find his housekeeper tonight and ask her. If necessary we'll roust someone from his bed to talk to him."

"Sir."

After watching the constable on his way, Rutledge walked back to the cell and looked in on their patient.

Toup was still restless, and the nurse, looking up as Rutledge quietly stepped into the room, said drowsily, "There's no sign of him waking up."

She had been nodding off, a shawl around her shoulders and a pillow at her back to make the station's hard wooden chair more comfortable.

He nodded and left.

But on his way back to the inn he wondered if it had been wise for him to send Pendennis to interview the vicarage housekeeper straightaway.

That left the woman watching over the vicar as the only line of defense, if whoever had attacked the vicar decided it was in his best interests to finish what he'd begun. If Toup regained consciousness, he would very likely be able to identify the person.

Rutledge turned, walking swiftly back to the police station.

There he sat behind Pendennis's desk until Mr. Daniels, the nurse's husband, came to spend an hour with her. Daniels was a large, burly man, and Rutledge left him to it.

As it turned out, the person who was rousted out in the middle of the night was Rutledge himself.

He woke to a pounding on his door, and had to fight sleep for a moment before he called, "Yes? Who is it?"

The door swung open, and Daniels stood there foursquare in the glow of the lamp hanging by the head of the stairs.

"Mr. Rutledge, sir? The vicar is showing signs of regaining his senses. If you want to speak to him, you'd better come."

"Yes, thank you, I'll be right there."

He threw back the covers and dressed hastily, then set out for the station at a run.

Daniels, Rutledge discovered, had fallen asleep in the chair he'd set next to his wife's, and never stirred until she'd shaken his shoulder and told him to fetch the man from London.

Mrs. Daniels met Rutledge at the police station door, which she had apparently locked as soon as Pendennis had called it a night, and she locked it after him as he came in.

"He's waking up?" Rutledge asked, following her back to the cell.

"I wouldn't say waking up, exactly, sir. But there are Signs." Her inflection capitalized the word. "The coma isn't as deep. I wouldn't be surprised if he could hear your voice."

They had reached the cell. Toup's condition appeared to be unchanged to Rutledge's eyes. He sat down where Mrs. Daniels had kept watch while husband and wife stood in the doorway, anticipation on their faces.

"Mr. Toup? Inspector Rutledge here. How are you feeling? Are you in any pain?"

There was no immediate response. And so at a nod from Mrs. Daniels, he reached out and took the vicar's thin hand in his own. How many times had he given what comfort he could to maimed and dying men in France? And sometimes a touch was what they needed, a reminder that they were alive and among friends, that help was on the way. Or that they wouldn't die alone . . .

He could hear Hamish in the back of his mind, and he struggled to keep his thoughts focused on the bruised man on the cot.

He began to talk, starting with Mrs. Terlew's mother-in-law. "Bad cough, but I don't think she's any worse."

Mrs. Daniels nodded again, in encouragement.

"I spoke to her daughter-in-law. They'll be happy when you can stop by. Mr. Terlew was away, looking to buy some ewes. I gather his wife—or perhaps his mother—is something of a weaver. I saw the wheel and the loom. It was her son who found you, by the way, and came for help. Dr. Carrick was here to have a look at you. He says you'll be uncomfortable for a little longer, but you should heal quickly. Except for the broken leg. You'll be giving your sermons from the rood screen, not the pulpit, for a few weeks. But that's all right."

He went on in the same vein for another five minutes, beginning to think that Mrs. Daniels had misjudged her patient's condition.

And then just as he was about to give up, Toup spoke.

His voice was no more than a tired thread. Rutledge had commented on the fact that it was a cool evening, casting about for different topics and settling on the weather.

"Morning. It's morning. I've only just had my breakfast."

Rutledge realized with a start that Toup was talking about their conversation at the vicarage door.

"I know, sir. I was commenting on last evening," he improvised.

"Forgive me. I've a dreadful head."

There was silence for a time.

"Did you see George St. Ives? Is he walking noticeably better these days?" Rutledge asked. He'd avoided mentioning the beating. He wasn't sure whether Toup had got that far in his memory.

"Angry. He was angry." The vicar's swollen face twisted, and Rutledge realized that he was trying to frown. "Why? Not God's curse . . ."

It was garbled. Rutledge was no longer certain that Toup was talking about the previous morning's encounter.

"I've never met him," Rutledge said. "Tell me, how does he look?"

"There's pain. I can tell."

His own? Or St. Ives's?

And then the vicar's body lurched, and he made a futile effort to lift his arms above his head, as if to protect it. He cried out once, a cry that tore at the silence of the police station, a mixture of deathly fear and anguish. He lost consciousness.

"Poor man," Mrs. Daniels said softly. She stepped forward, settling the coverlet again and making soothing noises. Straightening up, she added, "Poor soul. He doesn't know."

Rutledge wasn't certain what she meant—that Toup didn't know where he was, or that he couldn't tell the Inspector anything at this stage.

He waited for another half an hour, but wherever Toup was, it was not in the police station in the middle of the night. At length he thanked Mrs. Daniels and got up to leave.

"Pay no heed," she said. "Head injuries don't always come back to us the first time."

"Yes, I'm sure that's true." And then on an impulse, he asked, "Do you know anything about George St. Ives?"

"I do, poor man."

"Have you seen him walk of late?"

"I saw him one night. It must have been almost a year after he came back from the war. He was struggling down the road to his father's house. I asked if he needed help and he nearly took my head off. I was coming back from a lying-in, you see, and I was tired. I didn't need to be told a second time to mind my own business."

"Have you seen him since then?"

She looked away. "If I have, I've said nothing. Strange things walk at night. I mind my own business and pay them no heed."

"What sort of strange things?"

"My father met a piskey once, coming back from Padstow. He knew what it was straightaway, because it wanted him to turn off the road and go another way." She glanced at the vicar. "*He* wouldn't care to hear it. But my father was an honest man, and if he saw a piskey, it was true."

"I wasn't asking about your father. What have *you* seen?"

She answered him with reluctance. "Shadows where there are none. Shapes on the horizon. Sounds that shouldn't be there. You look away before you see too much."

"Why isn't George St. Ives fearful of piskies and the like, if he wanders about in the middle of the night?"

"You must ask him."

It was good advice.

"I have walked at night—and I saw nothing on the road but a farmer coming into the village."

She studied him for a moment.

"And you're sure it *was* a farmer?" she demanded.

He couldn't tell her it was Trevose he'd been watching. Letting it go, he left her to sit with Toup and went back to his bed.

14

But instead of his bed, Rutledge left the motorcar in the village and walked toward Padstow Place, listening to the night sounds around him as he made his way there. He could hear scurrying in the dry autumn brush on either side of the road, and louder sounds in the farther distance. The wind was still, and he couldn't hear the river from here.

A nervous man, he thought, would find meaning in those stirrings by the roadside. Or the odd outline of a misshapen tree. Even the fleeting image at the corner of his eye. A night bird rising from the scrub, but easily mistaken as someone vanishing in the dark.

I looked away . . .

Superstition was the perfect shield for anyone who didn't want to be seen.

There were some who claimed the piskies were the old gods, diminished in size and importance once the missionaries came to Cornwall from Wales and Ireland. Playful now, mischievous sometimes, but powerless to influence human affairs. Others believed them to be the souls of babies who died before they could be christened. Either way they were not to be trifled with.

George St. Ives, educated far from Cornwall, wouldn't share those fears.

Who else was not afraid of the dark?

It was something to consider.

He had passed the turning to the Grenville landing and then the gates to the house and was well on his way toward Chough Hall when ahead of him, where the road angled slightly toward the river, Rutledge caught sight of a figure just disappearing around the next bend.

Too tall for a piskey, he told himself, amused. But it had been the merest glimpse, and he wasn't certain how that person had been walking: well or with an effort.

He picked up his pace, but whoever it was had disappeared. By the time Rutledge reached the gates, he was sure he had lost the figure he'd been following.

Had it been George St. Ives? He would have known of any shortcuts to the house, where he could quietly enter a side door without awakening anyone. Walking down the drive, he risked being spotted by someone who couldn't sleep.

Cursing himself for not thinking about that sooner, Rutledge retraced his steps, carefully searching for a half-invisible track leading into the estate from the main road.

He didn't find what he was looking for. But that didn't mean such a track didn't exist. As a boy, he himself had learned how to slip in and out of his parents' house with great stealth. Growing up at the Hall, George St. Ives wouldn't be the first of his line to know how to come and go without being seen. And such access would have been available longer if it didn't shout its presence to gardeners and family alike.

So much for that. But it proved that the son of this house might walk without his father's knowledge.

Rutledge wondered if St. Ives had questioned his son about such nighttime forays, or if he was so certain they didn't happen that he had never broached the subject. He leaned toward the latter possibility—if St. Ives had brought up George's walks, very likely they would have stopped for a while.

St. Ives, like so many parents across England, had had to deal with the aftermath of the Great War in unexpected ways. Their hero sons had returned covered not in glory but in swaths of bandaging. If they returned at all. But it was easier to mourn a memory that had marched away in the autumn of 1914 and never come back. He was still the handsome young man in uniform that families last remembered, smiling at the photographer, eyes alight with the excitement of going to war. The shattered remnants of their child, coming home so utterly changed, was a very much harder cross to bear.

Rutledge could remember thinking, as he lay in his cot in hospital, haunted by France, still living in the trenches, that at least his parents weren't alive to see him there. For they would have come to hospital despite his pleas for them to stay away, and the pity he would have seen in their eyes would have devastated him. It had been bad enough for Jean to see him at his worst and flinch at his thinness and the dark circles beneath his eyes, so different from the strong, vibrant man she had kissed good-bye at the railway station that last December day.

He turned to begin the long walk back to the village, watching as a badger trundled quickly across his path, intent on the hunt. He hoped it was closer to its sett than he was to the inn.

As it was, Hamish was his constant companion on the journey, the distant sound of gunfire and a vicious shelling occupying the back of his mind. Rutledge fought hard against the invasion, but afterward there was a section of the road that he had no memory of walking.

Back in the inn, his last conscious thought before falling asleep was: What if that hadn't been George St. Ives rounding the bend ahead of him?

Dr. Carrick determined the next morning, when he came to look in on David Toup, that the vicar could be moved from the police station to his own bed at the vicarage.

"He may improve faster there. He's stable, I think, and the risk is small if we do it in easy stages."

Rutledge objected to taking the vicar out of the cell. "Granted it's not the best place for an injured man to be treated. It's confined, and there's little fresh air. But I think he should be left there for a few more days. At least until we have some idea of who did this or why. We can lock the station door at night, when Pendennis goes home. It's safer."

"It's also not the best place for an injured man's health. God knows what germs are crawling about the place. We had no choice in the beginning, there were no stairs here, but now we do. I'm putting him where he can be cared for under far cleaner and more salubrious surroundings."

Rutledge argued, but the doctor was not to be moved. And he could see why. He understood that part of it completely. What the doctor didn't seem to understand was that there were other risks besides infection.

"If it will make you any happier, I'll ask Carstairs to send a constable down here to keep watch. Someone must have been very drunk to attack a man of the cloth, possibly someone he knows very well. He won't wish to be caught trying it again."

"Not another constable," Mrs. Daniels said firmly. "They'll be putting in a cot for me. They can add one more for my husband. He's the match for anyone wanting to reach Vicar. I'll be more comfortable with him than with any stranger in the house. And besides, himself knows the village. He'll have a fair idea about who should come through that door and who shouldn't. What's more, he knows better than to get under Mrs. Par's feet. And people are already asking to bring broths and jellies and the like to help Vicar get well. It's for the best. Truly it is."

Mrs. Par was the vicarage housekeeper.

Knowing he'd lost, Rutledge put the best face on it that he could, and volunteered his help.

Later, when told that his patient had appeared to regain consciousness briefly during the night, Carrick shook his head. "I doubt he was able to make sense of what happened or where he was." Rutledge said nothing.

The vicar's housekeeper arrived to collect the bedding for washing, while Mrs. Daniels, her husband, Pendennis, and the doctor began the careful transfer of the vicar to a stretcher, which was then carried to the station door, where Rutledge's motorcar was waiting.

He was eased into the rear seat, and Rutledge spared a moment's thought for Hamish, banished from there for the duration of the journey. But it was not far to the vicarage, and there the process was reversed.

It was impossible for Pendennis and Mr. Daniels to carry the stretcher up the fourteen steps to the first floor and the vicar's usual bedroom. But that had been thought of too, and a bed had been made up downstairs in the sitting room, willing hands helping to remove pieces of furniture and bring down a bedstead.

Preparations and transfer took well over an hour, but the vicar appeared to have made the transition without injury. It had taken a toll nonetheless, and Mrs. Daniels, drawing up the coverlet to his chin, said, "Poor lamb. I doubt he'll stir for the rest of the day."

Watching her, Dr. Carrick said, "I shall start to worry if he doesn't begin to wake up sooner rather than later. It was beneficial, at the start, giving his body a chance to recover from the shock of his injuries. Now, we'll just have to see."

The two men left the vicar in Mrs. Daniels's capable hands, and as they walked out together to Rutledge's motorcar, standing by the vicarage steps, Dr. Carrick changed the subject.

"There's some concern in town that the four women accused in the death of Harry Saunders are still at Padstow Place."

"The decision to leave them there is mine, and not for public opinion to judge. There's new evidence that casts doubt on how Saunders died. I can sympathize with his grieving parents, but I am not convinced that we know the whole of the story."

"What new evidence?" Carrick retorted. "That man Trevose had no reason to lie. He swore to the fact that he believed there was an attempt to kill Saunders, and although it didn't succeed at the time, he died as a result of what happened in that boat. I should think the situation is quite clear."

"Do you know Trevose? Can you vouch for the fact that he has nothing to gain or to lose from giving his evidence? What's more, I'm not satisfied about the sinking of the dinghy."

"There *was* no dinghy. Saunders was in the boat with the young women when they decided to kill him."

"You're behind the times on your facts," Rutledge said, bending to turn the crank. The motor caught on the first try, and he rose to watch the doctor's face as he added, "The dinghy was retrieved from the river where it had sunk, just as Miss Grenville and her friends had described."

That was news.

Carrick stared at him. "No one told me that. The general feeling in Padstow is that you've dragged your feet because you have a connection with one of the women involved. Is it true?"

"Which one?" Rutledge retorted, with an effort keeping his voice level.

"Does it matter?"

"I believe it does. I have never met three of the accused. The fourth is a cousin of someone I knew before the war. Hardly a sufficient connection to warrant allowing four murderers to go free. I wonder who spread such a rumor?"

"One of the staff overheard an argument in one of the public rooms at Padstow Place, and told a cousin who lives in Padstow. *She* told one of the maids working for Mr. and Mrs. Saunders. She believed it to be her duty."

"Quite. Duty is often the finest of excuses for passing on gossip. Especially if it's hurtful. You may tell Mr. and Mrs. Saunders for me that hanging the wrong person will not bring their son back. Nor will it be justice."

They had been standing on either side of the motorcar. Rutledge gestured toward the door, and after a moment's hesitation Carrick got in. Rutledge waited until he was settled and then got behind the wheel.

"Do you think this assault on Toup has any bearing on what happened to Saunders? I've heard that you are now in charge of both inquiries."

"For very good reasons. But not because I see an immediate connection. Whoever did this to the vicar is still out there. And no one knows—yet—why Toup was the victim. Was it personal? Was it random? Will whoever it is try to finish what he's begun, or has he long since left the area? This is why I objected to moving Toup. We don't know."

"I shouldn't like to tangle with Mr. Daniels myself, and I hardly imagine anyone else would."

"Whoever did this thrashed the vicar within an inch of his life. Literally. One or two more blows of that sort would surely have killed him. There was fury behind the blows. A vicious fury that didn't take anything else into account. Anyone could have come down that path and seen what was happening. But whoever it was wasn't satisfied with a beating. He kept at it, blow after blow, never letting up until whatever drove him was assuaged. That's a dangerous man. Come with me and I'll show you what Pendennis and I found."

"I quite agree," Carrick said. "I treated Toup. You needn't persuade me. But I know these people, Rutledge. I can't find one person in Heyl or Padstow or even in Rock that I feel would be capable of what was done."

"That's encouraging to hear. But I need to ask questions. Where did the vicar live before he came here? Was there something in his past that we don't know about—and someone finally found out where he was serving? Did Toup recognize his attacker? Did whoever it was say anything to him that would explain the attack? And the best person to answer my questions is lying in his bed unconscious. We've looked at everyone in the village and the outlying farms. There's no indication on their knuckles or faces that Toup attempted to defend himself. But he must have done. It's human nature to put up a fight, clergy or not. Once he realized that he could very well be killed if he didn't."

"You are aware that he will very likely have an imperfect memory of events leading up to and including the attack?"

"That," Rutledge said as he drove into the square by the police station and stopped, "is what I'm most afraid of."

When the doctor had gone and the police station was empty and quiet once more, Pendennis said to Rutledge, "I did as you asked. I spoke to Mrs. Par."

"What did she have to say?"

"That Vicar found a note in his door that morning, asking him to call on Mrs. Terlew."

"Did he, by God! Where is the note now?"

"She doesn't know. It's likely Vicar took it with him. And I searched his clothing after it was removed by the doctor. Nothing was missing. Nor was there any note."

It hadn't been a chance encounter, then. Someone had indeed lured the vicar to that rendezvous.

"Good man. Now I want you to talk to as many people as possible and document when and where they saw George St. Ives walking in the night. Or in the dawn, for that matter. And I want to know if Mrs. Terlew is quite certain it was St. Ives she saw the morning of the attack."

"Are you settling on it being St. Ives?"

"Far from it," Rutledge said easily, concealing what he really thought. "I'm looking for a pattern. And any anomalies in that pattern."

"You aren't forgetting that Inspector Carstairs saw St. Ives on the road to Padstow?"

"On the contrary. The question is, did he see St. Ives clearly enough to identify him? Or did he make the assumption that it was St. Ives he must have seen?"

"I'm to question the Inspector?" Pendennis asked warily.

"He won't bite. And I need to know if St. Ives was on that road. When, and where he was going." To drive holes into the bottom of Harry Saunders's dinghy?

Pendennis, not best pleased with his orders, nodded and went to fetch his notebook.

Meanwhile, returning later that morning to Chough Hall, Rutledge tried again to gain access to George St. Ives. This time, instead of asking to speak to the father, Rutledge asked for the son.

The maid shook her head. "He's not receiving visitors, sir. You'll have to come back another time."

He decided that this was as good a chance as any to try a more roundabout route. He'd been wanting to take out the Grenville boat to see how it handled, and the tide was right. Leaving Chough Hall behind, he drove past the gates of Padstow Place and found the rutted lane again that led to their landing.

The boat was still there, and he launched it without too much trouble. Accustomed to rowing, he found it easy to guide the craft out into the current and then pull upstream. He discovered that he couldn't see Padstow Place from the water, but where the terrace of Chough Hall overlooked the river, there were gardens that ran partway down to the water. The rest was rough ground, and where that began, a path appeared to lead through the scrub up to the house. A small stretch of sand made a rather narrow but nice strand, and to his surprise he saw a man standing there, watching him as the boat drew even with the grounds.

It wasn't the father. Therefore it must be the son. What's more, the resemblance was strong. The same build, the same set of the shoulders and head, the same height.

Rutledge maneuvered the boat toward the sand and, kicking off his boots, got out and pulled it up far enough that he could trust it to stay there. Then he turned.

"That's the Grenville boat," the man said, an accusation rather than a statement.

His face was terribly scarred, deep gouges in the flesh that ran diagonally from his forehead to his chin, drawing his eyes downward and slightly twisting his nose and mouth. On the right side they went on down his throat, disappearing into his collar. And the ear on that side was ragged with scar tissue.

"As a matter of fact it is. I'm afraid I've borrowed it without leave."

"And you're trespassing."

"Actually, I rather think you're the man I've come to see."

There was sudden tension in the man's body. Rutledge wondered if he was about to bolt. On the strand beside him lay a pair of sticks, the ferrules still bright, with no signs of wear. Were they new? He couldn't be sure. St. Ives might own several pairs. He was wearing gloves and a light jacket against the wind.

And that was frustrating. Rutledge couldn't tell if his hands or forearms were marked. There was no reasonable excuse to ask to see them.

"My name is Rutledge. I've come several times to speak to you, but your father refused to let me in."

"I watched you pulling upriver. You know how to handle those oars."

"Long practice. Was it your father's doing or yours that prevented me from seeing you?"

"You don't sound Cornish. And so you must be the man from London he was so angry with."

"Scotland Yard."

The man nodded. "I thought as much."

"I understand you were out walking early on the morning the vicar went to call on the elder Mrs. Terlew. Her daughter-in-law told me that she'd seen you pass by."

He regarded Rutledge for a moment, then said, "I wasn't walking in that direction."

"There are witnesses."

"Witnesses be damned. It's not true. Is this what you've come for? I thought you wanted to ask about Saunders. And my sister."

St. Ives hadn't moved. Not even to shift his weight from one foot to the other. The stance of a man who had troubles with balance?

"What can you tell me, then?"

"My sister has never hurt anyone in her life. She's hardly likely to kill someone she knew, like Saunders."

"How well did she know him?"

"Not the way you're suggesting. We grew up in this house, she and I. Of course we knew Harry Saunders. For that matter, what reason would any of them have for harming the man? It's beyond belief." He was angry now.

"Yet there's a witness—another witness—claiming he saw the attempt to kill Saunders. First by shoving him overboard, and then using one of the oars to strike him in the head."

"Trevose," he said, his mouth turning down. "Why should you believe him, against the word of my sister? Or for that matter, the word of Miss Grenville? He was wrong about the dinghy, wasn't he? He said it wasn't there. And yet the divers found it just where it should have been."

"Four witnesses against one? Good odds, except for the fact that they happen to be the accused. It's expected that they would want me to believe their version of events."

"You're a fool, then," St. Ives said contemptuously. "And not a very good judge of character."

"Perhaps that's true. Could I trust you to tell me the truth if I asked if the rowboat came up as far as this house, on the Saturday in question?"

"No reason to lie about that. Yes. I was on the terrace."

"They called and waved. You didn't respond."

"Who else would it have been?" he snapped. "Sitting there?"

"Your father. A friend."

Goaded, he said, "If you want the truth, I was desperate to be out there on the water as well. But the doctor refuses to let me. I don't have the strength to swim if something went wrong." It went against the grain, Rutledge could tell, to have to make that admission.

"Can I have your word that Saunders wasn't in the Grenville boat at that time?"

"He was not."

Rutledge found he believed him. And it corroborated what he already knew.

"Why do you walk at night? Even your father wasn't aware of it, but a few people have seen you. Pendennis, for instance, and Mrs. Daniels. They aren't all liars, are they?"

"Look at me. If you looked like this, would you stroll into the village at midday?"

"Inspector Carstairs in Padstow has even seen you walking in that direction."

"He must be joking. I can't possibly make it that far."

"Have you seen anyone else walking late in the night?"

"I didn't look for them. I wasn't interested in having company."

"Surely your father has told you about Mr. Toup. How badly he's been hurt. I was hoping you might have seen someone else on the path that morning. That you could help us find the man who did it."

"I haven't seen Toup in months. Nor he me. He was told not to come to the house. I didn't need spiritual guidance. God forsook me a long time ago."

Hamish spoke suddenly, jarring Rutledge.

"He's denied having seen yon vicar. But he hasna' asked why you would think he wanted to harm the man."

It was true. Nor had he responded to the question about seeing someone else on the track.

"Looking at the facts of your sister's case," Rutledge said, "they point to the possibility that she and Miss Gordon and Miss Langley had no real reason—that we've discovered so far—to want to kill Saunders. And there's no doubt it was Miss Grenville who refused to help drag him into the boat—"

He thought for an instant that George St. Ives was going to swing at him, leaving him with no option but to drop the man in his tracks. The anger that had been seething under the surface had very nearly boiled over into action. But St. Ives had caught himself in time.

"She's no murderer," he said savagely. "Damn you, if you're half the policeman you're supposed to be, coming down here from London to find out the truth, you'd know that." He reached down for his sticks and nearly fell. Recovering through sheer willpower, he caught them up and turned his back on Rutledge, hobbling swiftly toward the path that led up to the terrace.

It was a shambling walk, unsteady and uneven. But Rutledge had seen the anger in the man and felt the frustration he had fought down. There was enough of both that he could have lost whatever control he'd had and attacked. But his opponent this time was not a frail clergyman, it was an able-bodied policeman with the advantage of height and reach. And St. Ives had recognized that.

Yet in spite of the anger in the man, it didn't explain why he might have wanted to kill the vicar. The only thing that George St. Ives *had* betrayed in their conversation was the fact that he was in love with Victoria Grenville. Hopeless though it might be. The only reason he'd been willing to talk at all was to learn what evidence the police had and how they viewed it. As if the secondhand accounts given to him by his father hadn't satisfied him. He'd wanted to see for himself what danger his sister and above all Victoria Grenville stood in.

Rutledge watched St. Ives almost to the terrace, to make certain he got there, then turned and launched the boat again.

He looked down at his wet stockings and trouser legs, and then ruefully shook his head. He hadn't gained as much as he'd hoped for by coming here. And while he was inclined to believe St. Ives when he said he hadn't been on the Half Acre Farm track the morning the vicar was beaten, if that was true, who had Mrs. Terlew seen?

Hamish said, "Have ye no' considered the possibility that he attacked the vicar to draw suspicion away from the four lasses?"

"It won't wash. For one thing, it wasn't a methodical beating, it was a furious one. For another, he must know that since he failed to kill the vicar, as soon as Toup regains his senses, he'll point St. Ives out. If St. Ives did try to kill the vicar, there was another reason for it."

But Hamish persisted, like a niggling doubt in Rutledge's mind.

"Unless he saw Victoria Grenville damage yon dinghy. And he believes the vicar also saw her out on the road that night. He walks in the dark, he couldha' followed her."

It was five or more miles to the cottage. A very long walk for Victoria Grenville. And an even longer one for a man whose legs were so damaged. But she could have done it. And St. Ives needn't have followed her all the way. He could have watched her go and come back, and then put two and two together much later.

Then why wait so long to silence the vicar?

Perhaps no one had considered Inspector Barrington a threat. He'd been ill, he died, the statements had disappeared, and there was an end to it. But Scotland Yard had sent someone else to Cornwall, and Rutledge was a very different man.

Jealousy was a powerful emotion. But again it hadn't seemed likely to Rutledge that Victoria Grenville had cared so deeply for Harry Saunders. What did lie between them, then? If it wasn't jealousy, what was it?

As for George St. Ives, love was nearly as powerful. He would perjure himself for Victoria's sake. Why not kill for her? He'd been in the war . . .

But even knowing this, Rutledge could still find no way to save Kate, or Sara Langley or Elaine St. Ives. It was still very likely that if one was convicted, the other three would be as well.

What was the key? The one small fact or motive that would put him on the right track?

After changing out of his wet clothes, Rutledge looked in on the vicar. No improvement in his condition, Mrs. Daniels assured him, although the poor lamb was restless still.

Rutledge thanked her, then went on to search Toup's study.

There was nothing in the desk or any other part of the room to put Saunders, Victoria Grenville, and the vicar in the same picture. The vicar's accounts, his diary—plainly just that, a list of his daily comings and goings—and his correspondence yielded nothing more than the usual activities of an Anglican vicar. Rutledge found no secrets in the man's bedroom upstairs. That was more monastic than the rest of the house, a spartan room with only the necessities of a simple man and his calling. A crucifix; a Bible on a tall stand, smaller than the one on the desk in the study; his clothing tidily hung in the armoire or folded neatly in the drawers of the single tall chest.

Rutledge went so far as to search the pockets of his coats.

There was a scrap of paper in one with an address in London. In Mayfair.

There was no way to judge how long it had been there. Or if it had any significance at all. A friend? A fellow priest? A relative?

Satisfied that he had done all he could, Rutledge made certain that he had put everything back just as he'd found it, and left the bedroom.

He was on his way down the stairs when Daniels appeared and jerked his head toward the door.

Rutledge followed the big man outside.

Daniels stood for a moment looking down toward the village streets, as if trying to find the words—or trying to set himself apart from what he was about to say.

"She doesn't sleep well," he began after a moment. "Not when she's on duty, so to speak. It's possible she was drowsing off again, and thought she heard it."

"Heard what?" Rutledge prompted.

"Someone trying to get in the door there." He gestured over his shoulder to the house door. "And then he tried a window. But he never knocked, which someone would have done if there was an urgent need for Vicar. For that matter, most people know what happened. They wouldn't have come seeking him."

"Yes, I agree. What did you hear?"

"That's just it. I never heard a thing. But she was worried enough to go round making sure all the locks were closed. That's what woke me. To please her, not because I had much faith in what she was telling me, I went outside to have a look round. And I didn't see anything to worry me." He looked up at Rutledge then. "Still. I thought it best to tell you."

"You did the right thing," Rutledge agreed. "I'll take it that she did hear something—if only to make certain we don't let down our guard out of complacency."

"Aye, that's true enough." Daniels paused again. "When I was a lad there was some who said the vicarage was haunted. I never got head nor tail of that. Mama wouldn't talk about it. And she was a maid in the house."

"What was the story? There must have been a reason for people to believe it."

"A vicar three before this un lost three babes to diphtheria. The well had gone bad. His wife went mad with grief, wandering the rooms looking for them. Vicar had to have her put away, for fear she'd harm herself. They brought her back after some years, but she was never the same. She would sit in a rocker in her room and rock back and forth, back and forth. She said it made her easy, but some thought she was rocking one of the babes. It was sad. One of my cousins told me the story."

"Very sad, but our ghost, if he was there last night, is all too real. You have only to look at the vicar's injuries to know that."

Daniels nodded. "Well. I should be getting back. She's turning Vicar on his side every two hours to prevent fluids settling on his lungs. Time to do it once more." He turned and walked up the steps, disappearing inside.

Rutledge watched as the door closed behind Daniels, listening for the sound of the bolt, and he heard it slide home.

He found, ghosts or not, he believed Mrs. Daniels. She was a level-headed woman who took her work seriously, and he couldn't imagine her being routed from a patient's bedside by any spirit.

He walked around the house, looking for signs of someone's presence, but found nothing, not even Daniels's footprints until he reached the door to the kitchen garden.

He was about to turn away when Hamish spoke, pointing out several drops of candle wax on the step in front of the door.

"If I was set on breaking in," he went on, "I'd bring a stub of a candle to gie me light while I tried to open yon lock. It wouldna' do to break the glass and reach inside. Too noisy, and it'ud leave a trace."

Rutledge knelt to look more closely at the lock. Hamish was right, the only onlookers here were the tombstones in the churchyard.

But he couldn't be sure someone had meddled with it. Still . . . Rising, he dusted off the knee of his trousers and went back to his motorcar in the drive.

Daniels had been awakened by his wife's movements as she looked at each lock, surely including this one. With the household stirring, whoever it was would have gone away.

But if the attempt was real, if the candle wax was fresh, then whoever it was would try again.

A stranger in the village, even at night, would surely attract attention. But George St. Ives was known to walk then, and villagers were used to his presence, seeing no need to report it.

Rutledge spoke to Pendennis, warning him to be on his guard.

The constable, apparently taking the warning with a grain of salt, said, "It's a terrible risk. Coming into the village like that. And the wind was up last night for a bit, with a shower. It could have been the wind Mrs. Daniels heard."

"It could," Rutledge responded. "But if whoever it was came down through the churchyard instead of up from the village, there's no one to see him but the dead."

Pendennis went to stand in the square, looking up at the church and the vicarage. "Aye," he said thoughtfully, his gaze on the rough land beyond the churchyard, sour land that no one had ever plowed to his knowledge. Furze and broom dotted it, with a half dozen wind-twisted trees. "It's the long way around. But he'd take it, wouldn't he, to stay out of our way." He walked with Rutledge to the motorcar. "I'll keep a watch."

Rutledge drove on to the telegraph office in the railway station in Padstow and sent the address he'd found in the vicar's pocket to Sergeant Gibson in London.

He was just stepping out of the station doorway when he thought he saw a familiar figure rounding the next corner.

Frank Dunbar, the householder he'd spoken to out where Saunders had kept his boat?

Nearly sure of it, he seized his chance and went on to the cottages on the outskirts.

The man in the third cottage didn't answer Rutledge's knock. And it had that empty feeling that houses often have when no one is at home.

Rutledge turned and went to the cottage where Dunbar had claimed the two spinsters stayed over the past summer. He found that the lock yielded easily to persuasion, and he stepped inside.

The rooms were decorated in simple chintzes and inexpensive carpeting, both chosen to give the appearance of a cozy holiday cottage. Shades of rose and pale blue and cream and a soft yellow enlivened the otherwise plain furnishings, and the overall sense was of comfort. Views from the windows more than made up for any lack of elegance, and he stood for a moment looking out at the headland on the far shore of the estuary. There appeared to be a ruin on the seaward side, and he could pick out people walking along the strand below. The deceptive silting that was the Doom Bar, the sandbar that obstructed the harbor, was invisible as the tide ran out.

There was nothing personal left anywhere. If there had been family photographs or small treasures or even books, they had been taken away by the women who had let the cottage. The drawers and shelves and even the crevices between the seat cushions and the frame were empty. Someone had come in and given the rooms a thorough cleaning and draped dust sheets over the upholstered furniture. The mattresses in the two bedrooms had been rolled up for airing, and the doors to the cabinets left open as well.

The only conclusion he could draw about the former occupants was that they had not been demanding in their needs, and they had felt at home in these surroundings. Hardly the sort a siren would let, a woman who would find it amusing to steal the heart of a banker's son while spending the summer in the wilds of Cornwall, flaunting her conquest in a village church, and then walk away, leaving his heart broken.

And yet when he opened the armoire in the larger bedroom and peered inside, the delicate scent of an expensive perfume wafted up to him. The sort of perfume his sister, young and single, might choose to wear, floral with a hint of spice. Not one elderly spinsters, as Dunbar had described them, would be likely to use. He went back to the armoire in the smaller bedroom and looked inside a second time. But he could smell only the cedar of the wood and a slight mustiness.

A slim bit of evidence—that one person and not two had taken this cottage. Hardly admissible in court.

Smiling at the thought, Rutledge looked out to be sure it was safe to leave unobserved, and then closed the door, relocking it.

Going around to the dustbins in the back, he looked inside the barrels, but they were empty. Must have been since September, for there was an inch of rainwater in the bottom. They smelled of long use.

A last glance as he was turning away—and something caught his eye. It appeared to be caught on a rough place along the inner wall of the dustbin. Leaning into the barrel as far as he could reach, his fingers just touched it. It took a full minute to work it clear and then wriggle it up the side. His greatest worry was dropping it into the filthy water below.

Finally it was far enough up that he could use his other hand to secure it. Clutching it, he went directly to the motorcar and prepared to leave before Dunbar returned. It wasn't until he was well away that he pulled to the verge of the road to look at what he'd found.

Someone had torn a page from a magazine into little pieces, then put them in the dustbin. Only one piece had survived. Rutledge looked at both sides. One showed water of some sort, but the place was unidentifiable. The other showed a window surrounded by white walls. A house? An hotel? The sepia tones of the reproduction and the condition of the paper made it difficult to be sure.

Turning it over in his fingers, he decided to visit the estate agent he'd spoken with before, on the off chance the man could identify the scene this represented.

Rutledge found a place to leave his motorcar and walked the short distance to the agent's office.

He was not in, but as Rutledge turned to leave, he saw the man trotting toward him.

"Sorry. I went to see a friend. Decided to spend a summer in sunny Cornwall, have you?"

"I'm in need of answers rather than cottages," Rutledge said, and followed the agent inside.

"Too bad. There's still a good choice just now."

Rutledge handed him the bit of paper from the bin. "Can you identify this?"

The man took it, then looked up at Rutledge with a grin. "Exciting lives you Inspectors lead, hunting down such frightful miscreants as this. Oh, yes, it's got around, who you are. Where did you find this bit?"

"I'm not at liberty to say. It's not particularly important," he added, not quite sure he trusted the man to keep quiet about his visit. "But I'd be remiss if I didn't follow up on every possibility. You'd be surprised how tedious that is."

"Well, this will fail to help you, I'm afraid." He stood up and went to a row of shelves in the back of the agency. Searching around, he found what he was looking for and brought it over to hand to Rutledge. It was a broadsheet along the lines of *The Sunday Pictorial.* "Look at page three. There's an article about Cornwall, with illustrations. You can see why I might have kept it."

And there it was, when he turned to page three: the photograph of a large white building bearing a sign reading THE FOWEY HOTEL. On the reverse were other photographs, and the one matching the window of the hotel showed the sea at Fowey. The theme of the article was Cornwall as a holiday center for war-weary Britons.

Going back to the front page, he saw that the date was the spring of 1919.

A back issue, then. If someone had been intrigued by this article, he or she might have looked for other accommodations and in the end, rented one of the cottages belonging to Frank Dunbar.

"You're right," he said, handing the broadsheet back to the agent. "A dead end." He thanked the man and left.

What disturbed him most about this inquiry was that whatever direction he turned, there wasn't a shred of evidence that he could take back to London with him. Nothing that would be useful to counsel chosen by the families of the accused.

Except for the holes in the dinghy . . .

It all seemed to come down to who had put them there, and why.

For if that dinghy hadn't sunk in the middle of the Camel, leaving Harry Saunders to drown, there would have been no need for rescue, and no accusations of attempted murder, no suspects waiting to be turned over to the police.

Harry Saunders could have drowned at sea, with no one the wiser until his body washed ashore somewhere along the coast.

Walking back to his motorcar, Rutledge remembered one of the legends about the sea here at Padstow. About the mermaid who had fallen in love with a fisherman, but he spurned her, and in her grief and fury, she had created the Doom Bar to close the estuary. Mermaid stories seemed to be popular in villages near the sea, and as a rule, a fisherman fell in love with one and when he'd been tempted to follow her into the deep whence she'd come, he drowned.

He recalled the scent in the armoire. Perhaps it *was* a mermaid who had lived there, and Harry had been destined to die in the sea where she'd come from. A fanciful thought: the woman who had let the cottage had come down a road to reach here, not up from the depths.

But it was an interesting possibility. After all, many such legends had some basis in fact. Who, in this story, had fallen in love with the wrong person? The man? Or the mermaid? She had come for the summer, and at its end had gone away. Unhappy? Or angry? Or with no reason to remember the man who kept his boat on the strand below her door?

Hamish, good Covenanter that he was, raised objections to this talk of mermaids. Rutledge tried to ignore him.

Perhaps he'd been wrong about jealousy leading Victoria to murder.

It was the vicar who could tell him more about this mysterious young woman. And whether she had tried to bewitch Harry Saunders, punching holes in his boat when he spurned her. Perhaps Toup had not wanted to drag her back into the affairs of the village, suspecting that she had already done enough damage.

But David Toup was in no state to answer him.

He stopped at the telegraph office, on his way through Padstow, to ask if there had been a response to his message to the Yard.

It was too soon, much too soon, but Rutledge was anxious now to find any lead that would help him sort out facts from possibilities. He had a bad feeling about where this inquiry was going, and he didn't like it.

15

Grenville was waiting for Rutledge when he returned to the inn from Padstow.

He had been pacing in front of the door, and he was not in the best of tempers. But he controlled it as well as he could and said, "I'm worried about this attack on the vicar. In fact, I've been to see him. Will he come through this?"

"Let's walk down to the water," Rutledge suggested, getting out and waiting for Grenville to join him. When they were out of earshot of the inn and the people going about their business in the street, he continued. "Carrick is optimistic. At least physically, that is. Heaven knows what his mental state will be. It's possible he won't remember the attack."

"But surely you have some feeling for who did this?"

Rutledge remembered that Grenville was the local magistrate. "I've questioned the Terlew family. The first they knew of his intended visit was when a son of the house found Toup bleeding and unconscious just off the path to the farm. The vicar had promised to call, but there had been no date set. Mrs. Par, Toup's housekeeper, tells us there was a message for him in the door that morning, but whether that was why he set out for Half Acre Farm we don't know. We haven't found the message in the vicarage, and it wasn't on his person. What's more, the only person the Terlews saw that morning, before or after the beating, was George St. Ives. But he swears he was nowhere near the farm."

"George?" Clearly Grenville hadn't been expecting that. "I thought—I'd been told that he refused to leave the house."

"Apparently he does, for exercise, after dark." As if changing the subject, Rutledge paused and then asked, "Were he and your daughter close? I'm aware of the connection between Miss St. Ives and your late son. I wondered if it was true of St. Ives and Miss Grenville."

"Yes, of course, the four of them more or less grew up together. School holidays, and the like, they were inseparable. I was rather surprised that my son had grown so fond of Elaine. But that summer of 1914 a good many decisions were made, for fear time had run out. And if Stephen was happy, I welcomed it. God knows, it was the last happiness for him."

Rutledge himself had proposed to Jean Gordon in June of that fateful summer. He could in a way sympathize with Stephen Grenville.

"This business with the vicar—it doesn't have anything to do with the death of Harry Saunders, does it?" Grenville asked. He was an intelligent man as well as magistrate. It was not unexpected that he would consider such a possibility.

"So far, there's no indication that it has any connection. The only obvious one of course is George St. Ives passing by a little before the attack. If you discount that, until the vicar recovers his senses—possibly his memory as well—we know very little about what happened there in Terlew's field."

"Yes, well, I'd welcome any news that would free my daughter and her friends. Not that I wish anyone else to suffer. There's been enough of that already. I sent a message of condolence to Saunders's parents. They refused to acknowledge it. Not that I can blame them. When word came that Stephen was dead, I thought my own world had ended. What you learn, in times of great loss, is that the human spirit can survive the most terrible events in one's life and somehow go on." He took a deep breath, staring out toward the river. "Not that it makes anything any better. You just learn to tolerate the difference, the change. And then you get on with it." He turned to Rutledge. "Were you in the war?"

"Yes. In France."

"Was it as bad as we've heard? Worse?"

He wasn't asking for truth. He wanted reassurance that his son had not suffered as much as people were saying, now that soldiers had returned home and censorship had ended.

"I won't lie," Rutledge said quietly. "There were days that could drive any man mad with the horror of them. But that was not all it was in the trenches. You learned to depend on the man beside you, to trust him in ways you never trusted any other human being before that. You looked out for him and he for you. He was father and brother and son to you. It's what got you through, that friendship. Knowing that you weren't alone. And God willing, he was there when you were wounded or dying. Or there was a nursing Sister holding your hand."

It was mostly true. But dying was a lonely business even so. He didn't tell Grenville that.

The man looked away again, and it was a moment before he could speak. Then he said, "Thank you." And he walked briskly away, back to where his horse was waiting in the inn yard.

Rutledge stayed where he was until he heard the horse walk out of the yard and then pick up its pace to a trot.

Then he turned and went to the inn, up to his room, where Hamish was waiting.

It was late when he came down again. He forced himself to walk to the vicarage and looked in on Toup, but there was no change. The doctor had come again, and according to Mrs. Daniels, he'd made noises of concern.

"But he'll be all right. Vicar." Mrs. Daniels nodded knowingly. "There was Tommy, kicked by the cow. And didn't he come back to us again, and no harm done? Or Sam's girl, who fell out of a tree when she was ten. Knocked her senseless."

He couldn't be sure whether she was that sanguine or she was merely whistling in the dark. Studying the patient's face, ugly as the bruises and swelling fully developed, Rutledge had his doubts.

"Any closer to finding out who did this?" Daniels asked from the doorway.

"I'm waiting to hear from the Yard on several points," Rutledge said. It was true, but it must have sounded as hollow to Daniels's ears as it did to his own.

He went back to the inn and changed to dark clothing. Then, in a roundabout way, he circled the vicarage and found a vantage point on the far side of the churchyard, well concealed behind a tall, gracefully carved Celtic cross. He had made certain while at the vicarage that the hens were shut up for the night in their coop, well away from where he expected to be watching.

He had begged a Thermos of tea from the inn's clerk before going up to change, and as the night grew chill, he drank half a cup. Something scurried past his feet, and sometime later he heard an owl call from the church belfry. Night sounds that were normal. As he watched, the last lamp went out in the vicarage, save for a small shielded one that glowed in the downstairs sitting room window. As his eyes adjusted again, it was a pale beacon: it was the room where Toup lay.

Rutledge was tempted to stamp his feet, chilled by the cold ground he was standing on. Down in the village he could see Pendennis making his last rounds of the night, and after a quarter of an hour, the constable walked up the drive to the vicarage and tapped lightly on the door. The sound carried in the stillness.

An exchange of words, low and brief, and then Pendennis turned and walked around the house, testing doors as he passed. Satisfied, as he reached the drive again, he strode quietly back the way he'd come and turned toward his own home.

Another hour passed. Rutledge drank a little more of his tea, knowing it must last him until dawn, and dawn came late this time of year.

He heard the church clock strike three and almost decided to give up his vigil. Surely if anyone wanted to break into the vicarage, he could have come by now when sleep was the deepest and one's guard was down.

Just then a light flared in the sitting room. And as it did, it briefly outlined a hunched figure just passing outside beneath the window. It wasn't as bulky as Daniels. Rutledge hadn't seen anyone arrive, and he swore under his breath.

He moved fast, grateful for his own night vision as he avoided the headstones. He had reached the vicarage when he heard the front door open, and after an instant, someone shut it smartly behind him, as if to be certain nothing slipped in through the crack. Rapid footsteps echoed as someone hurried down the drive. Daniels? Where was he going?

" 'Ware!" Hamish shouted, but it was already too late.

The sudden sounds of departure must have alarmed the prowler, and now he was coming back round the corner in rapid retreat, just as Rutledge got there from the other direction. In that same instant, the oncoming figure stumbled over something in the dark and pitched forward, arms outspread and windmilling, plowing straight into him.

They clung to each other, assimilating the shock of physical contact, and then broke apart just as quickly.

Rutledge reached out to catch the other man, clutching at his coat, finding purchase, and holding fast.

The man spun away, leaving the coat dangling in Rutledge's hand, and in the same motion, his other hand swung around. Something cold and hard slammed into the side of Rutledge's head, dropping him to his knees.

Rutledge could feel the coat being snatched from his grip, and then a second blow brought down a heavy curtain of darkness.

He didn't know how long he was unconscious. He came to in waves of nausea and pain, his face buried in the raw dampness of fallen leaves that had blown against the corner of the house. He could smell their earthy wetness as he lay there for a few seconds more, gathering his wits, and then with an effort he got to his feet.

Swaying for a moment, he scanned the churchyard.

He couldn't see anyone—what's more, he couldn't hear anyone. Either his quarry had gone to ground, or he had made good his escape.

Still dizzy, he forced himself to move, and then he made a thorough search.

There was no sign of anyone.

If it weren't for the mad throbbing in his head, Rutledge could almost believe he'd imagined the encounter. It had happened so fast, neither he nor his quarry had had time to do anything more than react.

How could he possibly have missed him? he demanded of himself. How had anyone got past his guard? He'd learned in the trenches how to watch the lines and spot snipers making their way to their hide. Or listeners who sometimes crawled almost to the lip of a trench and eavesdropped on the talk below.

The only answer was, the man had settled himself somewhere just after Rutledge had chosen the Celtic cross, before his eyes had become fully adjusted to the night. And the same must have been true of the prowler. He'd had no notion that Rutledge was there.

But he must have had his revolver out, ready to use it if whoever had left the vicarage turned or in any way sensed his presence. And then very likely, he had been heading for the rear of the vicarage, where he could force his way in. With only a middle-aged woman between himself and his quarry, he could have dealt with both and still escaped before Daniels—or whoever it was—had returned.

It was why, Rutledge thought, the man hadn't shot *him*. It would have brought the village on the run.

The question was, he told himself, making his way to the rear of the house, how long had this intruder been stealthily watching the vicarage? Long enough to know who was inside and what the routine was.

He made certain the kitchen garden door was still locked, and then turning, he walked unsteadily back to the front door of the vicarage. Knocking briskly, he called out to Mrs. Daniels and identified himself.

He saw the twitch of a curtain as she first looked out the hall window to the left of the door, and then it was opened, the light from her lamp blinding him with its brightness as she stepped out, as if relieved to see him.

"I'm so glad you came—" She broke off as he moved toward her and the lamplight spilled across his face. Staring at him, she exclaimed, "You're bleeding!"

"He came back. And he was armed. He hit me with his revolver. Whoever he is, he must have been in the war."

"Is Daniels all right?" She peered past him, looking for her husband.

"He hasn't come back."

"Step in. Go on to the kitchen. I'll find a cloth to bathe your face. And something cold for it." With a wary glance around, she opened the door wider, and then after he'd crossed the threshold, she closed and locked it again. Following him down the passage to the vicarage kitchen, she clucked in dismay. "That will hurt like the devil tomorrow."

"It already does," he admitted, and sat down, grateful for the chair. He was dizzy and unsteady on his feet, and he wasn't sure just how much farther he could have walked.

She filled a basin with water, and did what she could for his face. "There's a terrible cut along your cheekbone," she said as she worked. "It ought to have stitches. But some sticking plaster will have to do." It was when she was trying to close the wound that he winced, and she discovered the bloody knot on the back of his head. She cleaned that as well, and then stepped back. "That's all I can do for the lump, short of shaving your head. I'll put the kettle on. You've had a shock. Go on into the sitting room. He's awake. The vicar. Or he was before you knocked at the door. I'll bring the cup and a compress in there to you."

Surprised, Rutledge said, "Is he indeed? Is that why Daniels left in such a hurry? To find me?" He stood up gingerly, found he could manage, and started toward the sitting room, not waiting for Mrs. Daniels to answer. Opening the door, he stepped quietly inside. The vicar lay in his bed, his eyes staring up at the ceiling, as if he didn't quite know where he was.

Rutledge drew Mrs. Daniels's chair closer to the side of the bed and sat down, saying in a normal tone of voice, "I'm glad to see you're back with us."

The vicar's gaze swept around the room, and then settled on Rutledge. "I don't sleep in the sitting room." His words were slurred by his swollen lips.

"You've broken your leg. It was easier to bring the bedding to you than it was to take you up the stairs. Do you mind?"

"My leg?" He tried to move it, but the coverlet didn't stir. "What's wrong with my leg?" he asked then, growing alarm in his voice.

"It's in a splint. Dr. Carrick's doing, I'm afraid. Do you remember how you happened to hurt it?"

The vicar stared at him. "I don't know. It wasn't broken when I had dinner last night. I could swear to that."

Rutledge took a deep breath. Toup didn't remember what had happened two days before. It was all a blank. There had been a chance that he might remember, and Rutledge had banked on it. Now there was nothing.

"I'm thirsty," the vicar said then. "Have I had some sort of apoplexy?" He put a hand up to touch his face, and quickly withdrew it. "What's wrong with my face?" Alarm was turning swiftly to panic.

"You've had a slight concussion. Nothing more," he reassured the man on the bed. Reaching for the glass of water on the table, he held the vicar's thin shoulders while he drank. Then he set the glass aside and lowered him to the pillows once more. "You don't remember?" he asked again.

Mrs. Daniels, standing in the doorway, said softly, "Poor man."

"What's wrong with me?" Toup demanded, ignoring the question. "I want to know. I need to know."

"You were set upon. On your way to the Terlew farm. Someone struck you down and then kept beating you until you lost consciousness."

"Dear God," Toup said in amazement. "I don't remember it. I don't remember anything."

"It will come back to you, if you don't let it worry you. Memory can't be rushed. Rest if you can. It's the best thing for you. Are you in any pain?"

"I hurt. All over my body. I fell out of bed, did you say?"

"No, someone struck you down," Rutledge repeated patiently.

"Why?" He lay there, his eyes closed, not moving. "Are you sure? I don't understand."

"I wish we knew why. But we're doing our best to find out."

"Thank you." He seemed to drift into a light sleep then.

Mrs. Daniels came into the room and set the tray on the table. She handed a cup to Rutledge. The tea was hot, strong, and heavier with sugar than he cared for. But he drank half of it. Then she put one cloth on his face and another on the back of his head. They were cold, and they felt good.

Someone began knocking at the door. Rutledge was about to get up to answer it, but Mrs. Daniels put a hand on his shoulder. "It's Daniels," she said. "That's his signal. I'd sent him to find you. He's been searching for you."

She was gone for several minutes, and when she came back, she said as she took the cup from Rutledge and lowered the lamp, "He's gone to bed. Upstairs. Why don't you take my cot for a bit?"

"I need to stay here. In case he wakes up again."

"The cot is just there. Go and lie down. I'll sit here and call you."

After a moment he did as she'd suggested. But even with the cloths his head was thundering. He put his arm over his eyes and lay there, counting the minutes.

He must have drifted off, for he came wide awake as a voice cried out in agony, and for a chilled moment he thought it was his own. Rising on one elbow, he looked across at the bed.

Toup was twisting in the bedclothes, crying out and begging for mercy.

"*For the love of God—enough, enough.*"

Rutledge got up too quickly. Fighting a sudden dizziness, he came to stand beside Mrs. Daniels. They listened helplessly as the vicar relived his beating in his sleep. Mr. Daniels, awakened by the cries, came to the door. Rutledge heard him swear under his breath, then realized it was a curse.

They couldn't make out most of it. A tangle of cries that were incoherent, the words tumbling over themselves.

Unable to stand it any longer, Rutledge reached out and touched the vicar's shoulder. And he screamed, high-pitched and filled with pain.

He woke with a start, staring blindly at the man from London, not seeing him as he said clearly, "Coward. That's what you are. If you have something to say to me, say it now and be done with it. Or I'll walk on." And then he shouted a name, breaking off as the first blow must have struck. "*St. Ives—*"

The three other people watched as he slumped back against his pillows. Mrs. Daniels stepped forward quickly, and put a hand to his throat. "He's passed out. It was too much."

They kept their vigil until the sun came up behind a leaden sky, hardly making a difference between night and day. But the vicar lay there like a man in exhaustion.

And then, warning Mr. and Mrs. Daniels not to speak of what they had heard, Rutledge finally went back to the inn.

He postponed walking through the inn. The side of his face hurt, and he knew he would be the center of comment as soon as anyone saw him.

Moving on to the deserted landing, he stood there for a time, ignoring the misting rain that had covered everything with tiny droplets of water, giving them a frosted look. To the west it was beginning to clear, a glimmer of blue out where the sky and the sea met.

He didn't mind the rain. It felt good. Closing his eyes, he tried to clear his head.

He could feel Hamish stirring. And he thought, *Not now, dear God, not now.*

But it wasn't the war that Hamish was talking about. And then he felt it.

He was being watched.

Opening his eyes, Rutledge turned slightly, looking around him.

There was no one on the river. No one at The Pilot, and as he looked toward the shops along the street, he could see no one at a window or in a doorway.

The feeling was so strong his first thought was whether he was in revolver range, if someone was preparing to fire at him. But he was out of range of the street or the river.

He couldn't have said afterward why he looked up toward Rock on the far side of the Camel. His gaze swept the town, moved east toward a patch of rough ground, and still saw nothing. But he knew he'd found his watcher.

He turned to scan the landing at his feet, but there wasn't a boat tied up that he could borrow. And even if there had been, he knew he couldn't have pulled across the river and climbed the slopes in time. His watcher would have melted away long before he could reach him.

Rutledge brought his gaze back to that rough patch of ground and stared intently at it. The man must have field glasses, but there was not enough light this gray morning to flash off the lens. It didn't matter. Rutledge knew he was there, and why.

He rather thought whoever it was had wanted to have a look at his adversary. To see him clearly in the daylight. And possibly to assess what damage he'd done with the barrel of the revolver.

Well, then, let him have a good look.

He was about to turn his back on the watcher and walk on toward the inn when something along the far shore of the Camel, where the scrub came down to the strand, suddenly caught his eye.

He could have sworn that the Grenville boat was drawn up there, hidden in the deeper shadows.

Rutledge went through the inn and out the back door. It was a long walk, but out of sight of the river, he made his way toward the Grenville boat landing.

Even before he started, he had a feeling he would be too late, that whoever he was after would make his way across the river again. While he couldn't see Rutledge, Rutledge couldn't see him.

His headache was raging by the time he reached the small landing where the Grenville rowboat was kept.

And it was there. Wary of a trap, he walked on toward it.

But there was no one near it.

The boat, when he got to it, was wet, and the sand under the hull as well.

He'd been right.

But there in the wet sand just at the prow of the rowboat, something had been drawn. It was a very rough sketch of what appeared to be a horse's head. But it had been done quickly, without stepping out of the boat, and the water was already smoothing across whatever it was. He could see the two small holes on either side of the figure, as if the stick that had been used to draw it had been thrust twice and with some force into the wet sand. Rutledge couldn't be sure what the intent had been in making the drawing.

But he knew very well what it meant. Someone was taunting him.

Straightening up, he looked around. But there were no identifiable footprints except for his own. Whoever it was had either walked in the water a little distance before coming ashore, or he'd cleared his tracks away as he left.

Rutledge did know that he wasn't being watched here. Whoever it was had done what he'd wanted to do and then disappeared.

He couldn't help but remember the first word the vicar had used as he began to relive his beating.

Coward . . .

Why had he called the man who faced him a coward?

Rutledge realized suddenly that it was important for him to find out.

Ahead of him lay the long walk back to Heyl.

Taking a deep breath, he set out. By the time he reached the inn, it was willpower alone that kept him going.

Rutledge was awakened by a knock on his door. Outside his windows the rain was coming down in sheets, with the force of wind behind it. He got up and went to answer the summons.

The man who stood outside his door stared at his bruised and swollen face, then cleared his throat.

"Inspector Rutledge?"

"Yes?" he answered, wary now. He didn't recognize the man.

"I've been sent from the Wadebridge telegraph office, sir. Special messenger. There is a telegram for you from London." He reached into the pocket of the rain gear he was wearing and brought out an envelope. "I've been asked to have you sign for it, sir."

Rutledge took the form the man held out and signed it with a pencil produced from the same pocket. "Thank you. Have something at the bar until the worst of this passes. Put it on my account."

"Thank you, sir." He touched his cap and turned to run lightly down the stairs.

Why, Rutledge wondered, shutting his door, had London seen fit to send him a telegram through Wadebridge rather than Padstow?

He opened the envelope and went to turn up the lamp. With the storm, the already fading light gave the impression that it was later than it was. Glancing at his watch, Rutledge saw that it was a little after five in the afternoon.

Gibson had written:

A request has come from Cornwall for you to handle the attack on the vicar of St. Marina's as well as the murder of Harry Saunders. Chief Superintendent not particularly happy with this, but defers to the Chief Constable. Inspector Carstairs in Padstow had requested permission to take over the second inquiry if you finish the Saunders case first and must return to London. Chief Superintendent has been asked by Grenville of Padstow Place to leave you on the Saunders case, although Major Gordon has requested that you be withdrawn. In regard to the elder Saunders and a farmer named Trevose, neither has ever been in any difficulty with the law, at least none reported to London.

That, Rutledge thought wryly, explained why Gibson had sent the telegram through Wadebridge rather than Padstow. It would not do for Carstairs to learn the contents.

It went on:

About the address in London, 12 Sutton Place. Mr. and Mrs. Wingate live there, no known connection with Cornwall. He is authority on Edward I, has written several studies of his life and court. Only son killed on the Somme, daughter married and living in Edinburgh. They claim not to know a David Toup, and cannot explain why their direction should be in his possession. General consensus is a respectable and respected family.

Then why, he asked himself, had Toup had that slip of paper in his possession?

Hamish said, "He wrote yon number down wrong."

The voice was as clear as if Hamish were standing just behind him, clear even above the sound of the storm outside.

"Or was given the wrong number. Possibly the wrong street as well?" Rutledge answered aloud before he could stop himself.

There was a final comment.

In regard to the earlier inquiry. Inquest brought in death by misadventure. The weather held responsible for his fall. It was never challenged.

Mrs. Grenville had told him the truth about what had happened at St. Michael's Mount.

Putting the telegram back in its envelope, he locked it away in his valise and went to find Pendennis.

Even with an umbrella borrowed from the inn, he arrived at the police station with his trousers wet almost from the knees down.

"Nasty day," Pendennis said as Rutledge set the umbrella aside and looked up.

"Good God, man, did you run into a door?" he added, seeing the side of Rutledge's face.

"There was someone outside the vicarage last night."

"That's what Daniels told me. I went up there this noon, to see how Vicar was. Mrs. Daniels tells me he came to his senses in the night and spoke to you." He was clearly asking to be told what the injured man had said.

Rutledge was pleased to see that Mrs. Daniels and her husband had kept their word. "He was confused to find himself in a bed in the sitting room. And with a broken leg among his other injuries. That tells me that he hasn't remembered the attack. Whether he will or not, I don't know. But he dreamed about it later, and called out in his sleep. Most of it was unintelligible."

It was the truth, as far as it went.

Pendennis nodded. "It's not surprising, is it, that the shock of what was done to him wiped it out of his memory. The wonder is, he's alive. Did you get a look at whoever it was outside?"

"Far too dark."

"Will he try again, do you think?" Pendennis glanced at the gathering dusk outside. "Should I count on staying there tonight? You look as if you could do with a rest. Sir."

"No, I'll go back myself. But he was armed, whoever he was, Pendennis. Remember that." He gestured to his face. "He hit me with a revolver."

"In the war then?"

"Possibly. Yes," he added, remembering the field glasses. "An officer."

"I've tried, but I can't think of anyone here in the village who would want to harm Vicar. People have come up to me, shaking their heads, as bewildered as I am."

"Have you spoken to Trevose?"

Surprised, Pendennis said, "As a matter of fact, I have. He appears to be in the dark as well."

"Whoever this is, I'm beginning to think he knows more about this village than he should, if he's a stranger. Why else would he want to be sure the vicar is dead? If Toup has never seen him before, he could be in Plymouth or Warwick or Carlisle by now and none of us the wiser. Even if the vicar can give us a description."

"I don't know what to think." He reached across his desk for his notebook. "I've been asking people about seeing St. Ives at night. The odd thing is, they don't want to talk about it. And I don't think they are afraid. At least not of St. Ives."

"What, do they think they've seen a piskey instead?" Rutledge asked, exasperated.

"It wouldn't surprise me," Pendennis said dourly.

"Does Toup have any family? Is there anyone we should contact?"

"An aged aunt in Ipswich. I didn't think we should try to reach her. There's nothing much to be done, and it's a long way to travel at her time of life. Dr. Carrick had said Vicar would live."

"Yes, quite right. And close friends? Is there anyone else he might wish to see? Did he have friends in London? I remember seeing a London address, I think."

"If there was, he never mentioned them to me. He's had very few visitors over the years. No family, of course, only a few men of the cloth who had gone to seminary with him. But that was early on. I doubt anyone has visited him since before the war."

"His cousin, the woman who sometimes came to services with Harry Saunders."

"Yes, that's right, I'd forgot her. But she didn't stay at the vicarage, and she left before the summer was over. Come to think of it, to my knowledge, she never so much as dined with Vicar."

And that, Rutledge thought, was very interesting indeed. The first real indication that her relationship with Toup might not have been as close as he'd claimed it was.

"Who is he close to in the village?"

"No one in particular. That he'd confide in, I mean. Vicar always struck me as a lonely man."

He thanked Pendennis, went back for his motorcar, and drove up to the vicarage. But aside from mutterings in his sleep, most of them unintelligible, Toup had hardly spoken the few times he had awakened.

"He asked for water, and a little after that, I gave him some broth I'd made up in case. He drank a little of that at two o'clock, then again a few minutes ago."

Rutledge went to the sickroom and looked in. Toup lay staring up at the ceiling. But he turned his head when Rutledge knocked. "Is that rain I hear?"

"It is."

"It keeps me awake. Picking at the window as if someone is there. I must attend to my duties. There are people who need my care. And who is to take the Sunday service?" His voice had turned fretful. "I don't know why I must lie here. But Mrs. Daniels tells me I mustn't try to get up. And why is my leg pinned down?"

"It's broken, and Dr. Carrick has put a splint on it to keep it still as it heals."

"They must be giving me something." His fingers worked at the coverlet. "I have such violent dreams. Will you ask Mrs. Daniels to stop?"

There were no medicines, not even for pain.

Rutledge said, "What sort of dreams?"

"I don't know. I can't remember them. But they frighten me. I want them to stop."

He said lightly, "It's the blow on the head, I expect. Don't let them worry you. If you remember any of them, I'd like to know. I might be able to help you to understand them. Will you tell Mrs. Daniels to summon me, if you do?"

"I don't trust her," he said, that fretful note still in his voice. "She must be drugging me. It's the only thing I can think of."

"I'll have Dr. Carrick look in on you. If there's anything wrong, he'll deal with it."

The vicar looked at Rutledge. "Thank you. It's most kind of you."

Rutledge rose from Mrs. Daniels's chair. "You will tell me, if you remember who attacked you? Even if it's someone you know?"

Toup said, looking away again, "I don't remember."

But Rutledge wondered if that were true. Something in the man's eyes was different today. He couldn't quite put his finger on what it was, but he found it worrying nonetheless.

From the vicarage, Rutledge drove on to Padstow Place and was admitted to the drawing room, where Mr. and Mrs. Grenville were gathering before dinner.

Mrs. Grenville put her hand to her mouth to stifle a gasp as she saw Rutledge's face. Grenville looked sharply at him. "What's happened?"

"There was someone outside the vicarage last night. I tried to stop him. It wasn't very successful."

"Was there, by God. Did you get a look at him?" Grenville asked.

"No, it was too dark. But there is other news of a sort. The vicar is awake. He appears to have no memory of what happened to him. He keeps asking questions about it. Do you know of anyone who could have done this? Someone who used to live in the village or in Padstow and had had words with Toup? Or confessed something to him that perhaps he later regretted?"

"I would have said," Grenville responded slowly, "that if any man in the county was less likely to have enemies, it was Toup. There's never even been a problem over the years. I can't understand it."

"Does he have friends who ought to be told what's happened? Perhaps someone in London? Relatives?" He'd already asked Pendennis but Grenville was likely to know more.

"His aunt lives in Ipswich. She's in her nineties by now, I should think. As for London, I can't remember his ever mentioning any friends there. I'm in town often, and he's never asked me to look in on anyone or carry a message for him."

Rutledge said, "On a different matter entirely. Who took your rowboat across the river this morning?"

"The rowboat?" Grenville's brows rose in surprise. "No one from this house."

"Not even one of your tenants, intending to visit a friend across the river?"

"To my knowledge, none of our staff has relatives in Rock." He turned to his wife. "My dear?"

She shook her head. "They come from Padstow or Wadebridge. There isn't that much exchange between Rock and this side of the river. Why do you think someone took it across there?"

"I saw it beached on the strand below Rock. And when I came out to look, it had been in the water. Very recently."

"I don't like the sound of this," Grenville snapped. "It's private property there, and that includes the rowboat." He was angry now.

"Perhaps one of the neighbors borrowed it without asking, knowing you wouldn't mind? St. Ives, perhaps?"

"Don't be ridiculous. He would most certainly ask. And in light of the role the rowboat played in the accusations against my daughter and her friends, I can't imagine anyone would think I'd give my permission to use it. For any reason."

"Any news regarding my daughter?" Mrs. Grenville asked. "Surely you've found something that would help us? This waiting for word has taken a toll on all of us. You must see that."

"There has been a singular lack of evidence to work with," he told her. "But someone had interfered with Saunders's dinghy. That's why it sank under him. The surprise is that he had got as far as he had before it took on enough water to go down."

Victoria Grenville's parents stared at him.

Grenville said, "This is the first I've heard of anyone meddling with the dinghy. Why wasn't I informed?"

"It was a police matter. There were holes in the fabric of the hull." He explained what he had found, and added, "This casts a different light on the circumstances surrounding why Harry Saunders was in the water to start with. The problem is, it doesn't explain away the injury to his head. And that is what killed him."

"On the other hand," Grenville said, his voice hard, "there is no proof that the injury didn't occur when he foundered."

"Will you trust a jury to make that choice?"

Grenville looked down at the drink in his hand. After a moment he looked up at Rutledge. "Then find that proof, Inspector. It's what you are here for."

He could have challenged that, but it would change very little.

"Have you found the missing statements?" Mrs. Grenville asked, quickly trying to shift the subject.

"I'm afraid not. But they become less and less urgent as we learn more. Do either of you know the name of the young woman whom Toup claimed to be his cousin, visiting in Rock?"

"We were never introduced," Mrs. Grenville said. "I found that rather odd, but she seemed to be such a shy little thing. I expect she was more comfortable at St. Marina's where no one pressed her with questions or invitations. And I remember too, speaking to Mr. Toup about her, that he said she had recently been ill, although she appeared to me to have fully recovered. Except for the shadows around her eyes. But you didn't notice them particularly at a distance."

Rutledge hadn't been told she had been ill. Was that another lie? Or the truth?

"Are you acquainted with anyone living in Mayfair?" he asked, and gave the name and street address.

Frowning, Mrs. Grenville said, "I don't recognize the name or the address. My dear?"

Grenville was shaking his head. "No one I know. The name isn't familiar."

So much for that. Then why had Toup kept that slip of paper in his pocket?

He thanked them and then asked to see Kate Gordon.

"It's the dinner hour," Mrs. Grenville said.

"I shan't keep her long," he replied.

Grenville sent for her, and allowed Rutledge to use the study for the interview.

When Kate walked in, she stared in horror at his face.

"Ian—what happened to you?"

"It isn't as bad as it looks," he said, smiling, though it hurt to do it.

She came up to him and examined the cut and the bruise more closely. He had forgot she met the trains with the wounded, and might know more about wounds than he'd expected. "That isn't true. Someone hit you, and very hard." She put out her hand as if to touch his face, then flushed a little and stepped back, letting it drop to her side.

"That's not why I came. Kate, you and Victoria Grenville have known each other for some time. Do you remember attending parties with her in Mayfair, at this address?"

He gave it to her. And he could tell, before she answered him, that it was not one she was acquainted with.

"Should I know it? I'm afraid I don't."

"No matter. Is it possible for any of you to leave Padstow Place, without attracting attention?"

She gave him a wry smile. "I haven't tried. I shouldn't care to face Mr. Grenville's wrath."

"Even Victoria?"

"I heard her complaining to him only yesterday that he was too strict, that she was heartily sick of her room. But he didn't relent. She wanted to come downstairs for tea, and to play the piano."

"Perhaps her mother is kinder."

"I don't quite understand why, but Mrs. Grenville appears to be even more worried than her husband, if that's possible. She is just as strict with the maids—they aren't allowed to linger in our rooms, or gossip."

He remembered that there was someone in this house whose gossip had reached the ears of the Saunders staff.

"Why do you ask?" she inquired, when he said nothing.

"It's my duty to be sure that the Grenvilles take theirs seriously."

He had one more question for her. "Have you ever heard Victoria speak of George St. Ives?"

"Only in passing. Remembering when her brother was still alive, mostly. I've never met him, but she has said he was badly wounded in the war and that we mustn't stare if we encounter him. I think she pities him."

And pity was something a man like St. Ives would deplore, if he knew. "Has Elaine ever commented on her brother's feelings for Victoria?"

Kate frowned as she searched her memory. "Several times she's mentioned how happy she would have been to be mistress of this house, and how she wished Victoria could marry her brother as well and live at Chough Hall. And then they could go on as before, the four of them, their children growing up together. Now, of course, Victoria will be mistress here instead."

Rutledge walked to the window and back. "In your heart of hearts, Kate, do you believe that Victoria wanted to kill Harry Saunders? She refused to go to his aid as the dinghy was sinking, and there's the business with the oar. I must find the answer to this question; it's the sticking point in the charge against the four of you. Trevose claims it was a clear case of murder, and no other witness has come forward to speak up for any of you."

"Victoria is moody at times. We've all been touched by the war, Ian. Even those of us who never saw France. Victoria told me once that every wounded man she saw might be her brother, their suffering his suffering. Even though his commanding officer wrote that he'd died instantly, facing the enemy with the courage he was known for, she had witnessed what happens to soldiers in the trenches, and she couldn't be sure it wasn't just a comforting lie, that he hadn't lain in the mud of No Man's Land, waiting for a medic who never came. I hesitate to say this, because it could well see all of us in the direst straits. But I've had a good deal of time to think, Ian, and I can't help but wonder. Was what made Victoria quite so rude toward Harry Saunders the fact that he spent the war safely in America, while Stephen and George and so many of our friends bore the brunt of the fighting, and were killed or maimed?"

Rutledge wanted to shut out her words, to will them away. But he had asked, and Kate had given him her answer. Victoria's motive.

And it was damning.

He had never been quite convinced that Victoria Grenville was the sort of woman who would want to kill someone whose affections had strayed, most particularly someone she didn't love and would probably not be likely to marry. It was even possible that knowing this, Harry Saunders had teased her by flirting with her, salvaging a little of his pride along the way. Attractive as she was, Victoria must have been accustomed to men throwing themselves at her feet and then turning to someone else after she had made it politely known that she wasn't interested. And a jury might be persuaded to believe she wouldn't have stooped to killing a rejected suitor.

Kate, watching his face, said sharply, "Ian?"

He managed a smile, striving to make it appear genuine. He had always known how to listen. And people had confided in him. He wished it were anyone but Kate speaking to him now.

"I was weighing what you've told me. It's possible, of course. Something to keep in mind. Thank you, Kate, for being truthful."

Relieved, she returned his smile. But he was afraid, once she was back in her room, that she too would realize what she had given him.

"I mustn't keep you from your dinner," he added. "Mrs. Grenville was very particular about that. And as always, you'll keep this between us?"

"Yes, of course I will." She walked to the door, and then said, facing it, her back to him, "Do you still love her desperately? Jean?"

He remembered in time.

"She was a part of my life before the war," he answered Kate with great care. "I think of her fondly sometimes, but I wanted her to be happy there in Toronto. She deserved that." It was the best he could do.

There was a silence between them. Then Kate opened the door, saying, "Good night, Ian." And it closed behind her.

He stood where he was for several minutes before leaving the study and then the house without speaking to anyone else.

Rutledge spent the night at the vicarage. But it was uneventful. Mrs. Daniels insisted on putting compresses on his face, saying, "Do you wish to go about looking as though a cow kicked you in the head?"

He remembered the expression on Kate's face. "No. All right then. Go ahead."

Afterward he wondered if Mrs. Daniels had slipped a little something else into the tea laced with a splash of the vicar's whisky. For he slept well enough. As did the vicar.

And if there was anyone prowling around the house, he made no effort to get inside.

As Mrs. Daniels said, when she brought Rutledge breakfast in the morning, "It rained in the night as if the heavens had split wide open. He's no fool, this man. He stayed snug by his hearth, like the rest of us. Or maybe he's decided Vicar isn't going to turn him in to the police after all."

"Why should he decide that?"

"You'd be knocking on his door, wouldn't you? By now?"

16

Before leaving, he went to sit once more with the vicar. Toup was lying on the bed, his eyes closed, but Rutledge could see by his breathing that he wasn't asleep.

Shutting the sitting room door, so that he couldn't be overheard, Rutledge drew Mrs. Daniels's chair closer to the bed, and began to talk.

"If I were in London," he said casually, as if carrying on a conversation with Pendennis or Sergeant Gibson, "it just might be possible for these three events to be coincidental. There's Harry Saunders's death. According to Trevose, four women of good family conspired to drown him. They are to be charged with murder, now that he's died of his injuries. But someone hadn't foreseen that turn of events. And so he—or she—dug holes in the bottom of Harry's dinghy, with the expectation that he'd drown somewhere between the row of cottages where it was kept and Padstow Harbor. Either whoever it was had miscalculated or the holes weren't large enough. He was well east of Padstow when it finally happened. Nobody has asked just where he was heading that afternoon. Possibly to call on George St. Ives. But then Harry died before anyone could ask. Is it possible that Victoria damaged his boat? A case could be made for that—she was against going to his rescue, claiming that he wasn't drowning."

The man on the bed hadn't moved.

"Or it could have been George St. Ives who tampered with the dinghy. That sounds rather preposterous, until one takes into account the fact that he is in love with Victoria and too badly wounded to consider asking for her hand. If he thought Harry was annoying her—or a rival not worthy of her—or even if he thought Harry had broken her heart, he might have been angry enough to do something about it. He walks at night, you know. St. Ives. And not just in the back garden of Chough Hall. In point of fact, he was seen not far from where you were attacked. Another coincidence? Which brings us to what happened to you. Someone wanted to kill you. But it wasn't a cold-blooded beating, was it? There was passion behind those blows. Anger? Jealousy? Fear? Whatever it was, it was a driving emotion that brought him back to the vicarage on two separate nights, with an eye to making sure you couldn't identify him. That put Mr. and Mrs. Daniels in jeopardy, because he would have had to kill them after he killed you."

It was not precisely accurate, this conversation, but it was purposely designed to capture the vicar's attention. And Rutledge thought he could see a movement of Toup's fair lashes. But he said nothing about it. "And there's another small mystery. One you have refused to solve for me. Harry Saunders might have told me what I needed to know, but of course he died before I could ask. Who was the young woman who took a cottage on the far side of Padstow, but chose to attend church here in Heyl, in order not to attract attention? And you have no memory of who attacked you. We can't go to his door and arrest him, because we have no idea who it might be."

He got to his feet, walking to the window to look out at the churchyard.

"Saunders is dead. Sara Langley, Victoria Grenville, Kate Gordon, and Elaine St. Ives are going to be taken to Bodmin soon. I've dragged my feet as long as I can. It's no place for a gently bred young woman." He had a sudden memory of another young woman who could have answered to that. "God knows what it will do to them—and that's not even taking into account their reputations. What worries me is that they will be convicted and hanged. Trevose will be very happy about that. Mrs. Grenville will understand why." He took a deep breath. "There it is. I don't know if you'll ever remember anything about your assailant. But he's a killer. When I saw what he'd done to you, I knew that he could kill and very likely would kill again. It's even possible, God knows why, that he meddled with the Saunders dinghy. If there's anything else you know, even if you don't or won't believe that it's relevant, it could save a life. Yours? Someone else's? Mine, even. If you opened your eyes and looked at my face and your own, you'd believe me."

He waited, but there was silence. Turning, he walked to the door, and his hand was on the knob when the vicar spoke. His voice was ragged.

"St. Ives. The only person I saw that morning was St. Ives. But I refuse to believe he would hurt me. In God's name, *why*?"

"I don't know." Rutledge turned. "Who was the young woman who lived in that cottage outside Padstow?"

"She's no one of importance," Toup said, looking at Rutledge for the first time. "I will swear to it if you like. A summer visitor. A young war widow." His eyes, the still-swollen lids twice their size, blinked several times. "Come closer. I can't see you clearly."

Rutledge walked to the bed and leaned over it. Toup raised his head to stare.

"Oh, my oath, Rutledge." He closed his eyes again. "Was it St. Ives? Tell me it wasn't."

"I don't know. Whoever it is, he was more agile. Or else driven by fear to do his best. But then the only time I've had the opportunity to watch St. Ives walk, he knew I was there."

"It will not save the women who are accused," Toup said. "How could it?"

A very good question.

Rutledge had no answer.

He went back to the cottages, but Dunbar wasn't at home. Rutledge waited for an hour or more, knocking twice in the event the man was refusing to come to the door.

But there was no sign of him. Looking in the windows where he could, Rutledge could see that the interior was tidy, the curtains open, a cup and a teapot sitting on the kitchen table.

Not dead in his bed, then, Rutledge thought.

He would have liked to go inside, but he couldn't risk it. He had no authority to be there, and if Dunbar came walking up the path, he would be well within his rights to call in the Padstow constable.

Frustrated, Rutledge gave Dunbar another few minutes, then left, following the road into Padstow in the event he could spot the man on his way back from marketing.

Driving on, he returned to the village. The street above the landing was busy, people going about their midday business. He was stopped once or twice before he could enter the inn by people wanting news of the vicar. The doctor had come again in his absence, and this had been worrisome.

"He's slowly recovering. He has no memory of what happened to him. The doctor tells me it probably will never come back."

His inquisitors shook their heads in sorrow, but Rutledge knew the news would be repeated over and over again until everyone had heard it. As he intended.

Several others inquired about his face, a mixture of curiosity and concern.

Rutledge said ruefully, "Serves me right, to go wandering about the Cornish countryside in the dark. Are there stones every quarter mile?"

And they smiled. If the Cornish countryside had one stone, it had thousands. The wasteland was full of them, and low-growing gorse and furze were a constant trap for unwary boots.

When finally he was free to go inside, Rutledge went up to his room and stood by the window. Across the Camel, rooftops and windows caught the sunlight, winking back at him.

Almost from the start he had been working under the assumption that the first act in this inquiry had been the death of Trevose's brother Paul years before on St. Michael's Mount. Even Mrs. Grenville had believed it.

But what if it wasn't? Setting aside Trevose and the charge brought against the women in the boat, what if Scotland Yard had been summoned to Cornwall after Harry Saunders drowned in the Camel, unable to swim away from his sinking boat, and the sabotage of the dinghy had been discovered as it was raised?

How would he—or even Inspector Barrington—have proceeded at that stage?

He would have traced the dinghy back to where it was kept, and looked closely into the inhabitants of those three cottages, with an eye to uncovering any connection with Harry Saunders. And in doing that, he might well have learned about Harry escorting one of the cottage residents to services at St. Marina's instead of St. Petroc's, and this would have led him to the vicar of St. Marina's, Mr. Toup.

The connection with Toup would have been reinforced as soon as the vicar had been beaten within an inch of his life.

He went back down to his motorcar and drove to Padstow.

Saunders's parents still refused to see him.

And so he went on to Dr. Carrick's surgery.

There was, Rutledge was told, a rash of chills making the rounds, and the doctor's waiting room was full.

"Is it the vicar? Has he taken a turn for the worse?" Carrick's nurse asked.

"He has not."

"Very well, you can make an appointment and return tomorrow."

"My visit will take no more than five minutes. But it is urgent."

He would have to come back. She was adamant.

Politely thanking the nurse, he sat down among the coughing children and feverish adults waiting to be seen, and ignored the frowns and curious stares sent his way. By his calculations, he was fifteenth in line to see the doctor. Four more patients came in after him, and one of the children began to vomit.

An hour and a half later, the nurse summoned Rutledge, and tight-lipped, she led him down the passage to the doctor's office.

Carrick was behind his desk.

"Are you blind? There are people out there who need care. What's so important that it can't be dealt with tomorrow?"

"I too have a cough," Rutledge said blandly, and proceeded to demonstrate just that. He sat down in the chair in front of the cluttered desk.

"All right, what is it? I'm told this isn't about the vicar."

"The summer visitors in the cottages let by Frank Dunbar. Were you ever asked to treat any of them this summer? Most particularly one who had been quite ill, and had come to Cornwall to recover her health?"

"Is that the only reason you've interrupted my office today?" Carrick was angry now.

"It will save time if you answer my question and I can leave. It's important. More so than you may realize."

"The answer is no. As far as I am aware, this summer's visitors were not in need of my services."

It was a dead end.

Rutledge rose. "Thank you. I'll leave you to your patients."

"Here. What's this to do with the vicar's injuries?" the doctor asked sharply.

"I'll tell you when I'm sure."

"I did attend Dunbar, if that's of any use. He had a severe attack of indigestion from dining on mussels. Harry Saunders had just brought that young woman home after attending church services, and they found him in great distress. Harry came for me, thinking it was a heart attack. I was just sitting down to my own joint, and I was grateful it wasn't more serious than it was. The young woman agreed to see to it that he took his medicines that evening. Pretty little thing."

"Describe her, if you will?"

"Slim, dark hair, a very pretty face."

"And she was staying in one of the cottages?"

"The middle one. I remember because she was close enough to keep an eye on Dunbar."

"Do you recall her name?"

"Sorry. I don't think she gave it. But Dunbar will know, certainly."

So much for the spinsters!

Leaving the doctor's surgery, he drove on to the police station. Inspector Carstairs was not in, and Rutledge spoke to his sergeant.

"George St. Ives. Anything in his past that I should know about?"

"Young St. Ives?" His surprise was genuine.

"Before the war. What sort of lad was he? Any trouble with his friends? The police? A reputation for being a troublemaker?"

"High spirits, sir, but nothing I'd call trouble. He and the Grenville lad were that close, birthdays in the same month, in and out of each other's houses. One Easter for a lark they tried to put a rooster in the church belfry." He grinned. "Rooster got the best of them, and the doctor was called in. On another occasion, they claimed they saw a ghost ship out on the Doom Bar, and when everyone rushed out to have a look, they slipped into The Pilot and drew themselves a pint. Young Grenville was sick, but St. Ives managed to finish his glass before he was caught. No report on whether he was sick later or not. They stole a pony from Trevose, when their fathers refused to let them take out the mare, and rode it to Wadebridge to see a man with a talking parrot. Trevose wanted to see them up before the magistrate, but as the pony suffered no harm, Mr. Grenville refused to hear the case." The sergeant studied Rutledge. "You could have asked Constable Pendennis, sir, and saved yourself coming into Padstow."

"I could have done," Rutledge agreed, "but I preferred to ask here. Since I have no immediate cause to think ill of St. Ives."

Sergeant Beddoes nodded. "I understand, sir."

And Rutledge thought he did. What's more, this information confirmed what he was beginning to suspect: that St. Ives was in the clear, in spite of what the vicar had cried out in his delirium.

"I'll tell the Inspector you called, shall I, sir?"

"Yes, all right. Where is he?"

He wasn't sure afterward why he asked. It was none of his affair, well out of his jurisdiction.

"At the moment, he's busy with what appears to be robbery that ended in murder."

"Here in Padstow?"

"Yes, sir. An elderly gentleman. He'd just withdrawn ten pounds from his bank yesterday, and he was set upon before he could reach his home. The body wasn't found until this morning."

It was Hamish's voice in the back of his mind that warned him.

"Anyone connected with the Saunders's case?"

"Not that I'm aware of, sir. Although he does live in one of the cottages where young Saunders kept—"

"Dunbar."

"Yes, sir, how did you know?" Beddoes was frowning. "Is there something I should tell Inspector Carstairs?"

"I don't know. I waited at Dunbar's cottage for him. Most of this morning. I thought he'd gone to market. Where is Carstairs?"

"There's an alley toward the end of the harbor, runs from there into the town. The man's body was discovered there some time ago, but it had been there for a while. Early risers thought he was a drunk. His clothes disheveled, his hat pulled down low over his face, a strong smell of drink about him. A Good Samaritan stopped, thinking he might be ill as well as drunk, and called the police. He was dead, he'd been badly beaten."

"Good God." Rutledge was out of his chair, on his way to the door. "Was there a weapon found near him?"

"I don't believe so, Inspector. But I've not seen the full report."

Rutledge didn't wait to hear him out. He was out the door, on his way to the harbor. He had no trouble finding the alley. The usual cluster of onlookers marked the place. As Rutledge came closer he could see that it was no more than a narrow space between the two buildings on either side, running up to the streets above and dark most of the day. He thought it might have been used by merchants hurrying to meet a ship sighted in the roads or fishermen's families coming to meet the boats and help unload the catch.

The smell of sour beer greeted him before he'd turned into the opening. Halfway along a body lay propped against one wall. Carstairs was standing over it, talking to someone.

"Here!" A constable rushed toward him, to stop him.

"Rutledge, Scotland Yard," he called, and went on into the dim shadows. The pavement was puddled, scattered windblown debris caught in cracks of the cobblestones and against the sides of the buildings rising overhead. A sad place to die.

Carstairs looked up as he approached. "I thought I told the constable to keep the alley clear, damn it." And then he recognized Rutledge. "What the hell brings you here?"

"I was at the Dunbar cottage earlier, waiting for him. I thought he'd gone into Padstow and would be returning sooner rather than later. But he never came."

"We're waiting for Carrick, damn his eyes. He should have been here by now."

"He's got a surgery full of ill patients. What happened here?"

"See for yourself."

Rutledge walked closer to the old man's body and squatted for a better look.

At the same time Carstairs leaned over and lifted the man's hat.

His face and head were bloody, his hands as well, where he had tried to defend himself. From the look of his coat, he'd died lying down, but had been propped up afterward to give the semblance of a drunken man slouched against the wall. It was filthy, and spattered with Dunbar's blood, already dark and drawing flies.

"He's been dead some time," Rutledge commented, reaching out to touch his swollen face.

"He went to his bank yesterday just before it closed. We've determined that much. His pockets are empty now. But he'd taken out ten pounds."

"At his age, someone could have robbed him without beating him like this," Rutledge pointed out.

"I've asked for torches. But God knows what we'll find in the filth underfoot here. Nothing of use, I'll be bound." His anger got the best of him. "Damn it, he was a harmless man who eked a living out of letting those cottages of his. Never any trouble, mind you. I'd run into him from time to time when he came into town, and he always had a good word. The weather was fine, his latest visitors were pleasant, he'd heard birdsong or seen a flower in bloom on his way in, or there was a new boat in. Something. Even if it was pounding rain, he thought it might be good for the crops."

"Know anything about the people who came to let his cottages?"

"Families, mostly, or older couples looking for an inexpensive outing to Cornwall. Never any trouble, either. Paid up on time, lived quietly, came and went without fuss. No rowdiness or the like. We were never called out there for any reason that I remember. If you were desperate, he'd make you a loan. If you couldn't pay it back, he'd wait patiently for it."

Someone came just then with torches, and in their garish light, Dunbar's injuries were even more ghastly.

Rutledge and the constable held the torches while Carstairs scoured the alley for clues of any kind. There appeared to be none. And then Carrick was there: he spent five minutes examining the body, and straightened up.

"I'll know what killed him when I have him on the table. Hard to say what blows there were to the body. That one head wound," he added, pointing where a flap of scalp had been torn loose, "is also a possible cause. Have him brought around." He wiped his hands on his handkerchief. With a nod to Carstairs, but not to Rutledge, he was gone.

The constable's torch swung in an arc as he stepped back to allow the doctor to pass. And that was when Rutledge saw it.

"Here—shine the light by Dunbar's right hand."

"Where?"

"Just by his thigh. On his right side."

Carstairs turned to look as well as the constable, who steadied his torch on the spot Rutledge had indicated.

Something had been scraped into the scum that covered the pavement. It was hard to read—or even to be sure it was anything more than a dying man's twitches.

Rutledge backed up against the wall beside Dunbar's body, and tried to work out the scratches.

"*W*," he said after a moment. "And I think that's an *A*. *R*? And an *N*. Then something I can't decipher."

Carstairs said, "Let me try." He took Rutledge's place. "I don't see any letters. You're imagining—no wait, move the torch a bit—no, this way. Yes, that's a *W*, I'd accept that." He studied the ground beside Dunbar. "Good God, he must not have been dead when he was propped up against that wall. *WARN*—what's the rest of it?"

"He didn't finish it. He tried. I can't make out the next line. *B*? *P*? *F*? The rest is unintelligible."

"He lived alone. I don't know that he had any immediate family. You said you were there at the cottage this morning. Anything wrong?"

"Nothing as far as I could see. No one came to the door."

"Hmmmm." It was more a grunt than a response. "Why were you there?"

"We'd spoken, Dunbar and I. Earlier. It was where Saunders kept his boat."

Carstairs gestured. "That's not an *R*. I'm not sure what it is, but I don't believe he was about to write *Rutledge*."

"No." Rutledge moved away from the wall. "I will leave you to deal with this. If there's anything I can do, you have only to ask."

Carstairs smiled. It was more like a grimace in the torchlight. Curled lips over clenched teeth. "I think we can manage."

With a nod, Rutledge left. He was eager to be away from that dank, dim, claustrophobic alley with the smell of urine and beer and death. And he didn't want to be there when—if—Carstairs recognized the similarities between the two beatings, Dunbar and the vicar.

Besides, with Dunbar dead and the police occupied with his murder, there was no one to prevent him from letting himself into the cottage, to look for anything that might be useful. Or anything to do with a *P*, a *B*, or an *F*.

Rutledge stopped short at the mouth of the alley, and turned. "Carstairs. Has anyone reported the theft of a Hobby Horse costume?"

"A what?" Carstairs stared at him as if he'd run mad. Padstow's Hobby Horse festival was in the spring. "Can't you see I have a murder inquiry on my hands?"

"The attack on the vicar of St. Marina's. I have reason to believe whoever it was, he was wearing a disguise."

Carstairs took several steps toward him. "Funny, that. A fortnight ago I think it was, two lads on their way home from school saw a man pull what appeared to be one out of a dustbin. One was my sergeant's son, that's how I got wind of it. They reported it, mainly because I think they'd have liked to be the ones who saw it first. Nothing came of it. Still. Vicar would have recognized the costume for what it was."

"Yes, of course. The point of it would have been to hide the face of his attacker. Do you think the lads could identify the man they saw?"

"I doubt it. A fortnight ago? At the time they could hardly agree on what he looked like. They were more interested in the possibility of recovering the costume for themselves. The black cloth is cheap and doesn't last long as a rule, although the masks are often passed down. My sergeant did question the householder to be sure he'd disposed of it, and he had. Something about a crack in the mask. If you want my opinion, it's a jealous man looking to improve his own costume by copying the discarded one. Ah, there are the men with the stretchers. And about time, damn it."

Rutledge thanked him, and made way for the stretcher bearers.

He walked briskly back to his motorcar, his mind busy with the initials. Whatever had driven the dying man, he had fought to stay alive long enough to leave a message. Not a clue to his killer, but a warning to someone.

For whom?

He ran through a mental list of everyone he'd met in Heyl village.

All right, he thought, if not whom, then why?

And he had no better answer for that.

The one name he couldn't check against the three initials was that of the young woman who had, according to Carstairs, lived in that middle cottage, just above the boat landing where the dinghy was usually beached.

Did Dunbar know his killer? Or did he know what it was his killer wanted? Two very different questions.

Rutledge turned the crank, got in, and drove sedately out of Padstow, following the gray walls and the dry leaves blowing in the light wind. As soon as he reached the main road out toward the headland, he picked up speed, moving as fast as he felt he safely could.

But it was already too late.

He could smell the smoke long before he reached the cottages, but he put that down to people clearing out their gardens before winter set in. It wasn't until he had rounded the last bend in the road that he saw the flames.

Dunbar's cottage was already engulfed. There was no hope of saving it. What's more, the flying sparks had caught in the roof of the next cottage. He could see smoke there now.

But it wasn't a spark that sent up a column of smoke. That cottage too had been set alight.

The old wood burned fast and well.

He got out and ran to see if anyone was around. If somewhere the arsonist waited to watch the end of his handiwork. With Hamish raging in the back of his mind, he searched even under the landing, anywhere a man—or woman—might hide.

But there was no one on that lonely strand of beach other than Rutledge himself and the distressed seagulls overhead. Nor had he met anyone on the road here. Or found footsteps he could identify with any certainty. Dunbar's? Someone else's?

The ceiling collapsed on Dunbar's cottage as the beams burned through, the roof following in a crescendo of sparks and flame and smoke.

Helplessly he watched, and the second cottage was not far behind now. The ceiling fell in with almost a human shriek as the beams went.

It took more than half an hour for the cottages to be reduced to smoldering, blackened rubble, where flames shot up here and there as they found something new to feed on.

Warn . . . warn who? The question ran over and over in his mind.

When it was finished, he went back to his motorcar, reversed it, and left. There was nothing to be done, and Carstairs would discover what had happened soon enough. Someone in Padstow must surely have seen the column of black smoke by now. If he, Rutledge, reported it in Padstow, there would be questions to do with his presence so soon after the fires had begun. To do with why he had gone directly from the alley where Dunbar's body still lay to those cottages on the strand. And he didn't have time to explain.

Better to let sleeping dogs lie.

He set out in the direction of Padstow, was relieved to pass it by without encountering anyone else on the road, not even a police constable headed for the cottages. When he reached the village, he stopped briefly at the inn to pack what he needed. And then with a fresh Thermos of tea, he was on his way to Wadebridge, and from there he took the road south.

He didn't think he would find what he was looking for in Fowey, but it was the only clue he had.

And at the moment, any clue would be better than what he possessed now.

With only Hamish for company, he began his long drive through the darkness of Cornwall.

17

It was very late when he arrived in Fowey. He'd had to stop for petrol and again for his dinner, and the great white bulk of the hotel, gleaming in the starlight, was dark.

He pulled into the drive that ran down to the hotel, got out, stretched his tired shoulders, and then walked around to the door that led into Reception.

No one was there, but he found the bell sitting next to the lamp and rang it.

After a time, a drowsy clerk came out of the inner regions and asked if he was looking for a room. It was asked in a dubious tone of voice, as if the hotel was full up. But when Rutledge told him that he was, the man nodded and went to pull the ledger out of a drawer and set it up where Rutledge could sign his name.

"The kitchen is closed, the staff working there lives down in the village, I'm afraid. But I could manage a cup of tea."

"Thank you. I'll be all right."

The man looked on the board for keys and selected one. "It doesn't face the water, that's extra," he said tentatively.

"Then I'll have one with a view," Rutledge said.

That key was put back and another chosen, then Rutledge was being led to the stairs and a room that was well aired and of a good size.

He took the key from the clerk, thanked him, and went to the windows. The hotel was high on the hillside above the town. He looked down on rooftops and gardens all the way to the church tower, and beyond that lay the water. At the far end it opened to the sea, and in the upper reaches it was nearly hidden from view by trees closing in on the banks. Across the way were other houses, most of them dark, but the ambient light glimmered on the water.

He took in a deep breath of sea air, then went to bed.

The problem that faced him over breakfast in the lovely dining room with its open windows, the white curtains catching the slight breeze, was how to approach the question he needed to ask. The hotel was well filled even at this time of year. How many guests had there been over the last one or two years?

"A needle in a haystack" was Hamish's comment.

When breakfast was over, he asked to speak to the manager and was taken to a small but handsome office down the passage.

The manager was an older man, middle height, thin, and already balding. He welcomed Rutledge with a smile, asking what he could do for him.

"It's a police matter," he began. "There was a young woman who rented a cottage just outside Padstow over the summer. She left in September, and the forwarding address in London that she gave to the local vicar has been sold. I have no reason to believe that this young woman is in any way involved in anything untoward, but there has been a death in Padstow, and I have a strong feeling that she might be in danger now."

"What makes you believe she is here in Fowey?"

"There was a cutting from a magazine. It featured Fowey and this hotel."

"But that was a year ago, if I'm right in assuming which magazine carried that particular piece."

"Perhaps she was here then. I am hoping you can give me a name."

"You don't even know her name?" the manager—the small sign on his desk identified him as Tolworthy—asked in astonishment. "How on earth do you expect to find someone whose name you don't know and whose whereabouts are so uncertain?"

"I was hoping you could help me."

"Dozens of people come to this hotel each week. Many of them to stay, others are here for luncheon or dinner. How can I possibly know which one you mean?"

"I have a feeling she's from London, that there was some misunderstanding over the address. She is quiet, keeps to herself, makes few friends, and prefers her solitude. I've been told she's dark rather than fair, and quite attractive. She is careful to give away little information about herself, and I expect she stays only a short time if other guests become inquisitive about her."

Tolworthy blinked. "She just left!"

"What? You know who she is?"

"She had been here through September and into October, giving out that she had been ill for some time and had come here where it was quiet, to recover. But she said she was from Leicestershire. The address she gave when she arrived was most certainly Leicester. And I recall a comment she made about the cathedral there."

The vicar had said she was from Norfolk.

"Where did she go from here? Has anyone else come to ask for her?"

"I have no idea where she went. And you are the first to inquire about her."

It must be the same woman, Rutledge thought. Chary with information about herself, moving on when she became wary . . . leaving no forwarding address behind, and lying about her home.

"Will you tell me her name?"

Tolworthy opened a drawer and took out an oak filing box, sorting through the cards inside until he found what he wanted.

"Margaret Eleanor Avery Haverford."

His heart sank. Where was the *P* or the *B* or the *F*?

Hamish said, "If she has given a false address, why not a false name?"

And Rutledge realized that Hamish was right. Why lie about one if not the other?

"When did she leave?"

"A fortnight ago."

"Was she traveling alone?"

"Yes, she told me her parents had died in the influenza epidemic. But she seemed to be quite accustomed to traveling by herself. She managed her arrival here and her departure with equal assurance."

Because she had learned to manage both. But for how long had she been doing this? And what was she running from?

"I have told you that she has committed no crime. But I know very little about her. Were there any problems during her stay here in Fowey? Any indication that she might not be the person she claims to be?"

"Not Miss Haverford. I would find that very hard to believe, Inspector. I have spoken to her on numerous occasions. She is a fine young woman."

And yet she had very likely lied about her name and her place of residence.

"As you say. I'm worried for her safety, nonetheless. And if you are concealing anything from me, I want to know."

"May I see your identification, sir?"

Rutledge handed it to him.

"Yes, Scotland Yard. She did not trust me with her plans. I'm sorry. And that is the truth, Inspector."

"Would it be possible to speak to the maid who took care of her?"

Tolworthy took out his watch. "She will be off duty in ten minutes. Her name is Maisy, and she's a local girl. If you would care to wait, I shall send her to you."

Rutledge thanked him, and sat there in the small office, outwardly waiting patiently, but worried and frustrated beneath it.

Maisy was a small, dark girl with a round face and kind eyes. She came into the manager's office with some trepidation, and Rutledge set about putting her at ease.

"Hallo," he said with a smile. "Come in and sit down, Maisy."

"I'd rather stand, sir, if it's all the same to you, sir."

"As you like. You're in no trouble, you know. The problem is, I'm worried about Miss Haverford. Something has happened in Padstow, and I'm afraid it could bring her to harm. And she's unaware of it. I need to find her and warn her."

The girl's eyes were round. "Miss Haverford, sir? But she's never been to Cornwall before. She told me so."

The truth—or another lie?

Persisting, he said, "That may be so, but it doesn't mean that she has no relatives in Cornwall. Or friends."

Relaxing a little, she said, nodding, "I hadn't thought of that. She never spoke to me about her family. She seemed sad, when I asked about them. Her parents were dead. That dreadful Spanish flu, and she has been ill herself. She'd never had a strong constitution, she said. Anemia, she told me."

Rutledge let the maid talk.

"I'm worried that she might not have enough money with her," he said. "Do you think she will be all right?"

"She had lovely clothes, sir. Quite lovely. I shouldn't think that money was a problem."

He had meant the question differently, but this was more information to store away.

"What was she like?"

"Very quiet, but very kind. When my mother had the toothache, she let me take the morning off to carry her to the dentist. And she never told Mr. Tolworthy. She said it wasn't necessary." Her color flamed. "I shouldn't have said that."

"That's between you and Miss Haverford," he said easily. "I see no reason to tell him. Did you notice anything unusual about her?"

"She was quite pretty, and I asked if she had a young man. She blushed at that, and told me that she was still in mourning for her parents and couldn't think about her future for a bit. Not till she was back in Leicester. She had the nicest luggage, Miss Haverford did. A dark set, except for her hand case. It was a very handsome red leather, and it had an initial on it. An *E,* set out in gold. She told me it'ud belonged to her mother as a girl."

Not a *B* or *P* or *F.* An *E.* It could well have been. Rutledge felt his depression lifting.

They talked for another ten minutes, and then he let Maisy return to her duties. He had garnered very little from her chatter, except for the initial on that case. And yet he had the strongest feeling he'd found his quarry.

He was leaving the office himself when Maisy came hurrying back down the passage toward him. "I've thought of something else. She had a car come for her. From the village. The driver might know where she went."

He thanked her again, and then as an afterthought, he added, "Don't talk about her to anyone else, Maisy. Will you promise me that? Someone else could come looking for her, and he might not seem dangerous, but he could well be. Keep that in mind. Or a woman, for that matter. I am afraid for her. I can't tell you why, it's police business. But you must trust me on that."

She promised, and hurried away to her duties.

He walked down the path between houses and back gardens, all the way to the gray stone church dedicated to St. Finnbar. It took him a matter of minutes on the main street of the village to find someone who owned a motorcar for hire.

When Rutledge knocked at the door to rooms above a shop, he heard boots bounding down the stairs, and a young man with the bearing of a soldier opened the door to him.

"Need transport, do you? I'm going to need a sign made. You're the third person this week who came knocking. Word does get about." He was dark, his face a weather-beaten red and his hands large and square. Rutledge was wondering where he'd got the money to buy a motorcar when he added cheekily, "You'll want to know if it's mine. It's his." He gestured up the stairs. "I was his batman in the war, and I take care of him still. He lets me use the motor to keep it running well. You can go up if you like. But he's been gassed. Talking is hard for him."

And now Rutledge could hear the harsh, rasping breath of burned-out lungs.

"That won't be necessary. I'm looking for someone. My cousin. I came to Fowey to spend a few days with her, but she moved on a fortnight ago, before she got my letter. It's still waiting on the desk in Reception, and she's elsewhere. Mr. Tolworthy is busy, and he sent me to you meanwhile. Miss Haverford."

"The pretty lady with all the luggage? I drove her to the train. She told me she was off to Plymouth, but she must have changed her mind, because she caught the train north instead. I was afraid she might not have understood the stationmaster—he's Cornish, and damned if I can understand him half the time. So I asked. She went to Bodmin, to change for Boscastle."

"Damn," Rutledge said under his breath, and it was heartfelt. How far could he follow this woman across Cornwall? Seeing the surprise on the driver's face, he went on, "I was just in Bodmin myself. We probably crossed paths without realizing it."

He was about to turn away, when another thought occurred to him. "Who else has come to hire a motorcar?"

"Two ladies wishing to be driven out in the countryside for a picnic. And an elderly gentleman wanting to be driven to his brother's house."

He thanked the young man and turned back toward the church. It was a warm climb for this time of year, back up to the hotel, but the sea lay at his feet, dazzlingly blue, and he could see the ferry leaving for Bodinnick across the way.

He told no one what he'd learned, shaking his head when Tolworthy asked if Maisy had been helpful.

"She did her best," he said, "but Miss Haverford was not one to talk, she said."

"Yes, that's a true description of her. Are you leaving us, now?"

"I'm afraid so."

Tolworthy nodded. "I hope you find her, and she's come to no harm. Do return, Mr. Rutledge, when you have time to enjoy the hotel and Fowey."

Rutledge drove up the steep little road leading out of town, and was soon on his way north once more. He debated with himself, and in the end, he decided to go on to Boscastle. It was not all that far from Padstow. But he found it interesting that Miss Haverford—or whatever her name truly was—would hop, skip, and jump across Cornwall, when it would seem wiser, if she was afraid, to go to Derby or Cheshire or even Kent.

Hamish said, "It's no' logic, it's safety. Who would think she stayed in Cornwall sae long, if she was afraid of being discovered?"

And what was she afraid of? Who hunted her—or to put it another way, who did she think hunted her?

But Harry Saunders had escorted her to church, and he was dead.

The vicar believed he knew who she was, and he had nearly died at someone's hands. Dunbar had rented the cottage to her, and he too had been murdered. The cottages themselves burned to the ground.

If his speculations were correct, there was someone who would not stop at murder to find her.

But what about Victoria Grenville and the charges against her and her friends? She could have nothing to do with these other events, not locked away in Padstow Place. Still, she had been close by when Harry Saunders's luck had run out and his dinghy had sunk.

Did that mean that she hadn't tried to kill Saunders? That it had all been an accident, as the four women tried to pull him aboard the rowing boat? Had Trevose lied? Or had he told the truth?

It would be necessary to confront her when he got back to the village.

It was late when he reached Wadebridge. Weary, hungry, and damp from a drizzling rain that had beset him some ten miles out, he stopped for a meal and found a room in a small inn. It was cramped, the wick on the lamp smoked, and the window refused to budge when he tried to open it. But he was too tired to care. He slept without dreams, for once, and in the morning, a gray, dismal beginning to the day, he set out for Boscastle.

It sat on the coast, a narrow inlet running in from the sea and protected by two stone arms. For years it was a haven for fishing boats, and for merchant ships bringing in coal and limestone, carrying away Cornish slate and any other cargo the locals wished to ship.

Buildings in local gray stone, sometimes brightly whitewashed, crowded down to the harbor, a pretty little town with a long history.

He drove down the road leading to the harbor, looking for a likely place where a woman like Miss Haverford might stay.

As he explored, Rutledge was acutely aware that he was close to the house on the cliff where Olivia Marlowe had lived and died. He fought against the memories, keeping his attention on the road. And then, far from the harbor, he saw a small sign advertising rooms and breakfast.

It was a low, pretty whitewashed house with vines over the door and a garden in front. Longer than it was tall, it boasted two doorways, one into a smaller section, the other part of the larger dwelling.

Rutledge stopped, pulling up in front of the house and getting out to walk to the main door.

He could see a curtain twitch in the smaller section, and he wondered if Margaret Haverford was peering out at him, wondering who the stranger in the motorcar might be—and if he represented a threat.

He lifted the knocker and let it fall against the plate. After a moment, a young woman opened the door to him. She was slim and pretty, blue eyes in a sun-browned face framed by fair hair fashionably styled.

"I saw your sign. I wondered if you had rooms for the night."

"I'm so sorry," she said with the slight hint of a Devon accent. "We're full up just now. My sister has come to stay with me for a bit. But I could recommend another house down the road."

He almost believed her. She appeared to be forthright and genuinely sorry she had nothing to offer him.

Instead of taking her at her word, he said, "I wonder if your sister's name is Haverford."

Her face changed. "I don't know who you are, but I can tell you my sister's name is not Haverford. Why you should think so is disturbing to me. Good day."

She was about to shut the door in his face, but he set his boot in the opening and reached into his pocket for his identification. Holding it out to her, he said, "I'm not a casual caller. My business with Miss Haverford has to do with her own safety."

"Anyone can forge such papers," she said coldly, barely looking at it.

"That's true. If you like, I'll stop in the village and find the constable there. He can vouch for me."

"He can vouch all he likes," she said. "He's no more acquainted with Inspectors from Scotland Yard than I am. Now remove your foot from my door and go away."

"I will, if you will answer my questions. I'm looking for a woman who had stayed in the Fowey Hotel, in Fowey, under the name of Margaret Haverford. I have reason to believe that that isn't her name. I also have reason to believe she's in danger. Mr. Dunbar, who owned the cottages outside of Padstow, has been beaten to death. The vicar in the village of Heyl, Mr. Toup, was set upon and was lucky to survive. Harry Saunders is dead as well. I can't protect her until I know her danger. I will leave now, and walk as far as the harbor. If the young woman I'm after is living in your house, she has already looked at me. She knows I'm a stranger. If she will come down to the harbor, or, if she still fears me, to the public inn I can see just above the harbor, I'll be inside waiting. If what I know can help protect her and she in turn can help me find a killer, I hope she will come down and speak to me."

With that he withdrew his boot, and before the door could close, he was already striding back to his motorcar.

He drove on to the harbor, and left his motorcar by one of the shops. For half an hour he walked down by the stables, as far as the first harbor wall, then retraced his steps, listening to the water by his side.

There was no young woman waiting for him.

He made his way to the inn, and found a quiet corner in the public room. It was dark, dark paneling and tables, lit only by a single shaft of sunlight coming in from the door.

Sitting down, he ordered a pint, and when it came, left it untouched. But he had paid for an hour at this table, and he was willing to wait.

Hamish, alive in his mind, gave him no peace. He tried to ignore the voice, forcing himself to relax and to expect nothing.

The hour was nearly up when he heard the outer door opening. A middle-aged man walked in with a white-and-brown-spotted terrier at his heels. He crossed to the bar, sat down in what must have been his accustomed place to the far right, and the dog waited until he was settled before leaping up to lie quietly in its master's lap.

The barkeep nodded to him and disappeared. A few minutes later he returned with a pasty on a white plate, and set it before the man, then drew him an ale.

The man began to eat, and the little dog never stirred.

"Anything wrong with your glass?" the barkeep asked, coming across to Rutledge.

"I wasn't thirsty after all," he said pleasantly, but reached for it.

The barkeep turned and walked away.

The outer door opened again, and this time the woman who owned the bed-and-breakfast walked in.

He was surprised to see her, but said nothing as she strode purposefully across the room and took the chair opposite him.

"Who are you? Really? Newspaper? Private detective?" She kept her voice low.

"I've told you. I'm from Scotland Yard. I have nothing to gain from coming here, and no one to report to except for Chief Superintendent Markham in London."

"There's no telephone in this village. There's no way I can find out if you're lying or not."

He took a deep breath. "I knew Olivia Marlowe." It was not quite the truth, but he thought, watching her, that the name meant something. "I investigated her death, and that of her brother, for Scotland Yard. You may remember the story. It was the summer after the war."

"Yes. Yes, I do."

"She was a great poet."

The woman said nothing. After a moment, she added, "The woman in my cottage is, in fact, my sister. She's not the person you're looking for. And you don't even have that woman's name right."

"It's the name she used in the Fowey Hotel up to a fortnight ago. I don't know what she called herself in Padstow. But I do know she's frightened."

"Why on earth should she be frightened?"

He shook his head. "I know only that she's hiding from something. Or someone. And she may well be in danger. Someone has killed Frank Dunbar and set up the circumstances for Harry Saunders's death. Someone nearly killed the vicar, Mr. Toup. And she had a connection with all three. I can't think of anyone else who does."

"Surely you don't believe *she's* a murderer!"

"Not at all. But she can probably tell me who the murderer is. I found you easily enough. If he does, then you too are in danger, and your sister with you. If he thinks you are keeping her from him, he will kill you as well. Who is he? A father? A lover? A husband? That's what I've worked out, sitting here."

He could watch her struggle with her own fears—that she would betray this woman—that she would be dragged deeper into her friend's troubles.

"She isn't here," she said again.

"What name was she using, if not Haverford? Dunbar, as he lay dying after that savage beating, tried to scratch her name in the muck of that filthy alley where he was cornered. He wrote the single word *warn* and then managed only an initial after it. I couldn't be sure what that initial was." He took a chance. "Neither could the policeman with me. But I believe it was an *E*."

He'd guessed wrong. The woman rose. "You're lying. She didn't use a name beginning with *E,* not in Padstow. I'm going to the police."

He rose with her. "Then I'll come with you. I have nothing to fear from the police." He tossed coins on the table beside his untouched glass, and followed her to the inn door. They went out into the sunlight blinking at its sharpness.

"If the name was not an *E,* it began with a *P,* or a *B,* or even an *F.*

But the maid in Fowey told me that the initial on the red leather case was an *E*."

She bit her lip at that. Walking briskly, she led him to the tiny police station. But the constable wasn't in. She backed out of the room, undecided, uncertain what to do now.

"You're going to have to trust someone. It might as well be the Yard. At least I can protect you."

Ignoring him, she walked away from the station, then suddenly swung around to face him. "All right. The man is—was—her husband. She's been granted a judicial separation. That means that he will have no contact with her whatsoever. They remain married in name only. There are no—rights—attached to that. He has refused to accept the judgment. He came back from the war a changed man. He abused her, he terrorized her, he accused her of having affairs and lovers while he was away. They married while he was on leave in 1916. A month before the Somme. She loved him, she prayed for him to return. When he did, some months later, she was appalled. Her uncle managed the separation early in 1918, but he couldn't protect her. No one could. For nearly two years, she's moved every few weeks, and if she's lucky, she can stay in one place for a month or more. But in the end she has to leave, before people begin asking questions, before they come too close, before he can find her again."

He listened to the ring of truth in this woman's voice. And it fit. Everything she told him fit.

"Has he killed before?"

"No—that's to say, I don't think so. But he has harmed others, trying to find her. And they have refused to press charges, because they're afraid she'll be forced to appear, to testify. And so she has avoided her friends, trusting to strangers instead. She stayed longest in Padstow, because she felt safe in that cottage. But he must have traced her there. If what you tell me is true."

"Why stay in Cornwall now, why not go somewhere else?"

"Padstow was as far away as she could get without leaving England. Fowey, because she didn't think he would believe she stayed in the Duchy. Here because she was exhausted and needed rest."

"He will find you."

"No, I don't believe he will. We went to school together, she and I. For five years, long ago. He would have no reason to know who I am or where I live now."

"I found you," he said again. "I found the Fowey Hotel, and then the maid who remembered that red leather case. Also the driver who took her to meet the train."

In exasperation, she said, "I've told her several times. She won't part with it. She absolutely refuses. It was her mother's case. Her name was Emily."

"What matters is, what are we to do now?" He kept his voice level, not pushing, merely asking.

"I expect I shall have to take you to see her." She looked away. "I don't trust you. I warned her not to speak to you."

He said nothing, leaving her to make up her mind.

After a moment, she said, "Oh, very well. This way."

They walked away from the village, up one of the valleys, the road twisting as it rose. A few minutes later she stopped in front of a small stone cottage, painted a pleasing yellow. It must, he thought, have only two rooms. The garden in front was dormant for the most part, but he could see the bare stalks of a climbing rose reaching up to travel across the doorway.

"My late husband left me this cottage. There's no way to trace it back to her. If anyone does track her here, I'll know where to look for the person who betrayed her." Her voice was fierce.

"You haven't told me your name."

"And I won't. Good day, Inspector. Don't bother to stop at the cottage to say good-bye." She strode off, head down, hands thrust in the pockets of her tweed jacket.

He could feel someone watching him from the little house. He stayed where he was, waiting, only moving to take off his hat, so that she could see him better. And finally the door opened. No one came out to welcome him, but he understood that it was an invitation to enter.

He had to duck his head under the lintel, and he found the tiny front room inside rather claustrophobic. There was a hearth, bare beams in the ceiling, and furnishings from another era. But it was a comfortable room, nonetheless.

Standing in the middle of it, her hands clasped together, was a slim dark woman whose worried eyes seemed to bore into him, as if trying to read the man before her.

Her voice when she spoke was low and husky. "Inspector Rutledge?"

He could understand, meeting her, why Harry Saunders had willingly escorted her wherever she needed to go, why the vicar protected her nearly at the cost of his life, and why Frank Dunbar had died for her.

"I'll be glad to show you my identification. I was sent to Cornwall—to Padstow—when Harry Saunders was injured in a boating accident. I learned of you quite by chance. Even then, I was more concerned about the inquiry into Saunders—"

She stopped him. "Is it true that Harry is dead?"

"I'm afraid so."

Moving for the first time, she gestured to a chair, then sat down in the only other one in the room. "How did he die?"

He told her.

"And finding the holes in the dinghy was your first connection with the cottages?"

"No. I came there to see where he kept the dinghy. I discovered the holes quite by accident."

"And Mr. Dunbar?"

"He was severely beaten in a dark, dingy alley. As he was dying, he tried to warn you." He told her what he'd seen.

"Bingham. That was the name I used in Padstow. Frances Bingham."

"And Haverford in Fowey." It wasn't a question.

"He hasn't come to Fowey?"

"Not yet."

"Well. I must leave here anyway." She turned her head toward the window. He thought he could see tears on her lashes. "I don't know where to go, that he can't find me." Turning back to Rutledge, she said, "I will write to the Fowey Hotel and give them a forwarding address. A false one, asking them to send on a glove I fear I left there. It might buy a little more time."

"He has killed one man, caused the death of another, and nearly killed a third. It's time to stop him, don't you think? Rather than run from him again?"

"You can't stop him," she said, sadness in her voice. "Even if you arrest him, he'll find a good lawyer and prove he was miles away at the time. He's a very clever man, Mr. Rutledge, and a well-connected one."

"I'm told you believed the war changed him."

She shook her head. "It's what I told the court. But there were—signs before that. Only I didn't realize it. I was glad when he went back to France. I'd rather hoped he'd be killed. So many men had been. Why not one more?"

There was a ruthlessness in her voice that stunned him. If she had felt so strongly, the wonder was that she hadn't tried to kill him herself.

As if to answer that question, she said, "I have grown hard, Mr. Rutledge. Out of fear and desperation. I keep a pistol now. It was given to me. If the time comes, I will use it. I couldn't have before. I believed him when he said it was all my fault. But that was never true, was it?" She bit her lower lip. "Harry Saunders was very kind to me. For no reason other than the fact that he was a nice man. The vicar tried to counsel me, because he felt I was sad. Mr. Dunbar's only sin was to buy food for me, so that I didn't have to go into Padstow quite so often. There have been others. In Devon, one man was found dead in a field. *His* sin was to allow me to use the Dower House for a time after the judicial separation was granted, and I was near collapse. And in Derby, it was a neighbor who wouldn't tell him where I'd gone from there. She didn't know, you see. I hadn't told her. He cut her throat and then ransacked the house, to make it appear to be a housebreaker caught in the act. And so I never confide in anyone now."

"It has to stop. You must know that."

"The only way is with a bullet. I'm sorry."

"And you'll hang for it. It's better my way."

"You don't *know* him," she said in exasperation. "You think he's like any other criminal, foolish enough to be caught and punished for his misdeeds."

"Then why did you agree to see me?"

"To learn if it was true about Harry and Mr. Dunbar and the vicar. Three more names on my conscience. Three more burdens to carry."

"But you keep running?"

"I'm still afraid of him. I haven't found the courage yet to face him. Even though I have that pistol."

"Then you're equally guilty with him. You could stop this. Now. If you will let me help."

She rose. "I'd rather hang. Then I'll know I'm safe forever."

He rose as well. "At least tell me your name."

She smiled for the first time. He saw the dimples then, and something of the beauty she had been before she married a killer. "And you will find him, and he'll kill you too. No, I think not."

"I don't believe he can kill me."

"Perhaps not, perhaps he'll choose someone you love instead."

"Was there someone you loved?"

"Someone I could have loved. Before he threw me down the stairs and I miscarried. In the doctor's surgery he swore to me that he was sorry. That he'd been so afraid that it was another man's child. That he was going back to France to die a hero, to show me how much he regretted hurting me. It would be his salvation. I think all he gained from war was learning better ways to kill."

He stopped at the door and reached into his pocket, drawing out the square of cloth he carried in his handkerchief.

"Is this scrap from a gown you owned? I found it in the sand by Harry Saunders's boat, along with one of the nails used to damage it."

He thought she was going to faint. As she leaned forward to see the bit of cloth better, she swayed, and put out a hand. He caught it and helped her back to her chair.

Concerned, he went out to the little addition on the rear of the cottage and drew a cup of water from the pump there, then brought it to her.

She was pale, her face drained of all color, her eyes stark in her face. Unable to hold the cup to her lips, she pushed it away, and he knelt beside her chair to hold it for her. She drank a little, and then sat up straighter.

"I told you he was cruel. That's been cut from the gown I was wearing when he shoved me down the stairs. I thought it had been burnt. I ordered my maid to burn it."

He had already folded the scrap away. But he thought she could still see it in her mind's eye.

When she spoke, her voice was a thread. "He left a bit of it in the house where my neighbor was killed. It was under her body. I was told later that the Derby police looked for the owner of that gown. And of course they never found her. He wanted me to *know* what he'd done."

Afraid to leave her alone, he sat with her for nearly half an hour. And then she seemed to rouse herself, and regain a little of the steel that had helped her survive.

"Thank you, Mr. Rutledge," she said in dismissal.

"Will you help me?"

"No."

"He may well find your friend. I did. Do you want her to die at his hand? And her sister with her?"

"He won't find her. I'll see to it. Thank you, Mr. Rutledge," she said again as she ushered him to the door, and then closed it behind him.

He stood for a moment by the steps, hoping she would change her mind. Even though he knew for a certainty that she wouldn't.

18

The drive back to Padstow didn't take very long. Rutledge spent most of it trying to work out a way to save Victoria Grenville and her friends. He had found no evidence to support the charge of murder against three of the accused. But there was no way around the murky issue of Victoria Grenville's behavior. How to separate the four cases, and convince Trevose, the Saunderses, and even Pendennis that the women should not be sent to trial together? That might well be the very best he could do.

Juries were not always predictable. Mr. and Mrs. Saunders were intransigent in their grief. Trevose was determined to make Mrs. Grenville suffer the loss of her daughter, and he didn't give a damn about the fact that his evidence might send all four to the gallows.

Then there was the murder of Frank Dunbar and the beating of the vicar. He could hardly tell the Yard that he'd found the answers by speaking to a woman whose name he didn't know and whose whereabouts were uncertain. Nor could he clear up the question of who damaged Saunders's boat without bringing her into the picture. And that was pressing.

The vicar, Mr. Toup, persisted in claiming that the only person he'd seen that morning was George St. Ives. But was his memory dependable?

Still, Mrs. Terlew had reported seeing St. Ives as well. And she was an independent witness. The only other possibility was that someone had used George St. Ives's known predilection for walking at night to disguise his own movements around the countryside. Hadn't Inspector Carstairs seen him in the vicinity of Padstow one night? He was easily recognizable from a distance, and people had grown accustomed to seeing him.

But how to prove that, without a name to put to the man behind the masquerade?

Sergeant Gibson could try to discover the identity of the mysterious woman's murdered neighbor. The question was, had "Miss Haverford" been using a false name at that time as well?

When he drove into the village, he found that the news of Dunbar's death and the burning of the cottages where he lived had already reached Heyl, and there was rampant speculation.

He listened to the talk in The Pilot, where he went to bespeak a late lunch, and gathered from what he heard that Padstow had put out no further information. It would have been impossible to stop the spread of such news, but Carstairs was doing his best to keep the inquiry close to his vest. Rutledge would have given much to go on to Padstow, but the less interest he appeared to show just now, the better.

He called first on the vicar. His bruises were fading but nearly as ugly as they'd been at the start. The yellowish-green and purple did nothing for his already sallow complexion, and his spirits were low. When Rutledge was ushered into the sickroom, his eyes were closed.

"I thought I'd find you upstairs in your own bed by now," Rutledge began briskly, sitting down where the vicar could see him more easily.

"It's the leg," he responded, a querulous note in his voice. "And I still have vicious headaches, even some dizziness. I'm not well enough to read."

"Have you remembered anything more about the morning you were attacked?"

"It's strange. I keep dreaming that the Padstow Hobby Horse attacked me. It comes running up and I fall and am trampled underfoot. Not the usual foolery with the maiden being drawn under his costume. It's me instead." He turned to look out the window. "I don't understand it."

The Padstow Hobby Horse was famous, part of the May Day festivities where the town was decorated with greenery and flowers, and a Maypole. The Horse was in fact a man in a garish, traditional horse head mask, whose hooped cape, draped in black cloth, snared young women passing by. Songs and drums and much laughter kept the day lively, and everyone came out to join in the excitement.

And Rutledge still carried the small square of cheap black cloth he'd found at the scene where the vicar had been attacked. The crude drawing of a horse's head in the sand by the Grenvilles' rowing boat was further proof. A taunt that a killer had not expected him to understand.

"Perhaps it's not so strange after all," he said quietly. "Perhaps it did attack you, or appear to. Perhaps the first thing you saw when you came up to the clearing where you were found was a Hobby Horse standing there waiting for you, his face hidden."

Restlessly the vicar shook his head. "No, no, I would remember that, surely."

"But you have. In your dreams." He waited. But Mr. Toup would have none of it.

"There's no Hobby Horse this time of year," he said. "It's in May, probably once a pagan feast. Why would there be a Hobby Horse in the wood, anyway? It's a Padstow festival."

He wouldn't be budged.

But Rutledge was fairly sure now that whoever had lain in wait, it wasn't George St. Ives. A nameless man had been there, and a coward as well, hiding behind the mask and cloak in case anyone else came along too soon.

Changing the subject, Rutledge said, "I found her. The young woman who lived in the cottages above Padstow."

Alarm spread across the vicar's tired face. "What have you done?" he demanded. "Dear God, Rutledge."

"It doesn't matter," he said, testing the waters. "She gave you a false name, and the hotel in Fowey another one. I could shout either of them from the rooftops, and it would do no harm. The address in London is false as well. But I have a feeling she might be at the bottom of what happened to you, as well as Dunbar's death, and the burning down of those cottages. Something is wrong, Toup. And *you* were wrong to protect her so vigorously when I asked about her."

"Dunbar is dead? But who would harm him—why burn the cottages? I don't understand."

"Her husband is driven by jealousy."

"Oh, I doubt that, Inspector. Her husband was a Naval officer, went down with his ship off the coast of Ireland. That's why she came to Cornwall, you know. She felt closer to him here. They never found his body. Her family wishes her to marry again, but she's put them off. It's too soon to think about another match, however fine it might be. I promised I'd keep her secret, if a young man came looking for her over the summer. Or even after it, for that matter. I felt it was wrong of them to push her into a loveless match before she was ready. I could see for myself the anxiety she suffered."

"Did Saunders know about her—er—past?"

"I doubt she told him very much. It would have been unwise for her to confide in him. Because he'd met her early on when he went to take out his dinghy, I asked him to escort her to Sunday services, and he agreed."

It was not the story she'd told the hotel manager in Fowey. Or what Rutledge had been told in Fowey. But perhaps it was one the vicar would have understood better, prompting him to offer his protection. This tall, gangly, awkward man would relish the role of her knight.

Still, Rutledge could hear Hamish in the back of his mind, casting doubt on all of it.

Persevering, he said, "But someone damaged that boat, in the hope that Saunders would drown at sea. We found the dinghy, and I've inspected it. She feels responsible for what happened to Saunders and to you, and to Dunbar as well. Despite what she told you, there's a husband, Vicar, who is searching for her. And he will have her back at any price."

"Did she tell you this?" He turned away again, his gaze on the world outside his window. "No, you must have it wrong. It's the suitor who is persistent."

Rutledge hesitated, unwilling to disillusion Toup, but recognizing that he had no choice.

"I'm afraid the husband is very much alive. There's a judicial separation: he has no rights, and he's refusing to accept the court's decision."

"Oh, dear. Now I don't know what to think. I was so certain . . . Was I so easily taken in? I find that hard to believe."

"She told the hotel manager in Fowey that she was mourning her parents' death from the Spanish flu."

They could hear voices in the passage, someone coming into the vicarage, speaking to Mrs. Daniels, the nurse.

"I'm sorry," the vicar said quickly, his gaze on the door. "I can't bear to think of that young woman as a liar. But can you be so sure that she hasn't lied to you as well? About this husband of hers?"

It was Rutledge's turn to feel an upsurge of doubt. He *had* believed the woman. She had been believable, and her friend as well. But Toup had also believed her—and the hotel manager.

"Why did you say that?" He'd risen and was moving toward the door, prepared to block anyone from coming in before he had finished his conversation with Toup. It was too important, it couldn't be put off until another time.

The vicar said, his eyes on Rutledge's face now, "I don't know. Except that you have made me very uneasy. And if it's true, how did I become so gullible? How did you? And what does this have to say about my beating, and that boat, and poor Mr. Dunbar?"

"I don't know. God help me, I don't know."

There was a tap on the door at his back. Rutledge hesitated and then opened it. A parishioner looked in, bearing a plate of biscuits and jam.

"Think about it," Toup said, and forced himself to smile in welcome as he turned to his visitor.

More shaken than he was willing to admit, Rutledge left the vicarage and cursed the village for having no telephone, and Padstow as well for having only a telegraph, with a prying man in charge of it.

He had never felt the need of the resources of the Yard more.

But there was nowhere to turn.

Reaching the landing, he walked down to stare at the water, his mind in Boscastle, reliving his conversation with the young woman.

He had met pathological liars before, but few of them were that glib, finding it that easy to prevaricate with such emotion and fear.

She *must* have told him the truth. But then, she was a practiced liar.

And so he was forced to doubt her. Judicial separations were hard to come by. But even if he asked Gibson to search out this case, he would have no name to give the sergeant.

There was nothing else to do but drive back to Boscastle. But he had a feeling that she had left there as soon as he was out of sight. And he had no hope of finding her now. Her friend would lie, would refuse to tell him who she was or where she had gone. The woman hadn't liked him to begin with.

Behind him he heard Constable Pendennis's voice speaking to someone, and he knew then that going back to Boscastle was out of the question. His task was here. Not in Boscastle or Fowey or London or any other place she might be.

He turned away from the water and took out his watch. Trevose would very likely be in from the fields in another hour.

Why had a man who was willing to dive into a cold river to save another man's life suddenly turned on the women who had apparently been struggling to do just that? At what point had he turned from rescuer to accuser? When he first saw the rowboat? Or when he recognized it as the one belonging to Padstow Place? Or in the crowded rowboat when he'd taken in the situation?

Rutledge wondered if Trevose himself could answer the questions. But there must have been a moment of decision, unconscious perhaps, when he realized that he had an opportunity for vengeance: Victoria Grenville for his brother. Certainly he had been steadfast ever since in his accusations. He hadn't relented, and he had shown no mercy toward Kate and the other two women.

Rutledge had intended to drive out to the Trevose farm and wait. But he changed his mind and went to Padstow Place instead. One more conversation with Kate, he told himself, and he would be better armed to deal with Trevose.

There was just time, if he hurried.

Kate, sensible, steadfast, logical. So unlike the mercurial Jean. He wished he could tell her about this woman and listen to what she had to say. Another woman's point of view. Somehow he felt that she would have an answer. And at the moment, he didn't. But that would not be fair to Kate.

He drove out to the house, and his patience was tried as the maid who came to the door went in search of Grenville to gain his permission for Rutledge to speak to Kate.

When at last he was taken back to the study, he waited again as she was summoned.

Kate Gordon walked into the room with an anxious expression on her face.

"I thought," she began lightly, to hide it, "that perhaps you'd forsaken us."

Rutledge smiled and led her to a chair by the windows, as far as he could manage from the door and prying ears.

"Far from it," he began, with a lightness of his own, even though he didn't feel it. "I've been busy. But I must talk to you, Kate. And I must have straight answers, if I'm to do anything about this muddle."

"You know you can trust me," she said. "I thought you always had."

"Yes, well. There has been a different turn of events, Kate. And once more it must stay between the two of us." He dropped his voice. "Has anyone told you that Mr. Toup, the vicar, was set upon when he was on his way to answer a summons from what he believed to be an ill parishioner?"

"Gentle God," she said softly. "The vicar? No. Nothing has been said to us. But who could have done such a thing?" And then it struck her. "You aren't saying that this is somehow connected with us?" She shook her head. "He had nothing to do with the boat. He wasn't even there." Watching Rutledge's face, she added quickly, "Was he there?"

"He wasn't. But there's more, Kate. Did you know that Saunders kept his boat near several cottages that were for let during the summer? He knew the place well, and it was ideal for him, instead of the busy harbor in Padstow. There was a young woman who had taken one of the cottages. And a Mr. Dunbar, who lived in one of them, appears to have owned them."

She shook her head. "I had no idea where he kept the dinghy. Victoria said something to me about a private landing. Like the Grenvilles'."

So Victoria Grenville had known that. One more strike against her. Aloud, Rutledge replied, "The dinghy was interfered with, Kate. By someone who knew where to find it. And Dunbar has been beaten to death, the cottages burned to the ground."

There was fright in her eyes. "I don't understand. Surely the police don't think that one of us—Ian, we've been locked up here since that Saturday evening when we left the police station. I'd swear that none of us has left the house. You can ask the Grenvilles, their staff."

"This is why I've been away. Trying to track down who's behind it. I'm fairly certain now it's a different inquiry altogether, but until I could prove that, there was a strong possibility that George St. Ives was somehow responsible. Trying to throw doubt on the charge against his sister and Victoria."

She was silent for a moment. "I don't know George St. Ives. But I find it hard to believe that he would do such a thing—according to Elaine he almost never goes out. And to attack the vicar? What good would it have done if he'd killed Mr. Toup?"

"If I'm right about what I've learned, he had no reason at all."

She said, "We live with silence. Mr. Grenville is careful not to overstep his role as our guardian. I hardly see my friends. My father is very angry, and he refuses to let my mother come to Cornwall. She feels Victoria ought to stand up and confess, clearing our good names at the same time. She believes it's the only answer, that Victoria owes it to us. You've been my only anchor through this."

He was touched by her words. "The problem is, there isn't a shred of evidence to support a charge of murder against three of you. But Mr. and Mrs. Saunders have joined Trevose in his call for a trial. And then you're in the hands of a local jury, which is uncertain at best. It may come to that, but I'd much rather it didn't. As for Victoria, she may not stand up and confess because she sincerely believes she has done nothing wrong."

"Ian . . ." She hesitated. "I have spent a good bit of time alone, thinking. It's worried me that Victoria was being so difficult that afternoon. I don't know why, really, we've never had the chance to talk about it. I don't want to believe she deliberately tried to harm Saunders. I don't think, to be honest, that she took his plight seriously until she saw us struggling to bring him into the boat. Perhaps that's why she belatedly thought about the oar, because for a moment or two, it looked as though Sara and I would be pulled into the water with Saunders. We couldn't have clung to him very much longer, and that's the truth. As it was, it took more strength than we realized we had to keep his head above water and his arms in our grasp. The thing was, we'd lost so many friends in the war, sometimes very quickly, often terribly slowly. The thought of letting go, of watching him drift away and drown, was insupportable. We were desperate to save him. At any price. Sometimes I've wondered if she dropped that oar to make us let him go, for our own sakes. Or if she was trying to put it in his hands, in order to save us. If he could just have held on to it, while we made for shallower water, we might have been all right. But he was too far gone. If we'd fallen overboard with all our petticoats and heavy autumn clothes, we very likely would have drowned too. Sara surely would have."

She looked away, fighting tears. After a moment, she went on. "If you ask, I expect all of us will admit to nightmares. Even Victoria. It was, actually, rather awful."

"I wish she had told me this at the start."

Kate shook her head. "I don't know that Victoria herself understands it. And there was no one from Scotland Yard present when we gave our first statements. We were surrounded by men, all talking at once, and the farmer was shouting murder, and we didn't know what was wrong with Harry, whether he would be all right. Someone thrust a pen into my hands, and gave me a sheet of paper, telling me to write down what had happened. I hardly knew myself."

A thought occurred to him. "Did you mention, in that first statement, that the dinghy had sunk in midriver?"

"Yes. But no one believed us. The farmer had told them we were pushing Harry Saunders out of the boat when first he saw us."

And when Inspector Barrington died, and no one knew if the Yard was going to send a new man to Cornwall, those statements disappeared, along with Barrington's notes.

He stared at Kate, hardly seeing her sitting there in front of him.

Bloody hell, he thought, realizing what must have happened. If those first statements were missing, no one would be able to say with any certainty that in them the four women had claimed the dinghy was sinking. It could be considered an afterthought, and a good prosecutor could very well have claimed they made it up later to save themselves. Even Pendennis had dragged his feet when ordered to bring in the salvage boat.

When Barrington collapsed, there must have been chaos in the inn dining room, and someone could have climbed the stairs, found Barrington's papers, and hidden them. Or taken them home to burn in the farmhouse hearth.

Trevose. He was the only person to have anything to gain by taking them.

He rose, had to stop himself from embracing Kate for her help.

"I must go. They'll be wondering why I have kept you so long."

Startled, she looked up at him. "Ian. Is everything all right?"

She knew him too well.

"Something has occurred to me. It might be important, it might not. But it's worth pursuing. Come on, we'll find that maid to see you safely upstairs again."

"You'll tell me, won't you, if it has helped?"

"I promise."

Rutledge was eager to be on his way, but he changed his mind at the last minute and asked to speak to Elaine St. Ives.

Waiting for her, he thought about what Kate had told him.

Hamish, in the back of his mind, was warning Rutledge that he must not weigh her words more heavily than those of the other three women.

"I haven't," he said under his breath, loud enough for Hamish to hear him. "But I know how to measure what she says against what I've learned. I can't believe she would lie to me."

"She was no' charged with murder before," the Scot said darkly. "In 1914."

And then Elaine was there, and he set aside the question he'd been about to ask her and instead said, in a voice that blended sympathy and knowledge, "Tell me what it was like during the war."

Surprised, she forgot her nervousness in remembering. "It was rather awful. We couldn't train as nurses, our parents forbade that. So we did what we could, what we were allowed to do. Mostly helping people cope. I didn't mind that. But it was hard, meeting the trains. The men going to France were often frightened, and trying valiantly not to let anyone know. Some of them were little more than boys, they'd never left their village before, and here they were on their way to war in a foreign country where no one even spoke English. We gave them tea and buns, and talked to them, jollying them a bit, asking if they had a sweetheart at home, telling them we thought they were the bravest of the brave."

Tears filled her eyes. And Rutledge thought, she should never have been allowed to do what she had done at the trains. It had taken too much of a toll on a sensitive and kindhearted nature.

"That was bad enough. The trains of the wounded were worse. Shattered bodies, burned or broken or gassed, bloody bandages, so much pain. And we smiled and welcomed them to London, telling them they'd be all right now. I lit cigarettes for some and put them in their mouths. I just held the hands of others. Or told them England would take great care of them. But I came to recognize the shadow of death. Some of them would never be all right. And sometimes when I was tired, I'd see George lying there, or Stephen. I was almost glad when I was told Stephen was dead, had died quickly, without pain. It was a relief. Such a relief."

Rutledge had written many such letters to the families of the dead, and it was a stock phrase, used over and over again by all the officers: *Your son—brother—husband died quickly, without pain, and his final thoughts were of you. He was a brave man, a good soldier, and I was proud to have been his commanding officer . . .*

Even when that man had died screaming in agony, cursing the war and the Germans. A kind lie, a last service for the dead.

And those at home had believed the kind lie, because they needed to.

"Tell me about Stephen Grenville."

"He and Victoria were very close. Just as George and I were. I think sometimes she wished it had been Stephen who'd been sent to America. I think she resented the fact that Harry had been safe and never fired his revolver at anyone."

"Was that why she didn't encourage his interest in her?"

"I don't know. She told me once even a conscientious objector did help win the war. He served in a hospital or drove an ambulance or was a medic. Something that didn't require him to shoot anyone."

"Do you think Victoria resented his posting to Washington enough to wish Saunders dead?"

Startled, Elaine said, "Oh—no—no, of course not. I meant only that having lost her brother, she probably couldn't bring herself to care about someone like Harry. I didn't see anything wrong with what he'd done—someone had to go to Washington, to convince the Americans to come into the war. It was important. Think what would have happened if they hadn't come in at all."

"Did Harry care for her?"

She gave him a wry smile. "In a village like ours, or even in Padstow, there aren't many choices for people like us. We're allowed to be friends with the vicar's daughter, the doctor's daughter, the squire's daughter. But Mr. Toup and Dr. Carrick didn't have daughters. I think that's why Victoria and Stephen and George and I were so close. As for poor Harry, there was no one. He could fish and sail with our brothers, but he was the banker's son, and not considered a suitable match for us. And I expect his father felt the same way, that he wished his son to marry well, in his own circle. But I don't think Harry was above teasing Victoria a bit."

It was said without arrogance or condescension. It was merely the quiet assurance of someone who had grown up in a house like Padstow Place and had been taught from the nursery on what was expected of her and the name she bore.

"Did you like Harry?"

"Of course I did. He was very nice."

It was time to ask the question that mattered. "Do you think Trevose—the farmer—did all he could for Saunders, once he got him into the boat?"

She shook her head. "I don't know. It happened so fast, everything at once, and there were Sara and Kate and the farmer floundering in the bottom of the boat, thrown there in a heap as Harry was pulled from the water. Someone kicked me in the shins as I tried to find the oars, and then someone stepped hard on my foot, and my hand got caught against a thwart. I could see that Harry was on the bottom, and I was afraid he couldn't breathe. We were rocking wildly all that time, and then Kate and Sara righted themselves somehow. But the farmer did try to get the water out of him. I do remember that."

"And it was successful?"

"Harry coughed a bit, as I remember. And that's when they turned him over, and I could see the wound in his head. Then I remembered Victoria and the oar. But she was trying to help, to give him something to hold on to. Kate and Sara would never have got him into the boat. He was too heavy, with all those wet clothes."

The maid who came to escort Elaine St. Ives back to her room was surprised when he asked to speak to Victoria's mother.

If Trevose had watched her carefully over the years, she must surely have watched him equally closely.

Mrs. Grenville was showing the stress of recent events. There were dark smudges under her eyes, and he guessed she must be having difficulty sleeping.

"I hope you've come to bring me good news," she said, trying to smile.

He said, "I'm sorry, I only have more questions. For instance, I would like to know if Trevose ever had difficulties with the elder Saunders. At the bank, perhaps?"

"I have no idea," she said. "You must ask Mr. Saunders, I think."

"It's understandable, but Harry Saunders's parents aren't speaking to the police at the moment," he replied wryly.

"Then I don't know where to tell you to turn. If a matter came to the attention of the magistrate, then my husband might be able to tell you."

But Rutledge had no intention of speaking to her husband about Trevose.

He thanked her and left the house, driving on to the Trevose farm.

The farmer hadn't come in, he was told by the housekeeper, Bronwyn, and she was holding back his dinner for him.

"It's you I've come to see," he told her, and watched the morose expression on her face change to one of curiosity and then dark suspicion.

"I have nothing to say to you."

"I've heard rumors in The Pilot about Trevose's dealings with the elder Saunders at the bank. I've come to give you a chance to refute them."

"Here. I don't know his business. It's not my place."

"You've heard him pace the floor and swear at the bank. It must have been difficult to get credit after the war. And Saunders doesn't strike me as a kind man. He knows the rules, he doesn't offer any respite over monies due."

"And that's the truth of it," she said, suddenly angry. "The sowing hadn't been done nor the sheep shorn. And there he was, knocking on the door, wanting his money. It'ud been a bad year for everyone, but the well was drying up and we couldn't pay to dig another one. And then the well had water again. Just after he saw the piskey."

With an effort of will, he managed to keep himself from reacting as her words registered. He said, "A piskey?" And made it sound as if he were amused.

"Don't make light of it," she scolded. "Trevose saw him, and the dog never growled. Next morning there was water enough to draw up. After that we got the seeds in and it was warm enough to shear."

"When was this?

"During the war. 'Seventeen, it was," she retorted. "Didn't I just tell you so?"

But she hadn't. For many people like Bronwyn, time was not marked off in numbers on a calendar but by events. The day the cow went dry, the day the rains spoiled the hay, the day the baby died . . .

But the spring of 1917 was too early. Rutledge had hoped for a more recent sighting.

He was about to thank her when she said, "And the piskey was there again."

"The same one?"

"That's daft, who can tell one piskey from another? It was the night before poor Mr. Saunders was pulled into the boat. Trevose said it was a sign. He is always one for signs."

"What sort of sign?"

"How would I know? He did say the piskey was too tall. But he was in no mood to quarrel over that."

Had someone been walking through the farm that night? *Too tall for a piskey . . .*

"Perhaps he mistook George St. Ives, wandering about in the dark, for one. I'm told he sometimes does take to the fields."

"I've seen St. Ives walking about. Face like a prune. Enough to sour the cow's milk. He didn't think I saw him, but I did. Trevose had told me he walked sometimes. You wouldn't mistake him for a piskey, would you? Not the way *he* walked."

Rutledge wasn't entirely certain if he could tell a piskey from a person. And he wasn't certain Trevose, accustomed to the superstitions of his Cornish upbringing, could tell the difference either.

But the question was, where had this "piskey" been going?

He all but forced his way into the Saunders home, setting aside the maid who had attempted to turn him away.

They were just sitting down to their dinner when he called, and turned on him as if he himself had killed their son, demanding that he leave the house at once.

Rutledge stood his ground.

"It's urgent, sir, or I would not have presumed to disturb you. How much does the farmer Trevose owe your bank?"

"It's confidential business in the first place, and I will not deign to answer you when I've already asked you to leave."

"I am sure London will provide me with a court order to examine the bank's books, and give me someone trained in doing just that. If I must turn to them."

Saunders glanced at his wife. "If you will forgive me, my dear, I will answer his question and we will be rid of him."

Tight-lipped with fury, she nodded. "This is a house of mourning. He should not be here. Give him what he wants," she went on after a moment, "and let's be done with it."

Saunders turned back to Rutledge. "I can't give you the exact sum. I don't carry such numbers around in my head. It's what I employ clerks to attend to. But he has had to mortgage his land. It's not the best land in the parish to begin with. Even so, one man can't farm there alone. And the men who worked for him left in 1915 to fight the Germans. It's a common story, I'm sorry to say. And the men haven't come home, have they?"

"Sadly, no."

"I have not foreclosed. But we have had to badger him for what payments he can make. A bank can be a charitable institution only so far. Or it too is finished."

"Thank you, sir. I will leave you to your dinner." Rutledge nodded to Mrs. Saunders, and turned to go.

Saunders had the last word. "I shall report this intrusion, nevertheless. It was uncalled for."

From the doorway, Rutledge said only, "You are required to help the police in their inquiries, and it is your son, after all, whose death we are investigating."

"Then take those murderers to Bodmin Gaol. Then I will speak to you." He turned his back on Rutledge and sat down at his table.

But Rutledge had got what he came for.

19

Rutledge ate a late dinner and went to bed. It was already past ten. He would have to speak to Trevose in the morning.

He seldom slept deeply since the war, although it was often only in sleep that he could escape Hamish's voice and the reminders of the war that it brought with it.

And so sometime after three in the morning, Rutledge awoke with a start.

He couldn't have said what it was that had brought him out of his sleep that abruptly. The inn was quiet around him, and the night outside his windows was quiet as well. He lay listening, almost certain he could hear the river as the tide turned to run out.

Hamish, lying in wait, was there in the darkness, the soft Scots voice low as it repeated his own doubts and worries in his ear. Try as he would, Rutledge couldn't shake it off and return to the haven of sleep.

Finally, he got up and dressed, then quietly let himself out of the inn to go and sit on the bench by the landing. There was a chill in the air, and he lifted his coat collar against it, crossing his arms. In the distance he could have sworn he heard rowlocks, but the moon had set and the ambient starlight showed him nothing, even though he looked upstream and then down.

Hamish, whose hearing was even more acute, said, "By yon ither landing."

Where the Padstow Place rowboat was kept? The man guarding it had been withdrawn long since . . .

He ran for his motorcar and cranked it, got in, and drove toward the landing. Unable to see the terrain, he left the motorcar close by the road and went in on foot, his torch in his hand.

By the time he reached the landing, the rowboat was drawn up onshore, where it was always kept.

But in the light of the torch, he could see that the hull was still wet, water dripping into the sand along the gunwales.

Someone had taken it out, and Rutledge would have given much to know who it was and where he had been.

"Upstream," Hamish said. "Where yon houses overlook the water."

George St. Ives, even though he was forbidden to go out on the water? It was said he loved the river . . .

Although Rutledge cast about for footprints, the loose sand refused to give up its secrets. In the end he walked back to the motorcar.

The steering wheel was wet, when he touched it after turning the crank. He looked down at his hands, feeling the moisture there, and then he reached for the torch and shone it in every direction. But no one was hiding in the rough grass or the low scrub that bordered the track just here. Turning the motorcar, he drove fast toward the gates of the St. Ives house, but he met no one on the road.

Nor was there any sign of life on his way back to the inn, except for a hare crossing in the glare of his headlamps.

He put the motorcar back where he kept it in the inn yard, and went up to his room. He didn't like what had just happened. And Hamish, in the back of his mind, had much to say about it as well.

After lying awake until dawn, and then waiting another hour until the inn woke up and he could smell rashers of bacon frying, he went down to breakfast.

The question on his mind this morning was whether he should take Constable Pendennis with him as a witness when he went to see Trevose. It would be expedient, but he rather thought the farmer would have little to say to him with a witness present. In the end, he went alone.

Trevose was in the little shed to one side of the house, the one with the cracked window glass, sharpening tools on a wheel he ran with a foot pedal. Rutledge could hear the high-pitched squeal of metal. Following the sound, he found his quarry before Bronwyn had spotted him in the yard.

Standing in the shed doorway, he watched Trevose putting a fine edge on a scythe, but the dog at the man's feet got up and stared at him. This caught Trevose's attention, and he took his foot off the pedal, looking around.

He must have expected Bronwyn, for his expression was impatient as he turned. Then, seeing who was there at the shed door, Trevose set the scythe aside and rose slowly.

"Looking for me?" he asked.

"I was."

"You came questioning my housekeeper last night."

"Did she tell you? I'm not surprised." Rutledge stepped away from the door, so that Trevose could move outside. The shed was filled with tools that would make excellent weapons, and he didn't relish fighting off the dog and a hand scythe or hammer.

Trevose walked into the yard and stretched. "What's brought you here today? Have you come to tell me those murderers are going to trial at long last?" His tone was sarcastic. "You stick together, your sort. I should have known."

"Actually, I'm prepared to report that they should be tried."

Trevose stared at him. "Are you now?"

"I've been busy searching out the truth, and I think I've found it finally." Over Trevose's shoulder he could see Bronwyn at one of the house windows, the white lace curtain pushed aside so that she could watch. "The fathers of the accused have sent for lawyers to handle the matter. London men, all of them. They won't know much about the ways of Cornwall, but they are well trained in the law. It should be a short trial."

"There was no truth to search out. I saw what was happening. I told everyone at the landing as soon as we were in shouting distance. Attempted murder," he said with satisfaction. "Clear as the nose on your face."

Rutledge smiled. "Yes, it probably was attempted murder. The report will state the facts. That there is no motive I can uncover for those four women to kill Harry Saunders." He watched the other man's smile change to a look of uncertainty.

"When they put me in the box, I shall make it clear enough."

"There's George St. Ives, you see. His sister and her friends rowed up as far as the St. Ives house to wave to him on the terrace. And it was quite obvious that Harry Saunders wasn't with them at that stage. Meanwhile, we've recovered the dinghy just where the accused told us it ought to be. At this point it will be equally obvious that Saunders was in the water and the women went down to rescue him."

"It changes nothing," Trevose said. "I saw what I saw."

"I think that's true. You saw an opportunity. Here was Harry Saunders floundering about in the water, and two of the women were trying get him aboard. Only they weren't strong enough to manage it. So you went out to help them, and between you and Miss Gordon and Miss Langley, you got him into the boat. That's when you saw to it that in the commotion, Harry's head was banged against one of the thwarts. Hard enough to knock him out. And then you proceeded to revive him. That's when you told the women in the boat that they had attempted to kill him."

"Not a word of that is true."

"But I think I can persuade the lawyers from London that you saw a chance for a little revenge. Against Mrs. Grenville and against Saunders's father. Mrs. Grenville was never tried for your brother's death, but you could accuse her daughter of the same crime. Rather a poetic justice, that. And by harming Saunders, even though you didn't realize he would die, you appeared to be his savior, which would put you in his father's good graces when you next failed to make a payment on your mortgage."

Trevose's eyes narrowed. "You're lying. Every step of the way, you're lying."

"The shoe is on the other foot. If I were you, I would begin to worry about perjury. If you're sent to Bodmin gaol for perjury, who will care for this farm through the winter? I'm not a justice, I don't know precisely how long you will be clapped up in prison. He very likely will take into account those stolen interviews in deciding your sentence. Quick thinking on your part, I grant you that. I expect they were lying there on the table beside Inspector Barrington's bed, in plain sight and tempting. You'd been wondering, hadn't you, how likely he was to take your word against that of Grenville's daughter, and so far, Saunders hadn't been able to talk to the police. But then Barrington's belongings were packed away, and you couldn't very well return the papers at that stage. What happened to them? I expect you burned them."

Almost at once, Rutledge could see that he'd hit his mark.

"Get off my land," Trevose said, his voice dropping as he made his threat. "Come again and you'll have a nasty accident. Farmyards are dangerous places." Beside him, the dog growled in its throat. "See, she knows what I'm saying. Whatever's left of you can be plowed under, come spring."

Rutledge stood there and laughed. "Threatening the police, are you? I'd as soon have a bruise or two to back up my account."

He thought for a second he'd pressed the man too far. But Bronwyn was watching, and he wasn't sure just how far Trevose could trust her, if he decided to act.

Rutledge silently counted to ten, then turned away.

"Think about it, Trevose," he said over his shoulder as he walked back to the motorcar. "You'd have been all right, you know, if you'd only accused Miss Grenville. It might have worked, sad to say. But it's too late. You were greedy and chose to implicate all four of those women. Their parents will see to it that you are punished for that."

He had left the motorcar running, and he got behind the wheel, looking back at Trevose. "A few days ago, I wouldn't have given the accused a chance in hell of being cleared. Now I'm certain it will happen."

And he drove away.

Hamish said, as Rutledge made his way down the rutted, muddy lane that ran from the house, "And who'll watch your back, when you walk abroad at night?"

It didn't matter. He'd given Trevose something to consider.

If the man had told the truth as he had witnessed it, he would go straight to Constable Pendennis, or even, if he was angry enough, to Inspector Carstairs, and report what Rutledge had done.

And if the man had twisted the truth to suit himself, Hamish was right. Rutledge could expect Trevose to be there one dark night when no one else was about.

The telegram was waiting for him when he got back to the inn.

It had been brought over from Padstow shortly after he'd left.

He looked first at the sender, expecting it was the Yard wanting a report. But it was a name he didn't know: S. Browning.

He must have followed you. He beat them, they are in Dr. Learner's surgery, Bodmin. If you come, I will accept any help gratefully.

It was signed *Margaret Haverford.*

The name she had used in Fowey. A name the gossiping Padstow telegrapher couldn't have recognized.

He hadn't been followed. Rutledge was certain of that. But he had told her: *If I can find you, so can he.* She hadn't believed him.

He went back to the motorcar and set out for Bodmin.

When he reached the surgery in a trim house not far off the High Street, Rutledge was shown not to the reception room for patients but into a sitting room in the house itself.

The woman whose real name he still didn't know sprang up from her chair as the door opened, and then relaxed a little.

"Thank God!" she said, and sat down again, rather heavily. "Every time that door opens, I'm afraid."

"How are your friends?"

"The doctor won't let me see them. I found someone to drive their motorcar and brought them here myself. There was so much blood—I hardly recognized them. It was awful."

She was drawn, and he thought she had gone without sleep since the attack had occurred. The smudges beneath her eyes looked more like bruises, and the whites were bloodshot. She kept her arms folded close to her body, as if she felt cold, although the room was fairly warm from the fire on the hearth.

"Tell me what happened."

"It was in the night—I think it was last night, I've lost track of time—I couldn't sleep and I went for a walk." She shuddered. "I could see Ronnie's cottage from the road, and the lamps were still lit. I thought perhaps they'd found it hard to sleep as well. Your visit had unsettled all of us. I went toward the cottage, thinking we might have tea together. But the door was half-open, and that frightened me. I didn't go directly to it, but to one of the windows. I couldn't see anything, and I tried another. That's when I saw Ronnie's feet. Veronica. She was still wearing her street shoes. And the room looked as if it had been ransacked. I dared not go in alone, I was afraid he might still be there. I woke up the constable, and he came with me." She stopped and swallowed hard. "It was so ugly. Blood everywhere, furniture overturned, Ronnie lying there, crumpled and hardly breathing, and Patricia hanging from her bonds where she sat in a chair, her clothes black with blood, her face so bruised, one arm dangling as if it were broken. Ronnie looked as if she'd been struck over and over again. *And they hadn't told him.* That was the worst possible part—they had not told him." She couldn't cry. She was beyond the comfort of tears. She stared at Rutledge, not seeing him, remembering that room and what she'd walked into.

"I have to ask. Are you sure it was your husband?"

"I couldn't ask—I don't think they were conscious. They whimpered all the way to Bodmin. With every movement of the motorcar. And at one point, Ronnie said, 'No, don't hurt me any more, Will. She hasn't told me.'" The woman's voice was a mere whisper as she finished her account, her gaze pleading with him to understand what they had endured. "William. My husband's name."

"What about the police?"

"I have asked the doctor to wait until they are able to talk. And then I am away. Dr. Learner only knows that they were attacked. Not by whom or why."

"That's foolish. Let the police in Bodmin handle this."

"I can't. I tell you they're no match for him. I'll be dragged into court. And who knows what will happen? I'll be blamed. Or they will be. He won't be caught, I tell you. He hasn't been caught."

He swore under his breath. She was right in some respects. But it couldn't go on. It had cost too much already.

"I want your name—your real name. Or I can do nothing for you."

"Alexandra Worth."

Rutledge went back to the surgery, found Learner working with his patients, and introduced himself.

"Yes, my nurse told me you were here. She's under orders not to admit anyone she doesn't know."

"This happened last night?"

The doctor nodded. "I gave Mrs. Haverford a sedative. She slept until just before you came but I don't think it did her much good. See for yourself why she can't rest."

He gestured to the two women who shared the small room, their cots almost side by side. They had been severely beaten. One of them, the sister he'd never seen, had a bandaged arm, and her head was bound as well, reaching down across her nose, although her swollen eyes were visible.

"A loose flap of scalp. A broken nose, broken arm. The other one is badly concussed, internal injuries including a broken rib or two, a broken hand, several teeth loose." His voice changed from that of the medical man reporting what he'd done. He said with anger, "I have seldom seen a man beaten this badly. Whoever did this is a monster, in my humble opinion."

"I have no doubt that he is. Will they be all right?"

"Yes. With time. The bruises will heal. The bones will knit. They'll be all right, no lasting damage. At least not physically. Emotionally? Who can say?"

Rutledge looked at the still forms on the beds. They were not large women; they would have been easily battered to death. It would be a long time before the emotional wounds healed. If ever.

"The odd thing," Dr. Learner added, "I found a scrap of cloth in the elder sister's mouth. It's a wonder she didn't choke on it."

He reached up on a shelf and brought down a small dish. In it was a bit of muslin, bloodstained but recognizable. Rutledge had a similar scrap in his handkerchief.

"His calling card. His way of letting us know that he did this. It must be turned over to the police. There has been a pattern of use, you see. It could damn him."

"Vicious brute," he said harshly. "I'll have it put in a bit of gauze for you."

"Yes. I think it best that I take Mrs. Haverford away from here. For her safety. Will these two be safe in your care? I don't think he'll come back to finish this. But he may come looking for *her*."

"But why has he done this? She won't tell me."

"He's her husband. There's a judicial separation. He's not having it."

"I hope he rots in hell."

"If I can find him, he will hang."

"Good. Let her say good-bye to her friends. They're unconscious, but I think sometimes a familiar voice gets through."

"I'll bring her in."

"You will let me know what happens?"

"Be sure of that."

Learner nodded and went back to bathing Veronica's face.

It took several minutes for Mrs. Worth to say good-bye. She was even paler as she came out of the little room. Rutledge said abruptly, "Have you eaten anything at all?"

"I can't swallow food. It won't stay down. I'll be all right." She preceded him out the door, and down the walk to the motorcar. When they were out of earshot of the house, she asked quietly, "Where are you taking me?"

"I've been debating that. You must leave Cornwall. You can no longer hide here."

"No. I won't run anymore."

"Nevertheless. I'm sending you to London." He couldn't ask his sister to take Mrs. Worth in, not after what had been done to the other two women. But he thought Chief Inspector Cummins might give her shelter.

"No." She spoke with a determination he had seen once before. "This must end. If I'd had my revolver when I reached the cottage, I'd have gone inside and shot him dead. But I didn't have it. I was careless, you see, I thought in the middle of the night there in Boscastle, there was no *need*. I should have known you were followed." There was accusation in her voice now.

"I was not. But the driver who took you to the station worried about you and watched to see which train you took. It wasn't to Plymouth, he said. It was to Boscastle."

"I thought he'd gone, that he'd left the station."

"And so he had. But he could see the platform. And he knew which trains came in that morning."

"I thought I was safe in Padstow, I thought I could move safely to Fowey. But there were too many people in the hotel, even at this time of year. I was afraid someone might recognize me. And when I feel the anxiety building again, I run." As he finished turning the crank and was preparing to drive away, she added, "There's Scotland, of course. But people would know I was a stranger, as soon as I spoke. At least Cornwall is accustomed to visitors; they make nothing of a London accent."

He was heading for the railway station, but she put a hand on his arm. "No. I tell you, I can't get on that train. And I have nothing, nothing but the clothes on my back. I can hardly sit there looking like this."

She opened her arms wide, and he could see that her sleeves and across her waist, the fabric was stiff with dried blood. She had kept her arms folded in the surgery. "Dr. Learner's nurse offered me something to wear, but sadly her clothes didn't fit. And I dared not go back to Boscastle."

Rutledge weighed the risks, and then made a decision. He turned away from the railway station, although he could hear the whistle of an approaching train.

"There's one place I can put you for the moment. This isn't the only inquiry I'm involved with, but it's fast becoming the most pressing."

"Where?"

"I won't tell you. I won't mention this to anyone. And you will not be able to."

She was wearing a hat, one not well suited to her, but he thought it must have come from the cottage where the sisters lived, caught up before the motorcar set out for Bodmin and the doctor's surgery.

Rutledge pulled to the verge and took a clean handkerchief. Folding it carefully, he turned to the woman beside him.

"No—" she began, and put up her hands to stop him.

"You must. If I'm the only person who knows where you are, you'll be safer."

They argued, but in the end, she allowed him to blindfold her and then pull her hat down closer to her face to conceal it from passersby.

"I'm frightened," she said.

"There's no need to be." He cast an eye toward the sky. In another two hours dusk would fall.

She couldn't see where he was driving. He found one of the tracks out onto the moor, and after traveling a little distance down it, he pulled off into a small space where he could turn the bonnet back the way they'd come. And then he shut off the motor.

"You've stopped," she said accusingly.

"Not for long, I promise you. There's a rug in the boot if you're cold. I want to be sure no one followed us."

"Oh."

He went around to take out the rug, and gently set it across her lap.

"Can I remove the blindfold?"

"Yes. For a little while."

She lifted it and took a deep breath, as if it had covered her face and she could breathe now. "Where are we?" But he refused to answer. Leaning her head back against the frame of the door, she said, "I am so very tired."

"Then rest."

She finally fell asleep. He had no water or tea or food to offer her, but that was how it had to be. He got out and walked a little way, stretching his legs. Moors had always interested him. Secretive and wild, they were places where unexpected things could happen, and he smiled, remembering the Conan Doyle story he'd read as a boy. The Baskerville Hound had fascinated him. It had been his earliest introduction to superstition, and he'd relished it.

But they were not deep enough into this moor to feel its spell.

Dusk came, and she was still asleep. He walked again, to stay limber, and then when it was dark enough that he could barely see the track they'd followed coming in, he carefully woke her, so as not to frighten her, and asked her to put the blindfold back in place.

Rutledge made his way off the moor, found the road to Wadebridge, and settled down for the drive back to the village. Well before they had reached the outskirts, where there was still nothing to tell her where she was, he asked her to climb into the rear seat and pull the blanket over her.

He could hear Hamish protesting even as she quarreled with him, but in the end, he had his way.

They drove on. It was well into the dinner hour, and the street was empty as he passed the inn, then the church, and pulled up in the rear yard of the vicarage.

There was a lamp burning in the kitchen, and he thought Mrs. Daniels and her husband must be having their own dinner after feeding the vicar his.

"Stay where you are," he said quietly. "There are people about." It wasn't actually true, but he hadn't spoken to the Danielses yet, and it was too soon to involve Mrs. Worth.

When he tapped lightly on the door, a shadow loomed large. It was the hulking form of Mr. Daniels, blotting out the lamplight. He opened the door a crack and asked, "Who's there?"

"Rutledge."

He held up a lamp. "No offense. I want to see your face." Then grunting in acknowledgment, he opened the door. "Can't be too careful," he said.

Rutledge stepped inside. "How is the vicar?"

"He's been restless. I expect he's got something on his mind," Mrs. Daniels said. "Poor man, he's not used to not seeing to his flock. But they come to him all the same."

"Any other trouble at night?"

Daniels shook his head. "Do you think he—whoever he is—knows the vicar can't remember?"

"I wouldn't be surprised," Rutledge said. "Still, have a look around the churchyard, will you? To be certain? Because I have another favor to ask of you both. Will you give me your promise not to speak to anyone about what I have to tell you? Most particularly not the vicar."

They agreed, warily. And Rutledge told them an expurgated version of events.

"I've brought her here because there is no other secure place for her. If no one knows where she is, if she keeps the shades down, I think she'll be safe enough for the time being. But the man hunting her has killed before. I am telling you the truth about that."

"You must do as you think best," Mrs. Daniels said quietly. "Can you spirit her in without anyone being the wiser?"

"I can. Tell me which room, and I'll take her directly up the back stairs."

"Yes, that will be best. I'll go up and see to it. Daniels and I have a room close to the stairs, so we can hear Vicar if he calls. But there's a lovely big room on the back, and only the one window to it. Would you like Daniels here to nail down the shade to be sure? Even if she does peek out, there's nothing to be seen but the corner of the sheds and the barn."

He agreed, and gave them a quarter of an hour. Returning to the motorcar, he said softly, "It's arranged. There's a custodian here, and his wife. They'll bring you meals. But you must give me your word not to do anything foolish."

Her muffled voice answered him. "Are you sure this is best? Please, I don't want anyone else to die."

"Nor do I."

When it was time, when Daniels had assured him that the churchyard was empty, he helped her out of the motorcar, shrouded in the blanket and with the blindfold firmly in place. The stairs were narrow, twisting. He had to lead her up them, and she stumbled once, but he caught her before she fell.

"A lighthouse?" she asked with a smile in her voice that he could hear. "But I smell food, my mouth is watering."

"You'll have something soon enough. All right, almost there. Good, now turn to your right and walk with me down the passage."

"Can I remove the blanket? Or at least the blindfold?"

"Not yet." A door was open just ahead of him, and within the room a lamp was lit. He led her inside, and shut the door. "Now."

He lifted the rug off her head and shoulders, and she pulled down the blindfold herself.

The room was papered in a pleasing shade of apple green with white morning glories climbing the walls. A darker green coverlet on the bed was the same shade as the ties on the white curtains at the single window. On the floor the carpet was a pattern of green leaves on a lighter field.

She said, "Oh!" as she looked around, saw the rocking chair by the table, a small desk, and a chest of drawers, a wardrobe against the far wall, and the bed in between that and the chest. "I was afraid you might—I thought a policeman would consider a gaol the safest place."

He smiled. "You will not leave this room. People come and go downstairs, and you will be seen."

She frowned. "Are we in an inn? A hotel? I didn't hear voices."

"It's closed this time of year," he said. "But friends visit the owners or come for tea."

She turned to him, her face haggard in the lamplight. "Will they be all right? Ronnie and her sister? The doctor told me they would, but I thought he might be lying to make me willing to leave them."

"He told me the same thing."

"I should have listened. But I thought, no one knows they are there in Boscastle."

"The local people did. They go to market. They're seen about the town. If someone asked questions, it wouldn't take long to discover who the visitors are, this time of year." He left her soon after and met Mrs. Daniels on the stairs bringing up a tray for her.

It had been a risk, bringing her here. But Mr. and Mrs. Daniels were reliable. They wouldn't talk, and the house was large, and very empty, save for Vicar. But he would have to depend on keeping the vicar and Mrs. Worth apart. Still, it wouldn't be for very long. Or so he told himself. Meanwhile, he would ask the Yard to begin a manhunt for Worth. He had a name, now, and Mrs. Worth could provide a description. It would be a start.

He left soon after, drove back to the inn, and took the stairs to his room two at a time, his mind on the telegram he would send.

The owner, Joseph Hays, stopped him in the passage. "I saw your motorcar coming in. There's dinner put aside for you."

"Thanks," Rutledge said. "I looked in on the vicar first. He's doing well enough, in my opinion. Dr. Carrick continues to be concerned about his memory, but his body is healing."

"Aye. That's good news," the innkeeper said, and went on about his business.

Rutledge took his meal in his room, composing the telegram he would send in the morning. He was tired, but there was much to consider before he made his next move.

He had done his best for Mrs. Worth. He could only pray it was the right course of action for now.

But Hamish, in the back of his mind, was raising doubts.

"If he canna' find yon lass, if he kens you were in Fowey and Boscastle as well as in Bodmin, he will come for you. And when ye send a telegram through yon meddlesome man in Padstow, you canna' be sure he willna' hear of it."

"I'm more concerned about the man in Bodmin who sent the telegram for Mrs. Worth. The only alternative is to ask the Chief Constable to contact the Yard."

Restless now, he would have liked to go out after his meal and walk for a time. But when he looked out the window, a mist was rolling in from the sea. Rock had disappeared entirely, and the river itself was hard to find.

Not a night for wandering about. Not when his revolver was in his London flat, in the trunk under his bed.

20

There was a pounding on his door in the middle of the night.

Rutledge, awake on the instant, thought, My God, he's found her.

But when the door burst open before he could set his feet on the floor, it wasn't Daniels standing there, a torch in his hand. It was a livid Walter Grenville.

"There you are, lying in your bed!" he shouted. "And all hell breaking loose."

Rutledge reached for the matchbox and lit the lamp. "What is it? What's happened?"

"She's gone. A quarter of an hour, that's all it was. A quarter of an hour."

"Where did she go?" He was already dressing.

"How the hell do I know?"

"Where is Daniels?"

"Daniels? Who the hell is Daniels?"

"Have you come from the vicarage?"

"I came from the Place. It's the bloody middle of the night."

"Who, precisely, is missing?"

"Kate—Miss Gordon."

Rutledge stopped buttoning his shirt and stared at Grenville. "What are you trying to tell me, man? Start at the beginning, damn you."

He did, launching in a nearly coherent account, this time.

"We let them exercise after dinner. We can't keep them shut up in a room day after day. With the fog, it felt close in the house, breathless. I let them go out to the terrace to walk up and down. One at a time. It's safer than the lawns. They run down to the river. First Victoria, then Sara—Miss Langley. After that, Miss Gordon. I timed them. I sat there in the room and timed them. When a quarter of an hour had passed, I went to the door and spoke her name. Quietly, sounds carry in the night. She didn't answer. I stepped out on the terrace. She wasn't there. We spent the better part of two hours searching the house and then the grounds. I went to the St. Ives house, thinking she might be there. God knows why, but I couldn't think of anything else. But she wasn't. They hadn't seen her. I even went down to the landing, for God's sake. And the damned boat is wet. Someone had it out tonight. You knew her before this. I thought she might have come to you."

"No. She didn't," he said trenchantly, tying his boots. "Why didn't you send for me at the start? Why wait until now?" He looked at his watch. It was nearly two in the morning.

But he knew why Grenville had waited. He was the magistrate, he was responsible for the accused put into his keeping. He had wanted to find Kate Gordon without any fuss.

And he had come to the man from London as a last resort.

Wasting precious time.

Without waiting for an answer, Rutledge said, "Quite. Do you let them walk every evening?"

"I've told you. They can't remain shut up into a room."

"Was there anyone on the river tonight? Did you ask the others? Your daughter or Miss Langley?"

He hadn't. Rutledge read the answer in his face.

"Who would be on the river in this fog?" Grenville asked after a moment.

"Someone was. Your boat was wet. Whoever took her, he came in that way."

Grenville ignored him. "Kate gave me her word. As did the others. She's broken it. There was no one else. My wife told me she was homesick for London. She must be trying to make her way there. In the dark, alone, without a penny in her purse."

"I doubt it," Rutledge said, going out the door. Grenville followed him down the passage, leaving the door standing wide behind him. "Kate Gordon isn't a fool."

But where to look? Rutledge asked himself as he went down the stairs.

He had no doubt at all about who had taken Kate Gordon.

And if he was right, there would be a message soon. He could have told Grenville what it said, without even seeing it.

Kate Gordon for Alexandra Worth.

Hamish had been right. Her husband had found out who had sent that telegram. And who had received it.

Rutledge searched Kate's room a second time, although it had been searched before, but there was no message waiting for him. That sealed his certainty. She hadn't gone off on her own. And she hadn't taken it into her head to play detective and help him find a way out of their predicament. She was too sensible for that. But by this time, he could almost wish she wasn't. It would have been simpler.

"I shall have to send for Gordon," Grenville was saying as they closed the door to Kate's room. They had already spoken to Victoria and to Sara Langley, but neither of them had noticed anyone on the river that night.

"But I thought I heard a motorcycle," Sara said. "I couldn't swear to it. There aren't many around here, I'm sure."

He wasn't convinced there had been a motorcycle. Putting someone bound and gagged on a motorcycle was a tricky way of going about a kidnapping. Still, he hadn't been told of a strange motorcar on the road. Rare as they were even in London, they were rarer still in these parts. But how else had Worth traveled to Boscastle, to Bodmin, and then here?

"Right," Rutledge said as he and Grenville came down the stairs again. "Do you have a map of this part of Cornwall?"

"From the turn of the century," he said, and led the way into the study. "You think someone's taken Kate. Why? What's this got to do with Saunders's death?"

Rutledge said only, "It's too long a story and there isn't time. But it has to do with the vicar as well as Saunders. I can set your mind at ease on one matter. Whoever it is doesn't want Kate. She's a pawn."

"Who does this person want?"

"A summer visitor."

Grenville, still asking questions, pulled open a long drawer beneath the table and took out a large map of North Cornwall that appeared to be from 1900. But Rutledge found that it held true, for the most part, despite the passage of twenty years. He could pick out roads, villages, even farmhouses and more than one of the sacred wells, dolmens, menhirs, and other relics of the past. It was amazingly complete. But he didn't have time to study it in detail.

"If you wanted to conceal someone's whereabouts, where would you go?" Rutledge asked, ignoring everything else.

Grenville cast him a sharp glance, then bent over the map spread across the table. Mrs. Grenville had come into the room and was standing by the fireplace. The fire in the grate was snapping sharply and taking some of the evening's chill out of the room.

"Bodmin Moor," Grenville said at once, a finger going to the moorland. "Or here." He pointed to the headland beyond Rock. "There's the ruin of an ancient fortress here. Certainly not medieval."

"The moor is too far. And the headland is a trap, he won't go there. What's this large spot?"

"That? An abandoned quarry. Cornish stone was taken out of the ground, leaving a layered pit."

"That's what, about fifteen miles from here?"

"Nearer twenty, I should think."

"Then that's where he'll take her."

Grenville was all for summoning St. Ives and Langley and doing a little reconnaissance in force. But Rutledge shook his head.

"No. We'll see what his demands are. She won't be harmed. Not as long as he believes he'll have what he wants in the end." But she would be frightened—and stoic. He could count on Kate.

"Why Gordon's daughter?"

"I don't think he cared whose child she was. Only that she was someone with a father who cared. He may even have mistaken her for the magistrate's daughter."

"He must be mad."

"Cunning is a better word." He didn't add the word chasing itself through his own mind: *dangerous*.

"But what has this to do with the charges against my daughter and her friends?"

"Nothing," Rutledge said, and started for the door.

"Wait," Mrs. Grenville said. "You say Kate—Miss Gordon—is a hostage. What does this man want?"

"His wife. He refuses to recognize a judicial separation."

"Do you know where she is? Will you take her to him, to exchange for Kate? It seems rather—cruel."

Rutledge had already considered that. "I can't exchange her for Kate. Nor can I leave Kate at his mercy."

"Then take me. Can you make me look enough like her? There's nothing to be done about height or size. But it could work."

It could. Mrs. Grenville had the same coloring and build. But he was reluctant to agree.

He knew why she had volunteered. She felt responsible for what had happened to her daughter. She was afraid to tell her husband. This was in a way her expiation.

Grenville was already protesting. "I won't have it. We'll go after Kate ourselves, and bring her back." He started for the door. "Be damned with this."

"He'll kill her," Rutledge said quietly.

Grenville stopped, wheeling to face him. "You can't be sure of that."

"I have seen what he can do. I won't risk it. Not with Kate Gordon."

"My dear, Inspector Rutledge will see to it that I come to no harm."

"No, I refuse even to consider this."

She put her hand on her husband's arm. "Give Mr. Rutledge your revolver. I don't think he will hesitate to use it."

"Absolutely not. If we must do this, we'll ask one of the maids."

"No. That would be very unfair. Think about it, Walter. I can carry it off. I've always been good at charades, haven't I?"

He smiled in spite of himself. "That's hardly a skill you will find helpful in dealing with such a person. No."

She wasted half an hour in persuading him. But in the end, he agreed. She went up to her daughter's room and came back with a selection of gowns, asking Rutledge which might be more suitable to Mrs. Worth.

He chose a blue wool with a short jacket, and then a hat that more or less covered her hair. A heavy cloak against the wind, and appropriate shoes—she had only one sensible pair, for walking out—and she might just pass as Mrs. Worth.

"I'm going back to the inn," he told her. "I must await the summons. Then I'll come for you."

Her eyes were worried, but she said steadily, "Of course. I'll be ready, Mr. Rutledge."

A boy from Padstow brought the message an hour later. He told Rutledge that the man had given him sixpence to bring the note and a shilling if he lost his memory on the way.

"And so I can't describe him, sir. I have taken his shilling."

"I'll give you a pound, if you tell me."

But the boy shook his head firmly. "No, sir. I have given my promise."

Admirable, but frustrating. It didn't matter, the man who had given the lad the message would have left Padstow before the boy reached the village.

Rutledge went up to his room and unfolded the square of paper.

You know what I want. If you are standing on the village landing at noon, I will give my word that she will come to no harm. For twenty-four hours.

Rutledge swore, but he drove again to Padstow Place, asked for Mrs. Grenville, and said, "I shall need you to stand on the village landing at noon. He has field glasses; you must be careful."

"Give me fifteen minutes to change clothes." She left the room.

Grenville said, "You have a message. Let me see it."

Rutledge gave it to him.

"Yes, all right, then."

Ten minutes later he and Victoria Grenville's mother were in his motorcar on their way to the village.

"You didn't need to do this, you know."

She smiled and shook her head. "You know I must."

"Your husband will understand."

"He will. And that's the worst part of it, you see. This way, I've done something to make amends for my part in what has happened."

They were silent for the rest of the way. Rutledge drove the motorcar directly to the landing, and got out.

"No, stay here," he said to her as she prepared to get down. And then he walked on to the edge of the landing. He didn't know quite what to expect. Whether the ruse would work. But he was counting on the man watching them to be hungry enough to take the bait. Unless, of course, he possessed a rifle, and what he wanted as well was revenge.

He was standing there, scanning the opposite side of the river when something caught his eye. It was a single flash. He located it in a small stand of wind-shriveled trees high on the slope.

The flashes started again.

Morse code, he realized as he recognized the flashes. He shook his head.

The flashes began once more, and this time he pulled up the code from the depths of his memory and began to read.

The quarry. Ten o'clock tonight. Come alone with her. If you fail me, you know what to expect.

Rutledge waited, but the message was not repeated. The flashes had ended.

He turned and walked back to the motorcar, thinking hard. Why ten o'clock? Would it take the other man that long to set up his traps?

He made a decision. He reached Mrs. Grenville's side, and leaned forward.

Very quietly, he said, "I'm telling you something. Listen to it, and then shake your head vigorously. Angrily. Can you do that?"

She leaned forward, as if hanging on his words, then moved away, showing distress and anger.

He continued to talk to her, and she appeared to burst into tears. At that point he walked around the motorcar and got in, driving away.

When they were safely away from the River Camel, Mrs. Grenville said, "Do you think he believed in me?"

"I hope so."

"I saw the flashes. What did he want?"

"Ten o'clock tonight. The quarry."

She bit her lip, then said with more courage than she must have felt, "Very well."

He spent another hour convincing Grenville. And then, drained, he went back to the hotel and up to his room.

"It's a verra' grave risk."

"I know. God, I could use an aircraft. I would give a great deal to see this quarry."

But there was no one he dared to ask, except Grenville, who hadn't been there since he was a boy.

"A great empty bowl," he said. "They scooped out the rocks like porridge, and left it. An eyesore. There's no place to hide."

"But he can see anyone approaching."

"Yes, that's right. I don't think anyone has worked there these past twenty years. There's talk of opening it again. Nothing has come of it. You aren't proposing to do this alone? You can't take the risk, Rutledge, with two women caught in the middle."

"It will be all right. He won't come near Mrs. Grenville."

Grenville was difficult to persuade, but Rutledge was fairly certain that Worth would be watching. A raiding party would be spotted, and it was Kate who would suffer.

They left in the afternoon, he and Mrs. Grenville. And her husband's revolver went with them in Rutledge's pocket.

He had a feeling that Grenville would break his promise and try to follow, but he hoped that he himself had had a sufficient head start to finish the business before the cavalry arrived.

Mrs. Grenville was quiet as he drove to Wadebridge and then turned back toward the sea. He had some difficulty finding the road to the quarry, abandoned and overgrown as it was. By that time, they were only two miles away from their destination, and it was quite dark.

"It will go as planned. As long as you don't speak. Cry, scream, but don't speak."

She nodded, and he thought she was too tense to reply.

The quarry was larger than he'd expected and deeper. Even in the dark he could see how raw the land was for some distance around it, bare of anything but scrub growth that had fought its way back through soil pounded down by wagons and horses, and the feet of men. Grenville had not remembered it well.

The quarry itself was a great black hole. He could see nothing below.

Mrs. Grenville spoke, keeping her voice low. "It goes down in descending circles, you know; as each level was removed, the next was narrower and lower. Like giant steps. I haven't seen it myself, but I remember now that Stephen came here once. For a lark. It would be easy to fall, I think. I can't imagine how unstable those stones must be, and in the dark. He has the advantage, doesn't he?" There was resignation in the words.

"He thinks he has. It's what matters."

"Yes. You must be right."

They sat there. Rutledge found himself considering all the things that lived in the Cornish night, and he wondered if a man like Worth was superstitious.

A voice came out of the dark, echoing oddly.

"Did you bring a torch? Shine it on her face."

"The battery is too low. I'll switch on the headlamps instead."

He did, the large, powerful beams lighting the night and making him blink.

Mrs. Grenville had thrown up her arm, as if the glare was too much.

"Bring her to the pit's edge."

"Not until I see that your hostage is all right."

A torch shone down into the pit. Rutledge could just make out the figure of Kate Gordon standing on one of the lower levels. It appeared her hands were tied behind her back.

But the torchlight had not come from the pit. *Where the hell was Worth?*

"Kate?" Rutledge called, getting out of the motorcar. He had pocketed the revolver. "Are you all right?"

"I am. Take care, Ian." As she spoke, the torch flicked off.

It was a warning, and he took it seriously.

"I will not leave her down there. She must come up. Or the trade is off."

"I'll kill her then."

"No, you won't. You don't have what you were after. Bring her up." His voice was hard.

The torch came on again. And with her hands still tied behind her, Kate Gordon started to walk.

Rutledge held his breath. It was dangerous, she could stumble and fall at any moment. She had no way to protect herself. But she moved slowly, resolutely. A stone spun out from under her foot and went down. It was a moment before Rutledge heard it splash in the darkness below where rainwater must have pooled in the depths.

He watched, powerless to help her. But it was the only way to get her out of there. If he went down to guide her, he left Mrs. Grenville alone. And down in that pit, he was an easy target. It wouldn't take Worth long to discover the impersonation.

He couldn't imagine the courage it was taking. He walked to the rim of the pit, and it was then that he realized that Kate Gordon was blindfolded. He began to talk to her. She reached the slope that led to the next level. Keeping his voice steady and his eyes on her, he guided her with words, and she listened as he warned her of obstacles, told her how far she had come, encouraged her away from the precipitous edge without frightening her, using the only weapon he had to keep her safe.

It seemed to take forever, that walk. But she must have been able to see under the blindfold—a little—to follow the shining path of the torch light.

One foot in front of the next, slowly, painfully, she came nearer. And he prayed that the cavalry would keep its distance until she was out of danger.

In the motorcar behind him, he heard Mrs. Grenville gasp as Kate's footing nearly failed her, and she lurched too close to the edge. She froze there, and Rutledge talked her into moving again, praising her, warning her, and cursing in his mind the man who had put her through this.

For once Hamish was silent. He seemed to be holding his own breath as well.

And Rutledge was grateful for the respite.

She was nearly at the top now. Another twenty feet and she would be off the ascending levels and away from the edge of the pit.

And then the torch went dark, stranding her there, and the voice said, "That's enough."

"Stay where you are, Kate. You're safe there. It will be all right," Rutledge told her. "Twenty feet more, that's all, and you're almost within reach. But don't move. Not yet."

The headlamps didn't reach her where she stood, but he could see her shoulders slump as she realized it was nearly over.

"You have what you want. Give me what I came for."

Rutledge went back to the motorcar and pretended to pull Mrs. Grenville roughly from it. "Struggle," he commanded in a fierce whisper, and she did, her fists pounding his chest and shoulders before he turned her sharply toward his best estimate of the source of the voice, and made her march beside him.

At Rutledge's urging, she kept up the struggle, for all the world a frightened woman who was resisting being traded for the girl on the pit's edge.

"When I say drop, go down," he told her softly.

She didn't speak. But he knew she had heard him.

He walked only as far as the light of the headlamps reached. There he stopped.

"If you want her, come and get her. She will run if I let her go."

"With pleasure."

Rutledge could hear footsteps in the darkness, crunching over the rubble, and then he realized that Worth was moving away, not toward him but toward Kate.

"What are you doing?" he demanded, his voice cutting the silence.

Worth had reached Kate, taken her arm, and pulled her in front of him, as a shield.

Mrs. Grenville said quietly, "I think—he's holding her at gunpoint now."

He had seen it as well. Rutledge swore again, but he had prepared for that too.

They moved toward him, the dark outline of the man Rutledge had never seen, and the slim figure of the girl who had climbed out of the pit alone and without anything but her own bravery to help her.

They were still out of revolver range.

And then Rutledge saw a single flash of light somewhere on slightly higher ground behind Worth, where the land sloped upward before falling away again.

He heard a sharp intake of breath beside him, and then Mrs. Grenville began to struggle against the light grip he had on her arm.

"No, no," she cried, her voice muffled by her shoulder. And before he could stop her, she broke free. He whirled and caught her up, and he saw the anger blazing in her eyes beneath the hat. This time there was no pretense. She struggled fiercely, and he had all he could do not to hurt her.

"Let me go," she said then, and as he realized what she was about to do, he let her break away again, and run headlong into the darkness, away from Worth and from Rutledge. Just as Mrs. Worth would have done.

He heard the man swear, his voice wild and furious. And then he dropped Kate's arm and started after Mrs. Grenville, raising his revolver.

Too late, Rutledge realized that in the darkness beyond the headlamps, she had misjudged her distances. She was nearer Worth now than he was, and in range while he was not.

Rutledge shouted a warning, already racing to intercept Worth, to bring himself into range, but the man was quickly gaining on Mrs. Grenville.

Raising the borrowed revolver, Rutledge fired, praying that it aimed true, and watched the shot kick up a tiny spout of earth ten feet short of the other man, barely diverting him from his target.

He wasn't going to be in time—

And Worth was steadying his own gun hand.

Rutledge fired a second time, had the satisfaction of seeing Worth duck. And in that instant, when the man's stride was off, a large-bore rifle fired, echoing through the darkness, and Worth dropped like a stone.

Shoving the revolver into his pocket, Rutledge changed direction and ran toward Kate, stranded near the rim of the quarry, still blindfolded and fighting her bonds.

"I'm here," he said, reaching for the blindfold, and then pulling her into his arms.

As he half led, half carried her to the motorcar, she twisted to see what had become of Worth.

"Don't look," he ordered, and she turned her face away.

Mrs. Grenville had stopped where she was, staring in the direction the shot had come from.

And then she turned and walked awkwardly back toward the motorcar as Rutledge freed Kate's hands.

She was laughing and crying in the same breath now, clinging to Rutledge, her face pressed against his chest as he held her.

"I didn't think I could make it," she said shakily, her voice muffled. "But I did, didn't I?"

Glancing at Mrs. Grenville, he smiled. "You were marvelous," he said to her. Then he turned to the woman in his arms. "He didn't hurt you, did he? Tell me, Kate."

He could feel her shaking her head. "No. He kept his word. Twenty-four hours." And then Mrs. Grenville was taking Kate from him and folding her into her arms.

Rutledge turned away, walking back to where Worth lay. Out of the darkness a figure materialized, and he froze, hand on his revolver, until he saw that it was Grenville.

He was holding up a rifle. "My grandfather's elephant gun. From his game hunting in Africa. He used it until he was eighty, God save him."

They stared down at the remains of a man whom Rutledge had never met, whose face was one he didn't recognize at all. Whose name he was not certain even now that he knew.

He had never seen him before. Their only contact had been at a distance, or secondhand as he looked down on what this man had done to someone else.

"Now you will please tell me the whole story?" Grenville demanded harshly.

"What he did to Kate was unconscionable. He's better off dead," Rutledge said coldly. "But I will tell you that he has killed, several times over. He would have been hanged, if he'd lived. It was this man who savaged the vicar, among others."

Grenville said contemptuously, "Leave him. I will send someone from Boscastle or Tintagel to bring him in."

"We can't. It isn't finished." He bent down and took the revolver from Worth's hand, passing it to Grenville. "Evidence," he said.

"You're surely not going to hold an inquest," Grenville said sharply. "He's dead, man, let it be."

"It has to be finished." He rubbed his face, feeling the day's growth of beard rough against his hand. "Boscastle isn't that far. Find the constable there, and send him back for Worth. Tell him—" He stopped, forcing his tired mind to think, trying to ignore Hamish, trying to find a way to reason with Grenville.

"Tell the constable in Boscastle that you have found the man who nearly killed those two women last night. Tell him you believe this is the same man who put holes in the Saunders's boat, and who attacked the vicar of St. Marina's. That he may well be the same man who murdered Frank Dunbar in an alley in Padstow. We have no proof, but it's likely. We tracked him here and tried to take him alive, but he was armed, and we had no choice but to shoot. He was too dangerous to lose in the darkness."

"What's his name? And what made him kill?"

"God knows. We don't." Rutledge frowned. "The war. Blame it on the war if you must. As for his name, let the constable search his pockets and find that out."

"Why were we following him?"

"I spotted a stranger near your house, and I wanted to question him. Someone had been moving around the village at night, and I was suspicious. I asked your help because you're familiar with the countryside. And Mr. and Mrs. Daniels can tell the police that he was prowling about the rectory several nights ago, trying to get at the vicar again."

"Is that true?" In the darkness, Rutledge nodded. "Who is Dunbar?"

"Inspector Carstairs's case," he told Grenville. "We've unwittingly solved it for him."

"It might just work."

"Some cottages were burned down. On the outskirts of Padstow. Dunbar owned them. Perhaps our man had been hiding out there. There's no one left who can contradict that." He turned to look back toward the motorcar, where the two women were waiting. "It has to work. Miss Gordon has suffered enough. It will not serve justice to have her give evidence at an inquest. It will not serve to have Mrs. Worth describe what her husband has done to her. But much of our evidence is circumstantial, of course. And I shall have to give the Chief Constable an explanation for much of what has happened, one he will accept."

"Very well," Grenville said after a moment. "I'll find the dead man's motor and drive on to Boscastle. St. Ives has already taken the horses and the elephant gun back to the Place." He grinned at Rutledge's surprise. "Cross-country. It was the only way to get here before you did. And I can trust St. Ives. You will see the women safely home."

"No, I should go to Boscastle. It's best. Someone will remember me. I was there only a day or so ago."

Grenville shook his head vehemently. "All the more reason for me to go alone. You've reported these crimes to me. I'm dealing with it. If you go, you'll be expected to answer more questions than may be comfortable."

It was true.

"Then be careful. It matters too much."

"I will."

They walked together toward the motorcar, and Rutledge passed the borrowed revolver to Grenville, who pocketed it with a nod.

As they came abreast of the women, Mrs. Grenville stepped away from Kate to face her husband.

"It was the right thing to do," she said.

"I must go to Boscastle, my dear. Someone has to collect the body. The man's motorcar is just beyond the mouth of the quarry. Rutledge will see you both safely home."

It was nearly dawn when Grenville returned to the Place, reporting to Rutledge privately that he had had no difficulties with the constable in Boscastle.

"He was relieved, I think. The village had been on edge since the attack on the two women who lived there. He will hold the inquest there, he says, since that's where the body will be taken. Just as well. He did ask what had become of a Mrs. Hargrove. I had no answer for him, and so I told him she was helping the police with their inquiries."

"Quite right."

"He's contacting Pendennis here. And Carstairs in Padstow. You might want to speak to Pendennis this morning."

"Yes. I'll tell him what we know. But not about Mrs. Worth."

"Agreed."

Half an hour later, over an early breakfast, Rutledge sat down in the almost empty dining room and told Grenville, his wife, and Kate Gordon about the woman at the vicarage, and the man who had hunted her.

Kate, drooping with fatigue, had said very little. He had not wanted her to hear the full story, but Grenville had insisted that she had earned the right.

Rutledge showed them the scraps of cloth in his possession. "We can tie Worth to the dinghy and to the attack in Boscastle. As well as to one some time ago in Derby. It is enough, I think, to prove our case. That leaves the vicar and Dunbar, but Mrs. Daniels and her husband can confirm some part of the story there. As for Dunbar, with the cottages burned and the dinghy interfered with while it was at the landing below the cottages, I think Carstairs will be satisfied as well."

"Leave him to me," Grenville said.

"This absolves my daughter from any charge of holing the dinghy," Mrs. Grenville said. "But she still faces a charge of murder."

"There's always tomorrow," Rutledge said with a confidence he was far from feeling.

"I must meet this woman, Mrs. Worth," Grenville said. "As magistrate."

"Yes. I'll bring her to you."

Mrs. Grenville rose. "Kate, you should be in your bed. And I should be as well. I hope you can sleep without dreams."

Kate smiled. "I'll try."

They said good night and left the two men together.

Grenville said, "Worth isn't the inquiry that brought you to Cornwall."

He was finishing the glass of whisky that had been served with his breakfast. "No. But I think that too may be in hand. There is still time."

"By any chance, do you know the story of John Tregeagle? His grave is in the churchyard at St. Breock. Near Wadebridge."

"A Cornishman who was shockingly evil but who did one good deed—for which he was spared and ordered to do endless, impossible tasks he couldn't hope to finish, in order to keep him out of the devil's clutches?"

"That's right. We will let the man who lies dead out there beside the quarry become a new legend. That's to say he's there if he hasn't already been carried to Boscastle. There will be stories told of him, I expect. Cornwall has an affinity for things that walk abroad in the night, and kill."

"There's something we must still address. How Worth got his information. He prowled the night, listening where he could. We do know that. But I expect you will find he bribed some people. The telegraph office in Padstow, perhaps the one in Bodmin. Someone in The Pilot. They won't come forward on their own. Others gossiped freely. One of the maids in your own house, for instance."

"Does it matter now? Worth is dead. It will only draw more attention to what he has done."

"There's the elephant gun," Rutledge pointed out. "Will that cause trouble for you?"

"Yes, well, I had meant to take my shotgun, and in my haste, I took that instead. Just as well, too, or I'd have not been able to stop him from reaching my wife." He tried to conceal a surge of anger, then said in a different tone of voice, "A shame, really, you had wanted him alive, but he was beyond the range of your revolver at that stage of events."

Rutledge wasn't sure if Grenville was telling the truth or not. He took a deep breath. "I promised Dr. Learner I would give him the end of the story."

"We will notify him that the two women in his surgery are safe, that we have caught the madman who attacked them. It will be sufficient, I think."

"I don't believe Worth was mad." He paused, then asked, "Why did you shoot to kill?"

"I didn't. He was a moving target, and I had only seconds before he shot my wife, still believing she was his own. It was my only chance, and I took it. It was you who put her in danger."

Rutledge said nothing. He knew very well why Mrs. Grenville had tried to protect Kate. She had failed to save Paul Trevose.

The church clock was striking ten as Rutledge called at the vicarage to collect Mrs. Worth. Without any sleep, he had gone first to speak to Constable Pendennis, and then briefly, on a pretext, to see Inspector Carstairs.

"No answers on Dunbar's death, so far," Carstairs reported morosely. "And two of the damned cottages burned down to the ground. I expect whoever it was wasn't satisfied with ten pounds."

"I understand someone in Boscastle has contacted Grenville. About the vicar and Dunbar," Rutledge responded. "There may be a link."

"Boscastle?" Carstairs asked, instantly alert.

"It appears he's struck there as well. Whoever he is." He had planted the seed. That was enough.

Neither Pendennis nor Carstairs had seen or spoken to Trevose.

Satisfied, Rutledge went to see the farmer.

He had not gone to the fields the day before, nor had he gone out today, according to Bronwyn, complaining vociferously about her employer being underfoot when she was planning to scrub the floors.

Rutledge walked into the low-ceilinged front room where Trevose was sitting, staring into space.

He looked up as Rutledge came down the half step into the room. "What do you want?"

"Either you confirm the charges against the four accused, or you withdraw them."

"How can I?"

Rutledge wasn't certain whether he was asking how to accuse or how to renege.

He said, "You must find a way."

That roused the man. "I'll be a laughingstock!"

"Not if you tell the truth. That you were unable to judge well in the frantic moments after you brought Saunders into the boat. That time has given you a clearer memory of what you saw."

"No."

"You will have to testify. There's no choice about that. In a courtroom full of people who know you well. And many more who don't. Unless you stop it now."

"The magistrate. I'll go to him. Not the police."

"Have it your way."

He drove the reluctant man to Padstow Place, and left him with Grenville.

When the two men emerged from the library half an hour later, Trevose looked like someone who had been pulled from the water just before he drowned. Pale, shaken, and angry with Rutledge, he got into the motorcar and held his tongue all the way back to the farm.

"You have what you wanted," he all but growled as he got out his door and then slammed it with some force. "Now get off my land."

"Tell me. Did you truly believe those women tried to kill Saunders? If you did, you should have told Grenville so. In spite of what I said to you."

"It's finished. Be damned to you."

Rutledge said nothing as he reversed the motorcar.

And then Trevose shouted, "Was it so wrong to want my own back? Look at what they've got. Look at what I have. And no one to help me. My brother's dead. I owe the bank more than I can repay, and the land is going sour, as bankrupt as I am. What's an honest man to do?"

Rutledge slowed beside him. "I don't know. I wish I did."

"Curse you all." Trevose turned on his heel and strode back to the house, slamming the door hard behind him.

Looking after him, Rutledge listened to Hamish in his head.

There was nothing he could do.

And he would have to tell the Chief Constable that he had found the inquiry had no merit.

But where in all this was justice for Harry Saunders?

Although, Rutledge thought, Victoria Grenville would carry the guilt of Harry Saunders's death for the rest of her life, like her mother's burden of Paul Trevose's death, wondering if something she could have done might have changed the outcome. For her, for her friends, for Harry and his parents.

But was it enough?

Mrs. Grenville had given him a veiled hat for Mrs. Worth to wear, and a coat against the chill.

He went up the back stairs and found her sitting at the tiny desk, a sheet of paper before her, a pen beside it. He could see that the paper was blank.

She looked up. "I'm trying to write to Ronnie. How do you tell someone that you don't know how to repay them for their sacrifice? They could have died, Inspector. I'd told them I was safe in Boscastle. That he would never find me there. And they kept that secret."

"If they hadn't understood, they couldn't have held out against him. I've come to take you to call on someone. Grenville is the local magistrate."

She tensed. "What is it? Has someone else been hurt?"

"He intends to help you." He indicated the coat and hat he was carrying. "You'll need this. Just as well for the village not to see you."

She looked around the room. Sanctuary, and she was leaving it reluctantly. And then, with a sigh, she allowed him to help her into the coat. Standing at the mirror afterward, she settled the hat on her hair. "Mrs. Daniels, bless her, found a brush and comb for me, and a few other things. I'm grateful."

They went down the back stairs and out to the motorcar. It was late afternoon, and the sun had vanished behind a heavy bank of clouds. There was rain in the air, and Mrs. Worth pulled her borrowed coat closer, then drew her cold hands into the sleeves.

Grenville met her alone, and she talked to him for over an hour.

Rutledge waited in the drawing room, pacing the floor for a while, and then sitting in one of the elegant chairs.

The door opened, and he rose, thinking it was Mrs. Worth. But it was Victoria in the doorway. She came in tentatively, and he saw that her eyes were red from crying. He stayed where he was, waiting for her to speak.

"I didn't kill Harry. I didn't even hurt him. When I picked up the oar, I thought it was the only way to save him, to let him cling to it while we pulled for shallow water. Otherwise we were all going into the river. Elaine might make it to shore, but I didn't think I could. Sara and Kate were already exhausted. It was our only hope. But as I lifted it to help him, I saw his face. Something was wrong. There was blood, and his eyes weren't focusing properly. I tried to swing the oar back into the boat, but it was too heavy. It came down on Kate and Sara instead, and they nearly lost their grip on Harry. I was appalled. I thought, if he drowns, it will be my fault. I let the oar go and sat down, trying to stay out of their way, praying for all of us. I knew if I went back to help them we'd tip right over. And all the while Harry was swallowing water. Then someone else was in the boat with us, and he had Harry in, almost on top of us. I thought, he came out of nowhere. It's a miracle. But it wasn't, was it? Harry wasn't going to live. And I felt guilty because I thought him a coward for going to America, when all the other men we knew were dying in France. I blamed him for living when my brother hadn't. But I didn't want this to happen to him. I swear I didn't."

After a moment, he said, "Why didn't you tell me this before?"

"They were accusing us of murder. There on the landing. The farmer, Trevose, told everyone we were holding Harry's head under, and when that didn't work, I'd tried to kill him with the oar. I was frightened, I wanted to deny I'd ever touched it. That other man from London, the kind one, Inspector Barrington, understood. I told him what I hadn't put down in that first statement. And he said it would be all right. But then he died too. And we had it all to do over again, and I lost my nerve because my father warned me you were a hard man and we must be careful what we told you. I just wanted to deny everything. My mother wanted me to tell the truth, believing I'd be safe. But I wasn't. I was going to be tried for murder. And even if the others managed to go free, I'd be hanged. Because of the oar."

Barrington's missing notes. Was *that* why Trevose had burned them? Because Barrington had believed Victoria Grenville?

What had begun as curiosity must have become a very real fear that Barrington had learned more than was safe. And with a new man coming to take over, it was imperative to keep him in the dark. Small wonder Trevose had felt free to challenge him. He thought he had the upper hand.

Rutledge said, "It might have given some comfort to Harry Saunders's family."

"They have shown no sympathy for us. They told Mr. Barrington that we had lured Harry into the rowboat to mock him for being provincial."

"Do you feel any responsibility for Harry Saunders's death?"

"My father told me the dinghy had been interfered with. We didn't kill him—we tried to save him. I wanted him to be all right. I shouldn't have blamed him for Stephen's death. I regret that. I should have been kinder to him. I wish I had been." She shivered, saying in a hoarse whisper, "I've seen men close to death. It still haunts me."

He let her go.

"Do you believe her?" Hamish asked as Rutledge walked down the passage toward the door.

Barrington did, he answered silently.

"That's no' an answer."

"I don't think," Rutledge said slowly, "that even she knows what happened that afternoon. Or why."

Grenville had told Mrs. Worth the story that had been agreed upon, leaving out that Kate had been taken in her place, saying nothing about the role Mrs. Grenville had played.

When she finally stepped out of the study, Rutledge could see that she was visibly shaken, unable to believe that her long ordeal was over. Grenville, coming out behind her, said quietly, "She does not intend to claim the body. There's a distant cousin in Oxford."

Turning to Rutledge, she said, "Could I ask you to take me back to Bodmin? To Dr. Learner's surgery? It's where I need to be."

"With pleasure. If you will tell me your real name."

She glanced at Grenville, then turned back to Rutledge.

"I have told you. Worth." She said it with distaste. "My name before I was married was Sedgwick. Alexandra Mary Elizabeth Sedgwick. I shall petition to use it again."

Mrs. Grenville was waiting in the hall by the stairs. She had packed a small valise with a few things, she told the woman she had impersonated, and with kindness and not a little curiosity, saw them to the door.

Rutledge drove to Boscastle first, where Mrs. Worth packed three valises, her own and one each for the two sisters. She was quick and efficient, and he could see how she had managed to survive on her own, a woman alone, for so long.

And then he took her to Bodmin and the doctor's surgery.

She held out her hand to him at the door. "I don't know how to thank you," she said, "but I shall always remember what you've done."

"In the line of duty," Rutledge answered, smiling.

"No. It was not."

"You will remember to tell Dr. Learner that it's finished?"

"Yes. Good day, Inspector."

And then she was gone, stepping inside the surgery and shutting the door behind her.

He turned the bonnet toward the west again, speeding toward Wadebridge and then the road from there to the village, but he stopped before reaching it, walking up to the door of Padstow Place, his hand on the boot-shaped knocker, hesitating. Then he lifted it.

Although it was very late, Mrs. Grenville welcomed him, her face alight with happiness. "My husband has told me. The charges have been withdrawn. Mr. and Mrs. Saunders were understandably upset, but in time I think they'll agree with the magistrate's findings. There will be an inquest tomorrow. Are you heading back to London? Or will you attend it?"

"There are a few matters still to conclude in the village. I must speak to the Chief Constable. But I'll be leaving tomorrow no later than noon. After the inquest. I thought perhaps Miss Gordon would care to travel back to London with me. If she has recovered."

He hadn't seen her since that night. The breakfast at the end of it. She hadn't come down the several times he'd been at the Place since then.

Mrs. Grenville shook her head. "Oh, I'm so sorry, Mr. Rutledge. Her father came for her late this afternoon, and insisted they leave at once for London. I'm afraid she's gone."

He wanted to ask if she had left a message for him. But he felt it would not be for the best.

"Excellent," he lied. "She'll be in good hands."

"And Mr. Langley is coming tomorrow—or is it today? It's after midnight, I think. Elaine has already gone home to Chough Hall." She smiled wryly. "The house is suddenly so quiet. That will take some getting used to. We are all so grateful, Mr. Rutledge. I waited for you, because I wanted to tell you so myself. It was a wonderful thing you did for Miss Gordon. And for Mrs. Worth. For all of us."

He thanked her, and left.

He hadn't wanted so much gratitude. He had wanted to see Kate, to be sure she had suffered no lasting harm.

And that was a lie too.

Very simply, he wanted to see her.

CHARLES TODD is the author of the Bess Crawford mysteries, the Inspector Ian Rutledge mysteries, and two stand-alone novels. A mother and son writing team, they live in Delaware and North Carolina.